KILL CLUB

DJSmith

Copyright © 2017 David Jack Smith

David Jack Smith has asserted his rights under the Copyright, Designs and Patents Act 1988 to be identified as the author of this work.

ISBN: 9781521341827

This book is sold subject to the condition that it shall not, by way of trade or otherwise, be lent, resold, hired out, or otherwise circulated without the publisher's prior consent in any form of binding or cover other than that in which it is published and without a similar condition, including this condition, being imposed on the subsequent purchaser.

'Kill Club' is a work of fiction and entertainment. While certain historical events, locations and people exist in the real world, their inclusion in 'Kill Club' is entirely within its fictional setting.

ACKNOWLEDGMENTS

No man is an island entire of itself; every man is a piece of the continent, a part of the main;

As such I would like to thank my main men, and friends:

Dr Neel Halder MB, ChB, MRCPsych, MSc, CT Dip., PGCert. Med. Ed. (Senior Honorary Lecturer and Consultant Psychiatrist working in a forensic setting) for his invaluable advice on psychiatric diagnoses and issues; and of personality disorders and their treatments.

Jo Czarnecki (my former ad partner and art director in crime) for the Kill Club cover design and artwork (jokarma@btinternet.com)

To all those who have faith.

It Begins

It began as a practical joke. A nasty, boys-will-be-boys prank. That's what the others thought.

A mean spirited affair which most would not be proud to confess to their mother. Who would want dear old mum to hear about a scare some poor bloke half-to-death gag? Point made, lesson learned, let's all move on and never tell.

The others.

The selected few revved into a cocaine-fuelled frenzy with vodka chaser and adrenalin kicker. The others did not know the true intent for which they had been so carefully selected. Until—

The First.

The instigator. The manipulator. The beguiling worm tongue burrowing sweet somethings into willing ears. This one had always known how it would end after he expressed his darker purpose. A victim strung up balls-naked, dangling from a meat hook. Terrified. Punched. Kicked. Bloody. Gouged. Stabbed. Slashed. Resigned. And about to be very dead.

The First's experiments started small, yet proved thrilling in demonstrating the power of his superior being. His early attempts involved the smaller mammals and their cute furry faces. He frissoned at the gratification he felt as their lives ebbed away.

To prolong the intensity he started using pain as a control element. He would bring the subject as close to death as possible, pulling back before the point of no return. But these creatures barely measured on the sentient scale. Soon he evolved to the more complex species of cats and dogs. Most of them so trusting.

Here kitty, kitty, kitty.

This too proved a spectacular success, made even more thrilling by another thought: the agony that the disappearance of a loved one would cause its sentimental owner.

But like all powerful stimulants, the kicks gradually faded and diminished. The craving for greater highs burned into his flesh like acid. For variation he left the decapitated heads of the creatures for their owners to discover. This was highly pleasurable for a while. Especially when he could lurk unseen and observe the shocking discovery.

A further refinement occurred to him. He could use his newly acquired video camera to capture the moments of anguish. That way he could relive his pleasure over and over. He found old women and their tabby cats to be a satisfying combination. The zenith of this childhood phase happened one warm summer's evening at Jordan Hill Cottage.

He spied on her for about a week. The short, squat Mrs Rooney: a loud shrew with tight-cropped, salt-white hair. Her back garden sloped gently downhill over a hundred feet, ending at the line of unkempt shrubbery separating her little queendom from the farm land rolling onto the horizon. Perfect cover to observe the old witch's routine of watering her garden between six and seven each summer evening.

The cottage was totally secluded, with no prying eyes overlooking it from the rear. He had taken *Lady* earlier, returning at the time he knew she was preparing supper.

He had never experienced this level of raw excitement

as he pushed the two wooden pikes into the ground, two feet apart, half way down the garden. Removing both cat parts from the horsehair sack, he stuck Lady's axed off head on one pike, and her bloody torso on the second. Satisfied with his handiwork, he hurried back to his cover, readied his video, and waited.

Right on cue, the old woman left her cottage. The anticipation was too much. His body reacted in such a new, highly pleasurable way as he gave in to the irresistible urge to rub hard through his pants. Her sharp cry made him rub even harder. When she reached his little surprise, he could barely control these accelerating new sensations. It was exquisite. Then something he hadn't expected. The old witch, who had already been reduced to a strangled whimpering, began clutching wildly at her chest, gasping for breath. The whole event lasted no more than ten seconds before she dropped. Old Mrs Rooney was quite dead before her head clunked into the rock hard earth.

This was the moment everything became one, forcing him to his knees as his body drained into the ground.

The revelation had dazzled him with its piercing clarity. He now knew precisely what his gift to the world was to be.

A day like today, in a place like this on the cusp of the brave new millennium; in a derelict warehouse on an empty industrial estate, on the edge of a nondescript town.

The First had lured the young man with a classic misdirection. An invitation to join the privileged few on the inside.

Hush-hush.

An exclusive hand-numbered ticket for the act on

everyone's must-see list. Norman Cook in his hit alias, *Fat Boy Slim*. A secret rave known only to the select few.

Tell no one.

One of the others had rigged up a few speakers to blast out an ersatz club anthem welcome. The First was thrilled by the surprise on the boy's face as he walked into the semi-darkness. It finally registered he had been tricked a moment before the others grabbed him, safely anonymous in their scary horror-masks with the hideous twisted, bloody faces. Oh, how he shouted and struggled against the unquiet night: signifying nothing, with the others all against one.

The First was ready with the duct tape. A floor-filthy old rag was thrust hard into the boy's mouth. That, and a few tight wraps around the head, soon shut him up. The others held him down as they stripped him naked, before the First bound his hands and feet with tape.

Yeah, right here, right now. It's really happening.

The abandoned warehouse was a treasure trove of useful implements for their makeshift shop of scares. The overhead chain and winch system were co-opted. A crate full of rusty but sturdy meat hooks lay nearby: all the better to dangle you.

The others had not consciously thought out the implications of the *prank*. They had not wanted to, as each had been secretly excited and stirred by memories of suppressed natural urges. Who hasn't fantasized about killing controlling parents? Stupid little sister. Irritating brother. Annoying next door neighbour? Sarcastic teacher? It was natural. Normal even.

When they had the terrified boy strung up like a piece of meat, did they think this would be it? It was all going to peter out after a few laughs? Seriously?

The others tentatively slapped him around the head,

laughing and shrieking like kids in the playground. Confident the meat could never identify them prancing around in their scary horror masks and crisp, un-bloodied black boilersuits.

All the while the First stood passively, making no effort to get involved in the physical activities which grew more daring by the minute.

One of the tormentors asked the First for another snort of his seemingly endless supply of primo cocaine. He cut long lines on a tray and invited them to have at it. A new bottle of Absolut was cracked open and passed around.

They became bolder.

One swaggered over and punched the meat in the stomach. Another took a run before attempting a flying kung-fu kick he had seen in a Bruce Lee video.

Then it was all hands on meat. This phase lasted quite a while. Got the others all nice and bloodied up. Got them back to basics. Lords of the flying kicks.

'Hey guys, watch this.'

The First demanded their attention. He opened his satchel and pulled out an outrageous military combat knife. Sturdy rubber handle. Ten inch long blade. Sharply smooth one side. Jagged edge on the other. Killing machine.

One of them laughed uncontrollably. 'Fuck me—it's a fucking Rambo knife.'

Another. 'This is fucking wild. I love it.'

The First could see that he had primed his initiates kill-lust to perfection. Only then did he deign to approach the meat, which pathetically tried to struggle when it saw the knife. No hesitation, the First sliced down from the meat's left shoulder to its right hip. Then the opposite move. He stepped back to admire his handiwork.

'X marks the spot.'

That move stunned them into silence. For a second.

Hyenas on downed prey as they swarmed: biting, kicking, punching and gouging the meat.

All the time, the First waited for the prime moment.

'For fuck's sake, let's finish this thing.'

They stopped immediately. Command and control had been established. The First walked up to the meat, ripping off his mask. He pulled the meat's head up from its slumped position on its chest, pleased to see the tiny flicker of recognition register in its one remaining eye.

Through the blood, the lost boy could dimly see the glinting razor point approaching. The blade stopped, a teardrop away. The boy thought of his mum and dad. His older brother. His baby sister. His beautiful girlfriend. He saw the arm twisting back—ready to plunge.

He screamed silently: *'Why me?'*

He screamed. No more.

The crowd went wild. The meat's twitching spasms went on for a few seconds. The First pulled out the blade which had gone straight through the eye-socket, exiting the back of the skull. He was surprised at how easy it had plunged in, and how little the blood had flowed. He had expected *Carrie*.

He thought of *that* other movie they had all seen recently. The pretty boy Hollywood knob-head. Dumb story. A bunch of losers getting off by beating the shit out of each other. How stupid was that? Where's the fun in that? No. No. No. That wasn't the idea at all.

But it did give him *the* idea.

The First faced his lowly initiates, ready to consecrate them. Vinculum per cruor. Bonded by blood:

He took the knife, stuck out his tongue and lovingly ran the flat blade over its surface. Tasting success. He luxuriated in it. The blood. The pain. The power. The control. The kill.

He let it all out, screaming like a man possessed:

'Welcome to Kill Club.'

1

'Any advice?'

Micah Ishmael Gunn glanced at his questioner. His kid sister Bathsheba was sitting in the passenger seat: all neat, pressed and nervous. Gunn had driven half-way across London, feeling her ratchet up tighter and tighter with each passing mile. She needed to relax to nail her audition.

'Do actually sis. Never buy a safe needs opening by scanning body parts.'

'What?'

'Hand, finger, eye.'

By now Bathsheba was so distracted she didn't get the point of her big brother's odd story. 'Why? I don't—'

Gunn lifted his right hand and waved it. 'Bloke ambulanced into hospital last week. Blood gushing everywhere. Not surprising.'

'Jesus. Mikey. No blood. No blood.'

'Sorry, forgot.'

That was not strictly true. He had not forgotten her haemophobia, but he wanted to snap the wire pulling her tighter and tighter.

'Anyway, said geezer was missing a hand. Works in a city bank with millions in the hi-tech vault. Except could only be opened with the code plus one of three designated palm prints. His truly being one. Dead of night, robbery crew breaks into his house. Lopped it straight off. Gotta hand it to them.'

Gunn tried to deadpan it, but couldn't hold back the

smirk.

'Bollocks. You made that up.'

'Yeah, okay. But had you going for a sec. And you're the actor in the family.'

'Not yet.'

Gunn pulled up outside the Royal Academy of Dramatic Arts on Malet Street, a quarter mile north of the British Museum. As usual, half of London's highways seemed to be dug up and diverted.

He had driven Bathsheba because of the tube strike, called overnight while she was staying at a friend's house, south of the river. They had crawled up Whitehall, past the Cenotaph, on towards Nelson looking down imperiously from his lofty perch. The plan? Park in Soho. Grab a coffee and a delicious pastry concoction at the quirky Maison Bertaux in Greek Street. Relax. Amble on foot the half mile up through Bloomsbury. It seemed crazy now as Soho looked totally no go.

There are many Londons. 2000 years of them. Parallel Londons that never meet. Winding Londons whose paths endlessly converge and diverge. Far too many Londons for any one person to know. Having worked as a motorcycle delivery guy, Gunn knew a few: the West End's streets and short cuts, at least.

At Trafalgar Square, he took the counter-intuitive route, racing his red 1990 Saab 900 sports convertible up Pall Mall towards Green Park. He cut across Hyde Park Corner and floored it up Park Lane past central London's major lung. Crossing Marble Arch, zigging east and zagging north, up and down the maze of one-way side streets behind Oxford Street, stretching up through Fitzrovia. The ersatz *Fitzrovia* name was minted by the artists and writers who flocked there between the two world wars. But as the rents rose, the artistocracy upped pens and brushes to find somewhere new, as they always do. Today's Fitzrovia, centred on Fitzroy Square, houses more dentists and doctors than a third world country.

Clipping the south side of Fitzroy Square, Gunn zipped east along Grafton Way before turning back south again into Gower Street. A couple of hundred yards further and he made it. He had successfully delivered his biggest and most precious package with five minutes to spare.

His kid sister was going to the Royal Academy of Dramatic Art. Maybe. She had been called back after her first audition a month earlier. Gunn could not believe it. His younger-by-ten-months brother Ezekiel had been the smart one. He was the practical one. The tough bro wearing the hard rep. No one messed with Gunn's bookish, clever sibling with the sly sense of humour, and great smile. Not virtues always appreciated in the rough area where they grew up in north London.

Gunn had half-known Bebba was into the arsy-fartsy stuff at school. He assumed it was a way to hang out with the best looking boys. Then his first big brother panic. Gunn knew scummy teenage boys. Seven years practice. That was him before he met Ginny. Even worse, he read the tabloids and their never-ending gossip about actors. He didn't enjoy the thought that his kid sister would be Lohaned.

'Sorry can't hang around and drive you home kiddo.'

Bathsheba seemed to have calmed to something approaching her usual, eighteen year old, laid back self: 'It's all right. Going to Lezzy Square after. Channing Tatum at the Odeon.'

Gunn was never the touchy feely type. As a little kid, whenever an over-enthusiastic adult tousled his cute locks, or attempted to hug his cheeky-chubby little face, he squirmed away from their grasp with the agility of a well greased slug. So he surprised himself and startled his sister when he practically leapt across the seat, grabbing her in a big papa bear hug and squeezing hard.

'Channing Tatum? Never heard of her. What's that the luvvies say? Break a leg.'

She mock gasped. 'Can't breathe.'

Gunn released his strong grip, pushing five crisp twenties into her hand.

'Take your mates for a bite. Soho nice. No Big Macs. And get a cab home.'

Bathsheba was half way out of the car, shouting back her thanks. In the space of five yards the tension flowed out of her body. Her initial nervous stunted stride, picked up to a cocky jaunt. What was that? Real? Or was she already acting? Keyser Söze?

Bebba paused for a second in the entrance before she disappeared into RADA, looking back to dazzle out the dreamy smile she shared with Ezekiel. Gunn was staggered by how much she looked like their mother at that moment. Their sad mother, before their loving, eccentric dad died when Bebba was four; and Gunn was seventeen. Before *she* immediately married *him*.

He knew it was his own stubborn fault he had missed most of the growing years of his baby sister's life. The idea that he could miss being part of the rest of it, ripped at his guts. It would never happen.

He wanted to linger longer, as if his very will could radiate out and make her succeed. But there was nothing else he could do to help. Gunn reluctantly pulled away from the kerb and hoped the Sat-Nav would compute a faster route back to St. Michael's Hospital.

It didn't.

2

—THWACK—

A frustrated Gunn encouraged the vending machine to drop the can of coke for which he had deposited his last pound coin. The mute metal unit was proving immune to a punch in the fascia. Gunn was so wrapped up in his heated discussion with the coin munching monster that he didn't notice the man approaching. Though he couldn't miss the unmistakable Belfast twang that boomed out at him.

'Try not to break the damn thing like you did with the blood analyser.'

'You know the review said it wasn't my fault.'

Gunn wanted to add *'You arrogant prick'* but thought better of it. The prick in question being Mr Stuart Roper, Consultant and head of St. Michael's neurosurgery department. Gunn being a mere scrub nurse at the famous St. Michael's Hospital, with its great views of Parliament from the river facing wards. Affectionately known to staff, patients, and locals alike as St. Mike's, St. Micks, Mike's or Mickies.

'Delicate touch of the army medic eh, Mick?'

Gunn hated talking about his ten years' military service, but had to put his record straight. 'Royal Marine Corps. Medical assistant. Not army medic. Marines don't appreciate no pongo army lingo. And it's Nurse Gunn by the way Mr Roper. Or Micah. Or Mike. Or Mikey. Only corps oppos call me Mick.'

While Gunn was indifferent to Roper, the neurosurgeon actively disliked State Registered Male Nurse Gunn. Gunn couldn't be bothered to work out why.

At thirty-five, Stuart Roper was near the peak of his considerable powers, having recently been approached by the prestigious Johns Hopkins University Medical School in Baltimore. If that wasn't enough, at over six foot tall, ragingly single, and damn good looking in his roguish Irish way, Roper also had the pick of the young female SRNs at his hospital.

What bugged Roper was the knowledge that he couldn't intimidate or charm Gunn into quietly kowtowing to him. Not like his coterie of ward dollies hanging on his every wink, or lingering pat on the rump. Hence the nickname bestowed upon him by the less impressed female nurses: Roper the Groper.

Roper picked up something in Gunn's demeanour that lit up in flashing neon—*don't mess with me*. This annoyed the hell out of the alpha male on a primitive, grunt testosterone level. Gunn's seeming indifference made it worse.

Gunn had stopped at the vending machine in the walk-in reception area. He was pulling an all-nighter starting in ten minutes, and needed an ice-cold coke to remove the exhaust fumes left in his mouth. Even that was denied as the machine refused to comply for him.

'My mistake. See you in ten days. I'm sure Ms Soresha will be a capable deputy in my absence.'

Roper turned to walk away, then span back on his heel. With his talented right hand he carefully applied pressure to the fascia. A second later, Gunn's ice cold can dropped down the chute.

He smirked as he walked away, 'All in the magic

hands, *Nurse* Gunn.'

A motorbike versus truck came in about 8 p.m. The rider and passenger had been thrown thirty yards on impact. One helmet flew off mid-flight. That is never good. The helmetless boy racer died in the ambulance. Roper's deputy, Amanda Soresha did the honours and saved the female passenger. As a recently qualified scrub nurse, Gunn's job was to assist in theatre by handing over the surgical instruments the surgeon demanded.

Gunn escorted the still sedated girl as an orderly pushed her trolley back to the neurology ward. Part of his next duties would be to monitor her vital signs. He would also keep an eye on her emotional and physical well-being as she recovered with the knowledge that while she lived, her boyfriend had gone to that giant bike race in the sky.

Gunn swore if Bathsheba so much as glanced at a motorbike ad, he would lock her in a padded room till she came to his senses.

It was 5.55 a.m. and a narco-tired Gunn was glad his long day/night was finishing. This was his last shift before his own two week break. Nothing planned except fourteen whole days when he could stop worrying about total strangers and concentrate on reconnecting with his sister.

Gunn grabbed his bag from his locker and took the lift to the ground floor. He turned left and walked the long neon lit corridor towards the Accident & Emergency exit. As he approached the line of ten curtained-off rooms used for emergency treatment, a bloodied young man staggered out from number two.

'Oi, where's the crapper mate?'

Gunn eyed the half-cut, half-wit who seemed oblivious to his two black eyes and flattened, bloody nose.

'Down the hall through reception. On your left.'

With a grunt, the end product of six million years of evolution continued his stagger in the direction to which Gunn had pointed.

That was it. Exit ahead. Fourteen days of freedom. Before he could move, a foul mouthed, Chinese-accented, female voice hissed from the other side of the next curtain.

'Yo Gunn, that you muthafucka? You gotta fucken see this. Man this is unbelievfuckable. Like something from fucken Jet Li movie.'

'Don't have time Ziya.'

A surprisingly strong, slender arm shot from behind the curtain and dragged him into the treatment room. Gunn enjoyed being woman-handled by the mid-twenties Nurse Ziya Zhang. A real looker. Like one of those actresses in weird Chinese movies, where everyone flies across buildings. Gorgeous and graceful and gung-ho. She continued dragging Gunn to the treatment table to the *thing* she wanted him to see.

It seemed he was seeing Freddy Krueger's handiwork. What remained of the man's blood soaked clothes lay discarded in a heap in the corner.

'Waaaasup Gunn! Someone go medieval on muthafucka's ass. Croaked ten fucken minutes after ambulance bring in. Man, what the fuck.'

'Ziya, stop effing and blinding. You're worse than the Friday night walking wounded.'

Ziya smiled sweetly: 'Not my fucken fault learn muthafucken English watching kickass American gangsta movies in Hong Kong. But I try. For you Gunn.'

He looked at her and laughed. Scarface and Pulp Fiction seemed to be the top two teachable movies for Ziya.

Ziya was frantic to go through all the gory ruin in great detail. There was no stopping her, so he didn't try.

'Look. Fucken lef—I mean left eye cut out. Both ears sliced off. Teeth smashed.'

'This guy was alive when he came in?'

'Oh yeah, walking too, like some fucken living dead zombie before ambulance pick up. But he never say word, because—'

Ziya leaned in to triumphantly lever open the dead man's mouth: 'Taa daaa, no fucken tongue.'

It wasn't the only body part he was missing. Ziya enthusiastically pointed out to Gunn what he was seeing in gorious 24-bit colour. The man's face was an unrecognizable mess. The fingers on both hands were bloody stumps down to the palm. The whole torso had been slashed repeatedly with a knife. But not randomly it seemed: as a giant 'X' had been carved from shoulder to hip.

'Unbelievfuckable. Right?'

'You said it Ziya.'

'You miss it Gunn.'

'Missed what, missy?'

'Ha. He lose things, but he got extra—'

'Gotta go Ziya.'

'Fucka got six toes on each foot.'

Gunn checked the feet again. One, two, three, four, five plus a big toe. It was called Polydactylyism, and it was very rare, but especially as a central postaxial hand and foot polydactyly, where the extra digit was a fully functioning finger or toe. Gunn had seen it before with a Royal Marine when they went through training at Lympstone together. He had an extra finger on each hand. Good marine. His nickname was the inevitable, not so flattering *Hand Job*.

'Spotted. Not just a pretty face eh, doll?'

'You think face fucken pretty Gunn?'

Gunn grinned. Ziya loved compliments. She fished for them, but in an amusing way, not a saddo creepy way. She knew she was good looking. She had to know as she had two functioning eyes and did not need glasses.

He shrugged exaggeratedly, and shook his hand in a so-so gesture. 'Meh, you'll pass.'

Ziya belted him on the arm with her small fist. 'Ow, that hurt.'

'Ha. Good. Liar liar, ants on fire. You know you want, Gunn.'

Maybe he did, maybe he didn't. But the chat was getting a bit too personal. 'Pants. It's pants on fire not ants. And shouldn't you be getting a move on?'

'Yes, okay, you fucken hold me up Gunn. Quick, now police here any minute to take over body. Why set pants on fire? Ants yes, cweepy cwalies. English fucken crazy.'

Ziya handed Gunn one of the hospital's plastic bags used to store patients personal items. 'Collect X-man's stuff while I do chart for police records.'

'Ziya, I was officially on holiday ten minutes ago.'

'Please Gunn. You know it need two here.'

Gunn pulled on a pair of surgical gloves. 'Okay, okay.'

The man was naked except for a nice looking watch. The small indignities of death. The dial whispered discretely *Patek Philippe Chronograph*. It felt solidly real to him, not a knock-off. Real would be a few thousand pounds, as opposed to the hundred Iraqi dinar asked by the dodgy street hawkers he remembered from Baghdad.

'Patek Philippe. Obscenely expensive. Looks genuine.'

He bagged the watch then moved to the corner of the room to collect the discarded blood soaked gear in which the man arrived. The trendy Calvin Kleins were sliced, diced and bloodied. Gunn noticed that there was no shirt or jacket. The pants had been cut off and were in ribbons, soaked with drying blood. Gunn had dealt before with personal possessions in police cases, so he knew what to do.

'Witness me checking his pockets.'

No wallet. No ID of any kind. The pants' pockets were empty. The *Paul Smith* waist label confirmed its expensive yet discretely trendy provenance. Gunn bagged the trousers. The final personal possessions were a pair of expensive looking shoes. He dropped them into the bag. After tying the bag ends into a knot, Gunn placed it on the table next to the body. At last, he could begin his deserved two week rest-fest.

That's when he saw it on the floor. 'Ziya, something here.' Gunn bent down and scooped it up. It was a medallion, about the size and weight of a two pound coin.

The medallion had—what did it have? He had thought it was covered in globs of dried reddish-brown blood on the surface, but it wasn't blood. It was excrement.

Gunn figured that he, whoever *he* was, must have had the thing inserted up his anus. Like all of us when we die, his body and its muscles instantly relaxed, including his sphincter which controls bowel movement. In the unknown X-man victim's case this meant the medallion was close enough to the anal entrance to plop out along with any other natural body waste. Even as a medical professional, Gunn found that an unpleasant thought.

Shock. Gunn felt the expensive weight of the medallion in the palm of his hand. An arctic chill stormed through his body. It felt and looked familiar, but that was impossible. Had to be. He went over to the small sink and turned on the hot water tap. He held the medallion under the water and vigorously rubbed it in liquid antiseptic soap until it was shiny clean. Gunn could see clearly the engraved relief of a haloed St. Christopher carrying a child across a raging river.

Denial. Gunn told himself there must be millions of St. Christopher medallions still minted, even if the saint had fallen from grace in some eyes. One problem: Moshe Goldberg, the talented Hatton Garden jeweller, promised the teenage Micah that the design was absolutely unique: a haloed St. Christopher carrying a child across the raging river. And that Moshe made them to special order, each medal having its own edition number engraved on the edge in Roman numerals. For Gunn's order, the number was MXXVII.

Gunn hardly dared turn over the medallion to look at the smooth flip side. But he did.

'Fuck no. Fuck, fuck no.'

There it was, as he knew in his guts it would be; the engraving he had watched Moshe expertly etch into the silver in 1997.

To my kid brother Ezekiel.
Your Guardian Angel. M.I.G.

Anger. Gunn punched the nearest object: a defibrillator hanging from the wall. The expensive piece of kit kerranged to the ground, as a startled Ziya jumped a foot in the air. Gunn slumped to the floor, leaning back against the wall. Ziya knelt besides him, placing her slender hand on his shoulder. He didn't flinch, for once.

'Wha—what's wrong Gunn. Scare me.'

Acceptance. Gunn opened his hand to reveal the St. Christopher in his palm. 'Gave this to my older brother Ezekiel. The day he left home for university. Swore he'd never take it from around his neck.'

'Oh, okay. So what? He los—'

'Murdered, my brother was—nineteen ninety-nine. Some random paranoid schizophrenic. Arrested him the same day after confessing. Been locked in a secure mental institution ever since.'

'So how did—' Ziya looked up at the already decaying body of the man who also looked like he had been tortured and sliced and diced: 'Fuck a duck.'

'Exactly.'

3

Gunn fished the iPhone from his bag. Three new voicemail messages waiting. *Bebba.* He had no time to listen as he started clicking off photographs of the body.

'Gunn you fuc—you can't take pictures of dead body. Hospital go nuts.'

He lifted the medallion from his pocket, waving it at her.

'Sorry love, not today.'

He made Ziya promise not to say anything about the St. Christopher to the police, who could plod in at any second. Nurse Zhang pouted. She was still on a temporary work visa; and was paranoid about doing anything that put her on the police's radar.

Ambulance crews work different shifts to nurses. Bravo Roster was due off at 7 a.m. Gunn checked his watch. Six forty: twenty-five minutes since random events put him right outside Room 3, allowing Ziya to yank open the memory curtain back to his brother's brutal murder.

Throwing his padded bomber jacket over his faded blue hospital scrubs, Gunn had raced the quarter mile down St. Michael's Road to the main ambulance station for Lambeth & Vauxhall. He strode into the ambulance station's admin office which overlooked the twelve parking bays. It was one minute to seven; the sun had been up for a couple of hours, but there was a refreshing chill in the air.

Station manager Dave Malloy's shiny dome glinted like

an oily peanut in the harsh light of his PC monitor. Dave already looked harassed as he gulped the foul brew from the station's instant coffee machine.

'Morning Dave.'

Malloy glanced up from the night's incident reports. 'Hey Mikey. Long time no see. On or off mate?'

'End of an all-nighter. Ask a favour?'

Dave did not have the time. But he liked and respected Gunn. 'Sure, if I can. What is it?'

'Crew brought in a bloke, really bad way. Fingers chopped off.'

Dave shuddered at the thought. He was an administrator not a paramedic. Nor a lover of bloody horror.

'Jockette and the Jolly Roger made the run. From what she described, amazed she managed to get him to A&E breathing.'

Malloy hesitated as a potential snafu scenario for his unit suddenly sprang up; ready to kick him in the head. 'Err, why? Problem?'

Gunn picked up Dave's jobsworth vibe. 'No mate, no probs at all. Nothing to do with the job. Personal actually.'

'In that case my son, don't wanna know. Shtum's the word. Jockette's rig is in bay seven.'

The ambulance's rear doors were open and he could see a shapely female bottom pointed in the air, its owner searching for something under a seat. The Jockette—as she was universally known—had heard the footsteps stomp along the concrete ramp, stopping outside her ambulance.

Her lard-thick Glaswegian twang, mixed with *sarf London Mockney*, cut through the bay: 'I cannae see ya, but ya nae betta be looking at ma arse ya mucky perv.'

'That would be the pure dead brilliant arse with the no entry sign on it?'

'Gunn—'

—*THWACK*—

'—shit.'

The Jockette scooted out backwards; rubbing her natural, strawberry blonde-haired head. She hauled herself up to her full five foot seven, waving in triumph the prize for which she'd been searching.

'Dropped ma engagement ring, can ya believe it?'

Gunn was embarrassed. 'Been meaning to say, major congrats.'

'Yeah well, ya nae took ya wee chance Gunn. Lasses cannae hang around forever. Coming Saturday night? Stringfellas. Free bar till eleven. Meet ma wee fella.'

Gunn smiled his standard non-committal way. 'Okay, try me best love.'

'Did I tell ya he's dead rich? Halffa St. Mike's coming by the RSVPs.'

Gunn and Jockette had been out and about a few times last year, but his never-ending pain over the loss of his girls throbbed hot and heavy. Gunn was looking for platonic female company to give him the public patina of normal. The delicious Celtic firecracker Kirsty Smith – the Jockette – was looking for love. He was moving on, but not that fast.

'Fancy a coffee at Gino's? My treat.'

Gino's is the local Italian café on Hercules Road, around the corner from the ambulance station. According to the real coffee-nut Gunn, Gino's served the best coffee in London.

As he gulped through his first mug of strong black, Kirsty bit enthusiastically into her breakfast: golden egg yolk oozed freely onto her chin. On her, it looked cute. Even this early in the morning, the place was jostling elbow to arse with its usual mixed bag. Doctors, nurses and ambulance crews coming or going off shift. Blue and white collar council types. Commuters walking down from Waterloo Station. Tourists up early heading to places they travelled thousands of miles to experience; like the Imperial War Museum ten minutes walk away.

Gunn felt good to be lost in this anonymous slice of normal. Watching her chomp through a delicious mouthful of her rapidly shrinking egg and bacon and sausage ciabatta.

'What's it all about Mikey?'

He got straight to the point. 'That rocky horror show you brought in.'

'Aye.'

'What can you tell me?'

She went to take another bite, but stopped and shivered. 'Jesus F. Christ. Really? Why?'

Gunn drained his mug, and indicated to the lurking young waitress for a refill. She smiled, took his mug and went to the counter. By the time she returned with another hit of his drug of choice, Gunn had regaled Kirsty with an abbreviated version of the events in Treatment Room 3. He could tell she was hovering on the edge of giving him a right bollocking for lifting the medallion. It was a totally sackable offence.

'Me and the Jolly Roger answered a triple niner called in by a passing motorist on his mobile. Driving down Milkwood Road, Brixton like, about fifty yards past Dylan Thomas Industrial Estate. Anyways, good sammy reports guy staggering. Checked his rear view, saw him collapse. We was four minutes out so look the call.'

'If he was that much of a Samaritan how come he

didn't stop and go check?'

'People dinnae wanna get involved.'

Munching her way expertly through the rest of the ciabatta, she ran through the timeline. The man had almost bled out on the pavement, and she had performed a miracle getting him to A&E alive.

Kirsty delicately popped the last ketchup-dripping morsel into her mouth as she completed detailing all the guy's bloody wounds.

'Mmmm, so good. And that was it. Jolly called it in en route, suspected attempted murder, and we were told cops would arrive post haste, when we'd have to give a statement. Hung around till shift ended, then youse turned up.'

Kirsty leaned across and squeezed Gunn's bear sized mitt with her china doll fingers. He smiled and she zeroed him right in the eyes. 'Look, you're pissed off big time, acted in the heat of the moment. Go back to the hospital. Bet the cops havnae even arrived yet.'

Forty minutes later, Gunn rolled his red Saab slowly to a stop, twenty yards past the entrance to the Dylan Thomas Industrial Estate. The early morning sunshine had given way to darkening clouds. Milkwood Road was south Brixton, but it may as well have been on the dark side of the moon. He worked on the south bank, and had recently bought a house in Battersea, but Gunn would always be a north London boy. What was he doing here?

He had not paused to think from the moment he turned over a medallion which had flipped his life. As a marine, and even as a nurse, he always had a defined mission. A goal. An objective. It may seem like chaos to outsiders: bullets flying, men dying, but there was a purpose; and the comfort of structure. So what was he doing? Parked here on his own. What was his mission? He had no idea. All he had was the hunger to do something, unlike the way he fell apart fourteen years ago.

Gunn did a 360-degree scan to take in the terrain. On the opposite side of the road, the shabby industrial estate was kept in by an ugly 1950s style prefabricated concrete wall, stretching fifty yards in either direction from the centre entrance gate. He had parked in front of a row of red brick nineteenth century terraced houses. They had low half-basements and high steps to their front doors. On his side of the road a few vehicles parked off into the distance. They all seemed to be shabby older cars: Toyota, Skoda, Yaris, Nissan. A dark Range Rover was the furthest away in his line of sight. Too far away to tell its age.

He checked his watch. Two minutes past nine. An elderly black couple shuffled slowly past his car chatting amiably about test matches and Darren Bravo. This meant nothing to Gunn as he was strictly a footy man. A Liverpool Football Club supporter like his old man: and the rest of his dozens of Scouser cousins back up north in Liverpool.

The pair headed past the houses towards the line of small shops on the next block. He held back until they were out of earshot then scooted out of the Saab, hurrying across the narrow road to the pavement opposite.

And there it was: the unmistakable stain of dried browny-red where the blood pooled after the mystery man went down for the last time. Gunn was amazed. He was standing in a crime scene, and yet the police were nowhere to be seen. Is this how his brother's murder was treated when he was stuck in Bosnia with his unit and could do nothing about it.

About ten feet up the pavement, in the direction of the gates, Gunn saw something else. Bingo. A two inch wide blob of the same browny-red residue. Then a staggered trail of smaller blobs leading back towards the estate entrance. He took out his phone and once again click-clicked each trace of something bad.

Gunn looked at the huge blue sign to the left of the gates. The name Dylan Thomas Industrial Estate and its list of occupants was half covered by a diagonal poster stating:

CLOSED FOR REDEVELOPMENT.
CALL 0207 225 7188
FOR INFORMATION ABOUT
NEW INDUSTRIAL UNITS COMING SOON.
CPH LIMITED, LONDON, NW10 5TZ.

There was another sign attached to the gate. It had a graphic representation of a snarling Nazi hell hound warning trespassers that this property was guarded by TipTop Security Ltd. The high metal frame double gates were hinged on rusty metal pillars, bolted either side of the concrete wall. Gunn could see the dripped blood trail continuing right into the dog-eared estate. The gates were padlocked shut. He paused. It wasn't too late to take Kirsty's advice and get the hell out of there. Leave it to the professionals.

Nah, fuck it.

He climbed over the gate and dropped down inside the estate. Gunn reckoned there were about thirty large industrial units, seemingly of a similar crumbling red brick construction, topped by filthy grey corrugated-metal sloping roofs, ingrained with grime pre-dating the Beatles. The windows were uniformly boarded up with plywood.

It was all very nineteen-fifties; except for the one taller, metal clad building standing out like a gold tooth in a mouth full of stained porcelain.

The businesses had all fled, abandoning signs with names like A-1 Brixton Motors Ltd, Advanced uPVC Glazing, FastaPrint Quality Printers Limited, Sign-A-Rama: We Specialise In Making You Look Amazing.

The pot-holed, broken tarmac surface went in about twenty yards before branching left and right. Gunn diligently followed the trail, which kept up the same regular deadly droppage. It veered left.

Sign-A-Rama was situated half way down the length of units. Gunn had walked twenty yards past and arrived at a right turn intersection. No more stains, which meant his last bloody clue was plumb in front of the sign makers. As he hurried back, Gunn noticed the *quiet*. Apart from the distant *clack clack clack* of trains on a railway line, there was barely a sound.

The unit was fronted by an add-on Portacabin acting as the office slash reception. The door was hanging open so Gunn strode into the gloom. He found the light switch. Nothing. Not that there was much to see: a smashed desk, a pile of old rags, scattered office bumph, overturned chair, and—

There it was, in front of the door on the back wall leading into the building proper: another darkish stain. Gunn's senses went hair-trigger and the switch came on. In an unthinking haste, he had gone off totally cocked, dressed in scrubs, bomber jacket and his work trainers. Now here he was with no idea what lay behind that door, totally unprepared and vulnerable.

Gunn rooted around his jacket pockets. A packet of chewing gum surfaced. Not exactly a defence weapon of choice. He scoped the office again. The smashed-up desk looked promising. He found what he needed: a solid metal table leg about thirty inches long and three inches in diameter. The rags were a pile of old T-Shirts with the logo Sign-A-Rama emblazoned on the front. A jagged piece of wood helped rip the material. He tied one half of the shirt a few times around his left knuckles and repeated the process with the right.

That was better. He put his head against the door and listened. All he could hear was his own thump-thumping heart, which Gunn reckoned had spiked thirty beats higher than his normal seventy beats per minute. *Calm. Calm. No noise Micky.*

Gunn gently pulled down the handle.

—CREAK—

He held his breath. Still nothing. He pulled the door open.

—SCREECH—

Jesus Gunn. Take out an ad why doncha?

He walked into the windowless bible-black. The available light behind him, leaking in from the Portacabin doorway. Ahead he could barely discern the layout more than three feet in front, as he crunched extra loudly on the scattered glass, and other debris littering the floor.

Advancing in further, Gunn could make out more features. To his left were some large machines, probably used for fabricating signs. This being a sign maker, and all. To his right a row of separate rooms running off into the darkness.

Gunn stopped and waited. Dead silence. He would have to go back and buy a torch from one of the local shops, but as he turned to go.

—SCRAPE—

Spinning around fast Gunn gripped his improvised metal weapon even tighter.

What the hell was that?

The noise had snapped out of the black, further in, from one of the rooms. He paused and listened. Glancing back for bearings at the hole of light, Gunn edged towards the first room entrance, a few feet up on his right. He leaned back against the wall. From his new perspective this was to the left of the entrance. There was no door, only the edge of gaping blackness beyond. Gunn took three long breaths to calm his heart and flood his lungs with air. He was ready: pivoting on his right foot he span 180 degrees around from the wall to stand in the door frame. Pitch black.

Gunn grabbed his phone and pressed a random key. The screen lit up, casting out a dim light. He held it out and scanned the room. Empty. Then the phone battery died.

Gunn spun around again, back against the wall, edging his way in a sideways shuffle, combat style, like he was back in Afghanistan. As he approached the next room's opening, it crossed Gunn's mind how silly he must look. It was probably a rat dragging away something for breakfast.

Still, when he reached the entrance he paused and repeated his pivot routine. This was better. A tiny sliver of light was breaking through from above, allowing him to see the office chair plonked in the middle of an otherwise cleared space. Gunn crunched the ten feet across scattered pieces of glass to the chair. He lowered himself to his haunches to check for any extraneous matter that may come from, oh—a man being slashed, tortured and mutilated.

Every hair on Gunn's body shot up like a moon rocket.

—*SMELL*—

The unsubtle scent of a man's splash-on fragrance, the sandalwood not quite masking its owner's sour sweat. Right behind. Feet away. Silent. Waiting. For Gunn? His back totally exposed.

Gunn forced himself to *grunt* quietly, as if sharing a private observation. Acting oblivious to the fact that someone had the drop on him.

Vulnerable. Open to someone armed with—could be anything. If it was a firearm, and *the smell* knew how to use it, then he was probably lost whatever he did. Gunn forced the issue by slowly standing up, as if he had finished his casual sherlocking. His single advantage was that the bloke assumed he had a clear ambush field. So he would not expect any resistance when Gunn scratched the back of his head with his left hand, as he made to turn around.

—*BLAM*—

The assailant catapulted himself into a massive blitz attack. But Gunn was ready. The implement flashed past his head as he swayed away.

—*THUD*—

Instead of taking a chunk from Gunn's skull, the dull axe slammed a glancing blow against his shoulder on its way down. The force knocked Gunn sideways. Tumbling backwards Gunn's head slammed against the chair, but he had already begun swinging his own metal weapon. He smashed into the axe-man's leg. Hard. Everything he had.

—*CRUNCH*—

The bone-splintering crunch unleashing a howl of shocked pain.

Instinctively raising his left arm to his head to absorb the impact, Gunn smacked the ground. He rolled a couple of times as he had been combat taught, cloth-wrapped hands skidding across the glass strewn deck. In between rolls he glimpsed the axe-man stumbling backwards rapidly.

The head smash had stunned Gunn, but he bounced to his feet gripping his weapon. Gunn sprinted from the room. He could hear the rapidly retreating foot thumps as the assailant headed towards the pitch-black rear of the building. Gunn dashed forward, following the racket, when

—*SMACK*—

straight into a toppled filing cabinet. Gunn tumbled head first over it. The chair leg flew from his hand, clattering into the gloom.

Seconds later he saw daylight flash as a door opened about fifty feet in front. It was on its third or fourth bounce back by the time Gunn barged out into the now pouring rain. The axe-man had vanished.

Ignoring the blood flowing from his head, Gunn sprinted past the side of the building, back towards the front Portacabin. He reached the exit road at the same instant as a black Range Rover tore across him, obligatory menacing tinted windows and all. Gunn veered violently left and managed to miss running head first into the vehicle which then slid right to take the exit road back through the gates which were now open.

'Shit.'

Gunn repeated the word three or four times, bent double, hands on knees sucking in air. He walked slowly back to the entrance to the estate; it crossed his mind that he needed to do some road work, pump up his cardio endurance rate.

The rain was washing away all the bloody evidence as he flipped through the past few hours. Brother's death. Stolen evidence from a murder victim. Some guy had tried to smash him in the face with an axe. Head bleeding.

Pissing down. And he had narrowly avoided being mincemeated by a speeding Range Rover.

Gunn checked the time. It was nine-thirty. The day was young, but at least it couldn't get any worse.

That's when he heard the rapidly approaching Tiptop Nazi hell hounds snarling and barking his way.

4

A warm breeze caressed Gunn's face. The evocative aroma of Jamaican Blue Mountain coffee (the world's most expensive) was unmistakable. That didn't make sense, because it was over a hundred degrees, and he was lying on a dazzling white beach in the tropics. Nicely shaded by the giant palm tree, surrounded by ten almost naked beauties of every nation, seemingly focused entirely on him. Gunn relaxed and thanked God the thing about Ezekiel was all a dream.

The radio on the bedside table popped into real life. It was *Wham* waking him up before he go-go.

'Mon, ain't ya gonna switch dat noise off, ya Babylon white boy?'

Gunn shot bolt upright. Sitting in the comfy chair opposite his bed was a huge black guy. He looked intimidating even wearing a three grand Gieves & Hawkes suit. Hell, at two feet long the bloke's dreads looked like they could hold their own in a bare knuckle brawl.

'White boy? That's real nice. Classy y'know. And please drop the patois. You're so Richmond Surrey, not Richmond Jamaica.'

'Jah know. Ma bad. S'in de blud.'

Eddie Bishop was Gunn's best friend. *Bezzy mucker* in Royal Marine lingo. He was crashing at Gunn's Battersea house for a few days. They had a *no questions asked* friendship since serving together. It was not as if Eddie lacked plenty of options; at any one time he was buying and selling a hundred properties dotted around the country. He had also gotten into financing interesting start-ups and was backing a couple of techno-kids straight out of Cambridge.

Eddie had sold him the house, after Gunn had finally worked past his vow to never spend the huge life insurance settlement he received following the death of his wife and child. That was hard, but Gunn needed somewhere nice with the space to get to know his kid sister.

Eddie gave Gunn a real wake-up call. 'Brewed up a pot a yer favourite wet.'

'Smell it from here. You're gonna make someone a wonderful wife some day.'

'Forget it Sir Elton. Told you, not interested.'

'Keep posting your bio on Gayboys dot com. No takers yet, huh?'

'For *dat* bludclot, pour da wet yersel.' Eddie yawned. 'By the by, Bebba's on her way over. Something about you ignoring her messages. Oh, and two big coppers is downstairs asking for youse. What naughties you been up to One Shot?'

'Shit.' Gunn bounced right out of his bed and winced. The delayed effects of being axed in the shoulder had kicked in with a vengeance.

'Jesus Mick. Hell of a black an' bluey you got there on yer lily white. Head don't look too tasty neither.'

Gunn threw on a pair of 501s and T-shirt, at the same time giving Eddie the fast forwarded highlights of the past few hours.

Eddie sat shaking his head in that semi-judgmental way he had towards anyone making poor life choices. Like many converts, Eddie was a fanatic. His conversion was to turn his life around from the petty crime he drifted into after leaving the Marines.

'Want me to call my lawyer for you mate? She's bloody good.'

Gunn considered it for a second or two. 'Be all right.'

Eddie was correct. The two Scotland Yard officers were big. The junior detective was a barrel of a man, almost as wide as he was tall. It was his six foot three colleague Detective Inspector Sam Wilson who did the talking, but not before Eddie walked in carrying a tray balancing four large mugs of the world's most expensive coffee. Gunn and Eddie exchanged smirky looks, as they both clocked the *make someone a good wife* reference.

Eddie handed out the mugs: 'Officers. One black, one black with sugar. Your usual One Shot,' then made as if to hang around.

The lanky Wilson in charge made their position clear. 'Thank you sir, if we could have a word with Mr Gunn in private, much obliged.'

Eddie raised his eyebrows to Gunn in a *still don't want my lawyer* question. 'Sure, be in the kitchen.'

Twenty minutes later Gunn was sitting in the back seat of a dark blue Ford, next to Wilson. They were heading up the Albert Embankment to Lambeth Bridge, then across to New Scotland Yard. When the murder team finally arrived at the hospital, Ziya crumpled faster than a Kleenex brick. Gunn had agreed to voluntarily accompany them to clear up a couple of things. He was not being arrested. Wilson was careful to emphasize that point.

Neither policeman spoke in the four miles to Broadway and Victoria Street, north of the river. Gunn recognized calculated psychological warfare when he didn't hear it. The campaign continued in the Yard as the silent Wilson escorted him to an interview room on the tenth floor.

—*CLANG*—

The door shut with finality. The room was harshly lit, no doubt to make its denizens feel uneasy and more compliant. Gunn sat on an uncomfortable plastic chair, at a metal table bolted to the floor. All four corners had a CCTV camera fixed at the nexus between wall and ceiling. No matter where he faced, someone could see Gunn's face. He wondered about all the killers who had sat here, in this very chair. No doubt they were thinking how best to phrase their lies. How best to manipulate the situation. Or maybe they were shit scared and ready to spill all. Gunn was none of these. He zenned out and thought of as little as possible.

About an hour had passed when the door opened. Wilson entered, followed by another man in a Marks & Sparks off the rack pinstripe. He carried a couple of plastic folders which he slammed down hard before sitting opposite Gunn. Wilson dragged the other plastic chair to the side of the table and clattered himself down.

The new copper smiled with all the sincerity of a hungry Cheshire cat to a mouse. 'Mr Gunn, I'm Detective Superintendent Bill Hickman, with the Homicide and Serious Crime Command. Inspector Wilson you've met.'

Gunn glanced to his left to see Wilson staring at him, unblinking. Check—glowering.

'You have not been arrested Mr Gunn, you have come here voluntarily. But to ensure you know your legal rights I'll read this to you.'

Hickman took a card out of his suit jacket pocket, although he knew the mantra by rote. 'You do not have to say anything. But it may harm your defence if you do not mention when questioned something that you later rely on in court. Anything you do say may be given in evidence. Understand?'

Gunn nodded. 'A whole Detective Superintendent for little old me?'

Hickman ignored Gunn's interest in Met ranks. 'Could you affirm you understand, verbally sir, out loud please.'

'I understand. I can ask for a lawyer.'

'Do you want a solicitor Mr Gunn?'

'Not at the moment.'

'Great, now we've got that out of the way.' Hickman opened one of the plastic folders and pulled out a pile of photocopied documents. 'What the hell are you playing at son?'

Gunn was doing lots of things today. None of them playing. They didn't expect Gunn's fist to slam into the metal table with a force startling enough to make both coppers visibly flinch. Zenned out no more.

Wilson leapt to his feet to tower and glower over the seated Gunn.

'Okay detective, sit down.' Wilson complied instantly with his boss's barked command.

Hickman returned with practised confidence to his semi-voluntary guest. 'Less of the histrionics lad. Look, we know you took a piece of evidence from what could have been construed as technically, but not yet considered a crime scene, as the victim had been transported by ambulance, and there was an unfortunate delay in the initial report making it here to the HSCC. In case you're wondering this is *the* murder unit for the Met—and we are investigating what in all likelihood is the murder of an unknown male in his early thirties who died at approximately 5 a.m. this morning. Awaiting the post mortem and coroner's report.'

The confident Hickman was speaking seamlessly and

without hesitation.

'Here's the one time deal which expires in about ten seconds. Hand it over right now and we'll say no more. Fuck me around and I'll throw the whole fucking book at your fucking head. Believe me, in my hands it's a dead heavy fucker that involves you losing your fucking job, which I hear from the delightfully profane Nurse Zhang you're good at and you love. Whaddya say son?'

Hickman had him and they both knew it. Gunn undid the top two buttons of his shirt to reveal a silver chain with the dangling medallion. Lifting it from around his neck Gunn handed the medallion to Hickman. 'Want that back as soon as. And I wanna know how come my brother's St. Christopher was stuffed up the arse of some dead body, when his so-called killer's been locked up for the past fourteen years.'

Hickman dropped the medallion into an evidence bag. 'I understand your concern Mr Gunn.'

'NO, I don't think you do Detective Superintendent.'

'Then why don't you illuminate me, sir.'

'Yeah, right, okay, why not. I wasn't happy with the original investigation. But y'know, what the hell did I know? Some skanky-arsed kid with a legal rifle and a licence to kill, given ten days compassionate leave to bury me brother. Now this.'

'The man being held indefinitely at Radcliffe for killing your brother, Rufus Wright. Based on this medallion thing, you seem to have convinced yourself he's innocent, right?'

Gunn glared straight back at Hickman. 'I haven't convinced—

For emphasis Gunn threw in the air-quote.

—myself of anything. It's not like a jury found him guilty, as he was judged unfit to stand trial. Yet you seem to have convinced yourself he's guilty, right?'

'I hear you. But did you know that Wright has killed again since? In the secure hospital?'

A look of satisfaction flitted across Hickman's face. 'Didn't know that, I see.'

Hickman opened another file and extracted a sheet of paper. 'On August 3rd, 2009, Rufus Wright was taking an art therapy class in Radcliffe Maximum Security Psychiatric Hospital. He was completing an oil painting. Style similar to Vincent Van Gogh, apparently. Big gobs of paint. Big thick oil paint brush, that's important Mr Gunn. Big brush. So, patient Ryan Sperling, an arsonist who fantasized about watching people burn to death, and who fire bombed five cars in the underground car park of a Sheffield high rise to see if he could bring the whole building down, along with the three hundred families who lived there. Inspired by 9/11, see. Anyway Ryan sees what Rufus Van Wright has painted and makes some comment. At which point Wright knocks him to the ground with his paint palette. BLAM—

Hickman chopped his hand violently in front of him, causing Gunn and Wilson to visibly flinch.

—takes his fifteen inch long paint brush and drives it pointy end through Mr Sperling's right eye. The force is so great that it penetrates the back of his skull. He spasmed around for about five minutes while the duty doctors and nurses tried vainly to save him. Sound familiar? Given the almost identical nature of your brother's murder, et cetera, et cetera. Need I go on?'

That news had definitely knocked the momentum out of Gunn. Marine training kicked in. He needed to regain the initiative right now.

'But—isn't it like, well-known, sending people to prison mostly teaches them how to be better criminals?

Because Wright killed someone else doesn't prove anything about the past. They call that a logical fallacy. Post hoc ergo propter hoc. And as I said, now this. Believe in coincidences in crime Superintendent?'

Hickman crossed his arms and shifted in his seat. 'There are a number of scenarios that could account for this.'

'Yeah, okay. But who is he? The bloke with my brother's St. Christopher up his arse. Bit suspicious don't you think?'

Now that Gunn had surrendered the evidence, Wilson gave up his silent intimidating pose. 'That's still to be determined Mr Gunn. No ID yet.'

'No ID? What's wrong with—'

The belligerent Wilson spat back instantly. 'You saw his face and fingers for Christ's sake.'

The still defensive Hickman jumped in. 'Mr Gunn the whole area is a notorious drug centre south of the river. Given the type of violence, one working theory is this is the start of a vicious turf war. Swear to God, London gets more like the Mexican drug cartels every day.'

They circled around the block a few times in similar style. Gunn kept steering the interview back to questions about how this murder intersected with Ezekiel. Hickman kept it about on-going enquiries and drugs and turf wars and gangs. It was clear to Gunn that Hickman was not going to give him anything.

Hickman went to the photocopied sheets of paper from the folder. He seemed embarrassed. 'Mr Gunn I see you've had, uh—had some psychiatric treatment over the years.'

Gunn's turn to glower. 'Yeah, and not ashamed of it neither. Went a bit crazy after Ezekiel died. A Marine shrink saw me through it, even suggested I do the medical assistant thing to focus me.'

'Look I only mention—'

'No, no, you brought it up. Obviously what happened to my wife and daughter is photocopied there. Copy of a copy. All nice and blurry. Filed away. Easy that way. Makes it all so.'

'We are aware Mr Gunn. Must have been hard.'

'Christ's sake stow the fake empathy Superintendent. Your file mention I still do regular group therapy with Dr Daniel Mosser? Got me down on paper as a nutjob. That it? Well I happen to lead the group. Mention that does it? I help others for crying out loud.'

Hickman was about as embarrassed as he ever gets, which is never, usually. 'One more thing Mr Gunn. Can't help noticing you've taken some sort of blow to the head.'

Gunn tapped his temple. 'Tripped over a patient at work, luckily the ground broke me fall.'

'Funny guy. These cameras?' Hickman pointed up towards the corners. 'Not recording. Strictly off the record, courtesy to you, for your service, and—well, your brother. So, bump on the noggin. Nothing to do with this little enquiry then?'

This was the point of no return for Gunn. A call to action if ever there was one. This was his out. Spill the truth and walk away. Simple. Leave it alone like he did fourteen years ago. Betray his brother a second time.

No sense in kidding himself. Reject that and he would be committed to his own path, which could lead over a cliff.

'Absolutely not. Now can I go?'

5

Gunn stepped out of Scotland Yard into the dripping air of central London. The morning rain had given way to a hot, sticky early evening. Trotting the few yards from Broadway to the intersection with Victoria Street, Gunn headed west towards Victoria Station. He checked his mobile for new voicemails and texts.

Voicemail: You have two new messages. Press five to—
Bebba: Hey bro. Where you at? Okay, audition didn't totally suck. On my way to your place. I'll let myself in. (PAUSE) As opposed to breaking in I suppose.

Ziya had also been in touch. She was contrite, but how much, Gunn found hard to decipher.

Ziya: Hey Nurse Watchet, guess fucken who? Give up? It fucken me, Ziya. Ha ha. Look, sorry about squealing, but muthafucken coppa stare at me all time. Force me tell all about thing. Come to Stringfellas, get fucken shit faced like Belushi. You know you want me.

How could Gunn stay mad with that? She made him

43

laugh out loud. And she was right. It crossed his mind that he did sort of want her. He was beginning to understand that he wasn't betraying his wife and child.

Black cabs zipped past but he ignored them, intending to catch a No. 44 bus which would drop him off near his Battersea house. Striding fast he was passing the former Army and Navy store when he heard the raucous:

—*BEEP—BEEP—BEEP*—

Coming up behind him fast. The black BMW 6 Series Coupé rolled to a sleek stop ten yards in front of him. *Yuppie dickhead* was Gunn's first thought. He glowered across at said *dickhead*, to see Eddie's beaming face as he stretched over to lever open the passenger side door.

A surprised Gunn slipped into the pristine work of art on wheels, which smothered him in that seductive new leather smell. Sumptuous. Eddie slipped the bird puller into gear and glided away.

'Nice motor.'

'Got it yesterday. Was on me to brag list, till we was sort of interrupted by your run in with our fine chappies in blue. Wait till ya see the number plate. It's eee, double dee, number one, eee—spells EDDIE.'

'No shit Narcissus.'

They had already turned left down Buckingham Palace Road heading briskly towards Chelsea and the bridge across the river to home.

'How d'ya know where I was.'

Eddie pointed at his phone nestled in the car's mobile docking station. 'Doddle mucker. iPhone's got this new app. EyeSpy. Pings someone else's mobile with their GPS locator switched on. Soon as you was on the move, it pinged you out. Just a matter of following the phone's Sat-Nav.'

'Shit, big black brother really is watching me.'

'Someone has to. Bathsheba's back at your gaff by the by.'

Gunn pinged panic. 'You didn't mention any of this.'

'What you take me for? Not a thing. But this *thing*, what? I mean what are you doing man?'

Gunn stared out of the window. *What was he doing?* The traffic was flowing nicely as they reached Chelsea Bridge. The dark opaque Thames below mirrored the muddle that was clouding his mind. 'Playing it by ear.'

'I've seen your ears. Think that's the smart move?'

'Point made Eduardo. Message received and understood. That said, need to investigate a couple of things. You in?'

Eddie had tried. But once your mate shouts for help on the battlefield, that's it. Especially when it's a mate who saved your life. 'All the way One Shot. You know that.'

'Don't you sorta know some copper at the Met?

'Have a source. Not high level but he hears things, y'know. Ear to the ground type.'

'Can you tap him? Find out if he can get anything on the case, the bloke who was sliced and diced. Like a name? Like anything on what's going on. Something's not right here.'

'Done.'

The second thing Gunn had in mind was to go right to the source. Rufus Wright, the supposed killer of his brother. Minor problemo. Wright was banged up indefinitely at Radcliffe Maximum Security Psychiatric Hospital. Gunn had a couple of ideas on how he was going to swing that. Both long-shots. One actually crazy. Which Gunn thought was ironic, given that he wanted to see a person the state had officially declared mentally incapable of pleading. Technical term: crazy. He could apply to visit Rufus Wright. But that wasn't good enough for what Gunn had in mind. He needed alone time. A hour minimum. The two of them alone, all cosy, lovey-dovey like. To finally confront Wright. Look him in the eyes. Grab him by the balls. And not metaphorically.

Eddie pulled up behind Gunn's Saab parked in front of a neat terraced house. The stone steps leading up to a solid mahogany door, painted deepest navy blue. This was the house Eddie had helped Gunn acquire for a snip and a few favours called in. Walking up the steps, key in hand, Gunn could smell the spicy aromas of Caribbean food wafting from the inside. He had hardly eaten a thing since a slice of crapolla from the hospital canteen yesterday and coffee at Ginos: his stomach gurgled at the promise.

'Kid sister can't cook for shit. Guess this is all your doing master chef?'

Eddie shrugged and smiled. 'Renaissance man of many talents mate.'

'Like I said, wonderful wife some day.'

They clopped their way down the wooden floored hallway to the large kitchen at the back of the house. Bathsheba was sitting at the rough oak table, with room for seven more. She had been listening to something punky on her iPod while skimming through a style magazine.

'Mikey.'

'Hey sis.'

Half an hour later the table was spread with Eddie's Caribbean feast, the three of them dipping and stuffing and laughing themselves to a frazzle. For a while Gunn forgot the last disturbing twenty-fours, losing himself with Johnny Cakes, Jerk Pork and Chicken, Sweet Potatoes, plantains, grilled goat's cheese. Heart attack food. Who cares as it all washed down with ice-cold Red Stripe?

Gunn marvelled as his sister held court, running through her second audition for one of the coveted thirty-four places starting next September at RADA. Who was this person who had brought a lump to his throat bigger than one of the spicy dumplings he had devoured? How did she do that? How did she become *Sophie* agonizing which of her children she would choose to send to the gas chamber, so her other child could live. Over the banana fritters and Blue Mountain brew she finally wound down a notch.

Eddie managed to get in an impressed word or two. 'Stewart? You met Patrick Stewart?'

Bebba laughed at the thought. 'Not exactly met. He was in the café downstairs after, chillin' on his tod.'

Gunn was so impressed with his little sister. 'Did you get his autograph?'

Bebba shrieked in horror. 'Totally not cool mate. He teaches a master class for third years. I'd die.'

'So baldy old Paddy'll be teaching you, two years this September?'

'Oh, dunno about that Uncle Eddie. Gotta get called back again. That'll be a short workshop. Get past that, and it's another whole day workshop. Who knows.'

Eddie dragged himself up from the table. He returned with three champagne flute glasses and a very chilled bottle of very expensive Louis Roederer.

'So you're half way there kiddo. Which still calls for some bubbly and a toast right Mick?'

'Too right mucker.'

Three glasses poured and raised. 'The honour's to you Sarge.'

Gunn raised his voice. 'To my kid sister, Bathsheba

Rachel Gunn. May she kick arse marine style. May she never change her name so we see it at the Oscars. May she be taught by Stewart in her third year at RADA.'

Eddie affirmed the sentiments. 'No doubt.' They clinked glasses and drank to that. They drank some more. They drank to good times with good company. They drank until Gunn had almost forgotten.

It was after midnight. Eddie had disappeared out to do his Eddie thing. Bathsheba had finally crashed out in the spare bedroom Gunn had for exactly this happy contingency.

Gunn had set up the refurbished large basement as his office cum den. He had Ikea-ed it out in functional flat-pack furniture. Desk, office chair, leather sofa bed, bookshelves. He needed to have a massive clear-out of the accumulated life junk. But not tonight. Tonight he stood in front of the large trunk stowed away a corner. Ezekiel's trunk. He hadn't opened it in over ten years. No need. That way his brother's life and death was kept locked up—safe, sound, and silent. What was that poem one of his posh Uni mates had valiantly read at the memorial service, in her wavering, tear-strained voice?

'Remember me when I am gone away, gone far away into the silent land; when you can no more hold me by the hand—'

Gunn remembered and opened the trunk.

6

1999.

She sort of hated the movie, being more a theatre buff. She had told her companion that, but the director Sam Mendes was from the theatre and she thought he may bring a touch of his theatricality to the film. She had thrilled at seeing Mendes's revival of The Glass Menagerie, at the Donmar, quoting verbatim the character Tom's opening soliloquy for *him*:

> *'Yes, I have tricks in my pocket, I have things up my sleeve.*
> *But I am the opposite of a stage magician.*
> *He gives you illusion that has the appearance of truth.*
> *I give you truth in the pleasant disguise of illusion.'*

Illusion of truth. Yes, most people settled for the illusion. But not Judith. She considered herself an individual, classical liberal in the mould of Smith and Locke. Which certainly went against the academic grain, which, to her mind, tended to veer to an untruthful left collectivist cul-de-sac. And to be truthful, although use of the blood red rose metaphor by Mendes seemed trite, she admitted that two aspects of the film excited her, thrilled her. The hidden and the dangerous, with the promise of taboo sex: the life-damaged older man lusting after the younger girl, almost a woman. Society related to that, but it was different somehow when it was a slightly older woman like herself, and a hard, relentless man young.

They had visited one of the huge multiplexes sited a couple of junctions down the motorway. They rarely went out together as a couple, what with the divorce negotiations and all. But that was not her interest in him anyway, doing the couple thing. Nor his in her. Doing the coupling thing, the fucking thing: that was the one thing that interested them both.

It was Screen 11, the living-room sized theatre for the artsy crowd. The popcorn queues for the year's mega hit *The Sixth Sense* snaked around outside. That film held even less interest for the supreme rationalist Professor Judith Mundy, D.Phil, D.Sc, logician, grammarian and all round professorial brainiac, with a speciality in statistical analysis.

She was still a woman though. Still not bad looking at thirty-*nice*. She had needs that were not being met married to the bag of bones who had a fine mind, even if it was not quite in her league as Professorial Fellow, Balloch College, Oxford. And he had the nerve to cheat on her with that mouse of a secretary. Outrageous. She had kicked him out. Let him suffer with a second-rate life. Their academic friends and colleagues had divided. Unequally so. Judith proved more popular as she was more powerful academically and intellectually. Not that the two necessarily went together. Add her new penchant for wearing tightish skirts and push-up bras, in what was still a male environment; and all in all, Professor Judith Mundy was doing alright.

Her friend ordered her not to wear any panties for the film. This was an exciting new game. She spent her life in the dominant role. But sometimes Judith craved not having to make the decisions, she liked being bossed for once. No longer the archetype, but the stereotype too. She could play both roles, have it all.

She wore them anyway in anticipation. He made her wait until the fantasy scene where the hot teenage virgin tease is in the bathtub, strategically covered with the red roses. She felt his hand slip under her skirt, which she had let ride to the top of her thighs. Now he had to push her barrier aside, roughly. If her faculty could see her now. See the real Professor Judith Mundy, D.Phil, D.Sc, logician, grammarian and all round professorial brainiac, with a speciality in statistical analysis. And insatiable sex God.

Judith had kicked her husband Malcolm out of their eighteenth century manor house with its six bedrooms and two acres. Even though it was purchased and mortgaged mainly with her money, her lawyer warned she might easily end up paying him for his infidelity. She was furious at her own blind stupidity, and ripe for a makeover. She would show him. Judith knew she was being irrational. So what.

She had caught him staring at her while she was rereading Emanuel Kant's Kritik der Reinen Vernunft in its original German. He was handsome. When he glanced over again, as Judith knew he would, she held his gaze. *Ripe for it.*

Of course, what she did not know was that she had not caught him. He had caught her. Clever him: to fool a very bright woman who read Kant in German, and understood every nuance fluently. Ripe and ready to fall.

She was in the city's recently opened new American import that was very old: a coffee house called Starbucks. *Plus ca change, plus ca meme chose.* It was full of loud students lolling around on comfy sofas, sipping expensive so-so coffee, and Judith was probably the oldest person there. She took him back to her newly empty manor house and they spent an intense hour having hot noisy sex in three different rooms. It would have been five or maybe six, but Judith had a lecture to deliver. That was nine months ago.

She made it clear from the start that no one could know. That was fine by him, which surprised her. She was also surprised that he was quite bright. Though not in her league. But he had been very helpful in one of her passions. Epistemology: the study of knowledge itself. It was an ultimate question and Judith thrilled at its icy discipline. What is knowledge? How is knowledge acquired? What do people know? How do we know what we know? Judith's publisher had been urging her to produce a pop-culture, self-help book to sell on the back of her regular BBC appearances. She had kicked around ideas, but always came up short. Until—he chipped in with a *what if*? What if she combined her epistemology passion with statistical analysis. See if she could relate the field of knowledge acquisition with actual personality types? Judith was not totally convinced, it all sounded unscientific, even new agey.

But her agent loved it. The publishing deal sealed. Her first task would be to organize a huge sample of detailed personality testing. The university would be her first laboratory. Given her position at the top of the faculty, it was no problem to persuade the Master about the efficacy of a university wide survey. This could also be useful for the institution to follow its loudly boasted mission for future diversity. A few questions could be cleverly disguised to reveal so much. Judith used her academic contacts with leading psychiatrists and psychologists to design a series of psychometrics: closed questions to reveal the true personality type of the respondent. Built in loop questions triple checked the truthfulness of the answers.

There were 247 multi-layered questions in total. A huge number requiring a reward based incentive for students to complete. By now, Judith had attracted interest from private foundations, and government agencies interested in the scope of the study. Raising money was no problem. Field testing determined that a fifty pound cash completion fee would prove a good incentive. A prize draw for all respondents, with a pair of round the world air tickets (donated by the airline sponsor) ensured 31% of the 20,639 student body took part.

The tests were supposedly anonymous. But given the funds involved, there had to be a method to access personal information for follow-up verification and IQ testing. Names, date of birth, education, college house, and discipline. Judith kept copies of all the data on her computer at the manor house. This was easily accessible to him, while she slept after their *fuck-fests*, her name, not his. She never doubted for one second that fucking was her real interest in him. He was only interested in the algorithm which revealed the personality type of the respondent, with a little help from pioneers like Jung, Eysenk and Benziger. He was also helped by the statistical knowledge that within every population there are probably ten percent who will have what society terms sociopathic and/or psychopathic traits.

He soon identified twenty promising candidates for his study. From these twenty, he had his club. Phase one was complete. Phase two occurred a few weeks later in an abandoned warehouse.

Now he was bored. And he needed to move on from Judith. Matter of fact.

The thrill of potential public exposure, and his clever fingers, had given her the orgasm she so richly deserved.

But Judith wanted him fully inside her that night. All night. He deserved his reward too. Driving him back, she did wonder whether she was becoming too—addicted? This secret life was beginning to require more stimulation with riskier behaviour, and the rising possibility of discovery. Did she want to find herself on the front page of the Sun as *Sex Mad Prof Has It Off*, even if the tabloid was consistently voted down from the Junior Common Room. Maybe tonight, over dinner she should make it a last, albeit long goodbye. Maybe.

He arrived at nine, as promised, with a chilled bottle of champagne in hand. Judith had laid out the dining table and prepared a beef casserole accompanied with rough-cut crusty bread, and a mixed salad. He opened the bottle and poured two glasses while she dished out the plain but tasty food.

Handing her the glass he flashed his perfect teeth. 'To us. The slutty professor and the lover.'

She didn't think that was funny, but laughed anyway, gulping down the bubbly. Judith sensed something was off, even as she drained the first glass. Jesus, did he think she was 'slutty'? Maybe tonight was the night to finish it after all. After one last fuck around, of course. It had been a good, no, a great nine months.

Except—she had recently noticed that new professor of ethics. A thirtyish bloke who had earned full tenure and who wrote well reviewed noirish crime novels on the side. He didn't wear a ring, and he had noticed her, or her elevated breasts at least. Maybe her bio-clock had not passed midnight and there was still time to bring a child into the world. It was all about choices. And she, Professor Judith Mundy, was spoilt for choice.

Maybe. They talked about the movie. Judith did most

of the expounding on the imagery and the how the destructive closeting of emotions leads inevitably to explosive violence. She thought that was good, and could bring it up the next time she appeared on *Art Attack*: BBC4's new culture show. He told her that was a great idea, excused himself and headed for the upstairs bathroom.

She cleared the table and prepared dessert in the kitchen. Fresh fruit tart, imported, hand-made Italian ice-cream, and her. She returned with the food and without her skirt and panties, replacing her blouse with one of his long T-shirts that hung a couple of inches below her bottom. He was back at the table pouring a couple of glasses of the vintage Chablis Premier Cru.

He gave her that look she knew well. Or so she thought. 'Mmmm, fucking delicious. Pudding looks great too.'

Now that was better. He handed her the wine glass and she took a long gulp, sitting back down to finish off the meal. She used her fork to hack off a piece of tart and scooped it onto her spoon with a dollop of ice cream. She managed to raise her arm as far as her mouth, before the limb ceased to work. It fell to the table. She saw it bounce twice before she realized her whole body was numb. She tried to speak but her mouth refused to move. As her body tipped sideways and fell to the parquet floor, her immediate thought was she's too young and active to suffer a stroke.

The side of her head bounced twice on the floor. She felt it too. But couldn't move it. Judith tried to scream but nothing came out.

Thank God he was there, at her side. Her lifeline. He would call an ambulance and she would get the very best medical attention the University's expensive private insurance plan could provide. He bent down and stroked her face.

'It's the Diazepam. Sucks to be you I guess. Slipped it into your wine glass. It dissolves very well in alcohol, and as you can attest, it's both tasteless and odourless. Brilliant muscle paralytic don't you think? Use it on horses as well. Makes the next part so much easier for me. Not so much for you.'

He was looking right into her eyes as he nonchalantly counted down what was left of her life. A single tear rolled down her cheek.

She heard the door bell ring and silently screamed, shouted, and shrieked to say anything to alert someone and stop this madness. He stood up and walked to the front door. *Please God, please God, please God, let it be the police. Let it be the police. Fuck, even Malcolm, I'll take Mal.*

Despite Kant, as a rationalist and logician, Judith had long since taken the only position a truly thinking human being could take regarding the so-called deity. Secretly agnostic. Why take a chance when you have nothing to lose but all to gain? A billion to one still beats a billion to none every time. Even so, for whatever reason, God did not heed Judith's call as she lay on her dining room floor. It was not the police. It was not her separated husband. It was a gang of others, dressed in black boilersuits, faces covered with hideous masks, wearing surgical gloves and carrying various bags and boxes.

One of them pulled off her T-shirt leaving her exposed for all to see. Ran a latex gloved hand over her breasts and down between her thighs.

'Sweet. Brilliant fuck I bet.'

She felt it. And another tear silently rolled.

One of them had a video camera. The lover returned, now also dressed in identical black boilersuit and mask.

He picked Judith up effortlessly and carried her upstairs. Her head lolled over his arm and she could see back and sideways to the others, as they all headed towards the bathroom.

Please don't do this. Please I want to live. Please I won't tell anybody. Please let me go. Her pathetic pleas bounced around her own head.

They would have laughed at her at anyway. Professor Judith Mundy, D.Phil, D.Sc, logician, grammarian and all round professorial brainiac, with a speciality in statistical analysis, finally understood that now. She stopped begging herself for her life. Now she prayed. Fuck Kant. Screw Dawkins. All praise Blaise Pascal. If there was God in heaven she prayed to him for her soul and the life everlasting. It seemed the supremely rational thing to do at the time. But almost as much, she prayed that one day someone would make this smug bastard suffer. All the smug bastards suffer. That he would die in agony begging for his evil useless life before going to hell. For that, Judith prayed knowing for a fact that her life would soon be ending. And for what?

She recognized what he had done to the bathroom. It was like a scene from *American Beauty*, red roses scattered everywhere. Where had he gotten the roses? The police would be on that—oh, from her greenhouse. He took them from her own greenhouse. The police would not be investigating anything suspicious. The free standing cast-iron tub stood in the middle of the room, four sturdy legs resting on the highly varnished oak floorboards.

The tub was filled with warm scented water and surrounded by lit candles. She could hear Brahms from her iPod. Her husband's old cut throat razor rested open on the side of the tub, waiting for her. She knew what was going to happen tomorrow, and that was unbearable.

Someone was going to find her in this kitsch, staged scene and the verdict would be suicide. That would be how she would ultimately be remembered. Silly cow Mundy couldn't cope after her hubby left her, so she ended it all after seeing a fucking movie, how pathetic. How ersatz. And he got the manor house too with his brainless tart. Her mother, her brilliant caring mother who had helped so many, and who had pushed Judith to be the very best she could be. The devastation this will wreak. Thinking she had failed her own daughter.

He slipped Judith into the bath, smiling at her. 'You should be honoured. This is the first official meeting of Kill Club in the field, so to speak. We took a vote as per the club charter, and you had to go. Sorry, but to be honest if you'd seen the state of the first guy, you'd be grateful. That was fun.'

He made a dramatic sweep of his left arm at the scene. Gesturing as if she should appreciate all the effort he had made to make her death more pleasant. 'This, it's just business, tying up loose ends.'

She was propped up in the tub: the water covering her breasts. The others stood at the tap end, even beneath their masks she felt them grinning like mangy hyenas closing in for the kill on their helpless prey. *Fuck you all* she screamed out, but it merely echoed around her exceptional brain. The one that never saw this coming.

He picked up the razor. Having taken time to read the official literature on suicide, he knew exactly what to do. She watched him pick up her left hand which had been under the warm bath water. He ran it across her wrist hesitantly and lightly. A line of blood oozed. These were the hesitation marks that would convince the police it was a genuine suicide. A sudden bout of depression following Judith consuming a bottle of champagne and a bottle of

Chablis.

The first cuts were not the deepest. The second was. He dropped her hand into the water. Judith's life draining into the reddening liquid.

Her strong heart betrayed her, as the one muscle the drug had not paralysed. It was fast pumping her life away. As her blood pressure slowly subsided the light-headed buzz in her ears began and her vision darkened. The bastards stood around laughing and chatting like they were at the pub downing a few. The last thing she heard was him telling the others to start wiping the place clean of fingerprints. Then it was all over for Professor Judith Mundy. Lights out.

He could not help himself and was compelled to watch. The fact it was risky was reason enough. No point being stupid though, it was a calculated risk. Setting himself up a hundred yards away, he waited behind the high bramble hedge in the field opposite. He had checked her diary. She had a lecture at nine, and a meeting with the Master at eleven. When she did not show, there would be a response. Sure enough, at ten o'clock, a small car turned into the driveway and rolled slowly towards the front door. He raised the video camera and zoomed in to watch Judith's round little assistant exit the car and approach the front door. She rang the bell and waited. She rang again. When the inevitable nothing happened, she rooted around in her massive handbag for the key.

Less than sixty seconds later, she tore out of the house and threw herself back into the car. He could see her hand up to her mouth for a while, her shoulders rising and falling.

An ambulance arrived nine minutes later. A police patrol car pulled in a good ten minutes later. Two uniformed coppers exited the car at speed as if they were here to save the day. They disappeared inside.

A few minutes after that, one of the uniforms strolled out, looking around furtively before lighting up a cigarette. The copper had taken a couple of drags when he dropped the cigarette on the gravel. Another saloon car was pulling into the driveway. Three middle aged men in dark suits exited the car. He didn't recognize two of them. But the third. Detective Inspector Walter Czarnecki. The very one he had been hoping for.

He should have left but couldn't drag himself away from the scene he had created. Knowing that the police would be coming to a conclusion that had been written and directed by him was delicious. *Nah nah nah nah nah, I know a secret.*

He had pushed it about as far as he dared and was about to scoot, when a silver Mini Cooper roared up, almost skidding into the drive. An elegant woman in her sixties shot out and rushed towards the house, to be stopped by the constable at the doorway. They spoke for a few seconds, before she half collapsed and had to be physically supported by the copper.

Perfect.

7

The trunk was open. Gunn was rummaging for a past he needed to get a handle on. Layers of his brother rose to the surface. The fossilized bones of a life once lived.

Ezekiel's first bible, given to him by their dad.

His spidery first complete alphabet which he wrote on lined paper when he was three years old.

A pair of baby's bootees no bigger than Gunn's thumb.

A shoe box with *OXFORD* scrawled in marker pen, full of photographs from university.

A typed list of Zeke's fellow undergraduates for Balloch College graduating in 2000 class. That was essential.

A pile of play bills advertising productions from a student group called Mametaliens. He flicked his way through, stopping on a couple:

>Moser Theatre presents
>May 18 - May 24, 1999
>SEXUAL PERVERSITY IN CHICAGO
>by David Mamet
>*Fuck Me??? Fuck You.*

>Old Fire Station Theatre
>Oct 13 – Oct 21 1999
>GLENGARRY GLEN ROSS
>David Mamet
>*Fuck The Machine*

Was Zeke a fan of this group, or involved somehow? He continued searching. Somewhere in here may be the spaghetti connections leading from his dead brother to an unidentified male body all these years later.

One of his questions was quickly answered with a cutting from the Oxford Express dated October 14, 1999. The headline: ALL GUNNS BLAZING IN MAMET TRIUMPH.

Gunn scanned the two hundred or so words on the yellowing page ripped from the local newspaper. His eyes formed a misty film that made it hard to read the paean of praise to his kid brother, or take in the half-dozen eager young faces in the photograph. The founder of the group, and also its star and director.

A feeling of stinging shame and self-loathing swept over him, Gunn's fury now being re-directed at himself. He knew next to nothing about his brother's life after he left home. Maybe that was forgivable. He was an immature self-centred kid wrapped up in himself. What was unforgivable were the following fourteen years when he made zero effort to discover the maturing Ezekiel. To keep that person alive in his heart. In fact, he had done all he could to shut his brother out. To keep him all tucked up in a dark trunk with a big padlock. He had managed to make his brother's death all about himself.

Gunn stacked the various items on the floor as he delved deeper. A scrap of lined paper ripped from a larger sheet. On it was written neatly in his brother's hand:

Life is fleeting, and death is but a short step behind, even for the most fleet of foot.

He kept digging and there it was: the card handed to

him by Detective Inspector Walter Czarnecki. *Pronounced Chair-nesky Mr Gunn.* Blue embossed logo of the Thames Valley Police. Central Police Station, St. Alban's Road, Oxford. Switchboard number and mobile phone number.

Gunn remembered the moment well. That and the long sequence of events which had led up to the card. His troop were out on patrol in Bosnia. They had been off base for an hour when a radio call came in to return immediately. A marine Chaplain was waiting as he disembarked from the armoured vehicle. Two hours later he was strapped into the webbing seat on a regular Hercules flight back to Brize Norton.

Everything about the next ten days was a numbing blur, but still stored at the bottom of a memory hole. He remembered Czarnecki. The way he constantly sucked on strong mints, even though the haze of peppermint could not mask the smell of alcohol leaking from every pore. How the Inspector had assured Gunn they had the right man in Rufus Wright. How Czarnecki gave him his card and said if he had any more questions don't hesitate to call. Gunn never called. What was the point? They had the killer. Now he had a reason to call. One tortured and battered body of a reason.

Gunn had lain down on the sofa bed to consider his next moves. Six hours later the bright morning light from his basement's high window was filtering in through the gaps in the slats of the wooden blind. He had slept the dreamless sleep of the dead, and he was pleased for that. Bebba was moving around in the kitchen upstairs. At least he assumed it was her, as Eddie would be gone till midday minimum. The comforting sounds of normality were a welcome distraction. His iPhone banged into gear loudly and insistently at him from somewhere below his ears, playing his ringtone *The House of the Rising Sun, Eric*

Burdon and the Animals. Gunn felt around the floor, picking it up without looking.

His phone screen flashed the task:
GROUP. 9AM. SNOOZE/DISMISS.
'Shit.'

Gunn bounced into the kitchen to see his sister sitting at the table in one of his spare bath robes. It was massive on her. She had been watching the small flat-screen TV while busy scarfing down a mix of provisions she had rustled up.

'Made a full pot if you wanna coffee.'

Gunn never needed any encouragement to OD on caffeine. He went straight to the machine and poured a cup from the Perspex jug on the hotplate.

'Cheers love. Look, sorry, forgot this thing I gotta do. Gotta fly in a sec. You okay?'

'Go bro. Gotta load on today anyway. Probably go back to mum's tonight. I'll lock up before.'

'Stay as long as you like, y'know that. Eddie'll be back later.'

'Yeah I know. About time you visited mum though, doncha think?'

Gunn cringed. He constantly guilt-tripped knowing he should see his mother more often, a mere three miles away in Kensal Rise. 'Will do. Will do. Next week maybe.'

Bebba flashed him a *better do it pal* fiery gaze. Gunn took a huge gulp from his mug, and almost scorched the lining off his throat. Time to go before he burst into flames.

8

Dr Mosser's chambers are located in an annex behind the public library, not far from St. Michael's hospital. Chambers sounds rather grand. Usually they are a rented space in a convenient site for patients and doctor.

Dan Mosser was talking quietly as Gunn whirl-winded in, disturbing the group of thirteen sitting in a semi-circle on uncomfortable looking wooden chairs. There were twelve regulars plus one newcomer. Gunn nodded to his friend: tallish, thirties, intense piercing blue eyes, and the brisk no-nonsense air of someone who liked to get to the heart of the matter.

When Gunn's wife and daughter were killed in a hit and run four years earlier, it ended his life in the marines. He couldn't function effectively any more as a soldier. He could hardly function as a human being. The marine psychiatrist recommended an honourable discharge, so Sergeant Micah Ishmael Gunn could recover from the second family trauma in ten years. Mosser was doing consultancy work for the armed forces after the Ministry of Defence had lost a number of high award Post Traumatic Stress Disorder cases. He was advising top brass on changes to front-line psychological monitoring when Gunn's name came across his desk. He was intrigued by a case in which a patient's home life traumas affected military life, rather than vice versa. Dr Mosser had the marine shrink recommend that Gunn continue out-patient PTSD treatment under his care. Mosser worked one-on-one with Gunn for a couple of months, with a minimum drug therapy regime. After showing significant improvement and developing robust coping mechanisms, Mosser suggested two things. That Gunn move into his small cognitive behaviour psychotherapy group, and that he consider pursuing a career in nursing. The next year, Mosser persuaded Gunn to stay on and help others as a group session leader. It was an hour a week, so how could he refuse?

Gunn assumed his usual group tone of *upbeat*. 'Hi guys, sorry I'm late. Decided to drive today. Big mistake.'

They acknowledged him back with combined hellos. That left the newcomer sitting mute, head lowered and wings clipped. Whenever Dr Mosser had a new patient he would sit in for the first session. Gunn knew it had to be that way, but always felt a bit annoyed ceding back his authority.

'Okay, everyone I'd like to introduce Christina.'

The session progressed with Gunn seemingly in control, but Mosser subtly asserting his overall leadership. The hour was soon up. The Victims of Alien Abduction Society had the room next, and they were straining to fire up the mothership.

Mosser caught up as Gunn was climbing onto his Saab. They were in the Sainsburys' car park, around the corner from the chambers. 'Hey Mike, gotta a sec?'

'Dan, really haven't, be honest mate.'

'Heard you walked in on an odd one in A&E. Would you like to talk about it?'

Talking about it was something Dr Dan Mosser had become very successful at in the past few years. He had his NHS clinic at St. Mike's. He was on call with the police as the first line on mentally disturbed offenders. He did therapy work at the Priory, helping celebrities kick their addictions: drugs, sex, gambling. As if that was not enough, Dan also had his three hour weekly radio show on London's biggest radio talk station ChatterBox, *Talk About It with Dr Dan.*

He was a one-man global mental health conglomerate. He made Gunn feel positively slothful. But Gunn didn't have the time or the desire to have a cosy session on how he *felt* about all this.

'No worries Nothing more to tell. See road accidents worse than that every day.'

The doc meant well, only doing his job, but Gunn wasn't going to tell him about finding his brother's medallion. This would open it up for Dr Mosser, who was still his psychiatrist, and still had a duty of care for Gunn as a patient.

'You say. But if you need to talk, call me.'

Thirty seconds later Gunn was back in his car, punching a mobile phone number into his iPhone: the number he had retrieved from the decade old business card of Detective Inspector Walter Czarnecki.

The metallic voice answered him. 'The number you have dialled is no longer in service. The number you have dialled is no longer in service.'

He cursed to himself. *Of course it isn't. That would be too frigging easy.*

The house was crushingly silent. His effervescent life-enhancing sister had upped stakes back to her mum's place—correction, their mum's place. Eddie was still out doing mysterious Eddie things.

Down in the basement he collected the various items he needed and placed them in the swish satchel gifted to him by Eddie. It still had that sumptuous new leather smell of Eddie's new beamer.

Half an hour later he pulled away from his house in the Saab, heading towards Richmond and back over the river to pick up the M40 motorway. He checked his rear-view mirror more often than usual. Going up the long steep incline between Junction 3, and High Wycombe at junction 4, Gunn thought he spotted a dark Range Rover keeping pace four vehicles back. By the time he was tooling along towards junction 5, the dark shape had disappeared. It's hard not to be paranoid after someone first tries to axe you in the head, then range rovers your arse, followed by your entire body.

9

Gunn parked on a side street, around the corner from St Alban's Road police station. In a city of dreaming spires, this building screamed functional dreary. Grey concrete blocks surrounding white framed windows and a transparent plastic canopy hanging like a used condom over the entrance.

The PC smiled in his best community copper training manner. Gunn wondered when they started employing 14 year old kids. 'Yes sir, and how can we help you today?'

Gunn explained his desire to talk to Inspector Czarnecki regarding an old case. This seemed to perplex the constable who was more used to hearing about a mugging outside MacDonald's, or inside the Ashmolean.

'Chair-Nesky?' He pondered. 'Don't think we have a Chair-Nesky on the force here. Gotta a Charman. Or is it Chairman? Except, course, he's a constable out Woodstock way. Nice fella.'

Deep breath Gunn. 'Is there anyone who might know someone who worked out of this station about ten years ago?'

After much deep thought, the child-cop remembered someone. A phone call later and a uniformed sergeant met Gunn in the staff car park behind the station.

'Gunn? Unusual name. A Gunn was murdered, year I joined the force. You related I suppose? About that is it?'

'Brother. And yes, need to talk to the lead detective, Walter Czarnecki.'

'Closure you want, I bet. See it all the time. Closure.'

Gunn decided it was easier to agree. 'Yeah, closure.'

'About a year after your brother's mur—investigation, Mr Czarnecki retired. Now—' Leaning in and looking around warily, as if his movements were being monitored, the sergeant dropped his voice and tapped his nose: 'The goss round the canteen was Wally was a bit too fond of the old—' He made the universal hand holding a glass of alcohol gesture, 'Know what I mean. Got caught, over the limit driving his police car.'

'No kidding.'

'Last I heard, about eight years ago, moved to Watlington, bought a nice little cottage.'

'Wouldn't know the address would you?'

'Matter of fact, I do sir.'

That was all the sergeant knew. That and the fact Czarnecki was considered a pretty decent copper, until he started taking the path of least resistance to the bottom of the bottle.

Now that he had the location, there was one more thing Gunn couldn't put it off any longer. He had never been to his brother's college, and Balloch was a few minutes on foot up St Alban's Road, en route to Oxford town centre.

It was a sultry day and Kamikaze bicyclists bombed past Gunn from every angle. Balloch College loomed up in front of him on Ward Street. It was an old building of four floors. He remembered the day Zeke received his offer. How his brother had excitedly told him Balloch college had been around since 1258.

The brilliant sun was baking the building's golden stones. A tower stood tall, dead centre, dividing Balloch's entire length, fifty feet above the eight wigwam-pointed roofs, four either side. Gunn headed to the gateway which ran through the tower's flag-stoned ground floor.

He walked through the gate arch into a passageway. The temporary cool shade opened out into Balloch's front quad. He knew it was the front quad because he was holding a six by six inch photograph taken by his brother from almost that very spot. Ezekiel having scrawled *front quad* on the back, along with the date *27/9/97*. Gunn shuffled through the other photos. From what he could tell, little had changed in the intervening years.

One picture interested him. His brother sitting on a grand looking wooden park bench with fancy wrought iron work. Zeke had his arm around a very pretty looking girl, about his age. Gothish vibe. They were posing straight to camera, heads leaning against each other in an intimate gesture. Next to them was another bloke their age. He had longish hair and a beard, and seemed oddly out of place in such an intimate pose. On the back Zeke had scrawled the words:

Me and Beth and pet poodle. Herbert Asquith Mem. Bench. Balloch Quad, Oct 1998.

Beth.

He recognized her as the distraught girl who read a poem at Zeke's funeral. Though there was no hint at the funeral that Beth was special to Zeke.

He studied the photo. Was Zeke happy? Gunn hoped he was. The girl had a delicate oval face and large mournful eyes, purple mascara and lipstick. It was the classically proportioned baby/child-like features which both men and women subconsciously find pleasurable. She had pale skin of Celt lineage, topped by a cascade of bright copper coloured hair in tight ringlets. In common parlance: a total stunner.

Gunn found the bench and sat down. It was forty

yards in from the gateway facing what Gunn knew was the college chapel on the west side of the quad. The whole scene was so English it was almost cliché. Gunn could have stepped through a time-warp to 1697. He breathed in the atmosphere Zeke had thrived in, recalling one of the few letters Zeke had written while he was in some Bosnian shithole. Zeke wrote about being terrified and elated to have found an environment which challenged him at every turn. Gunn could appreciate that now. At the time he looked at his marine pals and sort of sneered Zeke should try being stuck here in Bosnia if he wanted to be terrified and elated. Professors shooting barbed comments in tutorials didn't quite compare to insane scumbags trying to zap you in the head everyday.

It was an odd thing being constantly exposed to possible death. Soldiers developed a sense of when they were being watched: well, those who survived did. When Gunn picked up the irresistible idea he was being observed, he did not dismiss it as paranoia.

He pivoted around fast to glare in the direction of the gateway arch. The sun was beaming directly into his eyes, the passage through the gateway was in shadow. It took a few seconds for him to squint into focus. In time to see the back of a man rapidly exiting left into Ward Street. Gunn was up and racing to the gateway. Blasting though the passage, he barely managed to dodge a couple of female students ambling into the quad. One of them bellowed 'arsehole' as he hurtled left. The street was a frenzied piranha pool of people criss-crossing on foot and on bike. He ran another twenty yards before stopping. It was impossible to pick out one person he had caught a glimpse in the shadows.

Then the doubt crept in. How would anyone even know he was here in Oxford. Gunn didn't even know himself until a few hours ago. He had told no one. If someone had been watching him, he must have been followed from London. But how, and why? He thought of the black Range Rover on the M40.

Jesus Gunn, they're coming to take you away, ha ha.

10

Watlington is a tiny, self-satisfied market town, twenty miles south of Oxford. Gunn took the M40 back towards London and left at junction six. Ten minutes later he drove into Hunter's Wood, a narrow cul-de-sac. Number 13 was a desirable olde worlde thatched cottage, white with black oak beams visible. Looked very expensive. Is that what retiring on a Detective Inspector's pension gets you?

Gunn pulled into the small, gravelled driveway, which led up to the traditional white cottage door. By the time he had exited the car, the front door was already opened by a neat, well-dressed woman smoking a cigarette. The over-abundance of small wrinkle lines made her look about ten years older than her fifty-seven.

'Mrs Czarnecki?'

She dropped the cigarette into the gravel and stubbed it out. 'Who wants to know?'

Gunn approached her, holding out his hand. 'Micah Gunn.' The woman reluctantly extended a couple of limp fingers. Gunn reciprocated. 'I was looking for Inspector Czarnecki. Is he in?'

'As a matter of fact he is. What exactly do you want? You know he's been retired from the force, oh, about ten years now?'

Gunn was quite circumspect, and told her just enough about himself and the old case, in the hope she would invite him in. His ploy clicked like con-work.

She ushered him into the hallway, and indicated down

the hallway to an open door. 'He's in here. Can I get you a tea? Coffee?'

Gunn entered the large living room, tastefully decorated circa Antique Roadshow 1975. He clocked the Chesterfield sofa and the two velvet-backed easy chairs. The distinct linger of cigarettes permeated the room like a smoke house permeated a kipper. He couldn't see anyone inside.

'Sorry. I don't see—'

Mrs Czarnecki looked quite amused with herself as she pointed airily towards the coal fire, set but not lit. On the marble mantelpiece sat a carriage clock, a silver photograph frame, a few small figurines of indeterminate Victorian characters, and a foot-tall metal urn.

'There he is, my Wally.'

She walked over to the mantelpiece and gently stroked the cold metal. 'Nice and safe.'

'He's dead?'

'I bloody well hope so Mr Gunn, the way he went though that crematorium furnace.'

Gunn wondered whether he should smile. It was quite funny the way she had set it up. He threw in a quick smirk before sympathizing. 'I'm sorry.'

She shrugged and lit up another cigarette. 'It was a blessing. For him.'

'Was it, the drink. If you don't mind me asking?'

Ruby took a long satisfying drag, and the business end glowed red. 'Lung cancer. Funny thing is, my Wally never smoked a day in his bloody life.'

She saw Gunn look at the cancer stick in her hand. 'Everyone thinks that. That I bloody killed him, passive smoking. Specially his nasty mother. But he was never bloody home. To busy at work, or drinking himself silly.'

'Don't have to explain bizarre random events. I'm a

nurse, Mrs Czarnecki.'

'Call me Ruby.'

'Talking drink, make yourself at home while I put on that cuppa.'

Gunn liked Ruby. She was brisk, to the point and didn't give a hoot, telling it like she thought it was. She prepared the pot of tea and brought in home-made scones straight from the oven. He was well into his second scone, slathered with home made gooseberry jam, by the time he finished giving Ruby the edited highlights.

'So basically you think my Wally cocked it up. Arrested the wrong man.'

That threw him for a second. He liked her and didn't want to insult the memory of her dead hubby. Not to her face.

'Not necessarily, it might be there was more than one person. Something like that. Hoping Walter might have shed some insight.'

'Horse manure. He probably ballsed it up. Wally was drinking so much by then. The job. My son, his step-son. All pressure. Maybe you'd like to look at his case files?'

Gunn blinked as he took in what Ruby had said. 'His case files?'

'Yes, all his cases, those in the nineties anyway. Wally photocopied what he called his murder books for every case he worked on. Said he was going to write big best sellers when he left the force. Be rich and famous.'

'Okay.'

'Remember that old TV show. What's his name? Set in Oxford?'

'Morse.'

'That's one. Used to drive my Wally absolutely bonkers. Said he could write better crime yarns in his sleep than those convoluted plots. He got totally obsessed with the idea they based that boozing detective on him, which pissed him off no end. So he started to photocopy everything he worked on. Investment research he said. Finally gets the time to do something about it, then he ups and dies on me. It's all mouldering away, in the garage, in boxes. Want to go through them?'

Gunn could not believe his luck. He scanned the dozens of self-assembly, cardboard storage boxes stacked floor to ceiling in the double garage. They were in date order with the most recent at the front of the stacks. Gunn located seven with the dates 1999/2000 scrawled in marker pen on the box. The actual case it related to was neatly written on the lid. There it was: Ezekiel Gunn. Student. Balloch College. Murder. Nov 99. He lugged it back to the cottage, along with a few other boxes from around that date. No reason, but Gunn was curious to see what else the Inspector was up to at the time, in between boozing.

Ruby told him it was fine to set up on the table in the living room, next to Wally as, 'He'd like that.'

He took out a fresh, crisp Folio-sized Yellow Legal Pad from his briefcase. After writing OFFICIAL POLICE INVESTIGATION on the first page, Gunn lifted the lid off the box. Inside were a pile of A4 sized buff coloured folders, each with its designation neatly written in capital letters, in red.

Taking them out and laying them on the table, the folders all seemed quite empty to Gunn's untrained eyes. There were eleven folders in all. Witness Statements x 2. Interviews x 2. Coroner's Report. Police Doctor's Report. Psychiatric Report. DNA Evidence. Post Mortem Report. My Original Notes. And there it was. Murder Scene Photos. Gunn pushed that particular folder to one side and started sifting through the official investigation into his brother's murder. Every time he came across something that jumped out to his non-policeman mind he made a note on his pad. His first task was to uncover personal details about the man locked up for murdering his brother.

He opened the Psychiatric Report folder and skimmed the contents. The first page was a brief biographical and medical summary of Wright. All the pages were headed as coming from the Ashurst Psychiatric Intensive Care Unit, Littlemore, Oxford.

DUTY DOCTOR: Dr Francis Benson
DATE: 7/11/99
PATIENT: Rufus Gulliver Wright
DOB: 9/9/76
SEX: Male
ADDRESS: No Fixed Abode

HISTORY:

> *Mr Wright was officially diagnosed with schizophrenia in 1994 during his first term at Oxford University. Although it has since been confirmed by his parents and close friends that the patient's behaviour and personality started to change shortly after his seventeenth birthday. The patient continued as a student at the university, and the disease was stabilised by a regime of antipsychotic drug therapy including Seroquel and Risperdal, followed by outpatient care at the APIC unit at Littleton. Patient had a history of neglecting his medication, and was asked to leave the university in March 1996 due to inability to control his disease adequately. The patient returned initially to his parents' home where he received care and resumed his*

> *medication. By now his schizophrenia was manifesting itself with paranoid tendencies. He left his parents' care and was living rough at the time of his arrest for murder. The patient is not reported as exhibiting violent tendencies prior to the alleged incident to which it appears the patient has indicated to the police that he was responsible for the death of a young man named Ezekiel Gunn.*

This was the man who supposedly killed his brother. It sounded plausible, so far, given his knowledge of paranoid schizophrenia. He methodically skimmed the rest of the folder, which included the detailed hand written notes on the three sessions with Wright. At the end of which, the medical advice determined that Rufus Gulliver Wright was unfit to stand trial due to diminished capacity. After going through each folder, Gunn reviewed his own hand written notes.

ENTRY No.1/INVESTIGATION

SUSPECT – 23 yr old, Rufus Wright found wondering near murder scene, diagnosed with schizophrenia in first term at Oxford U/1994. got worse so had to drop out in 2nd year. Claims heard voices. Couldn't remember anything about the day. Stopped meds two weeks before.
DNA – cops found Zeke's blood on Wright's T-shirt. Lots. But nothing else in warehouse. Whole scene wiped clean of finger prints. ODD?? Why would he do that being mental??

POST MORTEM BODY – brutalised, tortured. On display. How subdued? Why did Zeke go there anyway? No sense. Maybe 5 diff shoe prints on body. HUH??

SCENE – clean, not one print, NO DNA EXCEPT E's. all wiped. OG (Our Guy) highly organised then. Knows procedure? Maybe OGs? More than one?

WHY – if not Wright – personal?
Random? NO... thrill kill? Knew killer?

OGs? – is this first murder? PM says Cant be. Too calculated. Too horrible. Takes long time to reach level of depravity. Must be others.

PHYSICAL – no phys evidence to link Wright to scene.

KNOWN FACT - someone other than Rufus W. took Z's St C. which ended up on a body yrs later???

CONCLUSION = no idea yet.

Wright's condition sounded all too familiar with what Gunn knew about schizophrenia. The nurse part of him felt compassion. Wright was a normal bright teenager when the symptoms started. That scenario is the usual timeline for most sufferers of this devastating illness. It's the time when the brain is reaching full maturation for the young adult. Then for some reason, the almost developed brain is hit by a disorder, affecting everything the rest of us take for granted to function in our complex society. Wright's perceptions, thoughts, feelings and behaviour would have been altered to a level it is hard for those not suffering to comprehend. Looking at the doctor's assessment, Wright had a history of hallucinations, primarily auditory: the classic *voices in the head* told him to do it.

He also exhibited delusional actions which fell into the two standard types Gunn had studied briefly during nurse training. Wright was *Grandiose* – he sincerely believed he was special by virtue of the extraordinary powers given to him by a higher being. In his case that was the Devil. And he was also *Persecutory* – convinced with all his being that people were out to get him. Eventually that turns into a self-fulfilling prophecy because the subject's very behaviour and actions draws the attention of others. Which in turn is perceived by the sufferer as an attempt to *get him*.

Gunn was thinking about Wright's illness, and one of his compassionate Dad's over-used sayings – *there but for the grace of God go me and thee* – when he noticed something else on one of the other boxes. Professor Judith Mundy. Suicide. Dec 1999. That name sounded familiar. He rooted around in his briefcase and found the item from Zeke's trunk. A slim glossy booklet with the title *Balloch College Prospectus 1997/8* printed on the cover. The index listed a section called *Balloch People* on page 10. Gunn flicked to it and scanned the list of Fellows. It was in alphabetical order, half way down. Mundy, Judith Diana Patricia: BA Oxf, MA Oxf, D.Phil, D.Sc. He checked inside the box and pulled out the coroner's report. It stated unequivocally that although she did not leave a note, the method of death was fully consistent with a suicide by a person suffering from depression. From what he knew of female suicides it fitted. Pills and wrist slashers predominate, no damage to the face. Unlike men, women have a great reluctance to shoot themselves because of their appearance in death. The coroner had noted that the hesitation marks were also a common occurrence. Still? Gunn put it on his list of things to follow up on. Though his new priority was obvious, he had to somehow get in to see Rufus Wright. Currently locked up in the maximum security wing of Radcliffe Maximum Security Hospital, in Radcliffe, Hertfordshire.

He couldn't put it off any longer. There is was, right in front of him, like a big fat wart on a beautiful woman's face. The more you try to ignore it, the more your eyes drift back. Gunn steeled himself and opened the folder. One good thing, the dozen or so sheets of paper were black and white copies. It distanced him from the event.

He made notes in his pad about the nature of the wounds shown in gruesome close-up. The first photocopy was a full body shot of his brother's hanging body, photographed from the rear. Gunn's eyes squinted. He bit his tongue to stay focused. A controlled fury swept through him like Katrina through New Orleans. He flicked through the next shots which were close ups of individual wounds, starting with the kill blow through Zeke's eye which pierced his beautiful mind. Each was more shockingly depraved than the last. Finally he pushed himself to turn over *the one*—

'Fuck.'

A giant X carved across the body.

He had assumed a few possibilities about the body in the hospital with the medallion. Obviously he could be the actual solo killer who got lucky. Or been involved in some way with Rufus Wright. He may have come across the medallion by accident, or from the real killer, again possibly with a link to the current perpetrator. Any and all of these theories threw a giant spanner in Czarnecki's investigation and court conviction.

But now? Years apart? To see his brother had been marked in exactly the same way as this fresh victim. Maybe hospital guy had been kidnapped by the real killer and found this trophy of previous murders.

He wrote that theory down too, and was trying to fathom it all when he heard the rattle of cups from the hallway. Gunn gathered up the shots spread out on the rather fine mahogany dining table, shoving them back in the folder.

'Fancy another cuppa dear?'

Anything to take his mind off the appalling evidence of Zeke's suffering. And of how he let his little brother down. 'Life saver Ruby. Look, mind if I borrow the rest of these boxes?'

'No difference to me dear. Was thinking of clearing them out anyway for the space. Don't suppose I could just put them out for the bin men. So help yourself.'

Gunn had all the info he needed at the moment and didn't want to recap any more. Sipping from the fine bone china tea cup, he looked to the mantelpiece and the photograph in the silver frame. 'That your son?'

It was a younger Ruby in a floral summer dress and large hat. At her side was a young man in gown and mortar board. Judging by the height of his mother, he guessed the man was about six foot tall. He looked familiar but Gunn could not quite place him. The taller, older man in the photo was not D.I. Czarnecki.

'Yes, Simon's graduation from Oxford.' She took a drag from her cigarette. 'Two thousand—my goodness, seems yesterday. That's Simon's real dad Nigel. Wally was—uh, well he wasn't invited. I was very angry. Wally was so hurt. But my son and Wally never got on since he was thirteen. Sons and mothers and step-dads. Can be tricky.'

'Can imagine.'

Czarnecki's stepson graduating in 2000 meant he must have been up at Oxford at the same time as his brother.

'What's your son up to now?'

Ruby visibly puffed up like a cooing dove. 'Oh, he's very talented. Fell in with the theatre crowd at Oxford. Started writing, directing, then acting. No idea where he gets all that arty stuff from, nothing on either side of the family. Funny isn't it dear, how things work out?'

Gunn was puzzled for a second, thinking he had never heard of Simon Czarnecki. Until he realized his mistake, and why Simon seemed familiar. 'Oh right. Your son is Simon Murphy? Don't watch much TV, but I've seen him. Isn't he in that show on the BBC, The Colony?'

Ruby was beaming now. 'They call it a dramedy. He's very talented, but you need luck in life. It was down to my Simon and this other chap for the lead role, and then this other chap goes and smashes his car into tree.'

'Seriously?'

Ruby pulled open the door in the oak sideboard, rummaging through.

'Oh yes, lucky to be alive apparently, but broke his back, poor dear. Crippled.'

'So Simon gets the lead?'

Ruby grimaced at the thought. 'I know dear, but that's life I suppose. One man's misery is another's opportunity.'

'True. See Simon often then?'

Ruby found the photo-album, and Gunn detected a slight defensiveness as if he hit a nerve. 'Oh, he's very busy. But calls me once a month at least. Keep it to yourself but he's auditioning for some big Hollywood picture. Next week. Screen test they call it. Pinewood studios. It's where they film James Bond, you know.'

She held up the ten by eight colour print for Gunn. 'See, here he is. That's my Simon rehearsing for his first ever play.' She pointed to one of the heads in the group shot of about ten students posing on a stage. 'Coriolanus. Course he was only a spear carrier or something.'

Simon was standing at the back of the group. Whether that was because of his height or his role, Gunn could not be sure. He was sure about the bloke standing in the front. It was Zeke.

Gunn pointed at the figure in the photograph. 'That's my brother, there.'

'Really dear? Small world.'

'Ruby, was Simon ever involved with a group, I dunno, acting troupe? Called themselves the Mamet—aliens?'

Ruby laughed 'Involved? Why yes dear, you could say. He started them. He brought most of the people in the photograph on board. I wasn't too keen. I'm not a prude, but there were lots of, you know what, words beginning with eff. On and on. Not really my cup of tea.'

That was an outright lie. The Mametaliens was Zeke's baby. Gunn was angered, not with Ruby. It wasn't her fault her son would build himself up like that. 'So Simon started Mametaliens? You're sure?'

Ruby was surprised by the question. 'Well yes dear. In fact, that was Simon's big break, when they were invited to the Edinburgh Festival in 2000, him being the star and all, he was offered that comedy show on Radio 4.'

'Ruby, do you mind if I borrow the photograph and get it copied? I don't have many of Zeke at Oxford. Bring it back promise.' It wasn't simply Zeke, of course. He wanted to reference all the Mametaliens. Especially Simon.

Ruby grabbed his hand in a display of solidarity at losing a loved one. 'Please do. Must have literally hundreds of pictures of Simon. He likes the camera, the limelight. Most actors do I suppose.'

No kidding.

Ruby had an idea. She went back to the sideboard drawer and removed a business card from a neat stack, before handing the card to Gunn.

'Simon's phone number. I'm sure he'd love to talk to you. He has great affection for his time in Oxford. Always says that's where he found his true vocation.'

Gunn smiled sympathetically. Ruby finished one cigarette and was in the process of lighting up another. He drained his tea, glanced over at Wally, all cigarette ashes to ashes.

Time to exit stage London.

11

2001.

Byron Goolsbee admired himself: reflected in the mirror above the sink in the staff toilets at his firm in the City. He liked what he saw. What wasn't to like? The great tan. The buffed body. The Hugo Boss suit. The TAG Heuer watch. Technically the fifty quid knock off, as opposed to the two thousand pounds an original would cost. That would be rectified when he could afford the real deal. Which would be after he received the promotion he so richly deserved. Which was probably very soon after tonight. Though deep down he still longed to be the successful actor he dreamed about at college. A Hollywood all-action A-lister. Either that or a glamorous spy.

Byron certainly had the perfect gleaming white teeth, which he was busy flossing with religious zeal. They were so dazzlingly bright, he had to wear shades. That was his little joke. For this outcome Byron thanked his American mother and American dentistry, which was now paying off big shine. If his English father had gotten custody instead, he would have whisked him back to Blighty for his childhood and teens.

That routine finished, Byron took a swig from his bottle of mouthwash, swooshing it around his mouth vigorously before spitting it out.

The door clattered open and another sharply-dressed man entered. 'Goolsbee.'

Byron glanced in the mirror. 'Brenner.'

Both men worked in the city for the MOR Group (Management of Risk Group), though at different levels. MOR was a kick-arse derivatives trading outfit with offices in London, Tokyo, Paris and New York. The firm moved billions around the world at lightning speed, making money all the way. The offices were the typical boiler room, high pressure environment with testosterone on tap. Staffed predominantly by men who called each other by their surnames. A quasi-militaristic camaraderie which didn't mask the ruthless ambition that happily stabs your colleagues in the back, then the front, then the face. Metaphorically. Usually.

The hyper-aggressive young turks who joined were treated like the 'fags' of some nineteenth century British public school. The lead trader (the captain) had lieutenants, who themselves would run a pool of boot-strappers like Byron doing the grunt work. Brenner was a lieutenant, but not in Byron's pool. By 'grunt' work, MOR meant they still had to quick on their feet. Byron's problem being he was generally a major league fuck-up in fast-thinking department.

The boot-strapper's salary was crap for the first year or two. There wasn't a year three. Anyone who hadn't clawed their way out of the primordial booze by then was adiós amigo. Go screw up somewhere else. It was pure Darwinism. Come the six-monthly bonus time, the top guy could make millions upon millions. A proportion of which worked its way down the line to the lesser mortals. Unlike some businesses in which it was frowned upon, in that hypocritical British way, to talk about what you earned, not here. The millions others earned was part of the job pitch.

Byron took a closer look at Brenner. Had he been

crying? What a wuss. Even so, Byron knew he had to say something. Something normal. 'Any more news—'

Brenner's voice was thick with raw emotion. 'Oh shit, you didn't hear yet? They said on Sky no one above the seventy-third floor got out before tower one went down.'

That was the bonus Byron had secretly been hoping for. The MOR group's New York operation was on the eighty-fifth floor at WTC 1. It was about three hours since they had all been transfixed as Tower Two collapsed across the twenty or so TV monitors on the floor. It had been a normal balls-to-the-wall workday, till right before two in the afternoon London time. The floor was packed with people making trades. As usual there was a surplus of monitors and television screens tuned to CNN, Sky, BBC, CNBC, and Bloomberg. A wire-report came in about a small plane accidentally crashing into the World Trade Center. That caused a definite ripple given the proximity to Wall Street and the start of trading, but no panic.

Then Sky flashed to a live feed from its sister channel Fox News in New York. It was looping a recording of an airliner flying out of a brilliant blue sky directly into one of the WTC towers. Not a light plane, but what looked like a fuck-you, fully-laden Jumbo.

Byron was on the phone when he heard a commotion by the wall mounted TVs on the far side of the room. One of the boot-strappers had a remote control and was wanging up the volume. A few minutes later the phones went even crazier when, live to the world, another plane flew straight into the second tower. All hope that this was a tragic accident evaporated. For a while people seemed stunned into a mute acceptance, carrying on as normal. Until people started jumping from the windows, again live on TV from 3000 miles away. News of the Pentagon attack sent a shock wave through the floor, rumours that the White House had been hit ricocheted around. By now people were mostly unable to work coherently as they half watched the TVs, or had their computer monitors showing a live end-of-the-world feed.

When the second tower started its agonizing death collapse, everyone stopped dead. There was a collective strangled gasp and the floor fell silent. A lone phone rang unanswered. Somebody bellowed *'Christ no. Christ no.'*

As the vast grey clouds mushroomed out of what would be dubbed *ground zero*, Goolsbee looked around at the dark sky of numbed faces. One woman screamed and half collapsed into her chair, babbling uncontrollably. No one took any notice. People started hugging each other randomly. Byron thought he had better join in with these displays of normal emotion. It would seem odd not to. Behind the mask he was thinking how great this was going to work out for him, especially after tonight's little bit of club activity had played out.

'Know anyone in the New York office, Byron?'

The fact Brenner had reverted to Byron's first name shouted out at him. He probably wanted to feel close, to share a moment of caring. No need for Byron to disappoint.

'Only by phone, y'know, not like I met personally. You, uh—Tom?'

Brenner's face crumpled as he tried to hold it together. 'Shit man, yeah. I did. Nina Murkowski—remember? Came over for a few months.'

Byron shook a negative, which registered a memory in Brenner. 'Course not. Before your time. You shipped in recently right?'

'A year now.'

Now Brenner looked surprised. 'That long huh? Me and her, we, you know—casual like, but—'

'Oh, right.' Then *Now please shut the fuck up about the dumb bitch,* flashed across Goolsbee's mind.

'Yeah, used get the Concorde over, Friday night. Then the French bollocksed that all up.'

Water welled up in Brenner's eyes. Byron never prayed, but he prayed the guy would not cry. His mobile answered by vibrating towards the edge of the sink surround.

'Sorry—better take this.' Byron grasped the phone as it seemed ready to shake itself onto the floor. He recognized the caller's ID.

Goolsbee:	It's me.
Caller:	Likewise.
Goolsbee:	Still on tonight?
Caller:	Why wouldn't we be?
Goolsbee:	Yeah I'm here with a colleague.
Caller:	See you at the pick-up point.
Goolsbee:	Okay, gotta go.

Goolsbee parked the Ford Transit van in Soho Square as dusk was creeping in over the city. He reversed the van up towards the tall black iron railings encasing the small park at the centre of the square. The mini lung is a favourite for day workers in and around Oxford Street to the north, Charing Cross Road to the east, and Greek Street leading south into the heart of Soho. On warm summer days the grass is barely visible beneath the litter of sunbathers: tourists, shoppers, and wage slaves soaking up the UV together. Although the sunbathers had long gone, the park was still busy. A few people were throwing Frisbees, shrieking and shouting. The sounds of an acoustic guitar playing leaked in.

Goolsbee gazed through the windscreen at the expensive buildings opposite. They did not look much to him, rather boring. But Soho Square was primo real estate in an ocean of Soho detritus. It had the highest square footage rents in London, less than fifty yards away from cheap hookers in tatty bedsits above sex shops. Or all you can eat for a fiver in a Chinese alleged food hole. What you were eating, you did not want to know. Though unwary tourists might get a chance to see it again, four hours later, slumped over the toilet in their over-priced hotel.

He was looking directly at MPL Communication, the vanilla named headquarters for a certain Paul McCartney. Goolsbee's hated father had been a big Beatles fan, Goolsbee hated the Beatles in retaliation. Yet because his father always had a cassette playing in the car while he was a kid, he had so many of their songs rattling around his head. It needed the slightest provocation for one to take residence for hours. He did have a soft spot for Helter Skelter, with the obvious Manson connection. *You may be a lover but you ain't no dancer. Helter Skelter. Helter Skelter. Helter Skelter.*

Two policemen sauntered past McCartney's building. Byron instinctively flinched and slumped down lower in his seat. There was no need, even if they had been looking in his direction. The nondescript white van was quite safe. One of the others had bought it nine months ago for seven thousand pounds cash from a builder in Luton. The vehicle was registered to a fake company with a convenience address in Barnet, north London. It was stored in a rented lock-up garage in Camden most of the time. All the transactions relating to the purchase had been paid in cash, money orders, or postal orders. All untraceable. As far as the police were concerned any check on the number plate would flash a legit vehicle with a legit company address. They all had fake Driving Licences, which can be easily bought if you know the right pub. The standard was high enough to walk away from any random traffic stop by the police. Further police follow ups would lead to dead ends, as no actual person would be linked to the van or the licence. But by that time, the van and the driving licences would be long burned out.

Byron kept a wary eye on the coppers. They crossed over and entered the park. It was the first project he had been allowed to plan solo after getting the Kill Club vote. Any project needed the unanimous approval of them all. But Byron knew there was only one approval he needed: the one who had guided them to eight successful outcomes since that first amazing night in the abandoned warehouse.

Byron was the last of the others to head up an official project, but he desperately needed this one. He had been at the MOR Group for a year and was humiliatingly still a boot-strapper working his guts out for peanuts. Nearly all his fellow intake had moved up. Then he takes one lousy week's holiday in Singapore, and one of his fellow strappers, who had been there under a year, makes a deal that should have been his. Martin Forbes, the prancing little queen, was about to get promoted to lucrative lieutenant.

He smirked to himself as the scenario played to the final act. 'We'll fucking see Forbes, we'll fucking see.'

BANG—BANG.

Byron jumped at the double thumps on the rear van doors. It was the others. He jabbed at the door-unlock button on the dashboard.

Showtime.

12

The sound system was deafening, pumping out the massive bass beat vibrating every organ in his body. Byron edged past the dance floor and headed towards the bar. He had memorized the location of all the CCTV cameras last week, and made sure none caught his face tonight. He was proud of the way he was putting his *tradecraft* into action. He loved the word tradecraft, picked up from spy world novels from writers such as Ian Fleming and Frederick Forsythe. He read those secret agent books as a kid, and had longed to be the dashing spy licensed to kill, and thrill. John le Carré, nah, not so much.

He was still bitter that his application for MI6 did not progress further than the standard Oxbridge interview with written and oral psychological evaluation tests.

The curt official letter from HMG declining his services was devastating; seared into him word for word *Thank you for your interest in a career in the intelligence services. As you know, HMG attracts applications from the highest calibre of recent graduates from all the leading universities. As such, in this year's intake we attracted twenty applicants for each open position. It is, therefore, with regret that I have to inform you that we shall not be inviting you to the next stage in the rigorous selection process.*

Fuck them. Being a dual US and British national, he was thinking of applying to the CIA. His mom's brother in Maryland worked for *the company*. They had been reasonably close when he was growing up on the outskirts of Baltimore, Maryland. Roguish Uncle Ted would hint at the dark deeds he had been up to on his long mysterious absences in the Middle East and Central America. While Byron's middle school contemporaries were goofing around with kid's cherry bombs in toilet bowls, unknown to his mom, Uncle Ted was in his garage showing the twelve year old Byron secret agent tradecraft. Such as mixing common household chemicals to create powerful explosives, like the ones later used in the 7/7 London underground bombings. Then they would be out in the woods, where Uncle Ted would let Byron shoot his Sig Sauer handgun at people shaped targets. It was all great fun for a growing boy.

He could see himself as the heroic spy. Wet work. Black ops. Mysterious death of a South American leader. Car bombing in Caracas. He would love to serve his first country in a capacity for which Byron Goolsbee knew he was totally suited. Killing enemies. As tonight would definitively prove to *him* and to the others.

It was about eleven o'clock, and the dance floor was getting wild, as if nothing had happened in New York. He loathed clubs at the best of times. The noise, the sexed-up pick-ups, the drugged-up drones: and that was the straight clubs. A gay club was even worse for him. He had wanted one of the others to do this part of the op, but the consensus was that he was the one with the experience, having had almost a practice run at a gay club the previous year.

A massive cheer blasted from the floor from the mass of men gyrating to Geri Halliwell camping it out with *It's Raining Men*. Centre stage, one man was swaying side to side in his T-shirt, and nothing else. Another guy was on his knees giving him a blow job while the crowd cheered on. Byron shuddered. He was committed to *the* job, but had not thought he might have to go that far into tonight's role.

He was dressed in the Banana Republic/J.Crew preppy, pretty boy look he knew the target wet-dreamed over. A rush of excited clubbers impeded his progress. They were all gagging to check out the source of the grunting and manic cheering. Nothing like a free sex show to get the folks rubber-necking. Byron spotted the target. Hard to miss. Gaunt face topped by a shaven head. Pierced ears and two nose rings. Spiked dog collar. Heavily chained leather jacket. Tight leather pants with a bulge that could be a Prince Albert.

Byron made an executive decision and *accidentally* bumped into Adam Hanna, the off-on-off boyfriend of Martin Forbes, the mincing queen who was getting the golden job that was rightfully his.

Acting embarrassed that Adam had recognized him, he paused to mutter 'Sorry,' before continuing on his way to the bar, giving a quick glance behind to make sure he was watching him. Adam was. *He* was a great actor though.

Leaning against the bar he ordered two bottles of San Miguel. Waiting for the drinks he quickly texted his progress so far. Geri had finished her weather report and Kylie was bemoaning that she *Can't Get You Out of My Head* when Adam materialized right in front of him.

'Hey, it's Byron, right?'

He acted surprised. 'Yeah—do I—'

'We met.'

'Yeah right, the Christmas do. You're—'

'Adam. Marty—Martin's boyfriend. Ex boyfriend. I dunno. We split up couple of weeks ago. Sort of, I think. We do this all the time.'

Byron already knew this. Probably everyone at the firm knew this. Byron seethed that Martin never shut the fuck up about his love life. He was so far out past the closet he was out of the cosmos. It was this pathological and obsessive need to talk about Adam that became the genesis of the plan. When it happened, everyone would say, *'Y'know what, now I think about it, doesn't surprise me.'*

'Oh, sorry to hear that. But now you mention it, he did mutter something about some new guy.'

Adam's face hit the floor, bounced a couple of times, before settling on squashed pumpkin. 'Fucker, fuck, fuck, fucker. Seriously? Pardon my French.'

Byron shrugged his fake sympathy. 'Yeah sorry dude.'

Adam looked even more crushed than Byron dared hope. 'Fuck him.'

This was going great. Byron picked up the spare San Miguel and wafted it in Adam's direction. 'Hey, have a beer. Drown your sorrows.'

'Yeah, cheers man.' He grabbed the bottle and glugged down a big mouthful. Byron could see Adam's wheels turning. 'Jesus, you're teeth are so white.'

'Yeah it's called dental hygiene shithead. You wanna try it sometime.' That was what Byron wanted to say, instead of 'Thanks. I try.'

Adam looked him up and down. *Nice.* 'Look, be upfront here, thought you were straighter than Mick Jagger.'

Byron's modulated reply carried the right degree of uncertainty to get Adam all hot and bothered.

'I, uh—I am. Totally.'

Adam smirked and put a squeezing hand on Byron's shoulder. 'Oh sure, that's why you're on your own slumming at G.A.Y. Queer central for London.' He laughed for emphasis. 'Thought the blow-job on the dance floor might've been a dead giveaway?'

'Well I—y'know.'

'That's it, I do know.' Adam took another slug from

his bottle. 'Look man, we've all been there at some point. Look around.'

Byron followed Adam's dramatic arm sweep. 'See him, good friend of mine.' He pointed at a balding middle-aged man dancing with a young muscle hound. 'Married, three kids. Corporate lawyer. Took him till last year to come out. Going through his wild phase at the moment. Making up for lost time. So there's nothing to be ashamed of—experimenting. I mean, how d'ya know till ya try, right?'

'Well yeah, that's—'

Before Byron could finish, Adam leaned in, grabbed the back of his head and planted his long pierced tongue firmly into his mouth. Byron had thought he would be more repelled. But what disgusted him was the halitosis. So when he staggered back in response, Adam took that as a sign of his own irresistible gayness and a happy ending tonight.

'Fancy a boogie then lover boy?'

Byron checked his Tag Heuer Thai knock off which informed him it was five past eleven.

'Dance? Yeah, okay. Gotta go to the can first. Wait for me.'

'Wait for you? Aren't you adorable? I could eat you all up. Promise.' He winked. Unadorably.

Byron made his escape. He headed towards the ground-floor toilets, until he was out of Adam's sight. Then he veered left to the stairs leading up to the balcony of the former cinema. It was dark and gropey upstairs. He had a good view of the bar below as Adam stood waiting, swigging from the bottle. Byron took his Nokia from the Mulberry leather satchel slung over his shoulder, texting out the message *20 mins*. Then he fished out another phone. It was the one he lifted from Adam's leather jacket during the session of forced tonsil tennis. That was a bonus. Thinking on his feet. *He* would appreciate that. Scrolling through the address book, Byron found Martin's number. He already had the message down: *@GAY picked up pretty boy gonna take home2fuck silly jealous???*

That finished, Byron turned around to check on his new friend at the bar.

PANIC.

Adam wasn't there. Byron raced down the winding stairs to the ground floor action.

'Sorry—sorry.' He side-swiped a pile of people walking up as he checked his Tag. The timer countdown feature was racing down.

18:07:95

'FUCK.' Byron ordered himself not to screw this up. *He* would be incandescent with rage. No telling what he might painfully do to him. That solo incident with the girl 18 months ago was bad enough. The club members had taken a vote and Byron lost, but Byron could not leave it alone. She had rejected him and had to be humiliated. Suffer a living death with something that would haunt her forever. He knew how, but the others said no, it was too risky after the meat. Well, all except for that other one who liked to watch. Perfect for operating the camera. So he went ahead, him and one other. It was perfect and had the desired affect of killing someone inside. But when he found out (*he* always knew everything somehow) Byron was genuinely scared. He had no wish to be the one dangling from that meat-hook, it was way more fun when it was someone else.

He scoped the bar. No Adam. He scooted to the dance floor where Madonna was *Vogueing*. Bodies swirled and jived around him. His head felt the same. Still no Adam. Five minutes ago he was king of Kill Club. Now some crazed disgusting fag was gyrating in front of him, pouting his collagen enhanced lips.

16:31:88 pulsated menacingly.

The luminescent green numbers reflecting on his retina. Another Byron fuck-up. He felt a hand grab his crotch from behind. That was it, he swung around fast, fist clenched to land one.

A grinning Adam boogied in front of him. Two cold ones in hand and waiting. He handed a bottle to Byron.

'Jesus mate, thought you'd been jumped in the loos. Shoulda warned you, they're like animals in there.'

Byron fake laughed. 'Yeah, now you tell me.'

'Shit man, where were we then?'

'Experimenting. And that's okay. Right.'

'Too fucking right. Let's gerroff the animal floor.'

They found an empty table in a dark corner and sat. Adam took another swig, but he could not hide the fact he was salivating at the thought of the virgin newbie. When he began to feel light-headed as the room swayed, he put it down to his heart racing with anticipation.

It wasn't that, of course. It was the *Flunitrazepam*, Byron had slipped into the first beer he handed to Adam twenty minutes earlier. Also known as *Rohypnol*. Also known as a *roofie*. Also known as the date rape drug of choice. As part of the Benzodiazepines family, Flunitrazepam is a powerful sedative. It gradually incapacitates a person, usually taking full effect between twenty-five to forty minutes after ingestion. It was this indeterminate time frame which put Byron on a tightish schedule.

11:17:56

He had to get this fake *seduction* up to the next level. Fast.

'Whoa, you're making my head spin pretty boy.'

Byron switched on his million megawatt mouth. 'You spin me right round like a record.'

Adam shook his head, as if that was going to clear it. 'Fuck, that's one of my favourite songs. Guess we click.'

Time to move in for the kill. 'Whaddya say we get outta here Adam?'

This was going even better than Adam thought. For sure he reckoned it would take a couple of E-tabs to loosen up his confused new friend. Which is why he had slipped one into the San Miguel he handed to Byron. 'Where to lover?'

'Car's parked in Soho Square.'

He swayed again and grabbed onto Byron, more to feel him up as to steady himself. 'Fantastic. Like a man who comes well prepared.'

'Meet you outside okay?'

'You don't wanna leave with me?'

Adam did not realize how right he was. Although he would in a few minutes. Byron had to eliminate any chance they would be caught leaving together on CCTV. 'Honestly, no I don't. Not yet anyway.'

'Yeah, sad when you gotta hide who you really are.'

Byron smiled at the irony. If only Adam knew.

Two minutes later Byron led his erratic new pal away from the former Astoria cinema on Charing Cross Road. They cut through Sutton Row and into the Square. The park was empty and gates bolted. A group of toga clad, billiard-ball headed Hare Krishnas were ringing bells as they chanted their way home to the temple in Soho Street. Byron had not eaten anything since breakfast. The hunger inducing aroma of spicy Indian food was wafting over from Govindas, the restaurant butting up to the temple.

The effects of the roofie were showing more now. Adam's brain synapses were being flooded with inhibitors urging him to close his eyes and slip over the cliff into the beckoning total blackness. He was becoming more spacey, his speech slurring and his judgement impairing big time. The van was a few yards ahead.

'Byron, Byron he's the man I could've had hey Byron did you slip me something you naughty boy course you didn't you're choir boy you look like a choir boy I like choir boys they're so fucking peachy ripe peachy their arses are so ripe and peachy weachy you know what I'm gonna teach you to fuck whata you think of fucking that.'

They had reached the back of the van. Byron quickly scoped the square and the park to make sure no one was looking in their direction. All clear. 'I think—'

—THUMP—THUMP—THUMP—

Byron hammered the van door. 'You're so fucked Adam.'

'Oooo, not yet swee—URGGGHHHH.'

The breath shot out of Adam's body as he sagged forward. Hardly surprising as Byron had slammed his body weight behind a punch straight into his flabby gut. The van door opened and two sets of arms grabbed Adam, dragging him inside. Byron leapt in, slamming the door shut. The whole thing took less than five seconds.

Adam was on his back, like a helpless turtle flipped over on its shell. One of the others sat on his chest as he tried to kick out. Another had a hand over Adam's mouth. His flailing legs losing steam by the second as the roofie invaded even more of his befuddled brain.

Byron slipped on surgical gloves and took the rubber ball gag from his satchel. Glancing at the one person in the world he cared to impress, Byron went all master of the universe, barking out orders.

'Hold his head up. Make sure you don't mark his body. Yet.'

He felt fantastic. His body flowed with energy and confidence. It was the ecstasy, though he didn't realize Adam had dosed his beer.

Byron taunted Adam with the gag. 'Bet you're familiar with this little toy, eh?' He wished he could slice out his disgusting tongue. But that didn't fit in the Forbes project which called for more subtlety and finesse.

The ninja-less turtle squirmed and tried resisting. Byron forced open his unwilling mouth, shoving in the hard-rubber ball. He pulled the studded leather strap behind his neck, above the dog collar, belting it tight on the fourth strap hole. By the time Byron had manacled his hands and feet with stainless steel handcuffs, all the fight had gone out of Adam. All that remained was a bug-eyed look of resigned terror. Then that was gone as his eyes rolled up and his lids fluttered close. Fully roofied.

Fifteen minutes later the van pulled up outside Adam's flat in a quiet road off the Archway, past the two towns, Camden and Kentish. The set up had been easy. Byron had lifted Forbes's mobile from his office desk while the whole floor was watching the towers fall. The text he sent from GAY was received in the van. It established an unassailable time-line, and a location for both phones which the subsequent police investigation would undoubtedly uncover. It also established motivation and opportunity. The police love that sort of stuff when they make an arrest. Especially as one of the others had instantly texted back to Adam's phone: *fuk u queen bitch u said u love me, wots the point of iyt all.* A bit melodramatic, but goes to state of mind, M'lud.

Now came the tricky part, which *he* had pointed out at the initial project planning meeting was the one weak spot in the plan. Shifting Adam from the van to his flat without being spotted. In the end, they went for the clichéd classic. Four of them were on van ops. One had been on target surveillance outside Martin Forbes's house in Highgate making sure he had stayed in all night. Marty was well motivated to wait for '*Dennis*,' the young man he had been messaging via the chat-room at the popular social pick-up website *manhole*. The fake identity for *Dennis* had been created weeks earlier by Byron, who had also been grooming Martin for *his* first visit for a one-on-one bit of man pleasure. If the police tracked the IP address for 'Dennis' all they would find is a trail leading back to the huge EasyInternet café on Charing Cross Road. A dead end.

Byron and two others manhandled Adam into a double-sized duvet cover, pulling it straight over his clothes. It would be burned later, along with their work gear. All set, they rolled him up into the seven foot long rug, £64 from IKEA off the North Circular Road. Byron gave the all clear and the op was green for go.

They unravelled Adam in his flat hallway, the other two carrying him feet first to his bedroom. The power and control flowed through Byron as he directed the others to remove Adam's left shoe.

'Stand him up by the chest of drawers.'

They hauled his dead weight up vertically and held him up under his armpits. Adam's eyes fluttered slightly. Byron pulled open the middle drawer of three.

'Now push him forward so he drops and smashes his head against this drawer.'

—*CRACK—THUD—*

Adam's body crumpled onto the carpet, forehead blood oozing into the wool pile. They dragged him up and dropped him on the mattress of the sturdy old-fashioned brass bedstead. Byron undid the handcuff on Adam's right hand, pulled his left arm back and up, handcuffing it to a brass strut. Removing the cuffs from his ankles Byron put one bracelet round Adam's wrist leaving its twin dangling. He forcibly chaffed his wrist with the metal. The scenario playing out exactly as Byron had imagined it these past few weeks. He preened. All that remained was to plant the evidence.

And kill Adam.

The horror-masked others stood back allowing Byron to strut his carefully planned stuff. One of them videoing as usual. From his satchel he pulled out a sealed, clear plastic bag and a pair of tweezers. Two weeks earlier, Forbes had gone to lunch, leaving his classic with a twist *Paul Smith* pullover draped over his desk chair. Byron took the opportunity to scratch and pull out some material from the shoulder. He unsealed the bag, then used the tweezers to pick up one of the threads of black merino wool. Lifting Adam's right hand, he pushed the thread under one of his dirty fingernails. He did the same with each finger until the hand was fully prepped. Who says physical evidence doesn't lie? The police and Crown Prosecution Service, for two. The Forensic Science Unit. The tabloids which will avidly follow the salacious *Bondage Freak Kills Gay Lover* trial at the Old Bailey. Everyone. Except the guy who had been framed. The gay lover already pronounced guilty. Even his lawyer won't believe him because physical evidence doesn't lie.

Byron took Martin Forbes's mobile phone from his satchel, dropped it on to the carpet. 'Gimme his boot.'

One of the others handed him the well scuffed Doc Marten. Byron smacked the phone twice with the heel, before hand kicking it under the bed. Almost there. Byron carefully replaced the Doc Marten on Adam's foot, and tied the boot lace tight. Turning round to the others, he caught his mentor smiling approvingly. He had done well. One more task remained. The premeditated act that *Martin* was about to commit, instead of the *spur of the moment assault and hands around the throat and before I knew it, he'd stopped moving* job.

Byron undid and pulled off the studded leather belt from around Adam's waist. He did the same with the spiked dog collar around Adam's neck. Pulling on a pair of leather gloves over the surgical gloves, Byron climbed on the bed and straddled his chest. He leaned back and put all his weight into smashing his fist into Adam's face.

—CRUMP—

The nose broke and blood sprayed out, a few stray drops shot right onto Byron's mouth.

'Fucking hell Byron he's probably got AIDs.'

The others laughed convincingly at the First's joke. It was expected.

'Jesus don't say that.' Byron frantically wiped the blood off, before looping the belt around Adam's neck and pulling hard and tight with both hands. The leather dug deep into his windpipe crushing down mercilessly into the already necrotizing flesh. Even with a ball gag restricting airflow, it's still hard work strangling the life out of someone. Two minutes in, Byron's arm muscles were flooding with lactic acid, causing them to tremble perceptibly from the effort. Adam was not so lucky. His face glowed a grotesque reddish-purple and his body sagged into the mattress as his last few breaths were choked out of him like water from a damp rag

Byron knew it was all over – they all knew – when the god awful stink hit them. Adam's bowels had opened involuntarily as his life left his body. Byron gagged so hard he thought he was going to puke.

They looked to the First for a response, as they always did. 'Shit.'

They laughed. One of them wondered, 'What's that line from St. Augustine?'

Byron knew that one. 'We're all born between shit and piss.'

But *he*, naturally had to show off his superiority. 'Actually it sounds much better in the original Latin: inter faeces et uriname nascimur.'

They nodded in concurrence, two of them knew the Latin quote, but knew better than to step on his line. It was easier that way. Not so deep down they were all terrified of him.

'We're done here. Let's go.'

They left.

13

Detective Inspector Bill Hickman almost gagged as he walked into the bedroom. Two reasons. The smell. And the man sticking a long spike into the body lying face up on the bed. The body also appeared to have a ball gag stuffed in his mouth. 'Morning Doc. How are you?'

The police doctor looked up. 'Meh.'

'Meh? That a good meh or bad meh?'

'Irrelevant. No point telling people your problems. Half don't give a shit, the rest are thrilled you're finally getting what's coming.'

'Cynical Doc.'

'I am the guy who loves the smell of excrement in the morning.'

Hickman felt the bile rise into his mouth. 'Jesus that's horrible. I just ate breakfast.'

The Doc beamed inappropriately, then nodded towards the body. 'Imagine how he feels. No shreddies for him.'

Hickman scoped the room and noted what looked like the results of some sort of struggle. 'Any prelim thoughts on exactly when our friend here stopped feeling, period?'

'Liver temp, cold room, lividity, I'm guestimating, probably between eleven last night and one this morning.'

Based on the compelling forensic evidence found at the murder scene and on the victim's body, Hickman brought in Martin Forbes to help with his enquiries. A day later in the presence of his solicitor, Forbes was charged with the murder of his former partner. The same day, Byron Goolsbee temporarily stepped into Forbes' position at the MOR Group. None of this played in the national press of course. Only one story mattered half a world away in New York.

Forbes' hired the best solicitor, who appointed arguably the best murder defence barrister in London, Samir Shah QC. Forbes protested his innocence vehemently to his defence team. Mr Shah QC, told his client that while they would give him their best shot, much of the evidence was direct and damning. Although Samir, who had a nose for these things, and was rarely wrong, wasn't able to get his usual read on Forbes. He had the profile for the murder, a crime of passion that morphed into cruelty, which he could have stopped just after the belt was wrapped tightly around the victim's throat. It can take a long time to choke the life out of a fellow human being, it gives one time to reflect.

Seven months later, following a ten day trial at the Old Bailey, the judge sentenced Martin Forbes to life in prison. At the recommendation he serve a minimum of twenty-two years, Martin collapsed sobbing. Samir Shah QC was truly disappointed. Innocent or guilty Martin would have received the same ferocious defence. It's just that Martin was the first client to be convicted whom Samir thought innocent.

Watching in the gallery, Byron smiled. Later that evening they cracked open the champagne. Two bottles. Kill Club was on a roll, and they all needed clear heads for the next project.

14

Another London day was folding into a golden dusk memory file as Gunn parked outside his house following his long day in Oxfordshire. Eddie called as Gunn was passing the Heathrow junction on the M4. A British Airways 747 lumbered alarmingly overhead, in what seemed a couple of feet above the car. Through the scream of four Rolls Royce engines, he could barely make out Eddie shouting that his police contact had come through. Then the call dropped off. Sounded promising. A text bleeped out as he was zipping along the Hammersmith Flyover. He did a naughty, clicked it open, and hoped Inspector Wilson wasn't out on patrol looking for him. It was Ziya. Two words. All caps and exclamation marks. FUCKING STRINGFELOWS!!!!

Sitting in his car outside the house, he deployed the iPhone, punching in the number on the business card Ruby had proudly given him. The receiving phone rang four times, before it clicked into voicemail.

'Simon Murphy can't take your call at the moment, please leave a message and I might call you back.'

BEEP.

Simon's voice was deep, reassuring and trustworthy. The message? Gunn marked it maximum arse-hole. He recognized the voice from television commercials, that big car insurance company for one. Gunn bet Dr Harold Shipman sounded very trustworthy as he injected lethal barbiturates into over 400 elderly patients. Then sat back, calmly watching them take up to half an hour to breath their last.

'Hi Simon, you—uh, this is Micah Gunn, Ezekiel Gunn's brother. You remember Zeke, from Oxford. Was speaking to your mum today and she said I should give you a call. So I have. Ring me back. Cheers mate. Bye.'

Gunn thought better of adding *we can chat over old times, and oh, by the way, just wondering if you had anything to do with me bro's murder, old chap.*

Normally he wouldn't have wondered twice why the lights were on in his living room. But given the past couple of days, Gunn was acting with extreme caution, his painfully axed shoulder and bloodied head reminding him to be wary. And to take another tab of Codeine. Opening his front door stealthily, the silence washed over him.

'Oh Eddie darling, hubby is home.'

Nothing. *Cut the homo-erotic subtext One Shot.* Eddie had been and gone. The note on the kitchen table was a useful start.

Source in Yard, says shit has hit the wind-machine. Torture boy with Zeke's medallion had been ID'd as one Byron Goolsbee, yank. Plus – major flap on involving a new surveillance system called SPI/GLASS. Couldn't get source to give more details.

Goolsbee. He knew the name. Gunn had a phenomenal memory, so good it had its own medical term: *Superior Autobiography Memory.* Very rare. That was the derivation of his marine nickname 'One Shot' Gunn. It wasn't because of an above average prowess with firearms. Gunn heard, read, watched, or was told something once, and it would stick for later recall. Goolsbee was on the list of Oxford students he had seen in Zeke's trunk.

He checked his watch. It had gone nine, which meant he should have been gone ten minutes ago. He'd check out Goolsbee later. Some loud, tacky club was the last place he wanted to be, but Ziya was going; and Gunn couldn't deny a sudden, overwhelming desire to be with her.

15

Gunn spent most of the tube journey in a reflective fog, making notes in his yellow pad. He felt like he was trying to pin down jelly. No sooner did he discover something concrete, like Walter Czarnecki's murder books, something else popped up to churn everything around.

His favourite Hendrix track popped into his head: *there's too much confusion, can't get no relief.* He doubted a visit to a boom-booming club would clear the fog. Especially with Stringfellows penchant for employing tall Amazonian women to strut around wearing nothing but black leotards and knowing smiles.

The tube train rattled into the Embankment. Next stop Leicester Square. Gunn stopped jotting and reviewed his spidery scrawl.

ENTRY No. 2/EDDIE'S CONTACT
1. Police ID hospital body
2. Byron Goulsby, american – check Zeke's Oxford connections again.
3. Had same sliced X as Zeke, could be victim of same killer. Obviously not Wright
4. Get photo of G.
5. GOULSBY/zeke? 2 links...
G. had Zeke's St. Chris. Trophy from Zeke. How. Why?
G. had X carved on body – I now know same as zeke. Wonder if Hickman knows this. Tell Hickman?
6. Eddie's contact says POLICE in panic mode. Why?? what are they hiding? What's spyglass?

7. Two murders 14 years apart sharing characteristics, like x carved into bodies: GOULSBY links both somehow – FIND THAT LINK. Have to get into to see Wright asap – how??? Ask Mosser? NO?? NOT easy.
8. See Simon. Call again.

Thanks to Eddie, Gunn had a name to go with a body. Goolsbee was linked directly to Zeke through Oxford in the late nineties. There are no coincidences and even an untrained non-detective like him could work that one out. He also deduced there was no way Detective Superintendent Hickman was going to keep him in the loop. But Gunn no longer cared what Hickman did or said. He was on his own, with a little help from his friends. He was going to handle the rest himself. How he was going to do that, Gunn was not exactly sure.

Nor was he sure about what happened next if he discovered someone else was involved in Zeke's brutal murder. Except that it was likely to involve someone paying. Violently.

On that thought, the tube door opened on to a platform at Leicester Square. A blast of stale hot air was pushed over from a Northern Line train arriving at the opposite platform. It brought Gunn back to the evening's festivities.

16

Gunn edged down the stairs to Stringfellows' basement venue. He had flashed his private party invite to the huge muscle at the velvet rope baring the way to the door, near the corner of St. Martin's Lane and Long Acre.

The crowd were mostly fellow nurses, ambulance crews, and lots of the younger doctors. Plus one senior. Gunn was surprised to see Stuart Roper. On second thoughts, no he wasn't. His consultant boss had four mid-twenties women draped over him in one of Stringfellows' famous private booths. Two of the drapees were young nurses from St. Mike's. Gunn scoped the other guests. They ranged from heavy-set builder looking types, to the more moneyed classes.

The Human League, ripped into *Fascination* as Gunn scanned the crowd for Ziya. No appearance as yet. For some reason the iconic 80's band kept everyone's attention as he propped up the bar with a cold one.

When Kirsty Smith's mega-rich husband-to-be found out how much she loved the Human League, it was a money-no-object, done deal. He would do anything for Kirsty.

The League were well into *Hotel Bar*, when Gunn spotted a familiar face striding his way.

'Micah—Mike.'

Although they had become more than doctor/patient, this was the first time Gunn had seen Mosser outside work. It was always in his own one-to-one therapy, or leading group therapy sessions with Mosser's patients, or in St. Mike's when he was on psychiatric call. To share a drink with your psychiatrist was like going on a date with your sister. Though not as illegal. But this was good. On the tube over, Gunn had confirmed to himself that his next move was to somehow get in and question Rufus Wright. The problem was Wright may as well be in Guantanamo Bay for all the chance Gunn had of getting in on his own.

He had considered mentioning it to Mosser, then unconsidered it. Gunn needed a private one-to-one with Rufus Wright. Nothing less. He needed a big favour, which he knew breached medical ethics. Perhaps Dr Mosser was just the man he needed.

'Hey Dan. Wanna drink?'

'Yeah, non-alcohol beer.'

'Kidding right? You're not on duty. Go for it. Getting a drop of Scotch meself.'

Dr Mosser hesitated for a nanosecond, then conceded. 'Oh alright then. Whisky. On the rocks.'

This was heresy to Gunn. But if the psychiatrist was nuts enough to ruin perfection, who was Gunn to argue? It was a free bar and Gunn had spotted a Glenne Spenny, at £170 a bottle: the same nectar he remembered his troop leader, Lt. Mackie, receiving from his mother back home in Ayrshire. The Lieutenant had shared a tot each with his troop the day before he was burned alive in Iraq. *Slainte Mr Mackie*, one of the best. He told the barman to give him a double Glenne Spenny, and added a double Dewars on the rocks to waste on the good doctor.

The League segued into *Love Action*

'Cheers Dan.'

—*CLINK*—

'Cheers.'

The smooth nectar of the Gods slow burned its way

down and ignited the warm glow suffusing throughout Gunn's body. He knew he'd have to get Dan Mosser on board in his capacity as a psychiatrist. Having already decided on exactly how much information he was going to share, Gunn gave Dan the edited highlights of finding Zeke's medallion where it should not have been. Going through Zeke's things for the first time in a decade. Driving to Oxford. Calling in on the widow Czarnecki.

Mosser listened, never interrupting. Nodding sagely every so often. Gunn knew that Mosser's concern would shift from that of mentor to primary mental health professional. Gunn didn't mention the strange encounter in Balloch college quad when he sensed he was being watched. That smacked of paranoia, one step away from a voice in his head telling him what to do. Not things you wanted to hint at to a psychiatrist.

'Long story short, I think it would help if I could see Rufus Wright. Put this to rest, in my mind. Suppose I can request a visit. But how long's that gonna take, and how's he gonna feel about seeing me? So I was wondering if you have any sway in Radcliffe?'

'I am concerned Mike, I have to admit. It took you a long time to come to terms with Ezekiel's death. Then your wife and child. Now this. I can see it's starting to churn all based on finding a St. Christopher's medal which may or may not—'

'There's no *may not* about it. And honest mate, I am fine.'

'Of course you are. Even so—' The pause was enough for Gunn to know what was coming next. 'You know how much I respect your progress in the past few years, it's my professional opinion we need to—uh, talk. Make sure this isn't taking its toll. Again. Then maybe we can consider something with Rufus Wright, in a week or two.

You know there is a programme where victims of crime and the perpetrator are encouraged to meet? It's a bit trickier when mental illness is involved.'

It seemed easier for him to agree with Dan's assumptions, and seemingly acquiesce to leave it for a week or two. 'Okay.'

'Excellent. I'll clear something in my diary.'

Gunn was glad when *Don't You Want Me Baby* turned out to be the rousing finale to the first set. Most of the guests had been singing along as Phil Oakley conducted the chorus. As he said 'Thanks, you're a great crowd, see you all later' a beaming Jockette materialized from the crowd which rushed the bar.

It was nearly eleven thirty and still no Ziya. He had texted her twice and no response. He was happy to be here, especially after the Glenne Spenny. But she was the main reason. At Jockette's insistence he and Dr Mosser had piled into the happy couple's private booth. Once her fiancée, Jimmy, found out what Gunn was drinking he ordered the whole bottle.

Jimmy was a nice guy, but once they had exhausted the topic of how great Kirsty was and how they met (again), conversation waned. Gunn went onto movies and football, two of his favourite subjects but Jimmy had no great interest in either. Dr Mosser was no help in the meaningless chat arena. Some people are not wired that way. Maybe Dan was so used to listening to patients talk, he had forgotten how social chit-chat takes two to lingo. Still, there was always the Glenne Spenny, so smooth it hardly touched Gunn's sides on its effortless slide down. Even with that buttress it was a relief when Jimmy spotted an old pal at the bar, and zoomed off for a chat.

Before Gunn could say a word, the Jockette chimed, and not to him: 'Has he told ya Dr Mosser? About—a certain uh, body.'

'Yes, he has Kirsty.'

'And?'

'And what do you think?'

'I think he should leave it to the police.' She looked at Gunn. 'Which is what I shoulda told him the other morning. You're a dead brilliant nurse fa shite's sake, not bloody Columbo. Pardon ma French Dr Mosser.'

Gunn could not resist. 'Columbo's dead love.'

'My point exactly.'

Mosser had been watching and listening with his usual professional detachment. Gunn expected him to agree with the Jockette. Wrong.

'What's the risk here Kirsty? Anything Mike finds independently he'll be turning over the police, right Mike?'

Gunn took hold of Jockette's hand and squeezed, and lied. 'Course. Besides I've heard the police already know the dead guy's name. I expect it'll be wrapped up soon. This Hickman all but told me they had a handle on what was going on. Drugs apparently. So this could all be moot anyway. No worries, see.'

Gunn winced at telling his whopper, but on the inside. It did the trick, and Kirsty visibly relaxed.

Mosser backed Gunn up. 'See, that little fact's not even been in the papers. You don't know what's going on half the time.'

'I cannae argue with that. Had me in the cop shop near half the day, statement and whatnot. Called in some mumbo-jumbo memory expert to go second by second through everything that happened, from when we got the call. Look at it like a fillum he says. Frame by frame. Said they even use hypnosis because people may have something unconsciously remember something.'

Dan smiled sympathetically. This was his field of expertise. 'I see where he's coming from. The mind's a complex, delicate instrument that does a decent job of protecting itself.'

'Honest I was thinking this is a waste of time, then lying in bed last night, running through it in ma head like a fillum, like he said, and something popped up. Vague y'know. Just as we was turning into Milkwood Road, this fella is jogging towards the scene, I look out my passenger side window and he glances across—'

Gunn jumped right in. 'What did he look like?'

'That's what I'm saying, it's sorta vague. Think I should mention it to the cops?'

Before either Gunn or Dan could answer, hubby-to-be Jimmy was back. He grabbed Kirsty's hand and pulled her up. 'Sorry mates, I'm dragging this gorgeous creature away for a boogie. I believe the DJ is about to play our song. I do have some sway here you know.'

Gunn felt a pang at the all-too-true our song scenario. He and Ginny had a song. A good one too that happened to be playing when they spoke for the first time.

There is a house in New Orleans, they call the Rising Sun. and it's been the ruin of many a poor boy, dear Lord I know I'm one.

It was a good memory that he could handle these days. He even had the song as his ring tone on his mobile. A continuous reminder of good times.

The party crowd parted, applauding the happy couple to the dance floor. Gunn was thinking they made a great couple when his phone Eric Burdened him to flag up a new text message had arrived.

'Missme I fuking here were u???'

Gunn laughed, and felt the need to explain to Mosser. 'It's uh—Ziya Zhang. Nurse at the Mike. Don't think you know her.'

Dan shook his head in affirmation as he picked up the bottle of Glenne Spenny, refilling Gunn's glass, and his own. For a bloke whose arm he had to twist, Dr Dan was now all whisky a go-go. The good stuff too.

She was poised at the top of the stairs, looking for him. Crouching tiger, hidden pleasures. Ziya was the real essence. Eddie would understand that bit of marine slang. A vision of beauty. Exactly as he'd felt when he first saw Ginny.

She was wearing a full length azure blue silk piece, so tight Gunn thought it must have been spray-painted on to her body. The thigh to ankle split on her left side accentuated her long legs. The shoulder to waist split, from covered left shoulder to waist highlighted Ziya's other charms. Her raven black hair was no longer in a tight, pulled back, doubled up pony tail, it cascaded half way down her back.

Gunn was transfixed, and it was not all due to the five or six doubles. He could not be sure if her male patients saw Ziya like this whether it would cure them or kill them. Ziya spotted him, waving excitedly, she made her regal way down. Slow, the dress was that tight. Gunn looked around and noticed one of the stunning Angels had stopped whatever she was doing to look up at Ziya. Gunn gulped. And this china doll was heading his way.

Dan made a show of checking the time before standing up too. He leaned in close to Gunn's ear, and half-whispered: 'Have to go. The wife and little ones keep me on a short leash these days.'

He winked conspiratorially at Gunn. 'I am impressed. Well done. Real progress my friend.'

Mosser exited the booth moments before Ziya arrived, shouting back. 'We'll do that thing Mike, promise. Early next week. Okay.'

Dan barely registered. But Ziya did.

'Fuck Gunn, had to get fucken RICKSHAW. Believe that. Bike rickshaw in England. Driver white dude. Hilfuckingarious. You look shit-faced. It good look for you.'

'That dress. Good look for you too.'

'Nahhh, just something threw on—' Then the second wink in twenty seconds. 'For Gunn.'

But this one held out far more promise.

17

BLACK.

Gunn registered something warm and soft pressing against his body. It felt good. Right somehow. But unexpected.

He opened his eyes and the black merged into milky grey. He was under a sheet or blanket, of that he was sure. He slowly moved his hand until it hit naked flesh. He felt his own body. Naked too, except for his boxers.

He let his hand return to the bare, sleeping Ziya. It was the taut spot at the small of her back, and the start of the roundness. He remembered that spot, how Ginny loved for his hands to wander there, the spasm of pleasure that shot up her spine and tingled across her breasts.

She stirred, and he came to what he thought were his senses. What was he thinking? That was the problem, he wasn't thinking. It was the Scotch thinking for him. And it was the past few days which had blown apart his carefully reconstructed world.

His eyes had become accustomed to the dimness, helped by the flicking light of a small scented candle on the other side of the room.

Gunn could see it was a duvet covering them both. He slowly pulled it off him without disturbing her. He swung his legs down and on to the floor.

—CREAK—

The bare wooden floorboards ratted him out, each creak following his progress like a detonating nuke. He padded across the room to the table with the candle, intending to sit and decide his next move, but the doorless opening to kitchen-diner was right there. His head throbbed less than he could reasonably expect, but he still needed some clear water. The past few hours were a warm blur. He remembered Ziya's stunning entrance and Dan's exit. He was already nicely numbed by downing more whisky than was wise. They had gigglingly stumbled out of Stringfellows at about two a.m. Ziya hailed a cab which had taken them to her studio flat not far from the Oval Cricket Ground, Kennington in south London. He had helped unravel the double bed which was cunningly concealed in the sofa. Ziya had disappeared to the bathroom, so he lay down for a second and closed his eyes to stop the room spinning.

Then it was lights out.

He returned with a second glass to sip lying down. She was standing in the middle of the room. Like Eve. But after the fall. And no fig leaf.

'Gunn.'

'Ziya.'

'Like see?'

He looked her up and down. She returned the compliment. It was easier to see now, as Ziya had switched on the small lamp on her bedside table. He didn't have to answer as his body slowly started to betray him.

'Yeah, you like Gunn.'

She held his gaze, even in this light Gunn could see the self-satisfied smile of triumph playing across her lips. He felt his face flush slightly at her directness. Mission accomplished, she slipped back into her bed, pulling the duvet up to her delicate chin.

'Come bed Gunn.' She did her little trick of raising a

single eyebrow, a neat move if done right. It made her look incredibly innocent and yet capable of going all Karma Sutra in one second flat.

He also noticed the lack of the Tourette's expletives, specifically her facility with the F-word. He always suspected it was half an act.

'Fuckona twiglet you shittin' me Gunn.' That blew that theory.

He climbed back on the bed, laying stomach side down. They lay like that together for a few seconds, until Ziya leaned over and ran her delicate hand down his face and over his lips. It felt and smelt wonderful, but his unconscious flinch was like a slap in Ziya's face. He regretted it as it was happening. Too late. Then even worse.

'It's not you Ziya. It's me.'

Gunn could not believe he had uttered the weaseliest line in the history of weasel lines. *It's not you, it's me*??? She did a full body pout and flounced sideways to face away from him. Gunn realized he needed some instant damage control.

Rolling sideways to face her scrunched up back, he gently stroked Ziya's shimmering, silky black hair. 'I'm a total moron. You know that right?'

Ziya silently shrugged her shoulders.

'When moron becomes an Olympic sport I win gold, silver and bronze.'

She huffily adjusted her body so that they were spooning. While he was speaking to her Gunn noticed the small photo frame on the bedside table. It was a picture of Ziya – or so he thought at first. She looked gorgeous of course. Even in what looked like a rough, faded grey overalls. Then like a Spot the Difference competition, Gunn spotted a couple of subtle discrepancies. He was getting better at this detecting lark. It wasn't Ziya. But given the prominence of the photo it had to be someone very close genetically.

'Didn't know you had a sister? She in Hong Kong?'

She was still pissed off, acting the aggrieved child. 'Not sister—Mummy.'

'Blimey, looks like your twin. She uh—over here or China?'

'She dead Gunn.'

He could feel her stiffen when she said that. He held her shoulders. Tight. 'Ziya. I'm so sorry love.'

'Why? Not your fault. Don't even remember her. Fucken Chinese commie bastards kill her dead.'

Gunn felt the sob well up in her, rising till she was gasping for air as she choked it out.

'Ran—her—over—with—tank—she—so—brave—in—square—bastards—burn—mummy— body—in pit—'

Then Ziya couldn't speak as her throat almost closed. As had his. She turned to face him again. Even the stinging tears flooding her make-up into a mess, could not dim her beauty. He gripped her tight, holding her safe until she fell asleep in his arms. Only then did he lessen his hold, and stroke their pains away.

The salivating aroma of frying bacon woke him up. He was still semi-naked in Ziya's bed. This was nice. He could even make out her neat ordered studio flat thanks to the partially open curtains. In the distance he could hear a church bell chiming, reminding the parish it was time for morning service.

He padded over to the entrance to the kitchen/diner. Ziya was at the electric hob with her back to him, wearing a red silk kimono with dragon print. It looked totally unsuitable for frying up a full English breakfast, which is what she seemed to be doing. Including black pudding.

'Mmmm, that smells fantastic.'

She didn't turn around as he walked to her. 'Gunn, you awake. Good.' She was holding a black plastic spatula, pushing the bacon in the frying pan to stop it sticking. Gunn wrapped his arms around her shoulders and pulled Ziya gently back into him. He pushed his face into the crook of her neck, the one covered by her luscious locks, and breathed her in. It was the smell of warm summer's day. Sweet and sensual. She did not resist, but kept to the bacon task on hand. Perfumed but practical.

Gunn felt it was like a post-first-sex breakfast. Except they had not made love, had sex, done the horizontal tango, made the beast with two backs. Ziya had certainly been up for it. Except he Charlie Foxtrotted that up.

But something intimate had transpired. They had shared something human. Gunn felt exhilarated. It was a genuine emotional rush. It was real. They connected.

'You wanna shower?'

'Is that a hint?'

She laughed. 'No. It fu—it order.'

Gunn returned cleansed and refreshed and in the man's white towelling robe he found hanging on the bathroom door. It had the words Shanghai Hilton printed in navy blue, over the left breast. He wasn't going to say anything about it, even though he had a sudden pang of hoping it was a well past liaison. Not that he had ANY right to. But as he sat down to the plate full of bacon, sausage, scrambled eggs, tomatoes, black-pudding, mushrooms and dripping fried bread, Ziya piped in: 'Look good in my robe. Steal from hotel. Get twenty years in labour camp for that in China.'

Gunn was hungry, and twice as big as Ziya, but she

out-ate him. And that wasn't even with chop-sticks. She had doled out exactly the same portions, and out-scoffed him easily, and not in a gross fast-food eating way. Apparently she learned to love the 'Full English' in Hong Kong when she rented a room over a traditional English café, opened by an eccentric British ex-pat.

Gunn was being seduced by the ersatz normality after three days of near insanity. Perhaps they could pop down to the local for a relaxing drink. He'd bet a tenner Ziya knocked back a pint with the best of them.

What was he thinking? Gunn was aware he'd been asking himself that question more in the past few days than in the past ten years. And he wasn't that great at reading women back then. After last night, Ziya had beamed right back to the effortlessly up persona she showed the world. But he realized they had crossed a raw line together. She had bared herself to him. Vulnerable and at least as damaged as he was. Exactly where that line was, remained to be discovered.

'On police fucken radar now Gunn. Don't let them send me back to peoples' fucken republic.'

'Forget it love, no way will I let that happen. Don't be so paranoid.'

It was another new experience for Gunn to see Ziya with a worry frown. Though she still looked cuter than a bag full of kittens licking a very cute baby.

'Good. How about tell me what fuck's going on?'

This would be the third time he had been asked to explain events. He gave it another shot, but was thinking he'd be much better if someone explained them to him first.

'I wanna come with.'
'Come with where?'
'On case. With you. I'm on contract.'

'This is not a game love. Did you not hear what I said. Some guy tried to axe my head off. No—'

'Decision made Gunn. Get used to it.'

Gunn asserted himself. 'Forget it. No way.'

18

'Way.'

Ziya was sitting at the desk, back to him, typing furiously at the computer keyboard in Gunn's office basement. She had poutingly agreed not to take a week off and accompany him around like a foul mouthed Nurse Watson to his Holmes. Gunn tried not to pout back after he agreed to let her help him *research* at his place.

Gunn couldn't deny he needed help. He had quite a few mouthfuls left un-chewed on his plate. The biggie of somehow interrogating Rufus Wright alone. Digging up-to-date info on Zeke's contemporaries at Oxford. This detecting lark was laborious.

Not so long ago, if you wanted to find info about a person, it would need a private detective to dig around. Now first port of call is social networks such as Facebook, Instagram or Twitter. People were amazingly eager to give up the most private information about themselves to total strangers.

Twelve of Zeke's Oxford student friends had turned up at Kensal Green Cemetery for the funeral, plus at least one tutor and an official representative of Balloch College. They arrived in a mini-bus with the college's logo emblazoned on the sides. They were kids, Gunn was a kid himself. He remembered a group of them mumbling to him all to briefly. *'Sorry for your loss. He'll be missed. A brilliant student. Bright future. Senseless. Great friend. Can't believe he's gone.'*

Gunn was still too numbed to register the platitudes or the faces. They all looked the same to him. No doubt as his marine mates, in their full dress uniform, looked the same to them. He had long regretted never following up. Making the effort to get a real sense of his brother's Oxford life. They were a blur then, so they were a blur now, memory or not. But the girl who choked up whilst reading the Rossetti poem stuck in his mind. Thanks to the photograph on the quad bench, he knew her name was Beth. The man who seemed to be attached to her at the funeral was a mystery. Zeke had written Beth's name on the back, but referred to the bearded third wheel sitting alongside them as a *pet poodle*. It was hardly complimentary.

Time for Gunn to play amateur detective, based on years of world-class training watching crime movies. How would Jake Gittes proceed in Chinatown? How would Dirty Harry crack a case wide open? Motive and opportunity of course. Motive, as in Gunn recognized a lovelorn longing look when he saw it. Opportunity, as in they all lived and studied together in a closed community. The college being their world. Balloch College in the late nineties was the logical place to begin.

In the list of students starting in Zeke's year, three Elizabeths reigned: Brown-Symes, Minter and Monteretti. He was assuming Zeke's Beth had been an undergrad in his college and his year. Gunn had tasked Ziya with googling Goolsbee, or facebooking him on the PC, while he went after Beth on the laptop.

The printer started churning. It was everything Ziya had found on Byron Goolsbee. It wasn't much.

'Nothing on Facebook Gunn. What's up with that. Even fucking Queen on Facebook.'

'I'm not. Not Facespace. Mytwitter, or any of them.'

'You Godfuckinzilla Gunn.'

'Dinosaur. You mean I am a dino—fucking—saur.'

He scanned the pages on Goolsbee: mostly newspaper articles from the Financial Times, Investors Daily, Wall Street Journal.

Ziya was bursting more than Niagara Falls with her info. 'Hey, hey Gunn. Gotta photo here.'

She was feeling pretty pleased. 'His company sponsor London marathon for past ten years. Check London marathon website for runners each year. In 2006, Goolsbee listed as runner number 5062. Check results, he finish in time of three hours, twenty eight minutes. And here official picture of him crossing fucking line.'

Ziya clicked on the link and the head-on picture popped up of runner 5062, the Mall behind him with runners stretching back into the distance. There was no mistaking him now. He was older, sporting shorter hair, but Gunn recognized and remembered him instantly.

19

Gunn felt the house's silence smothering him like a wet towel. Bebba's last text informed him she was back at their mother's house, and possibly she would be crashing at his place some time later in the week if that was okay. Maybe it was best given his tasks at hand. He hadn't told her anything, and he wanted to keep it that way. The sin of omission being greater than the sin of commission.

Ziya had skipped out on him too, gone for her graveyard shift at St. Mike's. The taxi driver sat in the car while Gunn and Ziya stood there in his hallway. She like a prize possession, he like a prize lemon. The woman had stood naked in front of him less than twenty-four hours ago in her own bedroom. And he had still managed to find a way *not* to do that one thing which naked men and women with a mutual attraction invariably did.

He touched her arm. 'So thanks for the help. I'll uh—maybe we can, you know when I make some sense.'

The absurdity rolled over him, so he pulled her in by the waist and leaned down to kiss her delicious mouth. They turned their heads in opposite sync to avoid the dreaded butts. It lasted. Now Gunn definitely did not want to drag himself away. But the cabbie beeped.

'Fuck Gunn. Been thinking have stinky breath.'

'Nah, just me and stinky brain. Late lunch, early dinner, me and you, next week sometime. Local. There's a fantastic Italian on the high street. That's my high street by the way. I'll call. Okay?'

Then she was gone.

The big thing that stuck in his mind about Goolsbee were the teeth. Dazzling white in the London Marathon photograph, open mouthed crossing the line sucking in air. Exactly the same when Gunn saw him at Zeke's funeral. He was in the Oxford students group who mini-bussed it down. He would have recognized him at the hospital, except for the whole mutilated, bloated, battered face thing. He could no longer politely talk to Goolsbee, but now he knew the connections between his brother. Oxford and drama. The Mametaliens photo he'd borrowed from Ruby showed Zeke, Simon and Goolsbee.

He started on the three Elizabeths: Brown-Symes, Minter and Monteretti. Facebook first as they seemed to be touted in the press as the biggest with over a billion subscribers globally. Working alphabetically, Brown-Symes and Minter were still using their maiden names online. Unfortunately their pictures proved that neither was the Beth in the photo. The Beth who read the poem at the funeral. That left Monteretti. Close to Rossetti he supposed. If indeed, Zeke's Beth was in the same college and year. Facebook search drew a blank. There was no Elizabeth, Beth, Betty Liz, Lisa, Lisbeth or any derivative he could think of with the surname Monteretti.

He returned to Elizabeth Minter's Facebook page looking for her friends and contemporaries. Gunn scrolled down the date entries. Even fourteen years on, she still had lots of references to Oxford University and the people who were there. Elizabeth Minter had 212 Facebook friends listed. Gunn clicked on the link that said SHOW ALL. Another box popped up listing the friends alphabetically, Christian name first. There were two other Beths. But neither was *the* Beth. Gunn scrolled down towards the E's. One Elizabeth. An Elizabeth

Conway.

He double clicked the name and the new Facebook page opened. And there she popped: Zeke's Beth. She had hardly changed. Even her striking mane looked identical. The purple Goth look had gone though. Her short biography gave Gunn all the information he needed. Beth Conway was a literary editor at The Sunday Times. *Literary* sounded like his brother. What he would have been? Would Zeke be some megastar somewhere? Changing lives? Influencing opinion?

Beth had published her first novel to some critical acclaim, and even greater commercial success four years ago. It made big money and was being made into a Hollywood movie. She was currently completing her second, a sequel.

He clicked on Elizabeth's novel's title, *Panic Attack*, which was hyper-linked to Amazon. He had her name, her place of work, and her book publisher. He went to the Sunday Times website to check her by-lines and book-reviews. It took him a few seconds to discover Beth had a review in today's edition. He had a ton of information from which to track her down. But it was after nine on a Sunday evening. There was nothing else he could do right now about Beth, except trawl for internet info.

He scrolled through the list of Beth's Facebook friends to find any commonalities. Being a successful author she had a lot of 'friends': 87,391 to be precise. There was no way he could sift through them to find actual people she knew from Oxford, such as the identity of her and Zeke's pet poodle. Her personal status stated *In a Relationship*. Could it still be the lovelorn poodle? He had thought Conway could be her married name, but Facebook also had a facility to indicate *Married*. Gunn's musings ran wild.

Poodle was comforting her at the funeral. They were clearly all friends as the photo indicated. But he's the gooseberry poodle. He had to sit there day after day, and watch the girl he's in love with all lovey-doveying another guy. He can't take it, snaps, accidentally kills his friend Zeke, panics, makes it look like it was the actions of a deranged individual, like the convenient Rufus Wright.

It was a theory. Gunn jotted it down in his yellow pad. He read it back and had to admit to himself that it was not a very good theory.

ENTRY No. 3/PET POODLE
Mystery student in quad photo. Maybe has thing for Beth. Kills Zeke over it. REALLY???? We're talking Oxford students here.

Gunn was staring the monitor as if he would get an instant response. His iPhone rang. He hoped it was Bathsheba on her way over to stay the night. He was disappointed. He did not want another heart to heart with Dr Daniel Mosser currently flashing on his phone display.

He took a deep breath and clicked the green button.

Gunn:	Dan.
Mosser:	Mike.
Gunn:	Long time no see.

Dan laughed. It sounded forced, like Gunn's unfunny old gag.

Mosser:	Yes—about our last talk, the one involving a few glasses of that remarkable Scotch.
Gunn:	Okay, but I was thinking, you're

	probably right about me charging up to Radcliffe. Maybe not such a clever move.
Mosser:	Funny because I'm now thinking it's a healthy development. You know we've talked often about you confronting this particular demon. Face to face. The man who killed your brother.
Gunn:	True.

Except, not true on two counts. Gunn was keen to confront the man who killed his brother. But he no longer fully believed it was Rufus Wright, at least not alone. So Gunn was wishing he had never mentioned Wright to Dan at all. He didn't have a fully formed plan at Stringfellows. Now he had. Another idea, a crazy idea. And he wanted to handle it himself.

Mosser:	(DISAPPOINTED) Oh, really? But you know what, as I said, as your doctor, I seriously think we need to chat anyway. You never know you might change your mind about eventually getting closure on this.

Gunn shuddered because, despite mutely nodding to that police sergeant, he found the idea of closure a ludicrous concept. There's never *closure*. Not in this lifetime.

Mosser:	And to be honest Mike I am concerned, nothing more, what this is all dredging up. You've made so

	much progress since the bad year.
Gunn:	Yeah, okay.
Mosser:	I do have an hour that opened up. Eleven tomorrow morning? My house. You remember the address?
Gunn:	Actually, never been to your place.
Mosser:	Really? Okay, it's The Belfry, 8 Hilltop Lane, Hampstead Heath, NW3.
Gunn:	Be there eleven.
Mosser:	See you then. Bye Mike.
Gunn:	Bye Doc.

Gunn reflected that everything was working out perfectly for him. Hampstead was en route to Radcliffe. Dan had been his original Plan A to get in to see Wright. Plan B was even more of a long-shot he had half-planned for later in the week. It was half way to what he would be calling a Charlie Foxtrot, military letter code for cluster fuck. But it was something in his control. Other people always let you down in the end. Even friends. It was true that your enemies can never truly hurt you, only your friends can do that. Apart from Eddie.

It looked like the elusive Beth would have to wait another day.

20

'Never knew there was so much dosh in mental health.'

Gunn had been waiting in the study of a very grand, detached house over-looking Hampstead Heath. He had been let in by a middle-aged woman dressed in plaid, with a soft Irish accent. Housekeeper?

Gunn's eyes had bugged out at Daniel's house, which was nothing like his perceptions and preconceptions about his psychiatrist friend. In the hallway leading from the front door to the study, the quiet ambience was disturbed by the competing rhythms of four clocks of various antiquity. They looked very expensive.

The study was neat and ordered and full of elegant antique furniture. A magnificent writing desk dominated the room. Its highly polished wood reflected ridiculously expensive. The classic deep maroon leather Chesterfield chaise lounge looked right out of Sigmund Freud's Vienna. But it was the ticking collection of old clocks and various timepieces which caught his attention.

On the desk was a sloping stack of five pull-out trays. The plush black velvet type used by jewellers to display their wares. Gunn could see various timepieces for men and women with leather straps or bracelets in gold, silver, and other metals. The top tray displayed six classic looking watches neatly laid out. Gunn pulled out the second from top tray, there were another six watches. This was a serious collection. And they were all ticking away to various degrees of accuracy.

The wall opposite the desk was tastefully stacked with

an array of frames and plaques. He had already checked them out, purely out of curiosity. Not snooping. The centre-most frame was from The University of Edinburgh Medical School informing the world that Daniel Eccles Mosser had graduated from said institution with first class honours. He was duly permitted to claim the title of Doctor of Medicine, and to practice medicine in the United Kingdom and the British Commonwealth. Good to know.

He laughed at *Eccles*. Dan had kept that one quiet. There were three photo-frames on the desk. The photographs confirmed Daniel was married with a couple of small children.

'Dosh? Oh, you mean the house, and the stuff?' Dan gestured towards his many fine, expensive possessions.

Gunn felt silly opening his yap like that. 'Not that there's anything wrong with that.'

'You got me Mike. I do alright. Private stuff, the Priory. Radio. TV. Books. I like nice things.'

'So I see.'

'I know what you're thinking.'

Gunn smiled and seriously doubted that. 'Oh yeah?'

Daniel assumed a jokey serious tone as if he was dictating a patient's diagnosis into a tape recorder: 'Patient A. possibly exhibits symptoms of an obsessive-compulsive disorder. I'm right aren't I?'

Wrong. But Gunn laughed, embarrassed. He was beginning to elicit more personal information than he wanted.

'I love the beauty of old timepieces in their own right. Remarkable precision.'

Gunn mulled it. 'Suppose you deal with the chaotic unpredictability of the human mind, must be nice to count on unwavering precision in one area. Nothing as predictable as a clock.'

Dan seemed impressed. 'That's very perceptive Mike. Think it's more than that though. Don't believe in God, of course. What rational person does? But when you look at the craft, the workmanship, you can believe in an immortality of sorts. That the maker lives on in his creation.'

'God truly is in the details, eh.'

'Trust you to say that.'

'Expensive hobby.'

'Little secret Mike. Alicia, the missus, she's the big breadwinner. Corporate lawyer. That's the gig to be in. It helps me indulge my passion. See how that works?'

'Sorry?'

'Patients have obsessions. Psychiatrists have passions.'

'Got it. And psychiatrists with rich wives have expensive passions.'

Dan half-grinned as the study door swung open and the rich wife glided in. Tall, elegant, expensively dressed, with good taste, and clearly prepped to go out. Her almost shoulder length blonde hair looked natural. She was almost as tall as Dan. Despite the outward softness, Gunn caught a don't mess with me vibe. Directed at him or her husband, he wasn't sure. She was a lawyer though. No pity in that trade. But she sounded pleasant enough here when she told her husband: 'I'm off now darling.'

She extended her hand. 'Micah isn't it? Alicia Mosser.'

They went through the introductory pleasantries together before Alicia addressed her husband. 'I have no idea when I'll be back. These damn board meetings stretch till six, seven, if Sir Donald gets on his high horse. Nanny has the off-spring so there's no need for you to hang around the house. Eloise will be preparing supper for them for seven on the dot. After they've packed their gear for school. They leave tomorrow from St. Pancras, remember? We eat at nine sharp.'

*So that's how the other half of one per cent live*s? *Nannies, cooks and boarding school.*

Then Alicia Mosser was almost immediately bidding Gunn and her husband goodbye. With his wife gone, Dan relaxed back to his well crafted persona of laid-back competence and control.

'To answer your earlier question I inherited the house from my father. This is his desk. He was loaded. Stockbroker, that sort of thing. But as you probably guessed from the exterior, the old place is almost falling down in parts. Hence all the building work and scaffolding out the front. Oasis of calm on the ground floor, a total tip from the first floor upwards with crap from the attic conversion. Doing out the cellar too. Thing is we're in dispute with the builders and they walked out two weeks ago. Alicia is not pleased.'

Gunn was anxious to get moving he had things to do. Places to infiltrate. Lifers to grill.

Radcliffe Maximum Security Mental Hospital sits a mile north of the picturesque Hertfordshire village of Radcliffe. In Victorian times its full title was the *Radcliffe Lunatic Asylum for The Mentally Insane and Incurably Feeble Minded*. Better known as the loony bin, nut house, mad house, funny farm, crazy corner.

From Dan's house in Hampstead, he zipped up the busy A10. Soon he was past Enfield, crossing over the concrete ring of the M25. The edge of London giving way to the English countryside.

The therapy session went very much the way Gunn was expecting. He was also a pro at this stuff now. Dan probed him on how this sudden revisiting of past wounds was affecting his former patient. Gunn did his best to obfuscate so he concentrated on the Ziya angle. He knew the sex, or the lack thereof would arouse Dan's interest. What was it about psychiatrists and sex? Sometimes a cigar is just a smoke.

He was driving steadily up the A10, by-passing the small market town of Cheshunt. Thirty minutes later Gunn stopped a few yards before a large gate between the twenty-foot high brick wall stretching either side. In case people did not get the message, it was topped with four feet of razor wire. Radcliffe may be called a hospital but it was still a prison for some highly dangerous and notorious inmates. He turned the car around and drove back through the small village of Lower Radcliffe. He found a quiet lane, with semi-detached houses on either side. There were a few cars already parked, so it looked kosher. Gunn parked the Saab half on the grass verge, half in the country lane, then set about his final preparations.

He super-glued the tips of his fingers and thumbs and let them dry. Then he checked his small rucksack for the fourth time making sure he had everything he would need. He looked at himself in rear view mirror and ran over the sanity of what he was about to do. Satisfied with his handiwork, Gunn exited the Saab and walked the mile to Radcliffe.

Definitely nuts.

21

The original 1847 Victorian asylum exterior was virtually intact. A square, four story stone building, two hundred feet by two hundred feet. The east and west wings ran from the front entrance back to the rear wing, fully enclosing a square exterior courtyard. Various modern annexes and extensions had been added from the 1950s onwards, mainly branching out and back from the original rear wing.

As he sat on the uncomfortable chair in the reception area, Gunn remembered something Dan had told him about these places. They were never as grim as they looked from the outside. Maybe wearing his caring professional nursing uniform, that would have made him feel good. But despite what he knew, in all likelihood the guy locked up here for over a decade killed his brother solo, or with help. So who gives a fuck? Seriously. Gunn didn't. The grimmer the better.

A small, Gouda cheese shaped man approached. Even though he was pudgy, his off-the-peg suit flapped around on him a size too big. He had the facial look of a cartoon tortoise, topped off by the thickest pair of spectacles this side of bullet proof glass.

Gunn stood up on his fake name. 'Mr Callaghan. Harry, good of you to come. Pratck Chowdhury, Head of the Radcliffe Trust, amongst my many other jobbing sins. My Human Resources manager tells me you spoke to her.'

Plan B, here we go. Gunn extended his hand to Dr

Chowdhury. He reciprocated. Gunn could clearly see the brown skin was stained a dull yellow. That and the ashtray taste of the air told him Chowdhury was a smoker, and a heavy one by the fog of ash that emanated from his very being.

Gunn knew that secure psychiatric hospitals were notoriously difficult to fill with middle management medical professionals. It takes a special person to work these places. The units were filled with dangerous men whom society had deemed should not be in prison because their capacity was impaired when they committed heinous crimes. They were especially dangerous to females, being serial rapists and women abusers of every stripe.

When he phoned Radcliffe's admin offices, the recruitment officer seemed very keen to see a former special forces medic and current SRN working in a major London hospital. Gunn as Harry Callaghan had emailed his CV from an internet cafe using a newly created hotmail account, mentioning that he was on leave, and would it be okay if he popped in with a small amount of notice? Gunn was praying that there would be no checks to verify the credentials of a potential applicant until a job was to be offered. He also knew instinctively what buttons to push to get them interested in him, whatever his name.

Gunn towered over the diminutive Chowdhury, 'Yes, she was very helpful.'

Chowdhury's lack of physical prowess was made up for by his rapid fire discourse. 'I see reception has issued you your encrypted visitor's key card. Sorry about the naff photo. Keep that to hand—clipped to your jacket, or around your neck at all times as you'll need it to get out. Yes, do as I say not as I do, you're probably wondering where my key card is, in my pocket as I need a new strap. Thanks for reminding me.'

He laid it on thick for Chowdhury. 'Didn't I see your name on a fascinating article on art therapy in secure units?'

Chowdhury affected a false modesty at the welcomed praise. 'You saw my little piece in Psychiatry Today? It was my idea to hold an annual exhibition of Radcliffe art. Keep it under your hat, but next year we are hoping to do something in conjunction with the Royal Academy of Art.'

Gunn laid it on with a trowel. 'I've always been interested in art therapy Dr Chowdhury. Thanks for being so accommodating today.'

'The thing is Harry, may I call you Harry, we always have a need for nursing professionals with a more robust skill-set, especially in our Category A Wing which houses our more notorious patients.'

'Oh yes, wasn't there an incident a few years back. One of the patients killed another in art therapy class.'

Chowdhury's blinked rapidly for a few seconds at that unexpected reference. 'Oh yes. Rufus Wright. Textbook example of paranoid schizophrenia. But Wright is not one of our stars here. We have many more, more interesting subjects at Radcliffe. The infamous Beast of Barnet for one example. His necrophilia activities with the torsos and upper legs after dismemberment? Absolutely fascinating. He's channelling that rage into his art. It's very exciting. Are you familiar with Francis Bacon?'

Gunn hadn't realized there was a pecking order of celebrity killers. Was there a sliding scale based on victim count? You're a star if what? You butcher over five human beings?

'Now Harry, I thought I would personally give you a

quick tour. Lay of the land so to speak. I would not normally do this you understand, but when Sheila mentioned your remarkable skill set, gung-ho former SAS. I assume you were gung-ho, all special forces are from what I understand, fully qualified SRN at The Princess Alexandra, I thought to myself, Dr Chowdhury, you have to meet this person and get him on-board.'

Gunn was reeling from Dr Chowdhury's almost manic delivery, topped off by his creepy reference to himself in the third-person. That was rarely a good sign.

Chowdhury led Gunn down the long corridor which ran the length of the east wing of the original building. Gunn was half tuned out by now as Chowdhury fast forwarded himself explaining how the original cells (padded or otherwise) had not housed the detained since the 1960s. They had been converted into offices for administration and general support staff. The original stone cells mirrored in the three floors above, had been converted into single secure rooms (not cells) on the two floors above where the not-so-violent were housed. Gunn's other senses were extra acute as Chowdhury's voice faded down droning on about the history of Radcliffe. He noted how their shoes

—*SQUEAK—SQUEAK—SQUEAKED—*

all the way down on the lime green, linoleum flooring. The lingering smell of disinfectant and vomit. A printer in an office loudly churning out paper. Somebody on the phone talking loudly about office supplies.

At the end of the corridor, Chowdhury patted himself down, looking for his plastic key card to access the heavy duty security door. The one which should have been hanging by a strap around his neck.

'Forget my own noggin if it wasn't screwed on.'

Gunn seized the opportunity to try out his visitor key

card. The mechanism on the wall was a combination of a barcode scanner and a digital pad. Gunn flashed the key card over the pad above the lock and tapped in his temporary code: TEMP01. The light on the pad turned from red to green, and the door lock mechanism clicked opened, just as Chowdhury triumphantly retrieved his own key card from the depths of his suit.

'Oh, didn't know visitors could get through this first security check with a temporary key card. Have to look into that.'

There was a timed response. Gunn had waited for Chowdhury to pull open the door while he was busy chatting. The door locked again, and the light on the pad turned back to red. This time Chowdhury ran his key card over the scanner which pinged once. He then entered his personal six digit code in the pad next to the scanner. The light turned green and the door clicked open.

Once through, they turned left into another corridor. Gunn read the sign on the wall: *The Sigmund Freud Annex. Inaugurated by Her Royal Highness, The Princess Anne, March 28, 1988.* Gunn preferred the creepy old building they had left, to this neon-lit, nondescript concrete bungle.

Chowdhury explained that the Freud wing housed the patients convicted of serious crimes below the taking of life. But ultimately it was a judgment call made by the patient review board which decided on the status of every patient. On average those kept in the Freud wing would be in Radcliffe for less than four years. Gunn went through three more security barriers within this complex, twice he saved Chowdhury the hassle by using his temporary key card to open security locked doors.

Third time was not the charm. Gunn realized he was going to have to do something else, and more risky. The Freud Annex eventually led to a third security door which

Gunn's temp key card would not access. Chowdhury ran his card over the pad. The double door opened to a tunnel type construction with Perspex sides curving around to form the self-contained roof. The dull grey sky set the mood. A light drizzle was falling, with nowhere to go from the top but to flow down the transparent sides. Ahead and above Gunn could see through the droplets to the imposing modern concrete building. It looked more prison than hospital. And for good reason.

'And here we have our 'A' Block. As I said, it is where we accommodate our most fascinating cases Harry. As a senior nurse on an accelerated path to becoming Unit Nursing Manager at Radcliffe, you would be spending most of your working time in here.'

Gunn was not thinking of Chowdhury's celebrity zoo of fascinating cases. One patient interested him. And he was one key card scan away.

Chowdhury scanned his key card across the same type of scan pad as the security gate. Gunn tumbled down the rabbit hole.

22

Over the years Gunn had spent the occasional moment or two fantasizing on the number of different ways he could easily kill the man he had no reason to doubt killed his brother. No weapons except his own two hands and any old stuff that was lying around. Pen. Cup. Rolled up newspaper. Bleach. Credit card. Hard boiled egg. Match. In the right hands, the instruments of death were infinite. Credit card for instance. Bend it in half continuously, back and forth until it snaps into two jagged edges. Gripped tightly between thumb and forefinger, in a close quarter fight, one savage slice is enough to open an opponent's carotid artery in the neck, and watch them spurt blood to a fast death. Easy.

The extra ingredient needed to turn passive object into lethal weapon was desire. And total unwavering belief that it is you who is going to live, while it's the other sod who is going to die. Credit cards don't kill people, people kill people.

All his marine mates at one point had said the same thing to their comrade-in-arms, or variations on the theme: *Gimme five minutes in a locked room with the evil fucker. All over. End of story. Bury the bastard in a world of hurt.*

Marines tended to be very Old Testament about these things. As was Gunn. Eye for an eye. Tooth for a tooth. Life for a life.

That moment had arrived. Almost. It was surreal. Preposterous less than a week ago. Yet here it was.

Dr Chowdhury concluded his little sojourn with Gunn

prematurely, after receiving a call on his mobile regarding a patient crisis somewhere on site. Happened all the time, apparently. He deposited Gunn in Human Resources with his redoubtable Sheila, anxious to get the paperwork started. She was undermanned and overworked. This was going better than Gunn had dared hope when he first conceived his hare-brained scheme. His reasoning had been logical, or so he thought. Secure institutions secured themselves outwardly. Keeping those inside from getting outside. Not looking hard at stopping those outside getting inside. And Gunn was already exactly where he wanted to be. In.

It was nearly 3 p.m. Human Resources was located on the top floor of the original stone built asylum. Access was through the security barrier at the end of the east wing corridor. Left led into the Sigmund Freud Annex, right led to a short corridor with the clattery old lift which eventually hoisted staff up to the fourth floor. The lift door was open, and an out-of-order sign was taped to the wall next to the lift button. Gunn heard Chowdhury curse softly under his breath. Then explain:

'It's a pain, but this happens all the time. We'll have to take the stairs.'

The winding spiral slab steps were part of the original staircase built in 1847. They were constructed on a narrow steep incline, with built-in person sized recesses in between floors.

That was thirty minutes earlier. Gunn was sitting at a small desk, opposite Sheila Smith, Radcliffe's manger of Human Resources. He had been completing a series of forms for a job he had no intention of following up on. Sheila was a plump middle-aged lady of infinite patience, judging by the dozen phone calls she had fielded. Good news for him. Not so good news? Gunn was getting quite hot. A little bead of sweat had begun at the top of his shirt collar, held in check by his tie. It wasn't because he was feeling any pressure on the task at hand. He was resolute and calm on that front. He had faced the wrath of the Taliban. He could cope with the Radcliffe. There was no window, no fan and certainly no air-conditioning. But in reality, the hot culprit was Gunn's nurses' uniform which he was wearing under his suit.

PLAN B.

From the moment he entered Radcliffe, Gunn concentrated on noting the location of every CCTV camera, and assessing the area for blind spots. He had been into the Security Hub at St. Mike's, and listened to the security bods moaning about blindspots. This gave him a good idea of where they might occur in Radcliffe. He had no problem committing the locations to memory (One Shot, after all). But just in case, Gunn took out his yellow legal pad and took notes. Chowdhury assumed it was so he could remember the pearls of wisdom from his riveting commentary. He was wrong.

Gunn was as armed as he would ever be. It was time to make his first offensive move since he clobbered the bloke who was unreasonably bent on axing him in the head. Sheila seemed to be doing three or four things at once as she was down to a quarter her normal staff. When he handed her the completed forms, he made small talk until the inevitable occurred, the phone rang again. Before she could pick it up Gunn was ever so helpful.

'Hopefully we can take this further. Guess I'll be off then. Should I—' Gunn lifted his visitor key card hanging around his neck, waving it at her. 'Hand this in to reception on my way out?'

He had guessed that normally he would have been escorted out. But as they were not in a Category A area, he reckoned there was a good chance she would say what she said. He didn't have a Plan C. So this was all or nothing.

'Would you dear? Straight down the stairs, through the security barrier and straight up the east wing corridor.'

That was the very last place Gunn was going. For the next few hours anyway. He took the stairs down to the ground floor. The first thing he needed was to have it on record that his visitor pass was used to open the security door which lead to the reception and out. He lingered for a minute until the corridor was clear before he ran his key card over the scanner and tapped in the code. The lock disengaged, Gunn turned back to the stairs. He had to find a place to secrete himself pronto. There was only so long he could be seen wandering around with his visitor pass and a glazed expression. He wasn't a master criminal, so neutralizing an inconvenient person in 007 fashion wasn't an option. If challenged, he would have to get out while the getting was still voluntary.

Legging it up the stone stairs two at a time Gunn reached the third floor un-noticed. He had left a pair of glasses in Sheila's office, as an excuse in case she was coming down the stairs as he was racing up. On the way up with Chowdhury first time, Gunn had noted a couple of promising things. The light blue WC sign, indicating toilets on the third floor. A legitimate excuse for an unaccompanied visitor to be there. It was screwed to the wall, right next to the list of the other occupants on the floor. The list seemed exclusively pertinent to the health and welfare of Radcliffe's staff. Dental Surgery. Massage Therapy Room. Doctors Surgery. Staff Library. Television Room. Staff Kitchen. Gunn confidently pushed opened the unsecured door from the stairwell and breezed onto the 3rd floor as if he belonged.

Gunn hurried down a windowless corridor with fifteen foot high ceilings, the offices to his right. So far he hadn't seen any CCTV cameras in this staff area. The sound of a high-speed dentists' drill set his teeth on edge. The third floor was the doppelganger of the two below and one above, shaped in a full square. Ceiling signs hung down, suspended by two wires. They stated the function of each room, or set of rooms, with a red arrow pointing. He had not seen the sign indicating the toilets yet, so far, so legit. But he hadn't passed a suitable space either. He reached the end of the first corner, turning right to continue his clockwise tour. Still no one to pass, or pass him. Ahead the Staff Kitchen sign loomed. The door was partly open so he looked inside. *Great.* Empty. He went in and closed the door.

It took him thirty seconds to decide. In that time he checked for hidden panels, spaces behind cupboards, broom closets, the lot. Nothing doing. Then he looked up, to the suspended ceiling a few feet above his head. That probably meant a clearance to the original ceiling, assuming there was nothing else in between.

Gunn retrieved a small metal torch from his rucksack. Switching it on, he clamped it between his teeth before hoisting himself on top of the sink's work-surface. He pushed in on one of the two-foot square plastic ceiling tiles in its aluminium frame. Standing to his full height, Gunn stuck his head through the gap. Moving the panel had thrown up a mess of long accumulated dust and grime. The problem was the metal ducting attached by brackets to the original ceiling. It hung down to restrict the space, with one duct running right above his head.

Gunn was still considering his options when that decision was made for him. Voices clearly moving in his direction from the corridor. No hesitation. He reached through the gap to locate something load bearing. The ducting nearest to him was out: it was tissue flimsy. Rotating 180 degrees the torch arced around. He saw a series of old wooden beams fixed three feet apart in parallel. They were bolted into the two original stone walls which were a good fifteen feet apart. Maybe an older false ceiling had been fitted at a time when things were built far more sturdily. Gunn reached up and pulled down on a beam. It felt firm. It was all or nothing.

Hooking his arms over the top of the beam, he took a deep breath and hauled himself up. His left foot disappeared though the gap as the door opened and the voices entered. Still with his arms wrapped around the beam like a possessive lover, he swung his legs up to rest on the first cross beam. Now that his legs were supported, he loosened his right hand from double gripping the wood. As quickly as he dared risk, Gunn lowered his hand until he gripped hold of the ceiling tile, dropping it into its rightful place.

About thirty minutes in, Gunn was finally able to find the optimal position to perch in his nest high above the staff kitchen cum canteen. He had listened to the three men below talk for about fifteen minutes. No matter how loud they got, as they downed their tea-bag made sweet milky tea, Gunn dared not move a muscle. One slip and Humpty Gunnty would have a great fall.

The men finally finished their break. As the door banged shut, Gunn implemented his hastily drawn up Plan C-eiling. He had clicked off his torch when the men entered, so his eyes soon became accustomed to the gloom. This was helped by the six tiles with the built-in neon light source. Light leaked in allowing Gunn to peer to the far end of the ceiling space. About half way along, he could see what looked like a discarded sheet of half inch thick MDF board, about six foot by two foot.

He carefully inched himself along the wooden beams until he reached the board. It took him about a minute to raise the board and place it across three beams. The heat was stifling. He peeled off his suit, and then the nurses uniform below. Someone else came into the kitchen. Alone Gunn assumed, as there was no conversation. The kettle was filled. He checked his glow in the dark watch. It was five past four. Eight hours to kill.

Somebody else clattered in. 'That kettle on, I'm fucking gasping.'

'You look shagged my son.'

'Sitting next to Rufus Wright for three hours solid will do that.'

His fellow guard laughed. 'Oh God, I hate pulling that one.'

'Yeah, gets worse. The Dialysis machine was on the blink. So he's gonna be on the ward overnight, which means I gotta another five hours till some other poor sod gets the night shift.'

'Shit. Hope it's not me.'

The word *BOLLOCKS* flashed for Gunn. But there was no turning back now. He couldn't break in twice. The mission was now a go, plus twenty-four hours. In Afghanistan, Gunn had once hidden in a small hole in the ground for five days. 120 hours eking out six pints of water, minimum rations, crapping into a plastic bag. This was quarter less than that with about thirty hours to kill. Alone with his thoughts. Trying not to fall asleep in case he rolled over. Plenty of time to reflect on how crazy he must have been to think for one second this could possibly work.

At least he was in the very best place for crazy.

23

Gunn opened his eyes. He checked his watch. 12.06 a.m. He had lain concealed in the ceiling space for nearly twenty-four of the thirty or so hours. His last time check had been 10.36 p.m., the strain was starting to grip. Time to move from his current perch. but first he dressed in his nurses' uniform.

The night before Gunn had silently roamed the area. Stealing food. Collecting other provisions, including a bucket.

Now the mission was a go. The corridor was quiet and deserted as he hurried back in the direction of the stairs. All the offices were locked with simple Yale type locks in round brass handles. Gunn had a solution to that minor inconvenience, being part of a snatch squad in Iraq had involved learning new skills, such as lock picking. He was a bit out of practice, but he soon was pushing the door open and stepping inside the units dental surgery.

It was dark. Gunn deployed the pen torch from his rucksack and located the small toilet room. He closed the door and switched on the light.

—*CLANK—WHIRL—*

The small extractor fan kicked in. Gunn froze, for a second it sounded like a jet engine. When he had first arrived at Radcliffe almost thirty-four hours ago, Gunn had not looked his usual self. That would be the false beard, the brown wavy haired wig and plain-glass glasses he was wearing. What was the point of using a fake name without a fake face? In real life Gunn kept his black hair marine style, short cropped and squared away. He had that pale skin of the Celts, but with deep brown/almost starless black eyes. Being from Liverpool somewhere in his past the Welsh-Irish genes kicked in to give him the look of what some people called Black Irish. He was also clean shaven and had perfect sight. Little did Bebba know last month, when she spent a few hours showing him theatrical makeup, that he would be using it for this. Hell, little did *he* know. Gunn had removed the disguise after he first settled himself in the ceiling yesterday. He took a few minutes to transform himself back with the small bottle of theatrical glue.

Gunn retrieved Dr Chowdhury's key card from the rucksack. He had lifted it from the man's pocket as the heavy smoker had wheezed his way up the stairs.

Gunn examined it. It was clear that a close inspection by a guard would be an ignominious end of the mission. There was no way he could transform himself into a five foot five bloke of Indian extraction to match the photo. Absolute confidence in radiating the vibe that he totally belonged at Radcliffe – that would be the deciding factor here. People pick up on confidence. But in the event of an unwanted glance down at the key card? Gunn decided to improvise right now. Using a dentist's scalpel he carefully sliced around the laminate over the head shot of him taken 36 hours earlier, then heat laminated into a temporary visitor's key card. The photo had been printed onto the key card along with the I.D. barcode and his fake name, Harry Callaghan. Lifting off the laminate Gunn cut out the two inch square photo. He repeated the laminate slicing with Chowdhury's key card to unseal the photo. Using the theatrical glue, he coated the back of his photo face, then pressed it in place. Bingo. Okay, close up Gunn knew it looked iffy, but hanging from his neck? A few feet away? All the casual glance would show was a person approximating to Gunn, instead of a balding, tortoise-looking brown guy with huge glasses. At least Chowdhury wasn't a woman.

Gunn checked-listed everything off. Stashed his rucksack in the toilet's false ceiling. It was 12.55 a.m.. He was good to go.

Block A.

Chowdhury's key card did the trick – together with the six digit code he had memorized after observing Dr Chowdhury enter it several times. He couldn't have done it without his grand tour, that's for sure. That and the 1990s level of techno-security.

On the tour Gunn had gleaned the location of Rufus Wright. His forced extra-day stay enabled him to learn the shift changes at 1am and 7am. Lots of people moving around. Hiding in plain site was always the superior option in any mission. The fact that there were multiple shifts also helped. Faces came and went. And because one random member of staff failed to recognize another, would not throw up an instant red flag.

Given all that, Gunn was not on a suicide mission here. Risky yes, impossible no. He'd leave that for the fantasy movies, thank you very much. Gunn was fourth in line in the queue of staff waiting to key card themselves through. A minute later the guard in Block A. hardly glanced at Gunn as he breezed past. Heading straight for the medical room, he smiled appropriately at any staff he passed. No one thought it odd to see a nurse in uniform in what was still technically a hospital. Even more technically, enemy territory.

No dicking about. It was in and out unless events conspired. Gunn kept his head down, or found a way to obscure his face within range of the CCTV cameras. He had the disguise, but there was no need to make it easy later.

Once he had deduced what turned Chowdhury on, it had been easy to stroke his ego about his celebrity killers. The ones the press liked to attach catchy nicknames. Yorkshire Ripper. Beast of Barnet. Moors Murderers. Alluding back to his interest in paranoid schizophrenia with a personality disorder on the side, Gunn brought up Rufus Wright again. Even easier finding out he was in Room B 27 on the second floor. Gunn flashed the key card over the lift control panel, pressed the number two button, the twin-doors had almost closed in the middle when out of nowhere a hand shot in.

'Hold it.'

The Radcliffe security guard dived in wearing his standard issue dark-blue uniform with obligatory walkie-talkie. Karl pressed the button for the third floor and the doors closed.

Gunn went straight on the offensive. 'Hello mate. Not seen you before. Karl is it? Just started? Name's Harry by the by.'

In seventeen words Gunn put Karl right back on his heels. Even if he had been thinking *who the hell is this guy*, now all his brain could manage was to process the verbal barrage with its two questions and three declarative statements. In the seven seconds it took for the door to ping open for the second floor, he managed to confirm he was, indeed, Karl.

Gunn stepped out, smiled, and raised up the medical kit he had lifted from the medical room. The green coloured plastic box with the red cross on it screamed emergency. 'Urgent meds, psychotic breakdown, totally catatonic.' The lift door closed. Gunn had already turned on his heels, heading relentlessly for room B27.

Gunn clicked the door shut. Stone-still. Closed mouth. Eyes adjusting.

—*Rasp—Rasp—Wheeze—Wheeze—*

The snoring was regular and rhythmic. Opposite the door, the almost black of the clouded night, framed the high window with its bars. He could make out the shape of a metal-framed single bed, warm body laying on top. Look at him, all safe and sound and locked up and fed three square meals a day and some nice doctors working out how to make him all better. But you were never going to get better were you Rufus?

Wright was lying face up, mouth open. Lamp on a bedside table. His brother was in the cold ground, dead for all eternity, or judgment day according to their dad. And Wright had a lamp on a fucking bedside table. Glass of cocoa before warm beddy-byes? Karl tuck you in?

Keep it together mate.

Gunn rabbit punched Rufus once in the side, a hard smack on the kidneys. Not full weight. Nowhere near. He clamped his left hand over the mouth as Wright's eyes shot open. That tends to happen when awoken in the dead of night with a gut blow. Rufus squirmed. Gunn grabbed him around the throat with his right hand and squeezed. Not full kill weight, but enough to bloody hurt. It was pure primal aggression from Gunn. Darwin in action. After fourteen years someone needed to be hurt for Zeke. It rushed over him like rash. Even as he barely believed it was solely Rufus Wright any longer. But thanks to Hickman, he did know for sure that Wright had definitely killed another human-being. So fuck Rufus Wright and his temporary pain. The way it had to be.

Rufus wouldn't stop squirming. Gunn released his throat grip and punched him again, this time in the belly, a control blow, to take the wind out of his sails. That worked. Gunn grabbed his throat again, but didn't squeeze nearly as hard this time. He leaned right down and hissed in his captive's ear. 'Rufus, can you hear me. Nod your head twice if you understand my words.'

—*Nod*—*Nod*—

Inches from his ear, Gunn calmed his voice. 'Okay, here's what's going to happen Rufus. I don't want to hurt you but I fucking will big time unless you do what I say. And I won't hit you again if you promise to stop thrashing around, and not to say anything unless I ask you. Understand? Nod again if you understood what I said. Okay?'

In the gloom Gunn could see in Rufus's wild-eyed terror that he did not understand what was going on. How could he? But even the irrational will do the rational – if they *get* the fact that their reward is no longer receiving intense and sudden pain.

Rufus nodded enthusiastically.

'Gonna release me hand off of your throat, then mouth. Don't yell. Promise now.'

—*Nod*—*Nod*—

Gunn slowly released both his grips. Rufus gasped and spluttered for air. He grabbed his own throat, too terrified to even whimper.

Gunn perched himself on the side of the bed next to Rufus's head. Keeping the subject lying down in an inferior position exerted maximum dominance, leaving the victim with even more feelings of helplessness and hopelessness. It was all part of the psychological game that was as important as the threat of physical pain. Pain and psychology were the twin pillars of coerced interrogation without the niceties of due process.

One thing struck Gunn. Rufus Wright looked no more

than five foot six, and less than ten stone, soaking wet. Ezekiel was over six foot tall, and marginally less stocky than Gunn. Though he and his brother were opposites in temperament, Zeke had been as strong as him. Gunn had always been the in-your-face, better not mess with me guy. Zeke was easy going and passive, but he wasn't a pacifist. There is no way Rufus Wright could overpower Zeke single-handed. Not a chance in hell. Gunn started to leverage his aggression vibe.

'Rufus, do you know who I am?'

He was too terrified to speak, clearly mistaking Gunn's order not to yell to also mean not to utter a peep either.

'It's okay to answer. Promise.'

Through the pain in his throat, Rufus gasped out his two word answer. 'The devil.'

Gunn laughed. 'No Rufus, I'm not the devil.'

The wail from Rufus was guttural 'But I was promised.'

That was interesting. Rufus's answer gave Gunn another idea: in this line of work, you have to listen and act on the fly. Gunn was flying tonight.

'No—but me and him are really, really good mates, y'know. He sent me to talk to you. Check up on a few things.'

It was worth a shot to string him along if it got him talking freely. It wasn't as if Gunn had zero experience in the devil business. His dad's church had certainly believed in the devil and all his works made flesh. Possession, exorcism, demons. They were all very real to him growing up. Mumbo-jumbo, the rationalist might claim. But was it, Gunn had been asking himself? Wasn't the idea of the devil at least as good an explanation as *he had mummy issues so that's why he raped women. It was society's fault he slaughtered all those people.*

Rufus was wide-eyed and rapt with anticipation. 'Are you a fallen angel. Like Lucifer?'

Gunn hesitated. How far should he take this? Under any other circumstance, as a nurse, he owed the guy a duty of care. He had assumed Rufus would be on a cocktail of anti-psychotic meds. Plus any number of other drugs, dependant upon what the current diagnosis of his mental state happened to be. But his instant mention of the devil indicated that perhaps he was experiencing some of the symptoms of his paranoid schizophrenia. Or maybe he had undergone a genuine religious conversion since his incarceration. It has been known.

Gunn clicked through his memory cards and found the book he read when he was about eleven. The book was on his dad's bookshelf when he first sneaked a look at it. 'Yes I am Rufus. I'm Azazel, one of the Lucifer's most trusted acolytes—'

'LIAR.'

That was dangerously loud. Gunn's hand shot out to clamp over Rufus's mouth again. 'Quiet. Why do you doubt me Rufus. How did I materialize into your room? You know that's impossible, you've been here long enough to know that. How do I know so much about you? Is not our master also known as the Prince of Lies?'

Gunn loosened his hand. Rufus hisspered a surprisingly defiant response. 'Azazel told me others would pretend to be him, and that I must be vigilant for impostors.'

That threw Gunn for a loop. Not the response he had been expecting. Of all Lucifer's acolytes, he had to choose the one Rufus had actually been in contact with? Devilishly long odds. Maybe he should have said right off that he was the devil. Now he had to change tack.

'Very good Rufus. Azazel will be pleased. As you

guessed, I am but a humble servant, sent here by Azazel himself to test you and your loyalty.'

'I knew it.'

'How does Azazel usually communicate with you Rufus.'

'Don't you know?'

Yes, Gunn could see the logic in the illogic. But control was slipping. He had to re-establish dominance. As a marine and a nurse, he knew pressure points on the body that could cause extreme pain with the correct application of force. He clamped Rufus's mouth again, and gripped him under his arm-pit. An intense jolt of pain shot through Rufus's side and down his right leg. Almost as bad as a car-battery cranked up to zap down the electrodes embedded some poor bastard's skin. Tears leaked from Rufus's eyes. Gunn felt bad about it. Shamed in fact. But he was all in now. And it was for the greater good.

'How dare you question me.'

Gunn released his mouth clamp again as Rufus gasped out his humble apologies. He was beaten down. Compliant.

'He whispers things. Whispers to me. Explains things. Tells me things. The doctors try to stop him, but he's too strong. Too clever for them. You know that. What's your name? Please tell me your real name. Names have power.'

One Shot flipped through the memory cards again locked up in his brain. He had to get this one right. 'My name is Nisroch.'

Rufus contemplated the name. 'Nisroch. Yes, a third tier angel fallen from the heavenly host.'

'Second tier in all of creation, Rufus, behind Lucifer himself, but before mankind.'

'Second, of course, forgive me Nisroch.'

'Azazel is pleased that you have resisted his enemies. Do you remember when Azazel whispered to you in the art therapy class? Here in Radcliffe. About Ryan Sperling?'

Rufus preened at the name and looked very pleased with himself. 'Ryan insulted Azazel. Right to his face. I told Ryan not to, but he wouldn't listen. Cocky. Naturally he had to be punished. It was Azazel who suggested I use the brush to punish him. Artistic licence, he said. Ryan shouldn't have said anything. I told him. Told him Azazel was not happy. But he wouldn't stop, so I stopped him.'

That went well, so Gunn went for the big one. 'That's fantastic Rufus. Now, remember the warehouse.'

'Warehouse?'

'Yes, remember. The reason why you're in here. You know, the boy you, uh—killed. Confessed to killing anyway. The boy's name was Ezekiel.'

Rufus threw himself backwards, like he had been struck by a righteous bolt from heaven itself. 'No no no no. Not kill angel of God. Not kill angel of God. Not kill angel of God. Not me.'

'But you confessed Rufus. You confessed to killing Ezekiel. Why would you say that if you didn't do it?'

'He made me. The worm-tongue made me.'

'Azazel?'

Rufus looked around, swinging his head from side to side, desperately making sure he wasn't being overheard. 'No. Not Azazel. *Him.*'

'He whispered to you. His voice was in your head. Told you to confess.'

'Can't say. Can't say.'

Gunn didn't have the stomach to hurt the pathetic creature again. He took his hand instead. 'It's okay Rufus. We understand. Azazel understands.'

Out of Gunn's control, a break in the clouds allowed a brilliant shaft of light from the tiniest sliver of moon left in its old cycle, partly illuminated the room. Shadows danced crazily on the walls, cast through the leaves of the swaying trees in the slightest breeze. For a moment or two Gunn was as spooked as Rufus. The poor bastard swivelled his head to look behind him, like someone, or something, was about to leap out and devour him whole.

'Was sleeping. Hiding. The shouts and laughs woke me up. Saw. Watched—the one with the red eye. The single big red eye. From hell blinking open and shut, shut and open.'

Gunn was tense with anticipation. 'You watched? Another person? There was somebody else with you?'

Rufus calmed a tad as he recalled a good memory.

'Others. Many others. But the nice policeman, he explained it all to me later. Back at the police station. It was nice at the police station. We had a nice dinner. Fish and chips from the chip shop, and mushy peas. And a nice cup of tea too. I was dead hungry. I remember. He told me what to say, the nice policeman, like my dad. Nice like my dad, until I changed, then dad died and rotted away. He helped me write it all down, the policeman, not my dad, for the record he said. Had to be for the record. I offered to sign it. In blood. But he said no, that would not be necessary. It was nice and warm inside the cell. So cold in the warehouse in winter. It was all in Rufus's head, you see. He said. The nice policeman said. All in Rufus's head. The voices. I imagined it all. I did it. The others—they were all me. So I wrote it all down and signed in. In ink, not in blood. Though I offered.'

Gunn had let go of Rufus's hand as his almost stream of consciousness had burst over them like a breached dam.

'I did it. It was me, Rufus. But he found me. Later. After. Devil—visited me in my cell in the police station, then the prison. Can't say. Can't talk about it.'

Rufus looked around conspiratorially, once again checking for spies hidden in the shadows.

'It? What's *it*, Rufus?'

'Told you. Can't say. He wouldn't like it, the one with the knife. Big, big knife.'

In mid-rant Rufus's accent and voice pitch changed, as if he was channelling another person. *'Fuck me. It's a fucking Rambo knife.'*

If that creeped Gunn out, when Rufus did it a second time, as a second rogue entity, he almost freaked. Another imaginary person rose to Rufus's surface. Was it possible Rufus was also suffering from a Multiple Personality Disorder as well as schizophrenia? The second voice sounded younger, but not a child. *'This is fucking wild. I love it.'*

Two weird voices, random shafts of moonlight. They spooked Gunn alright. He snapped back. The reference to a *Rambo* knife was confirmation of sorts. The main weapon used to kill Zeke was never found. In Czarnecki's murder book, the police doctor's initial report, and the subsequent coroner's report, stated that the death blow was caused by a large, razor sharp knife, smooth edged one side, jagged the other, possibly military in origin. The only way Rufus would mention that, even as a second and third personality, would be if he was the killer after all, or he had been there and witnessed something. Most likely now the latter: Gunn could not reconcile the fact that Rufus would be coherent enough to get rid of the knife, yet manage to get himself caught near the scene, soaked in Zeke's blood, and confess. All within twenty-four hours.

Yet that's exactly what Czarnecki had fabricated. Why? He had been, at minimum, a competent copper. Was he protecting someone else? Who would a man be determined to protect at all costs. If not for him, then for his wife? Her son, his stepson? Simon Murphy?

That would be a good reason to frame Rufus Wright. What better than the nut-job found nearby who was already a danger to society.

'But you can talk about *it* Rufus. To me at least. You know that.'

'NO NO NO. He'll find out. Come and get me this time.'

'Azazel will find out?'

'No, not him—HIM.'

'Lucifer. The devil?'

'Not HIM. He's the devil in hell. The other devil. Here on earth. Better to reign in hell than serve in heaven.'

Rufus leaned forward and put his hand under the bed. He pulled out a well worn copy of the Bible and waved it in Gunn's face. 'It's all in here, foretold at the beginning of space-time, that was a long time ago. Book of Revelation, 13:18 *"Here is wisdom. Let him that hath understanding count the number of the beast: for it is the number of a man, and his number is six hundred threescore six. 6,6,6,"* you understand right?'

'Sure Rufus.'

'1999 reversed and inverted. Gives 666 and one. One is him. That was the year nineteen ninety nine. He is the one. Understand. He is the beast, understand. I am but a humble servant. You see it, right? One is first.'

Gunn felt like he had fallen into a real life version of the Omen. He couldn't use his real world logic with a paranoid schizophrenic, and whatever else Rufus's wired-wrong brain was experiencing. *Those voices. They're all in your head,* didn't cut it. Rufus World was an alien landscape. But it did have its own warped logic. He simply had to apply the irrefutable logic of that world.

'Okay Rufus. Now you know Lucifer is a very busy—uh, devil. Lots of evil in the world. Yada yada yada. But he's not God. Correct?'

'Angel of God.'

'That's right, Lucifer was an angel of God. God's favourite. Top angel. But that wasn't good enough for him. So he was cast out of heaven for insurrection. Like you said, better to reign in hell than serve in heaven. He knows that he, Lucifer, unlike God, doesn't know everything. He knows a hell of a lot, but not everything.'

Rufus was considering the proposition. 'Yes.'

'That's why he relies on faithful servants like you on Earth to keep him informed.'

'I am a faithful servant of Lucifer. Can I show you?'

Gunn shrugged a *why not*. He had Rufus drawn into his own logic and wanted to keep the spider's web tight. 'Yeah, okay. Quietly though.'

He let Rufus rise up from the subservient prone position, maintaining his marine wary status, but he let him alone, until—

'What the fuck you doing Rufus?'

Rufus had pulled off his white pyjama bottoms. His dingy grey Radcliffe issue Y-Fronts followed next, leaving him naked from the waist down.

'Need to show you —'

Rufus slid his hand behind him and under to his anus. Before Gunn could react, Rufus triumphantly dangled a small plastic freezer bag, clearly holding at least a dozen pills of various shapes and sizes. Gunn guessed that the staff must trust him because they gave him his medication in pill form and not as a liquid.

'—see, this is what the nurses make me take to stop my visitors coming. But I fooled them. They're trying to poison me. They spy on me behind my back. Watch me. Conspire against me. Nurses and doctors and guards. Why are you dressed like a nurse?'

Gunn had not expected that. But it helped explain Rufus's current disposition. Though he was correct. Rufus was being watched. It was a secure mental hospital after all.

'Disguise. That's great Rufus. Lucifer is very pleased with you.'

Rufus beamed at the news, before re-depositing his pills and pulling his underwear back on. 'He is? He has told me before, but it's nice to hear from someone else. I told Professor Mundy that Lucifer was pleased with me but that was a long time ago. And she didn't believe me. Now she's dead.'

Whoa. That name grabbed Gunn up short. 'Judith Mundy? You knew Professor Mundy at Oxford? She was at Balloch, but you were at Kings right?'

Rufus looked pained, as if he recalled the lost reality of a different life in which he was a star student destined to go far in the arcane but feverish field of the Philosophy of Logic. He returned to sounding quite normal, albeit an arcane professorial sort normal. 'Yes, but the study of logic is a small pond. Grammarians. We were fellow grammarians, though she was the Fellow, I was the student who followed the fellow. We shared an interest in the logic of grammar, Vic Dudman, and pioneers such as him. Have you ever wondered about *if?*'

Gunn zoned Rufus out as he droned on about Mundy and *if*. There had to be a link there, apart from Rufus.

For a few moments Rufus had regained his former

self, his inner being however we define that. But Gunn was relentless in his immediate task: deceiving Rufus. And that meant being the prince of lies.

'In fact, Lucifer told me he'd consider it a personal favour if you were to tell me, so I can tell him. What's this *it* you mentioned. The thing you didn't want to talk about.'

'But he'll kill me. HIM. He already watches me. He doesn't know I know about *it*. But if he finds out I know, he'll appear here and slit my throat, the guards can't stop the white coats. You know that.'

'But Rufus, if that happened you'll be dead. And when you're dead you'll be able to sit alongside me, below Azazel and within sight of Lucifer—honoured.'

Rufus considered this new revelation. 'I will? Be honoured?'

'Oh yeah. Totally.'

Gunn could see the cogs turning at the news. The spider had the fly. Rufus leaned in, he didn't want HIM, to hear this so he hissed it.

'Kill Club.'

'Sorry, what was that?'

Rufus channelled another voice, clearly different from the others. The one from all those years ago. The one the detective had told Rufus was all in his head. The one who seemed to know everything about him. The one who scared him. The one with the relentless single red eye.

'Welcome to Kill Club.'

24

1999.

'The inaugural meeting of Kill Club is called to order.'

He didn't have to say it a second time. Last week's little escapade in the warehouse had established his total dominance amongst *the others*. He was the first. The prime. The alpha. The hush fell instantly and obediently. There was something about the word *kill* that commanded attention. Especially as they all shared a dark joyous secret. Till your death do us part. *His* plan was to cement that secret in place. What better way than a secret society. Rules, regulations, agendas, minutes, goals. And membership has its privileges.

As do secrets. They're the powerful adhesive binding people. The cornerstone of civilization. A secret is merely an imprisoned fact waiting to be released. And therein resides a secret's one purpose. To escape.

Oxford was stuffed full of societies. Most not so secret, but they did have one thing in common. A discriminating shared passion for *something*. He imagined no one had ever seen anything like Kill Club. Not unless an Oxford branch of the infamous Indian kill cult, the Thugees, started operating in the early 1800s. Nothing new under the sun. He knew that was written in Ecclesiastes 1:9, about 3000 years ago. He knew because Rufus Wright told him, amongst his many babblings. *What has been is what will be, and what has been done is what will be done; there is nothing new under the sun.*

He had booked a meeting room above The Flying Horse pub in Ashdown Street, from 8.00 p.m. to 9.30 p.m. Every tradition starts when it is applied for the very first time. His tradition started with the first booking for The Oxford Borgia Society. Meeting compulsory. No exceptions. He admired the name he had chosen. It was redolent with dark deeds occurring behind closed doors, to the benefit of the chosen few who were bonded by blood. He liked that thought too. Bonded by blood: *Vinculum per cruor*. Kill Club's motto.

None of them had been in contact with each other since last week. His orders, which they had followed to the letter on pain of—something unpleasant. The arrest of the mentally disturbed Rufus Wright had been gratifying. The others were no doubt pleasantly surprised, and gut wrenchingly pleased. Once their blood lust high had worn off, the terror of reality would have hit them all hard. The fear of being caught, that is. Not any feeling for the meat they had despatched with some alacrity. As they didn't realize the scene had been written by him to play out like a Tarantino movie, they naturally would have started thinking about fingerprints, DNA, and other physical evidence they had accidentally shed at the crime scene.

He had not mentioned the little Rufus detail to them at the time, although he had planned it, naturally. His plans and desires had been evolving since the glorious awakening with Mrs Rooney. It was a process leading to perfection.

There had been one imperfection with Rufus. A minor, if unfortunate faux-pas with the roofie dosage. The *Rohypnol* laced cider had not knocked out Rufus for nearly as long as he estimated. But he had covered his tracks well enough, and scared the bugger shitless. No need for the others to know about that minor error. It might erode confidence in him. Unlikely, but why take an unnecessary chance? In fact, he had decided to leave them with the impression that Rufus's appearance and arrest was serendipity. That the accidental outcome had been the impetus for his novel idea of how to move forward for the club's mutual benefit. They were hooked. Now all he need do was reel them in.

The oblong room was about ten by fifteen feet. The wood panelling looked like it had been in place since the tavern first opened its taps in 1791: a very good year for bloody terror and mayhem. The solid oak table had been decked out by pub staff for an official meeting. There were two largish plates of freshly cut, crustless sandwiches covered in clingfilm: a mixture of ham and mustard, chicken and bacon avocado, cheese and salad, and tuna mayo. Three bottles of white wine in ice buckets. Wine glasses. And yellow, foolscap-sized, lined legal pads with accompanying black biros.

'Point of order Mister Chairman.'

'The chair recognizes the member.'

'On behalf of the membership we wish to offer our appreciation for all your sterling efforts. Both last week, and in today's excellent spread.'

The murmur of 'yeah yeahs' was reinforced by the banging of hands on the solid oak. One of the others was pouring the wine at the same time. They clinked glasses, offered salutations and glugged at the excellent New Zealand Chardonnay. Brave new world wine.

'Let's get on with the agenda. Item one, Kill Club rules. The floor is open to suggestions from the membership.'

Of course, he knew what the rules were going to be. But he had to lead them towards what he had already carved in stone. Like Michelangelo they would simply chip away to reveal his beauty beneath.

He was a meticulous note-taker and record-keeper. Order and structure are essential to the success of any enterprise. Pristine records being the historical record of that order. And yes, he was not blind to the irony. Clearly seeing the comparisons with the architects of the Third Reich. Seeing how their very obsession with recording everything made it so much easier to prosecute and execute them following the downfall.

He looked at the final rules which he had written down beautifully in his exquisite hand. After reading them out loud, dissatisfaction clouded his face. He took the paper and carefully ripped it into tiny pieces before placing them in his jacket pocket. The others felt a ripple of fear. Had they displeased him?

'That's all well and good. But too wordy. The rest is the mission. There's one rule to Kill Club. Betray Kill Club, you die. Agreed.'

They agreed. His idea had been gestating since the incident with the short, squat Mrs Rooney: the annoyingly loud shrew with tight-cropped, bleach-white hair. Not the name Kill Club. That came from the ridiculous film he had seen a few weeks earlier. That was the hook to catch the minnows. No. The idea of getting away with it. If someone was stupid enough to put themselves in a position where they could be harmed, then that was their own stupid fault. They deserved everything that happened to them. Asking for it. Why couldn't everyone else see that? The inferiors. They must be crazy.

It was like that throughout history. His philosophy was maturing and evolving through diligent study. He admitted that he could become obsessed with a particular subject. Sitting in the library for hours, reading every history book on the shelves. Some estimates had Stalin killing fifty million people. Well whose fault was that? Not Stalin. Same with Hitler. If those Jews wanted to hang around Germany then it was their own stupid fault if they ended up in a gas oven. He knew Darwin was right, survival of the fittest. When Darwin killed God, did he understand what he had done? What this meant? Those unfit did not deserve to survive at the hands of the more highly evolved. Not simply a whole species but the individual specimen within that species. It was necessary for the strong to eliminate the weak. That was so obvious. You have to be mentally unhinged not to realize that. And once you reject the silly notions of law and morals being derived from God, then what is the logical conclusion? There can only be one. They must be derived from homo sapiens: us. And who amongst us? He reached that level and became fully actuated soon after it struck him: one becomes the higher power by virtue of the fact one can. Quod Erat Demonstrandum.

Mrs Rooney had been a catalyst of sorts. The pleasure had been profound. A fragment of Milton came to mind as he remembered that first disobedience, and the fruit from the forbidden tree.

First Moloch, horrid kind besmirched with blood of human sacrifice, and parents' tears. Though, for the noise of drums and timbrels loud, their children's cries unheard, that passed through fire to his grim idol.

A few weeks later he was scouting some local woods, no particular reason but it was too baking hot in the library to concentrate. And he needed some action.

He had finished with the philosophies of others, and had been reading about the lesser others, who, while sharing his proclivities, lacked his vision. Dahmer, Fred and Rosemary West, Gacey, and most of them were always going to be the authors of their own downfall. They had all lacked the intelligence to think their actions through to the absolute logical conclusion. They did have the native cunning to select victims on the margins of society. People whom no one missed. But they kept their trophy remains near, and therefore easily able to be tied to themselves. Some essential verities had occurred to him. There was no crime if the police could not uncover one. There was no arrest if the police could not find a body. And there was no connection to him, if the authorities were guided in the direction of someone else to convict and imprison. It was all a process on the road to perfection. Though even then he felt that his perfection would always be undermined by those under him.

The memory tingled through his body. It came like he was gazing through a high definition time portal to the past.

The oppressively sticky weather had lingered all week, but today the air under the trees felt fresher and cooler as a breeze slipped in from the north. He moved in silence, stealthily. The gentle swaying of tree branches, and the sounds of the insects and birds were all that disturbed the hypnotic stillness. A distant cuckoo called out, rippling through the still air. The occasional sharp crack of dry twigs underneath his shoes. As he glided along, snatches of the intense-blue, cloudless sky sliced through the tree tops.

He had reached the ancient oak sentry at the centre of the wood. This was his secret impenetrable place. His Tower of London. He liked to stash his trophies in a deep hidden hollow in a nearby tree. Prized possession was the videotape he shot of Mrs Rooney as she found *Lady*. It was safely stored in an airtight Tupperware box, hidden at the bottom of the hollow, covered by leaves and a rotting dead cat. He needed to keep the tape, but he couldn't chance hiding it somewhere closer, where some nosy nabob would be bound to find it. He was leaning into the tree to pull the box out when he heard something creeping through the undergrowth. He scrambled down the slope to hide. A few seconds later the carefree youngster came into his line of sight.

The boy was the son a farmhand who lived in a tithed cottage on Home Farm, miles away. About seven years old with pudding-bowl cut blond hair, wearing tatty football shorts and a grubby Star Wars T-shirt. He had gotten lost and was well off his own well-beaten track. Though strong and stocky for his age, he was no match for a teenager, even if the older boy had not surprised him from behind with a tree branch to the head. The kid flopped forward, collapsing face down into the soiled earth. The single sound was a rasping gurgling seeping from the back of the boy's throat. The hot red liquid staining the leaves the colour of a New England fall. The surprising metallic smell jarred his nostrils, it wasn't unpleasant. He was transfixed at how easy it had been as he stood in an ecstatic daze, looking down at the boy on the ground.

It was the boy's own stupid fault for being there at his secret spot at the exact same time when he was there too. The boy was to blame for what happened. Not him. What did he expect? Mercy? Stupid boy. That'd teach him.

—*CUCKOO*—*CUCKOO*—

Snapped him back. Dropping to his knees, excited, he flipped the boy over to look at his eyes. He had missed that final pleasure with Mrs Rooney, but he now realized that he *needed* to look right in their eyes at the end. Like he did with his experiments, the cats and dogs. The last thing they saw had to be him. Their God. He cupped his large hands around the little boy's throat. He squeezed hard for what seemed to be ages. He was sweating profusely as the boy finally stopped twitching. Then they were both still. Both spent.

The missing boy was the lead news item for a few days. He followed it avidly in the papers, the TV, even the local radio. Then it fell down the newsworthy order. Still important, but other stories edged their way into the front. That disappointed him, as he never tired of hearing about it over and over again. The speculation. The theories. The parent's anguish. It was an exquisite pleasure. And he never tired.

He perked up after the BBC Crimewatch programme staged a re-enactment the following month. But he knew that the boy had been a long way from where he was last seen, so his final location was never known. Except to him.

Interest gradually faded as other more pressing news gripped a fickle nation. Until all interest ceased outside the family and the police. The parents were suspected, naturally. The semi-literate father was known to the police. He was drunk a lot. And he had a history of violence when drunk, the wife visiting A&E more than once, having walked into a door, or slipped down the stairs. However, no body, no evidence, no case.

This proved a valuable lesson for *him*. He had discovered that disposing of a body, even a small one was no easy task. And the police never stop looking. He pondered on that fact a lot – as another boy his age may ponder girls. A better idea, a *much* better idea would have been to close the case. How much more elegant for another person to be arrested, tried, convicted and safely imprisoned for life. Left to protest their innocence. A common occurrence amongst the criminal classes in prison, apparently. That was definitely the way forward. But it did sound hard work. Lots of planning. Lots of preparation. Lots of access. He pondered on that problem for a while as he was growing and preparing for adulthood. To become a man. All the time reading, absorbing knowledge. He read about secret violent organizations, like the Cosa Nostra, the IRA and the PLO. They liked to do what he did, on a much grander scale though. Maybe he needed to control a group of like-minded folks. Like a terrorist cell. Self-contained. Goal oriented. Secret. How would he go about recruiting? Something to think about. In the future.

'The chair recognizes the member.'
'Any other business Mr Chairman?'
He was not totally surprised that the others looked pretty vacant. They were bright. But needed a teacher. No matter, he had some unfinished business that was perfect to kick-start Kill Club proper.

He smiled paternalistically. They all had mummy and daddy issues, but he had successfully overcome his. 'Actually, I do have an interesting project I would like to put to the vote. Not that you have to vote yes because it's me.'

False modesty. Of course, that was not true. He knew that they did need to agree with him. The progenitor. The first. The prime.

He felt a grim satisfaction in suspecting they all knew that he was first amongst equals. They had to vote yes because of him. Why wouldn't they? Were they not in awe of him? Had he not opened them up to a brave new cold world.

One of the others responded. 'I think the club would all like to hear the proposal. Yes?' A murmur of affirmation rippled the room.

His false modesty knew no bounds. 'Well, I don't want to hog proceedings. This is a democracy after all. But if that's the will of the membership, who am I to object? I do have someone in mind, matter of fact. I'd like to propose a certain Professor Judith Mundy.'

25

Gunn finally left Rufus in his room slightly after a quarter to four in the morning. The bloke was becoming dangerously hyper. The last thing he needed was an over-agitated paranoid schizophrenic to become highly vocal after *Nisroch* departed this plane.

Rufus was most definitely suffering from a form of paranoid schizophrenia. It was all there—and more. Hallucinations, delusions, auditory and visual, feelings of grandiosity. And he was cunning too. What Rufus did not seem to be was a deliberate liar. He told what he thought was the truth. He had readily admitted that Azazel told him to give Sperling the brush off. Why would he lie about the warehouse and Zeke?

While he was distracted, Gunn grabbed Rufus in a choke hold again, and injected him with a fast acting sedative: The combined 5mg of Haloperidol and 2mg of Lorazepam was the standard Rapid Tranquillization in general use for psychotic patients. The drugs were part of the medical aid kit he had lifted from the medical room. The shot instantly relaxed Rufus, seconds later he was out. Given his smallish size and the single dosage, Gunn estimated it was lights out for a ninety minutes to two hours.

Gunn sat back on the floor in the quiet. The room was still partially illuminated by the moonlight, moon shadows played on the white walls. He was taking a few minutes to absorb what Rufus had revealed, specifically the ominous sounding *Kill Club*. Was it part of Rufus's delusion? Could be. The man was clearly not well. But it sounded real. Apart from the unblinking red eye.

His plan was to stealthily head back to the dental surgery and wait for the shift change. Then he would simply shuffle out as part of the crowd. Getting through the main gate might be tricky on foot. That part of Gunn's plan was still in the nebulous concept stage.

Block A was quiet. Almost 4 a.m. The dead time, the low point when the internal clock tells most of us that we should be deep in REM sleep. He had made it past the medical room and was almost out of the building. Good going. That's when he ran into Karl again, hand bleeding like a badly dripping tap, heading towards Radcliffe's medical treatment room. As supposedly a nurse on duty, Gunn had no choice but to accompany him.

Karl used his walkie-talkie to check in. 'Francis, over—with the nurse now.'

'Roger Karl. Take your time mate. No worries.'

It was a bad cut needing six stitches. That was no problem for Gunn. They had made small talk as Gunn did some basic nursing. He gave Karl a local to freeze the hand, before cleaning and starting the stitches on the wound across the palm. It was typical male talk. Football and cars.

So far, so good. If he could stitch and shift Karl out before anyone else breezed in, he was back on track. If Gunn hadn't leaned in and let his key card hang loose, right in front of Karl's eyes. Maybe Karl wouldn't have noticed the photograph but he saw Karl's eyes flick down.

'What did you say your name—'

Gunn went into auto-pilot and was already moving as it dawned on Karl there was something hinky with the key card. He was behind Karl in a blur and had him in an unbeatable choke hold. Gunn pressed down on Karl's windpipe, at the same time his forearm was depressing Karl's carotid artery, effectively cutting off the blood supply to his brain.

'Sorry mate, don't struggle. You'll be out like a light any sec. Not going to hurt you. Remember that okay, when you get your mates to set the dogs on me.'

As promised Karl sagged down and out. His brain, starved of two sources of oxygen, shut down to help preserve its life for the precious few minutes it had left. Had Gunn continued for a minute longer, Karl would have been quite dead. Instead Gunn went straight to his second involuntary sedative injection of the night. Karl would not be waking up till he had long gone. That was the plan. Gunn wondered what plan he was on now. K? L? Without pausing, he scanned the room for a temporary body stash site. His real concern was to position Karl so he could not accidentally choke on his own vomit. Gunn improvised. The examination table was perfect with its lower level to store various equipment and supplies. The drop covered the lower shelf and kept Karl nicely tucked away from view.

Next was the problem of the walkie-talkie. Francis, or whoever, would be checking in any minute. Gunn attacked the possibility head on again.

'Francis, this is Karl, over.'

There was a delay of a few seconds. 'On your way back Karl? Over.'

'Negative Francis, sorry mate. Nurse says she needs to check for tendon damage with the doc. Over an hour mate.'

'Bugger—okay that's that, suppose. See you later pal.'

That done, he took the second to reflect on the nut-cluster fucks that had occurred in rapid succession. 'FUCK—you moron Micah. Worse than Tora Bora.'

It was about to get even worse. Gunn was rethinking his exit strategy now that he had some new resources. Maybe this would be okay. He put on a fresh pair of surgical gloves, his sixth pair since he left HR and Sheila. The superglue on his fingertips covered finger prints, but he didn't want to leave palm prints. He also was careful to keep the gloves he discarded. Who was the paranoid now?

Gunn was weighing up his next move when it was made for him. Enter Nurse Louise Brenner. A six-foot tall, blonde Aussie with an accent wider than Sydney harbour. And she could talk the pouch off a kangaroo. It was her second day at Radcliffe, as a contract psychiatric nurse as cover for the next two weeks. It was 5.52 a.m. and Gunn had another hour until he could make the most welcome exit of his life.

Unfortunately no calls came in to drag her away, and she was still chuntering at 6.36 a.m.

Louise answered the call a minute later. 'Yeah—yeah—Jesus. You cut him down—Okay gotcha, defib. On my way.'

Gunn knew what was coming and was already at the crash cart on the word *defib*.

'Attempted suicide, daft bugger roped himself with a bed-sheet. Doc's on way.'

Louise grabbed the cart with its life-saving gear. Gunn made for the door to help her out. He glanced at the big clock on the wall. Not enough time. He had to get out of this place as of ten minutes ago.

'No worries mate, I got it. Room 27B on the second floor.'

While all the activity was heading towards Rufus

Wright's room, Gunn made his way back to the dental surgery. Time to get out of town. There was nothing he could do for Rufus, no matter how guilty he was feeling. At every CCTV camera location he was careful to obscure his face, or turn it away from the lens. This was getting bad. He was in serious crap. Correction, he would be suspected of being in serious crap. If he was caught on the premises then he would be in serious crap. All he had to do was get past that main gate and he would blag the rest. He took the old stairs two at a time back up to the third floor.

6.43 a.m. Walking slowly, about five yards behind a group of guards in the corridor. They seemed to be heading towards the kitchen, no doubt for a welcome cuppa. Stopping to bend down outside the dental surgery, he pretended to re-tie his shoe laces, while checking behind him. All clear. He slipped in.

6.51 a.m. Gunn clipped on the easi-fit navy blue tie. He looked at himself in the mirror above the small sink. The usual suspect stared back. The disguise was gone and Karl's uniform was a good fit, except that the steel capped black shoes were a little tight. Everything with which he had entered Radcliffe nearly forty hours earlier had been squashed into his small black rucksack. This was it.

7.01 a.m. He flashed Chowdhury's key card for what he hoped was the very last time. He had followed on at the back of a mixed group of staff exiting. Outside, the air was crisp and the early morning sun was bright and still low enough on the horizon be right in line of sight. He could see the staff car-park ahead to the east. About twenty staff seemed to be on the move too, either coming or going into the car park. No one looked twice at Gunn. He could see Karl's green Corrado. Now car-theft was about to be added to his crime-sheet. Assault, breaking and entering, theft, trespass. Eddie was going to kill him. He didn't even want to think of Bebba and Ziya.

7.04 a.m. On the back seat he found sunglasses and a Watford Town FC baseball cap. He put them on and started the car. Iron Maiden blasted out of the speakers at full belt. It was a bit early for the Ace of Spades, he lowered the volume and kept it on for comfort. Lemmy was oddly relaxing during a tense time. He had not felt this trapped since the five days in a hole in the ground, twenty yards behind a Taliban safe house.

7.08 a.m. Gunn waited behind three cars and a Land Rover. There was a man in the small booth next to the barrier. All Gunn had to do was flash his key card at the scanner and the barrier opened. If that did not work? Seriously, Gunn had decided he was going to test Karl's speed boast of 0-60 in 5.2 seconds. It was head down, foot down and straight through, like they did in the movies. It always worked then.

7.09 a.m. The barrier rose, the car in front edged out. The barrier dropped back down as Gunn inched forward. Gunn took Chowdhury's key card and flashed it over the scanner attached to the concrete poll at eye level outside his car window. For the other cars in front, the barrier had lifted about a second after the key card swipe. Nothing. Out of his peripheral vision, he clocked that the booth bloke had looked up from whatever he was doing. Various words crossed Gunn's mind, as he prepared to floor it for ten yards before violently hand-braking a forced sliding left turn into the lane. That's when they both heard the ambulance siren approaching fast. Booth bloke forgot the non-rising barrier. Instead he turned to check the entrance side. At the same time Gunn had pulled out Karl's key card and ran it over the scanner.

The ambulance, lights still flashing but siren turned down, had already pulled into the entrance side. Booth Bloke raised the barrier. By the time he had remembered Gunn, the barrier was already on its way back down and Gunn was gone. Well within the speed limit.

Gunn drove a mile past the village of Lower Radcliffe. The small B-road was perfect. He left Karl's car in the gate entrance to a field full of cows. The whole curious herd ambled over to investigate the action as Gunn stepped out to change out of the uniform, and back into his well-crumpled suit. He looked at their sad, trusting eyes. They should run a mile from any human being. *Poor dumb buggers. Don't you know humans are bastards.*

Gunn thought of the thing he learned tonight. Something called Kill Club. *Wicked bastards.* He reckoned he had a day before the police came calling again, probably a lot less. He better get cracking.

26

2005.

The razor sharp thorn sliced cruelly across Fletcher's face. It wasn't the first. He didn't care. He didn't slow down. Hell—it hardly registered any more. Under normal circumstances it would have hurt like a fucker, leaving him cursing like an enraged madman. Only a few things would prevent that. A local anaesthetic, or any numbing drug of some description. Being tightly gagged with duct tape. Or being shot in the head. Detective Sergeant Fletcher Hoodeson had experienced all three in the past few hours. Being chased by persons unknown (the ones who had recently shot you in the head) blocked out irrelevant extraneous stimuli not pertinent to his present predicament. In the scheme of things, it made crashing through the bramble infested undergrowth more like a genteel picnic at the Henley-on-Thames regatta. Not that Fletcher had ever been invited to a genteel picnic at the Henley regatta. Until last year he was one of the sweating and gasping guys on the coxless fours, representing the Royal Metropolitan Police Rowing Club, nicknamed *The River Filth*

He had been hoofing it for at least an hour and had lost the initial fight or flight adrenalin rush. His body had depleted its resources. As far as he knew he was still in Norfolk. Fletcher hated Norfolk. They talked funny. It was sodding wet. He hated the rain. Then there was the whole shot in the head vibe. Norfolk was proving one huge downer.

The horizon was flat and he could not see any rises in the land ahead. This was good. It also meant the chasing pack could not get the higher ground, and get the jump on him. He had to stop and get his bearings. Things were a little bit hazy still. He needed to think this through. And get his head examined. Literally.

He crashed through the last of the brambles and came to a clearing. Finally he had a line of sight to make out some features. The ground was soggy. His high end trainers were water-sodden, right through to his feet. It was bitter November cold out here. The canal, or waterway, or whatever the fuck it was, reared up twenty yards ahead. The silence was unnervingly deafening. He relaxed for a second, then out of nowhere:

—*HONK—HONK*—

Spinning around—three Canada geese—barrelling head height towards him in delta wing, lead goose formation. Fletcher threw himself to the soggy ground. Now his clothes were as soaked as his shoes. No time to feel sorry for himself, he was up and at the waters edge – although it was the Broads, and the water didn't need an edge out here. It was everywhere. This was his Thelma and Louise cliff. If the pursuers pursued him here, he could not go ahead. Left was off in a dead straight line, offering a perfect sightline of visibility for at least a mile; but right led to a not so gentle curve in the nebulous water's edge. He could be around the bend and out of sight in a couple of minutes. Right it was.

Fletcher had been trudging sodden for a while. He had not seen or heard anything since the kamikaze geese. No people and no water creatures, apart from the occasional, distant bird call. He had reached another huge curve in the canal, almost ninety degrees. Thank Christ, he saw the red and black of a houseboat. It was another quarter mile upstream. He liked that word, upstream. Made him feel he was back on the Thames water, rowing somewhere fast.

He boarded the houseboat, standing on the narrow railed deck, listening for sounds of life. There were none. He tried the door to the interior. It wasn't locked. 'Hello—hello.' nothing stirred. Fletcher did a quick recce from stem to stern. The houseboat was in perfect order. But there were no personal affects showing anyone living aboard. He went back to the tiny bathroom and looked in the mirror. Nightmare time. His face was ripped up pretty bad from the thorns. Back to the *overall scheme of things*: that was a good thing compared to the bloody groove above his right temple. He tried to get his mind around the fact that no more than two hours ago, he had been shot in the head. SHOT IN THE FUCKING HEAD.

The bullet had whipped across the side of his skull, causing a large amount of blood as it skidded off. The sight of him slumping to the ground, blood spurting had been enough to initially fool the shooters. He lay dead still hoping they assumed he was actually dead. It must have worked, because they left the derelict barn in short order, followed quickly by him, in the opposite direction.

Fletcher had made it a half mile before one of them spotted him legging it into the soggy Broads. The shot which pinged past his head made him think they had a rifle and scope.

He looked again at his face in the mirror. His thick shoulder length hair was matted with his own blood. The spider tattoo on his neck was almost obscured by the browning blood. After six months undercover, Fletcher looked the part of lowlife to a T. The bullet scar to the head would add to his street cred, if he lived that long.

Fletcher opened the small bathroom cabinet and spotted his first piece of luck in days. On the top shelf was a small bottle of green Dettol antiseptic, plus a few pads of cotton wool. There was no hot water, so he lowered his face into a sink full of ice cold water. The dried blood stained the water. Fletcher splashed a fair amount of Dettol onto a cotton pad and gingerly dabbed it on his bullet grooved skull. The pain felt reassuringly good to be alive. He tossed that old cotton pad and prepped a new one to also cleanse the random cuts on his face and hands.

This was bat shit crazy. The day before he had been acting the part he had been playing for six months. A low-level drug dealer in north London, working his way up the ranks thanks to his outstanding work ethic. Fletcher shifted all his product, he was never short with his money, and he was always on time. Drug Dealing Employee of the year. He was helped by the fact that he did not actually sell the shit. The Met took the drugs off his hands, and supplied him with payment in used notes. It turns out that so long as you paid your money to the top guys, they didn't much give a crap how you did it. As long as you did it.

His ultra-secret undercover mission had been two fold: to get recruited by the biggest drug gang north of the river, and then get actionable intelligence eventually leading to the arrest of the main guys. But no matter what he found, it seemed the top guys were always one step ahead. The obvious reason being they were getting their own actionable intelligence on the police from the inside. Very little of what he found out undercover would ever be usable in a British court with him as a witness. The courts don't operate that way any more. Ever since Scotland Yard's undercover debacle in the horrendous

Rachel Nickel murder, things had changed massively for any undercover op. Intel gathered had to be used to direct the Met in the right direction. That was all.

Fletcher's current predicament started two weeks earlier when he heard a whisper from a fellow scrote in the 'gang'. The whisper being that the top guy, Billy Ferguson, was heading up to the Norfolk coast. The kosher tip had Billy meeting up with a new Dutch partner on their first run, establishing a new cocaine pipeline into the UK. The gear starting in Afghanistan, magically transformed into ersatz clogs for the Dutch tourist trade; transported all the way to the Netherlands, then by small boat for the short hop across the North Sea. This was potentially huge. Fletcher should have reported that back immediately. A whole surveillance and snoop operation would have been put into place. But he couldn't take the risk that this info would be found out by the mole inside, tipping off Billy and blowing his cover as well. He decided to go it alone without backup.

Then fate intervened. Camden market. Tap on the shoulder. He'd been spotted as a copper. Luckily it was a colleague from their time as cadets in Hendon. The one always sucking on those mints with the hole, hence the obvious nickname of Polo. Bit of a posher who should be picnicking at Henley in blazer and striped shirt. But trustworthy.

As his official police cover, Fletcher had supposedly been seconded to the Strathclyde police in Glasgow, as the Met's liaison in helping coordinate a countrywide response to the multiple foreign gangs fighting for dominance. It was all a fake. There was countrywide coordination based out of Strathclyde, but Fletcher wasn't involved. His internal cover had worked well until yesterday. All calls to his personal mobile number were intercepted. His fake office in Strathclyde was manned by a lively Scot's lass at Scotland Yard. For all anyone knew when they phoned the Strathclyde police switchboard and asked for his extension, he was in bonnie Scotland. It had all worked well until—until Polo spotted him in Camden, seeing right through the long hair, neck tat, three-day old stubble, expensive street clothes, designer hoody, £200 trainers, latest mobile, the lot.

Over a coffee at a Camden Market café, Fletcher came clean about what he had been doing for the past six months. He felt a great relief in letting go a bit. It had been a big strain always worrying that no one had his back. And that his true identity could be whispered to some nasty guys at any moment. Which is why Fletcher had been trained and issued with an official Glock 19, semi-automatic Met firearm: sanctioned by the Home Secretary to be carried at all times for self-protection. Fletcher was permitted to use deadly force without prior authorization, subject to the full rigour of the law after discharge from his seventeen shell magazine.

Fletcher knew Billy Ferguson would be heading up the M11 out of London, up to Norfolk. He pre-empted the route by driving to Junction 6, parking on the small road bridge crossing the motorway. He waited patiently for Billy to pass under in the non-descript blue Volkswagen Passat. No gangsta car bling for Billy. He was far too intelligent for that. Fletcher spotted Billy's car approaching, tootling along at seventy in the inside lane, without a care in the world. Fletcher scooted back into his hire car, waiting a minute before rejoining the motorway a mile behind Billy. Knowing generally where your target is going helps in a tailing op. Fletcher closed the gap until Billy's Passat was in sight. He followed covertly with a gap of two hundred yards, as he had been taught.

It got a bit trickier once they left the motorway and headed deeper into Broads country. It was dark by the time Billy rolled into the tiny Norfolk village of Wytchum. He drove straight to the car park of the Wytch's Cauldron Inn, in the compact village square with its village cross. He had met his supposed drug-boss Billy a couple of times, so he couldn't chance entering the Wytch's Cauldron Inn. All he could do was wait in the King's Arms. He found a table by the front window, with a direct view of the Inn's car park. And waited. And waited.

He drank *no-alcohol* beers all evening, no danger of falling down on the job. Just when he was thinking it was a bust, Billy exited the pub and went to his car. The last thing Fletcher remembered was hurrying to his car around the side of the King's Arms, then black.

He regained consciousness in the boot of a vehicle moving on a very uneven road, probably a back lane. He could feel the rough material rubbing against his face, like a sack. His mouth was taped. His arms were bound behind him with the same material. Fletcher could feel that his Met issued Glock 19 handgun was no longer in his shoulder holster. This was not good.

They dragged him into some sort of building. At least two men. The sack-hood was still in place. No one spoke. He was hauled up onto a chair. The place felt derelict, and he could see a low light through the sacking hood. Turning his eyes fully downward, he could see past the bottom of the hood. He could make out filthy wooden floorboards, covered with sodden straw. Then a glimpse of the boots worn by one of the men. Fairly new boots he thought. A suedey golden-yellow, steel toe-capped workman's boots. The one with the boots took a roll of duct tape and ran it around and around Fletcher's torso until he was bound tight to the chair's back.

'Welcome to Kill Club fucker.'

Kill Club? Fletcher was thinking that didn't sound good either when the other laughing confirmed it.

'Yeah, it's murder to get in and there's only one exit.'

Then silence until he heard a car start up and pull away.

Naturally Fletcher struggled like crazy once he thought he was alone. But the tape was impossible to snap. He was gripped by the idea if he could get his hands free, the rest would be easy. He concentrated on working the tape loose by trying to twist his hands in opposite directions. Twenty minutes of effort and the bindings were starting to loosen slightly. He could feel his blood ooze as the tape cut into his flesh. Considering the coming alternative, this bleeding was incentive enough. No doubt he was not leaving this place alive if he stayed tied to this chair. Billy Ferguson must be fucking insane to even consider murdering a policeman in cold-blood. Fletcher thought of something he hadn't considered. Billy might not know he's a copper. Maybe Billy had spotted the tail and thought he was a rival gang member. Fletcher twisted on, perking up when he felt give in the multiple layers wrapped tightly around his wrists and hands. Another few minutes and he would be in with a real shout of getting the fuck outta here. Unfortunately Fletcher ran out of time as the vehicle crunched its return up the path.

The car doors slammed shut. Seconds later he heard something or someone else being dragged into his building. It was definitely a person from the audible *'Mmm—mmm—mmm'*.

—THWACK—THWACK—

A voice gasped: 'You two corpses know who you're

fucking with? I'm King fucking Billy. Billy fucking Ferguson and when I've ripped your fucking hearts out I'm gonna find your fucking families and I'm gonna—'

In rapid succession, two more blows or kicks connected with flesh, and Billy groaned. Now Fletcher was totally lost. Sounded like his target was also being held. It made no sense based on the facts. He continued twisting his wrists back and forth to further loosen the tape. He could hear various noises and draggings on the wooden floorboards. What the hell were they doing?

His hands were almost free when the unmistakable sound of a round being chambered into an automatic pistol echoed. Maybe his own Glock 19.

Fletcher couldn't see Ferguson, or the two men in black boilersuits, each carrying automatic handguns with long silencers attached to the barrels. The bloke holding Fletcher's Glock came and stood next to his chair. Behind his back, Fletcher was still slowly twisting his hands, weakening the tape. Another minute or so was all he needed. The other boilersuit went over to Billy. He dragged him up on to his knees. The boilersuit behind Fletcher raised his gun and Billy knew for sure now.

'Fuck y—'

—*PHUTT*—

The bullet slammed into Billy's chest from a downward trajectory and knocked him on his back.

'Get the fucker up again.'

The other guy pulled Billy back up into the same position. Billy did not give the shooters the satisfaction of one sound. The psycho had balls alright. At least he had them for another two seconds before the Glock was fired again, this time twice in rapid succession.

—*PHUTT—PHUTT*—

The first slug tore straight into Billy's genitals, the

second into his belly. Both nasty, bleed to death shots. And not so slowly, but so painfully.

What the fuck was going on? It did not cross Fletcher's mind that it was his turn next, until someone grabbed him by his hair through the hood, dragging him up. Fletcher couldn't see the other shooter, standing next to Billy's dying body. He dropped onto one knee before raising his gun in an upwards trajectory.

—*PHUTT*—

The bullet smacked into the left side of Fletcher's skull, skidding off. Fletcher dropped to the ground, blood spurting. He was lying face down in the filthy floorboards, holding his breath. For about thirty seconds he expected a double tap to the back of the skull, it concentrated the mind. It still did not make any sense – except one thing. The scene was being staged. He was not a detective for nothing. From the theatrics, it looked like he was supposed to have been shot by Billy once, while the gang leader lay mortally wounded by him.

Fletcher heard a phone buzz and one of the others answered.

'Yeah, done them both. Went perfect considering we're clearing up your fucking mess. You got the stuff? Stay in the pub car park and you can follow us back in Hoodeson's car. These two aren't going anywhere, believe me.'

Fletcher waited dead still, face down in his own blood, for as long as he could after he heard the car drive off again. It was when he started hearing a rhythmic *pitter-patter* of things scurrying across the wooden floorboards that he tensed. The noises stopped. But when something not that small ran up his leg, towards his torso, Fletcher was up in the air faster than a space-shuttle launch. He ripped off the last of the bindings, and pulled the hood from his head.

The huge rat flew off him. Fletcher looked over at Billy, there were four rats around his body sniffing him out.

'Sweet Jesus.' Fletcher felt the left side of his head, which now hurt like buggery after the initial shock had worn off. The blood was starting to congeal, slowing the flow. He had to get out of there now. The rats shot off Billy at his sudden movement. The guy was bleeding out in front of Fletcher's eyes. He looked dead, but if he wasn't, with those guts and balls shot out, he would be soon, no matter what Fletcher did.

Fletcher patted himself down looking for his mobile phone. No go. They had taken it. He looked at Billy again all glassed eyed and staring up. Bending down he went through Billy's bulky jacket pockets. No phone. He stuck a hand inside Billy's pants' pocket. Bingo. Fletcher wiped off the warm blood and checked the display.

'Fucking bollocks.' He looked skywards as if for divine intervention. 'Too much to fucking ask, really?' There was no signal. And the battery was pretty low as well. He switched it off to preserve whatever power was left.

'Sorry mate.' Fletcher stepped over Billy and fled into the dawn's early mist. But honestly? He was not sorry, not sorry one tiny little bit. *Rather him than me* Fletcher thought. He had seen the fruits of Billy's psycho labour. As far as he was concerned, the late, or soon to be late Billy Ferguson deserved all he got. But he, Fletcher Hoodeson most certainly did not. Whoever did this to him was going to pay.

'Polo. Thank fucking Christ, am I glad to see you.'

Fletcher's friend responded with a typical laid back

response in the posh accent for which he was famed: 'My pleasure old chap.'

After cleaning up his head as best he could, Fletcher had checked Billy's mobile phone. Powered up and the display again showed the little red no signal sign in the top right corner. A second later it shifted to active signal—he punched in 999—the signal dropped off again.

'Oh for fucks sake.' A *battery strength low* flashed on the phone's screen. The signal again showed on, a second later flicked to off. Fletcher was worried the phone could go dead at any minute. The signal was coming and going, an actual phone call seemed out of the question. *Think, think, think.* He had an idea. Send a text message requiring a couple of seconds to transmit to someone he trusted explicitly.

Fletcher's friend looked at the icky state of his face. It looked like something from one of Clive Barker's Hellraiser movies. Their five year careers had followed similar paths since they joined on the same day. Pure coincidence that they were both the new breed of Met copper actively being sought following a bad decade leading up to the third Millennium. High profile PR debacles had dented the reputation of Scotland Yard. Fletcher was studying for his M.A. in Medieval European History. He had intended to teach, maybe. He was not sure what he wanted to do. But then he saw that high flying university grads were actively wooed by the Met, so why not? Following a standard year on the beat like all PCs, they were then accelerated into an enhanced promotion process, designed to see them as Detective Inspectors in a much shorter time-frame than usual. They were already Detective Sergeants, five years ahead of the amount of service needed. This didn't go down well with the less intellectually blessed amongst the Met's ranks.

Hence the gay allusions directed at the likes of Polo. Not so Fletcher Hoodeson, he was a clever working-class kid, who talked street, specifically London street. He was one of the lads. That's why he knew ultimately he would always be one step ahead of his posh mate if they ever came up for the same promotion. Fletcher's ten year plan was to be fast-tracked to Commissioner of the Metropolitan Police, but entirely on merit. He, Fletcher Everton Hoodeson was going to be the first black Commissioner of Police in the UK.

Alas it was not to be. It's a moot point whether Fletcher recognized his friends gold-yellow, workman's boots first, or the Glock 19 pulled from behind Polo's back. The one being raised to head height.

'Fuck—'

In the second it took Fletcher to clock both and start to speak, the bullet had ripped through his right eye socket, passed through his brain, before taking out the back of his skull. Unlike fiction, Fletcher's life did not flash before his eyes. The one thing that flashed, apart from the boots, and the gun, was the insufferable smirk that lit up Polo's face. Then lights out.

The others were straight in behind Polo to clean up the mess and set up the scene back at the Barn.

27

2005.

He called a special meeting to go through the previous week's near disaster. The others had never seen him this angry. Not with them, at least. They were in the private Mackintosh Room, their usual haunt on the second floor of the Bysshe Club.

The room overlooked Dean Street in the heart of Soho. Now that they were all based in London, it was a civilized place to continue the regular meetings of The Oxford Borgia Society. The location had been the suggestion of one of the others, the creative one in the media. Their real club house was a two-bedroomed flat he owned in Camden. That was where all the meticulous planning for invited Kill Club *guests* took place. But they also needed somewhere pleasant to relax – have a bit of fun outside their usual high maintenance high-jinks. All in all, it had worked out to their benefit.

The room was perfect, with its elliptical shaped table, rather nice catering, and very good sound-proofing. It was pricey, but handy and Kill Club had plenty of cash on hand. Mostly thanks to the lucrative former relationship with Billy Ferguson, the Donald Trump of drug dealers. He had been considering what to do with that huge pile of cash long term. Commercial property was a good bet in London.

Unfortunately the Ferguson dealings had to end abruptly after it became clear the drug kingpin had been compromised. Billy Ferguson, you're fired. The worrying thing for him and Kill Club was that it had been discovered by chance. This was totally unacceptable. And the others had to be taught that while membership of Kill Club had privileges, it also had responsibilities. He had played out the scenario over and over in his head.

If Polo hadn't seen Detective Fletcher Hoodeson on the street, last week's little Norfolk adventure would have been cracked by the Met. Hoodeson would have caught Ferguson importing massive amounts of cocaine. Being a me-first scrote, Ferguson would bargain, giving up all selected easy contacts. Starting with Billy's Kill Club insider in Scotland Yard, to whom he had paid seventeen point nine million pounds in the past eighteen months. A good investment for the druggies with a return near the £800 million mark.

How long would it be before Polo himself also bargained and gave up Kill Club—and him? Five seconds? He had always imagined it would be Goolsbee who would fuck up. The early incident with the Oxford girl showed him that. He had told Goolsbee his proposal was too risky coming so soon after their initiation kill with Ezekiel Gunn. But the idiot went ahead despite the clear rejection of the plan by the membership.

This time he was forced to admit (to himself, not the others) that he had panicked, being forced to improvise the save on the hop. Making it seem as if Hoodeson was the bent copper at least a year earlier than his original plan. It was still clever though. That there was a falling out of thieves, which is why Detective Hoodeson shot Billy, before Billy got off a lucky shot that caught him in the head. Leaving the trail of incriminating breadcrumbs linking Billy to Detective Sergeant Hoodeson.

On one level it was exciting. The shock of the new. He

had maintained a flawless run since that first night in the warehouse. When he initiated them into Kill Club. Even the name popped into his head like it was meant to be. All the greats understood the importance of branding: Hitler, Mao, Stalin. Like *him*, they understood about inciting individuals to do things *en masse* that they may never do their own. Following orders. Lord of the Flies was on the next island and it was a short boat ride away. Once you make others complicit in your deeds, the rest is easy.

Relaxing around the convivial table in the Bysshe, a thought occurred. *'I AM GOD, AND KING, AND LAW!'* Where had he heard that. Shakespeare?

He was their maker. They were made in his image. He felt great pride in his creation, he knew how God must have felt on that seventh day. But unlike God, he never rested.

Anyone can kill. Look at the newspapers or watch TV for proof. Primitive stuff, unlike his sophisticated Kill Club. He had kept meticulous records of their twenty-two kills to date, each based on a member having a prior relationship with the inductee. That was the real thrill – a hidden pattern he had created. A code that no one could see, and therefore could never unravel hiding in plain sight. Unlike the currently incarcerated or dead: Sutcliffe, Bundy, Crippen, Brady, West, Dahmer. They all repeated the same ritual over and over. Until somebody noticed, tracked, hunted and caught them.

It was an intellectual challenge above all else. Each inductee was different. They had to be cleverly manoeuvred into place with cunning, imagination, drive, brio, heroism. *He* had pride in that. Then came the all-consuming satisfaction of seeing the life-force drain out of somebody. That was always the same. The power, the control and the glory forever and ever amen. Making the seduction different every time had the effect of making each experience the first all over again. As Madonna sang: *Like a virgin, touched for the very first time.*

And yet, with all that success, all that effort, events and fate and random acts conspired to challenge even the superior being. If there was one thing the previous week's near debacle had taught him, it was *exit strategy*. A fully loaded, ready to rock and roll plan to terminate Kill Club. Dissolve the entire club membership, minus him of course. And if possible frame someone else. One last Kill Club act. How fitting.

He called them to order. They were his children, and in order to learn, children had to fear their parent. True fear had to be realized through punishment.

So he reminded them: 'Only rule of Kill Club: *Betray Kill Club. You die.*

28

Gunn parked his Saab around the corner to his house, scoping out his street first and checking if anyone was lurking.

All clear.

The lingering aroma of ground coffee told him that Eddie had recently been and gone. Gunn was half glad that he had avoided his mate, and the bollocking Eddie was going to give him for the two day Radcliffe escapade.

Twelve new voicemails waiting on his mobile. Eddie and Bebba wondering where the hell he was. No Ziya. Disappointing. Maybe she was pissed off he hadn't called. He had deliberately left the phone in his car during his Rufus mission. He couldn't tell Ziya that was why he hadn't phoned her until now.

This investigation malarkey was a laborious process. You found some intel, you followed up. Time to deploy the yellow pad again.

ENTRY NO.4/LATEST INTEL
1. Rufus Wright says KILL CLUB???? Is this for real or crazy talk? Can anything a Paranoid says be trusted?
2. if real, how does KILL CLUB jibe with Goulsby? FOLLOW UP LEADS need speak to Simon Murphy. Need track down BETH, first find out who other guy in photo with her and Zeke. THE POODLE... find out any link between Goulsby and these two.
3. Call Ziya re: meal.

The Beth bit needed a kick start on the computer. Gunn went to the Sunday Times website and found the phone numbers for the newspaper located in Pennington Street, East London, not far from the bloody Tower. His call went straight through to voicemail. The past whispered in again, quiet and subdued, in perfectly enunciated English.

Beth: This is Elizabeth Conway. I am not at my desk at the moment, please leave your name, phone number, and short message, and I will endeavour to return your call.

Endeavour. Nice touch. Gunn complied. He lay back on the sofa, and closed his eyes.
—*PING*—
He received an almost instant text.
Micah. Terra TurrisEast.43 floor. Canary wharf. Beth.
This was good.

29

Canary Wharf is a wealthy enclave in the London Borough of Tower Hamlets. The borough was more akin to a third world country with a gated community of immense wealth and high culture, existing a sliver away from deprivation. One of the parallel Londons that only criss-crossed in the service industries: restaurants, shops, drug dealers.

Zipping past St. Michael's Hospital, about half a mile west of the South Bank arts complex, he thought of Ziya. He had been thinking about her a lot. Especially since she had stood shamelessly naked in front of him, strategically shadowed in the dim light. She was on duty till ten – maybe he could surprise her, grab a bite. Sleep deprived and energy depleted as he was, Gunn felt alive. Reborn. Revitalized. Re—Gunn couldn't think of another *re* but he got his own metaphor.

Twenty minutes later Gunn was looking up at the Terra Turris complex: the tallest twin apartment towers in London. They were linked by a *green* atrium containing the latest in fully serviced urban living for the mega-rich professional: three restaurants, gymnasium, sauna, swimming pool, and a small cinema.

Gunn sauntered into the atrium lobby. The place looked like a five star luxury hotel on the banks of the Amazon, except with far higher security. The soothing sound of cascading water washed over him. He expected a parrot to swoop down from one of the rainforest trees and greet him in so-so English.

The guy behind the reception desk, the one with the neck as wide as his shaved head, had been welded into a security uniform that looked a couple of sizes too tight. He smiled a smileless smile.

'Yes sir, may I help you?'

'Elizabeth Conway, flat 4312 please.'

All-Neck picked up the security phone. Gunn could see an array of small CCTV monitors running under the high plinth of the desk. He punched in a number while keeping his eyes on Gunn. 'And your name?'

'Micah Gunn.'

'Is Miss Conway expecting you sir?'

'Yes'

Gunn was kept waiting a good thirty seconds before he heard four dead bolts and locks clunking. The apartment door opened and there she stood. Zeke's Beth.

Her wild, untamed copper hair framing her delicate face. She didn't look a day older. No wonder Ezekiel had fallen for her. Who wouldn't? In the trunk where Gunn had kept Zeke safely locked away all these years, he found an art book on the Pre-Raphaelite Brotherhood. Zeke had indexed a page with a glossy reproduction of a painting. It was a young woman, floating face up in a stream, surrounded by flowers. The text identified the painting as *Ophelia* by *John Everett Millais*. He had recognized the similarity between the famous model Lizzie Siddal and Beth. But now? Standing before him was the living image.

'Micah. Come in.'

They made their awkward introductions and small talk. Gunn didn't come out straight away with the real purpose of his visit. While she was in the kitchen making them a cup of Earl Grey, he scoped out the view from the forty-third floor, the highest point. The floor to ceiling window told Gunn that his host wasn't an agoraphobic scared of wide open spaces. The panorama was impressive. Or as Ziya would say *it fucking fanfuckingtastico Gunn.*

London was laid out before him like one of those perfect miniature villages. The Thames winding its way back west, past St Michael's Hospital. Past the lumbering giant wheel that looked ready to spin across the Thames into the Houses of Parliament opposite.

She set the mugs down on the dining table. 'I've often wondered about you, you know.'

He cringed inside. That was more than he had reciprocated. 'Something unexpected has come up, about my brother.'

'Oh.'

'I need to ask you about your relationship with a bloke that Zeke called your Pet Poodle.'

Gunn was staring for her reaction. He didn't expect her eyes to immediately tear up. She took a sip of tea.

Beth's voicemail message had not done justice to her warm sibilant voice, with a precision of enunciation which seduced the listener. 'Oliver Boodle – Poodle. Yes, that was a cruel thing to call a friend. Really spiteful. Young people can do such thoughtless, nasty things. Capable of great compassion at the same time, of course. Great self-sacrifice, as you know from your time in the armed forces. It's a dichotomy. It was my joke, not Zeke's, but that's not even truly me either. Oliver was a good friend to me. A very good friend. For a while.'

'I bet he was. A very *good* friend. Oliver.'

Beth visibly bristled. 'Sorry?'

Gunn pulled out the photograph from his satchel, the one with the two lovebirds on the bench in Balloch quad, the cuckoo in the nest in the far cold corner, looking on longingly.

'I don't understand. I assumed you came to talk about your brother.' But Beth had been stirred. 'You were his hero, did you know that? I tried to talk at his funeral but you were a total basket case. Worse than me. I wanted to tell you how much I loved him, how much he meant to me. Now I can tell you Zeke is the only boy—only man I ever loved. Ever.'

Gunn wasn't buying it. He was on a roll now. A destructive role. 'I'll get to the point. I found out the mental case who supposedly killed Zeke, Rufus Wright, most likely didn't do it. So someone else did.'

He clocked her wide-eyed shock. 'I don't under—'

'Maybe someone like a pet poodle who moved in when the love of her life was out of the way. I may have been a basket case but I do remember who had his arm around you at Zeke's funeral.'

Beth laughed – but not with joy. 'So you're saying it wasn't Rufus Wright who murdered Zeke? The pathetic, mentally ill boy who confessed. But a fellow student so crazed with lust for me he was willing to kill probably his one friend, apart from me.'

When she put it like that, Gunn began to see the holes. Then his working theory fell into the Grand Canyon.

'Oliver was—is, gay. Did you know anything about your brother's life after he left home?'

Gunn was no longer on a roll.

'Olli fell for Zeke the moment they met during Freshers' Week.'

Beth saw Gunn's face fall. 'Jesus, relax, it was never reciprocated. But Zeke was sensitive about it. I was harder on Olli than Zeke was, and his name Boodle was so deliciously—apt, hence *pet poodle*. He was a very needy clingy person. Everywhere we went, Olli went. The week before Zeke died, we had had an argument over Olli. I told Zeke he had to stop towing him around after us, and until he did we should take a break. So I never—' Beth's voice choked slightly as she recalled. '—didn't see him that final week at all. Even after he phoned about a big surprise that night and would I come with him.'

Gunn jumped right on that revelation. 'What was that? Surprise? I never heard that before.'

'I told that policeman, the one investigating, with the funny name. Zeke said he was getting a ticket for a secret gig, remember that record *Right Here, Right Now?*

'Yeah, Fat Boy Slim.'

'But they had already arrested Wright, and didn't seem that interested. To be honest, I hadn't thought about it, till just now. There's a lot of other stuff from then I don't like to think about.'

'I hear you. I honestly do.'

'Anyway, Oliver was a friend, at the time, and after, you know. For a while anyway. He lost Zeke too but was much stronger than me. Why is any of this relevant? I don't understand.'

Gunn was annoyed with himself. He had constructed one theory in his head based on a single moment caught in a photograph. Her reply had thrown him right off his game. She seemed so genuine.

'I—uh, look, I'm sorry Beth. You're right, already found I don't know much about Zeke's Oxford life.'

'So where's all this coming from then?'

'I'll fill you in, promise.' Gunn pulled out two more photographs from his satchel, 'Know this bloke? He came down to the funeral with you.' The first shot was the finishing line photo of the London marathon. The other was the stage photo he had borrowed from Ruby Czarnecki.

Beth looked at the photographs. Gunn thought she

was going to keel over and do a head bounce off the dining room table. He had seen enough of physical *shock* to last a lifetime. Beth's face turned the colour of a debris cloud. Her hand went to her mouth and she started to sway. He was up and helping her without thought.

Gunn helped her across to the soft, brown leather couch. She lay back and closed her eyes. As pale as the dead. Gunn thought she looked even more like the lady in the painting floating in the stream. He checked her pulse (racing), and felt her forehead (cold and clammy).

'It's okay love, I'm a nurse.' She smiled weakly as if he was kidding. 'Seriously.'

She started shivering.

'You're in shock. We need to get you covered up.'

'Bedroom, left down the hallway.'

Gunn pulled the heavy wool wrap off the bed, he noticed the framed photographs on the bedside table. The big one was Zeke and her at a pub, probably in Oxford. Next to it were a couple of other photos of her as a young girl, with a man and woman he assumed were her parents.

Gunn placed the blanket around her. Whatever would cause a severe physical reaction like that had to be bad. Evil bad was his guess. He looked around with more seeing eyes. The location: forty three storeys up with the illusion you can see what's coming at you from the horizon. The security he had to get past simply to reach the lifts. Cameras everywhere. Now that he was thinking about it, her flat door looked like reinforced steel. Plus three heavy duty mortise locks. She seemed to work at home for most of the time.

Her voice was shaky and barely a whisper. 'You know him.'

'You could say.'

'Friend?'

'No way. And he's dead.'

Beth's eyes welled-up, it took a few seconds for her to start sobbing. Then the full Niagara. It seemed obvious now that Beth had located herself in a space where she could minimize intimate physical contact. He reasoned that letting her gush out by herself suited them both fine. It was when the sobs morphed into laughing, he worried it might be time for an intervention.

Beth calmed down and composed herself. 'How did Byron Goolsbee die?'

'Not well. He was—uh, pretty much tortured. Lost body parts, over half his blood. Had to be horribly painful.'

'Dead. I wish I could believe you.'

'Believe me. Saw the body. Touched the body. Even took—' Gunn stopped himself.

'Even took what?'

'You don't want to know.'

'Photographs. You took photographs? Have you got them. Can I see.'

'I don't think that's such –'

'<u>Don't tell me what I fucking think</u>. Have you got them or not?'

The smile on her face was genuine joy. Gunn understood perfectly why she had not stopped smiling since seeing the horrific damage to Goolsbee during his last painful hours – all in glorious Technicolor. After Beth finally revealed what the monster Goolsbee did to her, Gunn felt exactly the same.

30

'Fuck you looking at cunt.'

For tactical reasons Gunn had not been looking directly at the foul-mouthed flotsam. But now he stared right through the youth like an MRI machine picking out internal organs. Outwardly impassive, but that was the mask. Gunn was riveting down a real primal urge to hurt someone, anyone who absolutely had it coming. Goolsbee no longer being available, this repellent goon fit the bill.

Gunn considered the protective ribs across the youth's lungs. Kicked in with a roundhouse swing, they would do serious damage, a good chance of puncturing a lung. He visualized the shin bone smashed in two, bent like a banana after a savage downwards thrust from his steel toe-capped boots. Down and out. The nose pushed into the brain with a rapid thrust from the palm of Gunn's hand. His MRI scan saw lots of juicy targets. After what he had heard from Beth he would have no hesitation. The guy better back off right now while the backing off was still good.

Gunn had parked on one of the side streets radiating off the mile long Brick Lane, still in Tower Hamlets. The other name for Brick Lane is Curry Mile, famous for years as having the greatest density of Indian restaurants in Britain. Though the term *Indian* is a misnomer, as most curry houses in the UK are run by Bengalis from Bangladesh. Curry Mile and its restaurants are also getting another less flattering reputation. A hub for the crack cocaine and heroin trade taking over from the West Indian Yardies. St. Mike's A&E being one of the near shorelines upon which the human detritus of that business washed up. Working in the hospital you had to be deaf not to hear druggy patients talking about the £300 off-menu specials cooked up for drug dealers: samosas or onion bahjis spiced up with crack and heroin stuffing for resale on.

He was heading for where Beth told him the artist and apparent crack head Oliver Boodle had his studio in the newly trendified Brick Lane. His instincts had been right about Beth's psychological state. In the years since Oxford, she had gradually withdrawn into her hurt, slowly cutting herself off from the world, unable to get past it. You don't have to go to a desert island to do that. It's never been easier to establish virtual relationships. Her sudden bestseller exploits greased Beth's solo descent with financial security. The crooked grin of the city of London skyscraper line loomed south behind him. Like a rapper's mouthful of bejewelled, uneven but expensive teeth, gleaming in the late afternoon sunshine. Gunn squinted. He burned with the intensity of the sun at what Beth had told him.

Byron Goolsbee was a yank from Washington D.C., having been a Rhodes scholar at Peterhouse college when he met Zeke. They were both getting into the Oxford drama scene. Then Zeke and Beth became an item. Whenever Zeke was not around, Goolsbee would semi-proposition her, relentlessly and without any encouragement. She laughed it off, but he was one of those guys who had skin thicker than the walls of a nuclear bunker. When Zeke formed the Mametaliens, she joined to help behind the scenes. Goolsbee came on board too. Beth tried to make sure she was only around with Zeke.

When Zeke was murdered, Beth was all alone in a sea of self-absorbed students. Gunn agonized over that as she clinically described the events that haunted her to this day. His dead brother's girlfriend had been defenceless and all alone, while he was off fighting someone else's war. He couldn't protect her, let alone a foreign country full of people who hated his guts. As she half whispered to Gunn, he couldn't even look her in the eye. Ashamed at his unforgivable weakness.

In the weeks after Zeke's murder, Beth described her existence as a blur of unreality. As the bleakest November ever bled into December, she fled Oxford before Michelmas Term ended. Bolting home to her parents, staying until after Christmas and the New Year. Oliver had phoned her every day and was there to greet her when she returned for start of Hillary term in January. About a week after returning, Olli persuaded her to take a night out at Oscar's, one of Oxford's drag/comedy clubs. She remembered going, she remembered having a drink at the bar, then at a table. She remembered Olli seeing someone he knew and leaving her. Feeling a bit woozy. Then *blackness*.

Beth's voice grew stronger. She regained control. She told Gunn how she woke up head-befuddled in a bare room. The curtains closed, but she could see the daylight seeping through. She tried to shout but there was some sort of rubber gag strapped around her head and in her mouth. It took a minute to refocus, but when she did, Beth understood she was naked and chained to a bed. Her left wrist was manacled and the chain was attached to the brass bedstead. Her head throbbed horribly with pain. That's when she noticed some dry blood on the sheets, and felt her head, touching the congealed blood. That raised a vague recollection of slipping on some stone steps and smashing her head on the ground.

There was a television on a stand at the foot of the bed. A video camera was perched on a tripod next to it. Gunn could not even comprehend the terror Beth must have experienced. Naturally she thought she was going to die, in that room, all alone. Then it got worse.

The television came on. A recording started to play. It was her, Beth, unconscious on the bed. Gunn thought he was going to puke when she told him on the screen it was a man raping her to camera. There was no sound. At the time she didn't understand, but later she came to realize the purpose of the monster. It was to humiliate her. To violate her body. To pose her. To laugh at her. To show her the tape to destroy her very soul.

The coward monster in human guise wore a boilersuit and horror-mask at first. But he had to partially disrobe for the sustained physical assaults. Beth said she forced herself to watch by disassociating from what was happening to this other person. That's when she noticed small details as the camera zoomed in and out, and even moved around for a better shot. He was taking direction from the cameraman. There was a second person. Then she saw it. Discounted it, then saw it again. The ghoul dressed in human skin. The beast who should be put down like a rabid dog. He had six digits on either foot. Now Gunn knew. He wondered why the monster would go to all the trouble and then let that slip to camera?

Finally the nightmare recording ended. Only for it to play over again, and again, and again. For the first time Beth faltered as she described the monster returning in his black boilersuit and horror-mask, carrying a huge knife. This was it. She was resigned. He was going to kill her, and film it, and laugh over it. And she would be gone forever, consigned to oblivion and perpetual nothingness. Surprisingly to Beth, instead he forced a glass of water down her. That was the last thing she remembered before waking up back in her clothes, numb from cold, lying face down in a ditch about ten miles north of Oxford. Her head hurt worse than before.

She was outside the small village of Frampton. Finding a phone box she called Oliver who rushed to pick her up in his rickety 1978 Volkswagen Beetle. By the time Olli arrived, Beth's high at still being alive had collapsed into a pit of nothingness. When Oliver grasped what she was saying, she realized he was sceptical. It was too crazy for him. He'd flitted away after spotting someone at Oscars whom he had hooked up with the previous week at Heavenly Delights, Oxford's popular student gay club. The last he had seen, Beth was chatting to people. Then Beth was gone. He assumed she left with friends, finding a way to forget Zeke for a while and thought good for her. Oliver insisted on taking her to the hospital where his very good friend from Oscars happened to work.

Oliver's doctor pal was happy to help. He took her to a private examination room. He cleaned up the wound to her head, examined her for physical injuries. Beth said she was sort of wondering about rape kits, collecting evidence? But she was still in such a state of shock she meekly went along with a figure of authority. He was a doctor, after all. All the time he was asking her questions about her state of mind since Zeke was murdered. Did she remember suffering any bumps on the head apart from the nasty cut. Had she ever seen Zeke since he died? Crazy questions. That's when another doctor came in, a female. Beth felt good to have a woman near. She insisted on telling them what had happened, they listened sympathetically. Then they left.

Oliver came in a minute later and looked distraught. She was feeling sorry for him until Oliver's special doctor friend returned, except he wasn't alone. In tow he had a couple of large men in the clichéd white coats. The doctor explained that following concern from her friend Oliver, it had been decided that Beth should be detained involuntarily at a mental facility for her own safety. He hadn't found evidence of any sexual assault. And her one injury was something she vaguely recalled sustaining herself. The main concern being that she may self-harm in a state of clinical depression. It was madness. But merely the start.

Beth was kept under observation in Ashurst Psychiatric Intensive Care Unit, at the Littlemore Mental Health Centre, two miles south of Oxford. She was there for three days until it was determined she posed no threat to herself or to others. Unfortunately her clothes had gone missing in between the examination room at the Oxford general hospital and Littlemore. They loaned her some *leftovers*, as they called them, a jumble of eccentric clothes left behind by former patients.

Once she was released, Beth got the bus back to Oxford, refusing their offer to phone Oliver, who was on record as her contact. She went straight to the St. Alban's Road police station and demanded to see Detective Inspector Czarnecki; dressed in a collection that would have been burned as unwanted by the Oxfam shop. While he acted sympathetically, Beth was soon convinced that she wasn't being taken seriously by Czarnecki, but being humoured. It was five days after the rape: impossible to collect physical evidence. She was by her own admission examined by a doctor who found no evidence of assault, let alone rape. She had admitted the head injury was self-inflicted after falling on stone steps. She could not remember anything of her alleged abduction and confinement except this fantastical tale of video recordings that seemed out of a sick Hollywood movie.

Then there was her sectioning under the Mental Heath Act. Czarnecki shrugged and wondered what he was supposed to do. He asked if she really wanted to make a statement. That's when the truth hit her. Bad enough to have what happened happen; but for no one to believe you? It was the Kafka stuff of nightmares. And it was about to get worse.

Since a toddler Beth had been a real water baby. She loved to swim. To dive. To float with her head breaking the surface. She never felt more alive than when she was in the water.

Two weeks after her ordeal she summoned the courage to rejoin the Oxford University Ladies Water Polo team. It was a training session at the university pool. Beth was standing poolside after the session, when the Men's swim team started to appear, including Goolsbee. He saw her and came right over. He didn't say anything, he had that perpetual smirk he always had. He wanted her to look, see. Look and see that on each of his size twelve feet, he crammed in six toes. And there was not a damn thing she could do about it.

Beth left the city of Oxford the same day. She left the University of Oxford a week later and transferred to Harvard, after a little help from a family friend who was a major league donor to his alma mater in the 70s.

The front door to Oliver Boodle's studio was half open. It was on the sixth and top floor of a former Victorian warehouse first used for spices shipped up the Thames from the Indies. Gunn could hear voices as he approached the door.

He slammed in uninvited. He wasn't sure what a working artist's studio should look like, but this wasn't it. While the large space was filled with painted canvasses, they were strewn everywhere. The floor was a mess of fast-food wrappers, empty liquor bottles, wine bottles, and the detritus of drug-taking gear. Crack pipes, large metal spoons, needles, rubber hoses. The smell of urine and faeces was eye-watering. Gunn had never been to a crack den, he guessed he could check that off his *things not to do ever* list, right now.

He had no problem recognizing the man slumped back into the crazy looking leather sofa with half its cushions sliced open. But this Oliver was a gaunt, bone protruding version who looked nearer aged fifty than the thirtysomething he should be. The scumbag standing over him? He was a different story. Looked about twenty, about six foot, rangy, not over-muscled but youthfully fit, scar down one cheek, probably carried him street cred as a toughie. Gunn ambled over, keeping a peripheral eye on the scumbag, directing his gaze to the best advert ever against drug use.

'Oliver. It's Micah. Ezekiel Gunn's brother. Remember me?'

'Fuck you looking at cunt.'

31

Gunn had closed to within three feet of the sofa; an ideal distance for close quarter action against an opponent who looked under-prepared and over-confident. Even from the door, Gunn could see the black handle of a pistol jutting up from his belt. It was a semi-automatic, probably a 9mm with a magazine holding at least thirteen bullets. Once clocked, Gunn never let his eyes stray there again to tip off the scumbag he knew he was strapped.

The scumbag's body was positioned all wrong, facing Oliver sideways on to Gunn. Gunn directed all his attention to Oliver. 'Need to talk about some stuff regarding Beth, Zeke.'

'Said, what the fuck you—'

It happened faster than the scumbag could repeat his rhetorical question. Scumbag's left hand went towards his waist and he started to turn from facing Oliver to face the approaching Gunn head on. Gunn had two choices: disable the guy before he levelled the weapon at him, or take the gun off him. Gunn knew the big problem attempting the disabling move before the disarming move. Fail and the scumbag could clear his waist, 9mm in hand, and double-figures in the mag. Then all bets are off. Gunn knew he was not prepared to kill this particular scumbag here and now. His one real option was to seize control and secure the weapon by force.

Taking one step forward, he right straight-armed the scumbag hard in his left shoulder. This unexpected hit increased the momentum of the already turning bad boy, causing him to swing sideways, his own left hand slipping past the gun handle he was about to grip and lift. Gunn's forward momentum, with a right twist, enabled him to effect a smoothly rotated ninety degree counter-clockwise slide into the spinning scumbag, who was now disoriented and scrambling to grab at the gun again.

Gunn was already two moves ahead. With his left hand, Gunn grabbed the guy's trigger finger and bent it sideways ferociously. It snapped like a length of dried spaghetti. Same time: Gunn reaches across with his right hand, pulling the semi-automatic 9mm handgun from the now screaming scumbag's waistband.

Now the former hard-boy reels backwards holding his left hand, wailing with pain. Gunn steps back a pace to give himself room, seeing the safety is on, he flips the nine mil around to grip the weapon at the top of the handle, the heel of the rubberized handle grip now aimed like a hammer. Stepping forward again, Gunn smashes the heel of the gun across the scumbag's nose with devastating force. While the shocked scumbag is still digesting that blow, Gunn finishes the move by delivering a savage downwards chop stomp to the scumbag's left knee. Scumbag goes down, and with a hand, a nose and a knee out of commission he didn't know which injury to tend first with his one good hand.

The whole action lasted four seconds. To Gunn it was like riding a bike, the moves were memory and muscle imprinted. His body was fully automatic, ready to roll. He flipped the nine mil back, gripped the handle, and pointed the business end towards the prone figure.

Gunn dropped to his haunches and with his left hand, felt inside the youth's jacket. He found the wallet. Inside was at least £500 in used notes, plus his driver's licence and name.

'Honest to God Anthony, I don't give a flying fuck about a twat like you and what's going on here between you and a crack head. Seriously.'

With all the rapidly evaporating conviction scumbag could still muster, the final threat plopped out. 'You're fucking dead man.'

'Yeah yeah tough guy. Here's the thing little man, no doubt you'll be crawling back to someone higher up your poison chain, and no doubt you'll be tempted to mention today's unpleasantness. That would be a mistake Anthony. I don't care what porkies you have to spin, but grass me up, or Olli over there in any way shape or form, or if I hear of anything untoward happening to Olli here, then one dark and stormy night, about four in the morning, I'm gonna quietly break into whatever shithole you crash, and zap ya. But I won't kill you there and then. Nah, I'll put a two-two in your spine, between your seventh and eighth vertebrae. Hawking you forever. Anthony you'll be sucking food out of a straw, shitting in a plastic bag attached to your waist. The only thing on your whole body that moves will be your eyes controlling the computer you use to communicate with the world. You'll fucking wish I had double tapped ya.'

Gunn wondered if he was a bit too obviously melodramatic with the Pulp Fiction/Samuel L. Jacksonesque threats. But he had to sell it, because short of actually killing the bloke, he had to make sure the scumbag never mentioned what happened, to anyone. Gunn bent over him as the bloke was still oscillating between his nose, knee and finger. He pushed the barrel into his spine.

—*RATCHET—CLICK—*

The sound of him pulling back the firing hammer echoed with an ominous certainty. As the yellow liquid slowly stained scumbag's pants and steamed onto the floor, Gunn reckoned he had finally made his point. *Overwhelm. Dominate. Destroy.*

He pulled him up by his bad hand, then waved the scumbag's wallet in his face.

'You was jumped, okay. Four guys, took your shooter and wallet. No way no one's gonna dispute that, state you're in pal. Nod you agree that's what happened.'

Gunn pointed the 9mm directly Anthony's face.

Scumbag nodded, surrendering completely.

Gunn pulled the trigger.

—*CLICK*—

'Ooops, safety on. Won't be next time.'

Alone. Gunn was finally able to turn his attention to Oliver Boodle. The bloke had received every opportunity and break. A nice upbringing, top university, budding career as an artist, breakout show at the RCA in 2003, culminating in this, the crack den from hell. He was looking at Gunn as some sort of saviour and was anxious to spill his own personal tale of destruction. He hadn't painted for over two years since his crack habit took over. That's when he started dealing on the side. Oliver found it easy to buy wholesale and sell retail. That kept him supplied until his own personal habit started to eat more and more of the profit. Until the inevitable day when he owed more than he could bring in.

Gunn cut him short. 'Tell me about the day you took Beth Monteretti to the hospital. Actually tell me about the club first. The place you took her, you remember? You buggered off and left her there to be drugged, taken, raped, humiliated, terrorized to the point she was going to die. Like that's bad enough, instead of taking her to the police you took her to your doctor pal, who not only didn't believe a woman who said she had been raped, but went and got her sectioned for three days. What sort of doctor does that?'

Gunn was surprised Oliver felt much of anything anymore, outside the ever-shortening highs and the bottomless downers that left him craving another hit. But his gaunt, sallow face slowly imploded even more into itself. Then he broke down, gasping out his pitiful excuses.

'Never forgave me did she? Saw her at my RCA show in 2003, out the blue. Said she did, but she didn't did she?'

'Can you blame her?'

'I didn't know. She wasn't making sense, and I'd met this gorgeous guy, a doctor, so you know I thought wouldn't be a bad idea if she should see him first. Never guessed he'd do that. Commit her to a loony bin for crying out loud.'

'Yeah well, we all do shit we wished we could take back. You're looking at a prime example.'

'Any consolation I told Stuart I could never see him again. Broke my hea—'

'Stuart? Doctor was called Stuart?'

Olli shrugged wistfully, remembering better days. 'Yeah, my Irish Stew I called him. Dr Stuart Roper. Actually read some article about him in the Guardian last year, some brain gizmo he's pioneered. Rising young talent or some such shit. Seems to be doing alright for himself though. I called him, y'know, old times sake. Maybe go for a drink. Said he wasn't in my scene these days. Was happily playing the breeder field. Can you believe that? Talk about double life.'

Double life. Exactly what Gunn was thinking.

32

Of all the times for his car battery to go bye-byes. Gunn was still parked near Oliver's studio. He wanted to be at St. Mike's as of ten minutes ago, have a root around Dr Stuart Roper's office. Irish Stew A.K.A. Roper the Groper. The nice RAC lady on the phone promised to be with him within the hour. There was also the little problem over the gun. He opened the boot of the car, and pulled back the carpeting to expose the spare tyre/wheel clamped to the Saab's chassis. He quickly twisted open the wing-nut holding the wheel in place, wrapping the gun in the oily rags lying in the boot, he secured the gun in place.

He had gotten the spare wheel back in its slot when Eric Burden started singing insistently in his pants pocket. The iPhone display announced *Doc Dan*. Did he want to take it? He loved the guy, but this was getting ridiculous.

Gunn:	Mate, how's it hanging?
Mosser:	*(UPBEAT)* Oh you know, same old, same old. On a four minute commercial break, for my little radio show you may have heard of.
Gunn:	Honest to God Dan, prize media hog.
Mosser:	Try my best. Where are you?
Gunn:	Not far from your studios actually. Brick Lane. Battery's died, waiting for the RAC. Any particular reason for—

Mosser:	Okay—funny thing, had a phone call from a certain Detective Superintendent Hickman.
Gunn:	Oh yeah.
Mosser:	Your name came up. Apparently Rufus Wright tried to hang himself. Even odder, appears someone broke into Radcliffe. Don't know anything about that do you?
Gunn:	No kidding? Don't people usually try to break out?
Mosser:	Funny. Look, joking aside. Again. Should I be concerned?
Gunn:	No worries Dan.
Mosser:	Look, you know the drill. I've a duty of confidentiality. Anything you tell me remains between us. Doctor patient confidentiality. Did I mention the word *confidential*? Police will never know.

Gunn tossed it around for all of a second, he slammed the car boot shut with the carpeting back in place, and saw the flashing orange light of the RAC van.

Gunn:	(TENTATIVE) Mate, there's a whole big, big something else going on about Ezekiel's murder. Don't ask me how I know, half is guess work, but it all goes back to Oxford, the uni, y'know.
Mosser:	What goes back?

Gunn paused. He had reached the part he hadn't

wanted to mention. Maybe to Eddie—in fact definitely to Eddie, that was actually a priority. Except he was too far in now not to continue.

Gunn:	*(BIG BREATH)* Something called—Kill Club.
Mosser:	Kill what?
Gunn:	Kill Club.
Mosser:	Mike. Please.
Gunn:	Yeah I know. Sounds, uh-out there. Gets outier there-er. Think—uh, I think Stuart Roper may be involved.
Mosser:	*(AUDIBLE GASP)* Oh come on. Roper? He's a doctor for God's sake.
Gunn:	So was Shipman. And Crippen. And Mengele.
Mosser:	Yeah, but, come on Mike. Damn. My light's flashing, Back on air in ten seconds. Don't do anything rash. I think we need another one on one. Talk about what you're feeling.
Gunn:	Try mate. Gotta fly, guy's here. Cheers.

—*CLICK*—

The RAC guy confirmed the car's battery was flat, but only because the Saab's alternator connection had worked its way loose and had stopped charging. Ten minutes later Gunn was jump started back on the road, on his way to the hospital.

He had pressed the speed dial for Ziya's mobile, and it rang four times before going straight to voicemail.

'Not here. Leave message.'

He hung up. That was five times now. Maybe she had popped out for a quick smoke, along with all the other medical based nico-fiends addicted to the cancer stumps. He would surprise her instead.

Gunn fiddled around with the tuning knob on the car radio until he hit the 927 AM frequency for ChatterBox. Dr Dan's smooth, oh so mellow voice rippled out of the Saab's speakers. He'd never heard the show before, despite Dan's semi-regular enquiries as to whether Gunn had caught his latest edition of *Talk About It with Dr Dan*. All he wanted was some background to fill in the thoughts ricocheting around his head.

It took him a couple of drive-arounds to squeal into a spot in St. Mike's hospital car park. Dr Dan was still talking sympathetically to another caller. Gunn shook his head, switching off the radio before hurrying inside to toss Roper's office. Then surprise Ziya.

Stepping out of the lift on the sixth floor, Gunn turned right and headed to the neurology department's small, open plan public reception area. Good. No one manning the desk. Roper was officially on leave but Gunn still checked the large white board filled with information written in dry marker. One half of the board chronicled the thirteen patients on ward and their status. The other half showed bookings for the Operating Theatres, the procedure involved and the neurosurgeon's name. Roper's name was missing.

He had been in Roper's hospital consulting room many times in his capacity as a scrub nurse on his neuro-team. This was his first time as a cracked detective. Of course on those occasions he was not looking for anything. Not that he knew what he was looking for exactly. It would be one of those *I'll know it when I see it moments*. The desk seemed a good place to start. Gunn switched on Roper's hospital laptop and let it boot up while he rummaged through the drawers. Nothing popped.

He moved to the two identical slate-grey metal filing cabinets, with five drawers. Naturally they were locked. But Gunn had already found the key in one of the desk drawers. There was nothing interesting in the filing cabinets. He remembered the movies where people always taped incriminating or vital evidence at the back of the drawers. Handy in fiction but not today.

Stumped again, he sat back in the throne-like leather desk chair and contemplated his next move. Dan was right. Stuart Roper was a doctor, a star neurosurgeon for God's sake. Even Gunn had to admit he was an exceptionally fine one, despite his annoying attempt at the alpha male personality. But that could describe a high percentage of surgeons with the God complex. Something was nagging. What would be Roper's psychological motivation? The anti-superhero? Saved people by day, kill them by night. He would have to be a world-class malignant narcissist, like Crippen or Shipman. And an incredibly clever ruthless psychopath.

The laptop was fully booted. Stuart Roper's face beamed out from his monitor. Yes, he had a headshot of himself as wallpaper. No password protection though, suggesting nothing there. Gunn clicked away looking for something, anything. Clicking the icon *Filing Cabinet* opened another window with a list of sub-folders. He clicked on the one named Photos to display about thirty photographs stacked three across. Scrolling down he saw various Stuart shots. Stuart sitting on the Lincoln Memorial steps. Stuart outside Johns Hopkins Hospital. Stuart sitting at a restaurant table next to a stunning blonde. Stuart sitting at the same table next to—next to

Byron Goolsbee.

Fuck. They knew each well enough to break bread in the states.

Stunned. His eyes roamed across the desk: wire-mesh three tier letters rack, landline phone, and a neatly stacked pile of glossy brochures. He picked up the top one. It was a commercial property portfolio, the gold background had photographs of various commercial properties laid on top, the company logo at the bottom right a black circle with the name CPH Limited embossed in blood red.

CPH? That name rang a bell. Gunn had seen that recently. He was flipping over his mind's eye memory cards as he turned the page to see the first double page spread. On the left hand side of the page, the face of Dr Stuart Roper, Chairman of CPH beamed out – alongside the mission statement of the company; and a list of the current industrial and commercial properties in the group. In less than two hours Gunn had discovered mind-boggling details about his relentlessly hetero boss with the reputation for tapping anything in a nurses' uniform. He previously enjoyed the odd gay liaison. He was apparently a property magnate. And he may sideline as a psycho-killer.

Gunn scanned down the property list. His memory card focussed on a sign he clocked last week, right as he reached a familiar name on the page: Dylan Thomas Industrial Estate, Milkwood Road, Brixton.

Double Fuck.

Gunn debated whether to still surprise Ziya before her shift ended. The Roper revelations were bouncing around his head like an un-tethered balloon. He should be doing something. Calling Hickman?

He spent the next few minutes padding around St.

Mike's looking for her. If she was in the hospital then it defeated him. No one had seen her in the past hour. He tried her mobile again, but it went straight to voicemail where he had already left a pile of messages asking her to call back. He had a brainwave.

There he was, feet up on the desk in St. Mike's Security Hub. Phil was reading the Sun, behind him two seventy-two inch monitors displaying feeds from multiple live hospital locations. Phil held the newspaper open for Gunn. 'Seen this, two more of our boys fucking murdered in Helmand. Crime man, fucking crime. Nuke the place, finish the fuckers.'

Phil was a sound guy who had joined up to be a Royal Marine. A month into basic training at Lympstone, he had suffered a major head trauma. It left him nearly blind in his left eye. It meant he could no longer serve as a fighting marine. The only kind. He had total respect for anyone who had yomped it, especially for Gunn. Phil loved living the life vicariously through any exploits Gunn cared to occasionally share about some of his hair-raising battle tales, usually involving Eddie. In Royal Marine slang Phil was *corps pissed*. As in totally intoxicated by the life that passed him by through no fault of his own, but some Harry von twat who involved Phil in his cluster fuck.

Phil was soon accessing the archived footage. Gunn was impressed at the sophistication of the CCTV and computer recording system. Based on a running timecode, Phil was able to punch in an approximate time into a known location, say A&E, say a couple of hours ago. Phil used a computer wand to circle Ziya. As she walked down the A&E corridor, the computer seamlessly followed her from camera to camera. She headed towards the staff locker room first. Ziya opened the small padlock on locker number 219. She removed her bright yellow coat and put it on before picking up her handbag from the locker.

She took a familiar route leading to the forbidden zone – contaminated ground where the lower caste of smokers congregated to indulge their addiction. As the CCTV picked her up walking past Osteopathy, Ziya stopped for a second to fumble around in her handbag. She pulled out her phone and answered it. She started walking again while she was still talking. After a short conversation, Ziya exited the swing doors at the end of her trek which led her to the forbidden zone.

The screen went blank. Gunn knew why. Everyone in the hospital knew that the security guys had given up repairing the fixed CCTV camera pointed at that location. Gunn noted the timestamp 21:05:27, recalling what he was doing at the same time. The RAC man was driving away. He had gotten into his car. The car radio had defaulted back to its factory setting when the power from the battery went dead. He retuned it back to 927 AM as Dan gave a time check for nine oh, five, and resumed his show after the news at the top of the hour. Gunn worked out the sequence in his mind. It had taken him about twenty minutes to drive to the hospital, he had spent another forty-five minutes flaffing around in neurology and Stuart Roper's office. He had come down to A&E. He had found she had already gone. Was he feeling jealous?

33

Gunn called Eddie as he speed-walked back to the Saab in the hospital car park. Another one went straight to voice mail. *Don't people answer their fucking phones anymore?*

He left a message this time. 'Hey mucker, sorry been dark past couple, been eating the Harry von shite. Call a-sap.'

He couldn't get Ziya off his mind. What did he know about her? Not enough. As a colleague at work he had dismissed the sly intimate touches, the way she turned her body into him, and way she absentmindedly tugged on her luxuriant black hair as she spoke. 20/20 hindsight? Pretty damn obvious.

But he had no idea about her life. He hadn't even known why she left China, until she broke down over a photograph. Family here? Maybe that phone call was from an uncle or a cousin over in Chinatown. Maybe it was an ex-boyfriend. Maybe a current boyfriend. *Downer.* He wanted to know everything about her. And he wanted to tell her everything about him. Not the way he told Eddie, or Dr Mosser, or his sister. Gunn wanted to lie naked next to her again. Hold her. Confide in her. Really connect.

The naked desire frightened him. Not the thought of connecting after Ginny. It was the realization that he was opening himself up to loss again. *Gain and pain.* The human condition reduced to a verb, noun and conjunction.

Ziya's flat is in one of the narrow Kennington streets near the Oval cricket ground. The four storey Victorian house had long been subdivided into eight flats and bedsits, with Ziya's perched right at the top. He negotiated his way down the side of the house to the parking spots at the back. He thought she'd be home. She wasn't answering her phone. Or the door. This was crazy, he was acting like a loopy teenager besotted by his first girlfriend. He should get out of there right now.

Entering through the communal front door (around the back) was a cinch as Ziya had given him the code to the keypad which controlled the lock. Standing outside her front door, officially Flat H, was trickier. The hall light was movement controlled. He took a roll of black electrical tape from his rucksack, ripped off an inch, and stuck it over the peep hole to Flat G, directly opposite. The last thing he needed was the occupant spying out to see him picking locks.

Then he was in. No need for spy work now, he flipped on the light switch.

This is crazy nuts Gunn. What if she walks in? Acting worse than Tony Scarface Moreno. It was official. Gunn was jealous that she might have a significant someone else in her life.

The bed was out and the sheets unmade. It was obvious Ziya hadn't been back since she left for work. Gunn sat on the bed, then flopped back. He felt tired, washed out like an old pair of jeans. Her smell washed over him, subtle, evocative. The faintest aroma of jasmine mixed with something he couldn't quite place. Gunn buried his face in the sheets where she had lain.

That was something he had done before, albeit with someone else in another country that was getting harder to visit. He had loved to do the same thing when he was on leave and he could be with his wife Ginny, all too briefly. Her bed smelt wonderfully of her. Different to Ziya, but equally as pleasing, equally as feminine. When they died, his wife and daughter, he spent hours with his head buried in the sheets of her bed, the ones she had slept in the night before. He had carefully lifted the sheets and blanket from Megan's tiny bed and did the same for Ginny. Trying to bring them back to life the only way left. Unable to move and paralysed with despair.

When Eddie found him, he had to drag him physically from the room. He left, but only because Eddie promised to look after the only living things that remained of his family. Gunn had remembered something he read once, that two thousand years after dying on the cross, every breath everyone currently alive on the planet took, contained a least one molecule of air also breathed by Jesus. It was a nice story, maybe a fairy tale, and his dad would have loved it, true or not. Gunn had Eddie vacuum pack Ginny and Megan's sheets in a specialized plastic container. Their essence lived on in those sheets, now preserved.

Gunn breathed deep and was revived by Ziya's essence. He wanted her all to himself. No sharing.

The hands on Big Ben's clock turned unstoppably towards midnight as he turned left from Kennington Road, and sped past Waterloo Station. The Houses of Parliament on the opposite bank of the river rose larger. The exterior lighting bathed the old stones in their warm steady golden hue. His phone Burdened.

Bebba:	Hey bro.
Gunn:	Hey love, got your messages. Sorry, not calling you back. Where you at?
Bebba:	Your place. Uncle Eddie's here.

Gunn: Great. Back in twenty.

Relief washed over him. One good thing. He had to tap down the Ziya obsession. She was a free agent. Out and about in Chinatown probably. He was acting nuts. But—it occurred he was poking in shit with a big stick. Who knows what he'd disturbed? He had to protect his sister at all costs. He had a trump card. Eddie. Bebba adored Eddie. Who was *totally cool*. Unlike him, her big brother, who was so *tragic* Bebba had to help out as Gunn's own lifestyle advisor. But Gunn didn't mind as *cool* was not the effect he was aiming for.

34

—THUMP—HAMMER—BANG—

The battering on the front door reverberated through the house. Eddie had gotten Gunn's *Harry von message* and was already there when Bebba turned up. They were in Gunn's kitchen rustling up a quick snack. Having put his healthy appetite on hold again, Gunn gratefully grabbed a portion and headed down to the basement. Eddie was pressing for details, but it was tricky with Bathsheba in and out of the room.

Eddie cocked his head to one side. 'Stuart? Who's this Stuart character then?'

This detecting was hard work for a one man band. 'Tell you about it later.'

—THUMP—HAMMER—BANG—

Gunn and Eddie shared the look. The marines in action look. They didn't have to say it because they both recognized that level of aggression from their exploits in bad guy snatch squads in Iraq. If he didn't open the door, there would be no door to open.

'Think I know what this is about.'

Eddie slammed Gunn with his glare: 'Seriously One Shot. After last time? Really?'

'Need you to stash my sister, somewhere 100 percent safe. Right now.'

'Mate, what the fuck?'

'I know. I know. It's a Charlie Foxtrot.'

Eddie churned it around. 'Solved. Couple of guys house-sitting one of me properties out in leafy

Buckinghamshire.'

'Sound?'

'As a double tap. Gucci sound. Jim's ex-Corps. Paul's ex-Para. Both ex-bouncers at Peppermint Rhino. Both as bent as a nine bob note. No one's getting nowhere near Bathsheba.'

'Good. Major good.'

'Gonna have to tell her something One Shot.'

Gunn grimaced defeat. He had wanted to keep her mind focused solely on getting into RADA 'Okay. Tell her everything, starting with the medallion. She's gonna be pissed off big time.'

The noise became even more insistent. Gunn figured he may as well save himself the door replacement money.

He was greeted by the lanky Inspector Wilson. This time he brought along four of his uniformed mates.

'We meet again Mister Gunn.'

'Can't this wait Inspector.'

'Actually sir it can't. It's regarding a very serious matter as I'm sure you know.'

Eddie appeared behind Gunn. 'Don't say nothing Mick. Lawyer this time?'

35

The interview room was subtly different, though it looked identical. The same tenth floor. The same bright lights, the same CCTV cameras in every corner focussed on the suspect's chair. *Suspect*—Gunn mulled over the word. That was him. He was an actual *suspect*. Sounded fair, he was totally guilty of something. He knew that. He was certain that they knew that. Not guilty in a monstrous Goolsbee way. Not guilty in a natural justice way. But that wasn't the point. The point is what could they prove? The sole thing that counted in the justice sausage-grinder. That and what could he be charged with, if push came to shove him into prison and throw away the key.

There was the little matter of assault regarding Rufus Wright. Breaking into a secure government facility. Yes there was that. Choking a guard to unconsciousness. Stealing his car. They were his criminal starters for ten. How about him effectively putting a wannabe gangster into crippling rehab, and his urine caked pants into the drycleaners? For some outrageous reason, all this was also frowned upon by the powers that be.

Those PTB kept him stewing for over an hour. Gunn took the time to build an implacable walled redoubt in his mind. As a marine he had undergone interrogation resistance training that went far beyond what the police were allowed to do. The police couldn't even waterboard him.

Hickman finally crashed in, Wilson in tow, both lugging folders. Far from the desired effect of the room in making a suspect edgy and pliable, Gunn was seemingly in a relaxed state of trance.

Both coppers slammed themselves down menacingly opposite him. Hickman looked at Gunn. He was shaking his head disapprovingly, as if Gunn was a naughty child to be chastised. 'Mister Gunn, not keeping you from your beauty sleep I hope?'

'Am I under arrest Superintendent?'

'Not yet Mister Gunn, but the night is young and I can hold you for up to forty-eight hours.'

'For what?'

'You're helping us with enquiries into a very serious incident at Radcliffe Psychiatric Hospital. So once again I have to go through this little procedure *You do not have to say anything. But it may harm your defence if you do not mention when questioned something that you later rely on in court. Anything you do say may be given in evidence.* What can you tell us about the events at Radcliffe?'

'Err, nothing.'

'Remember our little chat last week Micah. How I was quite emphatic at how I would fuck you over. But you wouldn't leave it alone would you?'

'Has my lawyer arrived yet Superintendent? Can I get up and leave?'

Wilson went to one of the folders and pulled out a few eight by ten photos. They were all pulls from the CCTV at Radcliffe. 'Recognize this person Mr Gunn?'

Gunn was impressed at the pin-sharp clarity of him taken in various parts of the unit. In all photos his disguised face was also partially obscured by his hand. His care had paid off. There was no way they could use this visual evidence against him.

'Can't say I do.'

Hickman smiled. 'Have to admit, what you did. Quite

impressive. That'll be your marine training I suppose. Takes balls. Breaking *in* to what is essentially a secure prison. That has to be a first.'

'Again, Mr Hickman, Bill, can I call you Bill? I have no idea—'

Wilson tag teamed him with the threat. 'Your sister. Bathsheba? Actress isn't she? Else wants to be. Up for RADA we hear.'

'Leave her out of it.'

Hickman piled on. 'Can't if she was involved.'

Gunn continued to play a straight bat. 'Involved in what?'

Wilson took over again. They were trying to knock Gunn out of his stride.

'That disguise, quite clever. Your sister helped you didn't she? Knows all about theatrical makeup, and wigs and disguises to be an actress. If she did, and we caution her, then question her about it, that's what we like to call an accessory. That means most likely she'll be charged as well as yourself, you know. Accessory to a serious crime. Maybe a custodial sentence. Hard to get into RADA when you have a criminal record I guess. Hollywood, forget getting a visa to go to the States either. What do you think superintendent?'

'Impossible I would think, shame really, a talented career destroyed before it began. All so needless.'

Gunn could admire the move on Hickman's part. The way Patton could admire Rommel. Attack your enemy at his weakest spot and he will surely succumb. Gunn's weak spot had to be his sister. Bubbling below Gunn tasted the rage, any threat against his sister would do that, as it was meant to do.

Gunn smiled instead. Hickman was throwing out a head fake. Unless they charged Gunn, there was nothing they could threaten against Bebba. No crime, no accessory to said non-crime. By now, Eddie would have squirrelled her away safe from everyone, including the police. It was chicken and egg. And Gunn was one tough chicken. Hickman was operating with smoke and mirrors, trying to goad him into a slip they could leverage against him. At that impasse, the door to the room clanged open.

A uniform poked her head in. 'Have a word sir, please?' Hickman looked annoyed at the interruption. Maybe he genuinely thought a veiled threat against the sister would crack Gunn's seamless granite surface.

She followed for emphasis: 'Urgent like.'

Hickman left the room leaving him and Wilson facing each other.

'So Gunn, get anything useful out of Rufus Wright? Nuttier than a fruit cake, Super says after he spoke to him yesterday. Thinks he's the devil or something. Isn't that right?'

'Honest to God Mr Wilson, I don't know what you're on about. In all these years never once met the psycho who killed my brother, Radcliffe visitor logs must show that.'

Wilson smirked. 'Sure. But off the books Gunn, you should think of your sister here. You two've only recently reunited haven't you? Shame if anything untoward were to happen.'

It took all of Gunn's self-control not to vault the table and remove the smirking threat from Wilson's face. *What the fuck did untoward mean anyway?* Fortunately the door opened, and in stepped a stunning woman.

She flashed her dazzling smile at him and directed her fiery gaze at Wilson, as the peeved looking Hickman trotted in after her.

'Don't say another word Mr Gunn. Sarah Olongo-

Hitchens, your lawyer.'

A razor's edge shorter than him, about five eleven, with legs past her elbows, her delectable skin shimmered like the smoothest, most expensive dark chocolate the Swiss have to offer. Her shortish Afro emphasized her beautiful, classical African face.

'Superintendent Hickman, I am shocked to find my client all alone, being interrogated after two in the morning without his lawyer present.'

Sarah winked at Gunn as Wilson stood up.

'Hardly an interrogation ma'am.'

Hickman stepped forward. 'Let me assure you Ms Olongo-Hitchens, Mister Gunn is not being interrogated. He's merely talking to us as a possible witness to a major incident.'

'Is that correct Mr Gunn?'

Gunn shrugged, still seething at the implied threats against Bebba. 'Seemed like a bit of an interrogation to me. They did tell me my rights again.'

Sarah bristled to her full height of Masai warrior level. 'Superintendent Hickman. Inspector Wilson. This is not my first date. And you two aren't my first condoms.'

Ha. Gunn loved this woman already.

'This is beginning to look like harassment. I must insist that my client is allowed to leave immediately unless you are prepared to formally arrest and charge him. Maybe I should mention this to my friend the Home Secretary, next time we meet on his Justice Review steering committee, which coincidentally, is in—' Sarah checked her watch, '—seven hours.'

Hickman graciously conceded defeat. Wilson looked angrier than a baby denied the tit.

'Okay, let's not detain Mr Gunn any longer Inspector. Find a constable to escort him and Miss Olongo-

Hitchens out the building.'

Wilson outwardly seething as he scuttled out of the room.

'Really Bill, I'm surprised. Always thought you were a strictly by the book chap? A Superintendent and an Inspector in on a non-interrogation? Bit hands-on for you?'

'Can't say anything Sarah. Probably saying too much me saying that.'

Gunn was mulling over what that oblique comment meant when Wilson reappeared almost instantly with a uniformed constable in tow.

Hickman resumed his previous stance as hard-nosed copper. 'Okay Mister Gunn, you are free to leave, though we may need to speak to you again at a later date.'

'Only in my presence Superintendent, I hope I've made myself unambiguously clear on that point.'

'Crystal.' Hickman acted the gentleman and indicated the door for the lady to leave first. 'After you Ms. Olongo-Hitchens.'

She led the way as Wilson and the constable trooped after her into the corridor. Gunn was about to follow them out, when Hickman grabbed his arm, yanking him hard back into the room.

Hickman leaned in close to Gunn's ear. 'Kill Club.' Talk about stopping someone dead in their tracks. 'Mean anything to you?'

Gunn didn't have to say yes or no, his unguarded expression had already betrayed his answer to Hickman.

Hickman looked relieved, as if the doctor confirmed it wasn't a heart attack merely indigestion. 'Say no more.'

Gunn seized the moment to say more. 'What's Spyglass?'

Now it was Hickman's turn to betray himself in a look.

Gunn could see the cogs turning. 'Honest son, don't give a flying fuck about your Radcliffe chicanery. Needed to rattle a few cages a bit, find out how much you know. And others.'

'What the—what's going on Superintendent?'

Hickman put a finger to his lips. 'Shtum. Outside. Fifteen minutes.'

Then Sarah was back. 'Everything okay Bill?'

'Absolutely, Mr Gunn was just leaving.'

Wilson a few seconds behind Sarah. 'Problem sir?'

Hickman smiled. 'Not at all Polo.'

36

The cusp of dark and dawn. Night once again defeated by the bright promise of a newly minted day, ripe and lush with rebirth and hope. Gunn saw nothing but darkness, despair and the pits of hell from the video message on his iPhone.

An hour earlier, outside Scotland Yard, the temperature had dropped to an unseasonable chill. Gunn thanked Sarah for dragging herself out in the dead of night to help him, then she was gone. The way she rushed out for Eddie when all good folks have taken to their bed? Was anything going on between them. He hoped so.

A nondescript Ford Mondeo pulled up. Gunn slid in, and Hickman headed towards Battersea, flashing effortlessly through near deserted streets.

'Okay Mr Hickman. I'm all ears.'

Hickman's intake of breath was audible. 'You never heard any of this from me.'

'Heard what?'

'Synchronous Photographic Integration Generating Lateral Advanced Surveillance Systems. SPI/GLASS.'

Gunn was already brain-fuddled. This didn't help. 'Sounds great. So?'

'High quality CCTV cameras are everywhere right? Part of the official surveillance network, controlled by the government and state proxies.'

'Yeah, Big Brother's watching.'

Hickman chuckled. 'You ain't seen nothing yet brother. After the two-thousand five bombers, then the wannabombers two weeks later caught on that lovely Hi-Def CCTV, everything changed. All these images are out there, all accessible eventually; but generally after an incident has occurred. SPI/GLASS is going to change all that.'

'But how does that—'

'Look, every day, in every way, GCHQ's massively fast super-computer is trawling the planet sucking up video data from anywhere. Facebook, YouTube, social networks, ATMs, garage forecourts, supermarkets, buses, cabs, stores, speed cams, TV News, internet and other footage which never makes the air. Constantly running facial recognition algorithms, against live feeds – as well as archived material. Let's say known Islamic terrorist sips a cappuccino on the Piazza San Marco in Venice, SPI/GLASS can spot him in real time. Doesn't matter if Osama bin terrorist's in disguise or had cosmetic surgery. Ten minutes later, Italian special forces are rolling to take him down.'

'All very riveting nineteen eighty-fourish stuff.'

'You been following the Mandy Monroe murder trial?'

'Wasn't it adjourned week before last, some unknown reason?'

'Known reason. Privately. Whiz-kid film producer Lawrence Summers didn't do it.'

'The guy who's on trial?'

Hickman winced. 'Yeah. Was me personally got him for the torture, rape and murder of an almost famous model who had a bit part in his last film, who he then stalked for two months. Compelling, irrefutable DNA from all sources, blood, skin, hair placed Summers on top of Mandy Monroe at her painful, over-kill death. And his alibi is pitiful, like the plot of one of his movies.'

Hickman slammed on his brakes as traffic lights

changed to amber then red on Chelsea Embankment. There wasn't another vehicle on the road either direction. Gunn clocked Hickman looking in his mirror. He'd done that a lot as he'd been driving and talking.

'Summers admits to being a minor coke head and small-time semi-supplier to the Soho media crowd. Claims he gets a call at his Wardour Street office enquiring whether he was interested in carrying a bigger weight. As it happens he does need a regular supply to gift to A-list Hollywoodenheads when they sign on for one of his movies. Our hero thinks he can score major industry points, if word's out to the latest hot young American actors that he has a private supply.'

Finally something Gunn could follow. Again he worried about Bebba being sucked into this sleazy end of the acting biz. *All part of the package luvvie.*

The light changed to green. Another glance in the rear-view before proceeding.

'Coke to the stars?'

'Precisely Micah. That bit rang true. The preposterous bit is this. Summers says mystery voice tells him to meet in the underground car park in Chinatown, off Shaftesbury Avenue, at ten p.m. He's to get in the back of the white Transit van on sub-level five. So he turns up, and should have been shit scared but he's snorted a line in his office, which has him feeling Carlos Escobar like invincible. Even though the bloke in the back of the van has on a hideous mask.

'Mask.'

'Yeah, you know like they wear in horror movies, twisted bloody slashed face. Our masked druggie offers a kilo of pure uncut powder from Venezuela, price is a must-buy bargain. Forty thousand, which to Summers is a totally doable business expense.'

'He's admitting all this?'

'Better than a rape-murder charge. The tale continues with Summers getting a small sample to test the merchandise. Van stops and it's outside his flat in Neal Street. Course, he's already paranoid from his earlier coke, they know where he lives. Horror mask tells Summers to go in, don't leave as they're watching, try the merchandise and they'll be back later to seal the deal. He's a coke head so naturally he snorts. Total mindbuzzer, his words. That's the last thing Summers said he remembered till the next day when we battered his door down.'

'You didn't buy it?'

'Doesn't matter. We checked his story anyway. The route he walked from Wardour Street to the Chinatown car park had Met cameras pointed at traffic and not people. Forensics checked the recorded footage, but Summers never showed up anywhere. CCTV in the car park had been down the whole day. Nothing on Neal Street with his flat either. No street cameras for the alleged van. No one saw him enter his flat at around the time he claims.'

'Case closed then. Even I know that.'

'Yeah. Till ten days ago. Some techno-bod at the Met is beta-testing SPI/GLASS and picks the Summers case at random. It could have been any case. She inputs Lawrence Summers facial recognition algorithm, just to see what turns up on his timeline.'

Crossing over Battersea Bridge, Gunn stared out of the car window as the first hints of the new day percolated in. 'And something did?'

Hickman laughed. 'Something so random no one could factor for. Next door to Summers' house is a small block of flats. One on the first floor is a holiday rental, with balcony. The new occupants had arrived that day, couple from Cincinnati, Ohio with their eleven year old son. The kid's into the whole social networking bit. So he sticks his wireless outdoor webcam on the balcony and points it down into Neal Street, so all his pals back home could check out Cool Britannia in real time. leaves it on 24/7. At precisely 11.03 p.m. GMT it picks up a white van pulling past and stopping. Back door opens, a man exits rapido. He staggers, then looks straight up into the webcam. It's Lawrence Summers. Alleged rapist murderer. The digitally stamped footage was archived on the Facebook server in the States.'

'Jesus, wasn't Mandy Monroe killed around the same time? So it couldn't have been him.'

Hickman was impressed Gunn had that little detail. He was even more impressed with his logical deduction.

'So basically you're thinking—you're thinking the forensics are overwhelming, not even circumstantial. Yet there's absolute proof Summers was somewhere else at the time the girl was murdered Then. He was—is, framed. And framed in a dead sophisticated way. Right?'

'Excellent deductive reasoning.'

'Practice.'

'In light of this new evidence I ran Mandy Monroe's facial algorithm through SPI/GLASS. There were no hits of Mandy Monroe and Lawrence Summers in close proximity, let alone together. The so called stalker who was supposed to have made her life hell.'

'Which sort of negates the whole stalker's code, I guess. That is to stalk.'

Hickman pulled up outside Gunn's house. 'Now that doesn't prove anything either way. But SPI/GLASS did pick up one face with Mandy Monroe on six separate occasions, in and around the West End in the month before her sad demise. And a name. A yank, Byron

Goolsbee. Thirtysomething. Successful. Made a mint in the city at one of those dodgy derivative places, then moved on a couple of years ago.'

Gunn blinked once at the name. then gulped involuntarily.

"I guess the name Goolsbee means something to you. Right Micah?'

37

Gunn caffeined up. He should get a few hours of zeds, but he was no longer open to civvy options. State Registered Nurse Micah Ishmael Gunn was on extended leave. Sergeant Gunn had stepped up, yomping on regardless, hacking it marine style. Nurse Gunn knew he probably shouldn't consider taking the Dexedrine tablets resting in the palm of his hand. He was weighing up the risk of *not* dropping a 10mg tab of pharmaceutical grade methamphetamine, compared to the health risk of actually taking it. All drugs are risky depending on the individual and the physical circumstances. For Gunn it was vital to the mission he stayed wide awake, so that made it an easy decision. Many of the marines he knew had taken speed when they were on extended missions. Stay alive? Make sure you stay awake and sharp first.

He washed down the two tabs with a full pint of tap water, churning over all the information he had absorbed in the past few hours.

The other Goolsbee info from Beth was surprising, but not an actual surprise as Gunn knew what the evil fucker was capable of with his little Kill Club. At that point he couldn't see any upside in not telling Hickman he already knew Byron Goolsbee was the guy with his bro's medallion stuffed up his arse. But that was all he gave up to Hickman. He never mentioned finding Stuart Roper's long-standing links to Goolsbee. Rufus Wright's Kill Club references. Nor his visit to Beth and her Oxford links back to Goolsbee and to Oliver Boodle.

The last thing Hickman did was warn Gunn against playing vigilante. The last thing Gunn wanted were the police being one step ahead of him as he personally nailed anyone involved in Zeke's murder. That rocket had launched and he was orbiting his prey, ready for the kill.

Back in the basement, he began checking out Companies House online to see what he could glean about CPH Limited. Companies House holds all the records for limited liability companies registered in England and Wales. CPH was first registered in 2007 and began trading the same year. The latest accounts released by the company were only for 2007/2008. It took him a minute to discover that for any real company information, revealing the names of shareholders and directors, had to be paid for and could then be downloaded electronically.

Gunn deployed the credit card. As he waited for the files to be emailed, he chugged back another mug of strong black coffee, reading through the original CPH brochure he had lifted from Stuart's office. Nothing popped, except the thought of how did the guy get all the time to do all this, whatever he did? Whatever this *Kill Club* was. Whoever was involved. Goolsbee for sure. Now Stuart Roper?

The small print on the back page stated CPH (Casey Property Holdings) 4th Floor, Baron House, Lower Vauxhall Road, London SW1 9QL. Registered: 8168814.

Clearly CPH was an abbreviation of the official company name. He was still mulling it over when the PC pinged to audibly tell him he had new email. Six PDF files were attached to the email from Companies House. He wanted to see who besides Stuart was involved, so he clicked on the one called DIRECTORS. The files automatically opened. It was very frustrating. The shareholding comprised four ordinary shares. One held by Stuart Roper, one held by another three limited companies. Nowhere did the name Goolsbee appear.

All Gunn saw was another visit to Companies House website to drill down into yet another set of companies. And who was to say that he wouldn't face the same task of unravelling myriad shell companies hiding their owners. All hidden in plain sight. The best place to hide.

Hiding in plain sight. That's when it hit Gunn. Casey Property Holdings. He couldn't believe it. Then he did. Was Roper that brazen? That arrogant? Yeah well, he already knew the answer to the arrogance question. Now all doubt was removed.

Casey. Kay Cee. KC. Kill Club.

'You fucker Stuart Roper. You total fucking fucker.' Gunn almost shouted Ziya-like at the computer, the brochure, the world. No longer the mildly amusing Roper the Groper.

Gotcha. Now what? Decision time. What next?

Gunn's iPhone sparked into life, Eric Burdon belting out, *There is a house in New Orleans, they call*—he picked it up and nixed the ring, seeing that his phone's display was informing him he had received one video message.

If it was bad before, learning the truth about his brother, Gunn's life was about to turn into hell on earth.

38

In the early hours of the morning, St. Michael's Hospital basement seemed even more devoid of life than usual. Since Victorian times, St. Michael's had been the chief mortuary and cold storage unit for all suspicious deaths south of the river, so it made sense to base a futuristic forensic mortuary on the site. The entrance to the new Forensics Post Mortem Complex was at the end of a neon-lit corridor.

—CLOP—CLOP—CLOP—

The corridor echoed to the relentless momentum of Gunn's footsteps. It was a very movie moment. The iconic scene in *Point Blank* reverberated in Gunn's head like an unwelcome guest for Christmas lunch. Lee Marvin as the sympathetic, brutal criminal Walker. Ruthless with an eye for an eye code. Lee Marvin, the real life US Marine, the real tough guy playing Walker: walking, walking, walking along the seemingly endless corridor. The cold fusion light burning into Gunn's brain. Like Walker, relentless, remorseless, emotionless. Less than human.

—CLOP—CLOP—CLOP—

It was exactly the state in which Gunn had imagined himself to be. When he had finally hunted down Stuart like the rabid beast he was. When Gunn killed Kill Club. All of them. He no longer cared what happened to him. That ceased to be a defining factor the moment he recognized Zeke's St. Christopher's medal. He was all in: buried deep in someone else's shit. Now it was his shit.

Before he had taken the backstairs down to the basement, Gunn paid a quick visit to the Hospital security hub. His mate Phil was still on duty. Gunn strode into the Monitor Room, all business like. Phil and a younger colleague, in his pristine uniform, were drinking something hot and hideous from the multiple-choice vending machine outside in the corridor.

'Mick? Jesus, how you doin' mate?'

Gunn's stone face gave nothing away. 'No worries pal.' Then he locked on Phil and made with the eyes to indicate he wanted rid of his young oppo. 'Got some scran corps talk if you're interested mate.'

Phil got the message. 'Time we had a sweep 'n' check on the car park. There's a good lad.'

The kid looked pleased to get away from Phil and his boring stories. Gunn waited till his footsteps faded out of earshot and got straight down to it. 'You up to be my oppo on a top secret mission, mucker? Life and death. No fucking about.'

Phil instantly straightened up Colour Sergeant ramrod style.

Gunn used the restricted area key card to unlock the main door and enter the dead zone. The harsh florescent lighting was even more dazzling than the outside corridor. He had changed into the spare set of blue nursing scrubs he always kept stored in his staff locker. The surgical mask, operating room skull cap and gloves completed the uniform. He was heading down the main interior corridor which ran at a ninety degree right angle to the outside access corridor, and the main security entrance. He had his target: the cold storage units at the farthest end, which meant he had to *clip clop* past the six post mortem rooms. At the door he paused for a second. Crap—this was not good. It was occupied, this early too. The dull intonation of a forensic post mortem bled out. The voices, or rather one main booming voice was coming from Forensic Suite 3. Gunn stopped for a quick glance in through the clear glass porthole window.

Gunn's phone vibrated in his pocket.

'Yeah Phil.'

'Probably nothing, two obvious coppers drove into the main car park in a dark blue Ford Mondeo.'

Gunn was already on the move as he clicked Phil off. The booming voice receded at pace and then Gunn was standing outside a set of double swing doors. The sign on the wall above the doors helpfully informed Gunn he had reached the BODY STORAGE UNIT, as far the CCTV coverage reached. He was on his own as he swung in and looked around for the location of Cold Room C, Tray 7. The air was cold. *Dead cold.* The chilling effect had made his boots echo even more loudly on the hard, non-slip floor with its dull maroon finish.

C7. It wasn't difficult to locate the body as the system was idiot proof, which was just as well because he was acting like the world's biggest idiot. His first call should have been to Hickman. Gunn convinced himself to ignore that instinct. This was the only way. Then he bounced back to *that's crazy*. But the whole thing was a crazy situation, so maybe *crazy* was also the solution.

Cold Room 'C' contained fifteen coffin sized stainless steel containers on the wall opposite the heavy, see-though plastic swing doors leading in. The containers were in a row of five, stacked three high: *stack 'em and rack 'em.* The numbering ran from top left to bottom right, and each cold unit had its large number stamped in the metal door, then embossed with navy blue, acrylic metallic paint. Gunn went straight to number seven, almost dead centre in the middle row. On the door were a number of items vital to the forensics facility. A small digital readout displayed the individual tray's temperature at minus 20 degrees Celsius. In the six inch by three inch metal card holder below it, a handwritten card had pertinent details written in a blue biro.

PERSON UNKNOWN
Arrived – 16/5, 11.31
Post Mortem – 18/5, 15.05
Cold Storage – 18/5, 20.27

Gunn opened the door and pulled on the metal handle. The spring-loaded trolley rolled out slowly, revealing its dead weight. There he was, or what was left of him. Byron Goolsbee, mass murderer of this parish.

The frozen stiff body was laid out on a linen sheet which stopped the body adhering to the metal tray. Gunn knew that the police had identified Goolsbee a few days ago. The fact that Hickman was keeping the ID under ice-cold wraps as an *unknown*, could only mean one thing. Hickman must want the person who had tried mightily to make Goolsbee a non-person to continue thinking he had succeeded. But Gunn knew something Hickman did not. The name of Goolsbee's killer. Stuart Roper already knew his former Kill Club comrade had been identified. And he also seemed to know he had missed something on the body. Goolsbee had dragged himself with inhuman strength from his killing room, taking something else with him besides Zeke's medallion. Something Stuart did not want to chance trying to retrieve himself. That made sense.

The wounds were grievous, but he had no doubt the brutal, wicked things done to this particular meat suit were richly deserved. He had no duty of care to this monster. He was glad Goolsbee suffered so much before he died. After what he had done to Zeke. And Beth. He hoped Goolsbee's torment went on for a long time.

The Y shaped wound on Goolsbee's chest had been roughly stitched close, following the removal of the heart and the other organs for analysis. Unfortunately the body was the wrong side up for Gunn's purposes.

It's not so easy flipping over an evenly spread dead weight of about fifteen stone. Rigor mortis had long since dissipated, but the body was frozen. Even in the chilled air, Gunn worked up a quick sweat trying to get Goolsbee over onto his stomach for easier access.

He finally had the body flipped, and was reaching into his rucksack for the vital implements picked up en route. *Shit on a stick* – his mobile phone vibrated again.

Gunn:	Phil.
Phil:	Sarge, them two coppers are at reception. Heading down for a PM.
Gunn:	Cheers marine. Nearly done.

—WHOOSH—THUMP—WHOOSH—THUMP—

Everyone panics. Gunn knew that from front line experience. And everyone is scared. Anyone who says different is either lying or on excellent drugs. The hero is the one who panics and nobody knows. The hero is the one who is scared shitless, but carries on regardless. Gunn forced himself to stop dead in his tracks. He relaxed his hands and shook them, as if casting water off his skin. It was a familiar and comforting ritual. He did the same to his arms, gradually working his way through his torso and legs until he had relaxed his whole body. At the same time he took long deep breaths in, exhaling slowly.

The room quietened. Gunn removed the chrome plated rectal spreader from the rucksack. Spreading Goolsbee's legs, he inserted the four pronged end into the body's frozen anus. The turning handle on the spreader worked on the slow ratchet principle, necessary when the subject is alive and the doctor wants to avoid accidental tearing. Gunn turned the handle as fast as he could go and was soon ripping the dead flesh open, stretching past the point it would normally be safe. He stopped when Goolsbee's anal passage had cracked open to fist size. Even with his high tolerance for gross, Gunn was hoping whatever he was looking for would simply plop out. Like the medallion. No such luck as whatever it was had been frozen in place, like a lolly at the bottom of a freezer. He had to stick his hand up Goolsbee's rectum, right up to the wrist. Gunn poked around and there it was.

He pulled and pulled and pulled. It took tremendous effort until Gunn finally yanked the small plastic freezer bag from Goolsbee's arse. Holding the object at arm's length, he hurried to the small stainless steel sink, running hot water over the bag until he was satisfied he had washed away all the ick factor. The visible ick factor. Only then did he open the clip-seal bag to see exactly what he had retrieved. Two red USB thumb drive memory sticks. They must have been important given the extreme lengths (and depths) Goolsbee had taken to hide them. Gunn didn't have time to return the body into the same position as he found it. Time to get the hell out of there. He was about to push the tray back into its compartment and close the door on Goolsbee when—

'Who the bleeding hell are you sunshine?'

39

2007.

Something was not right. Samir Shah QC knew that. He had felt it for a long time. Nothing tangible, merely a nagging doubt, and it always seemed to revolve around the same department in Scotland Yard. He had a nose for these things.

As a successful barrister for many years, he had defended the innocent and the guilty. He always knew which was which. There was rarely ambiguity. No Hollywood movie doubt. He had heard colleagues claim to maintain a detached air, a Chinese wall over their clients innocence or guilt. That was a fairy tale they told themselves, perhaps so they could sleep at night. They knew. But that didn't matter to Mr Samir Shah QC. He had been sworn to offer the finest defence a client's money can buy at the dynamic *Advocacy Chambers*, Lincoln's Inn Field. That had been his job. And he was very good at his job. Juries liked him because he was sharp, witty and personable. His tanned complexion with a hint of the Med, jet black hair and piercing blue eyes gave him the look of a movie star, even in his late forties. Some thought he was a dead ringer for Johnny Depp. Others mentioned Al Pacino in his Godfather days – one and two, of course. Not three.

So life was good for Samir Shah. Until that fateful day when Sammy (everyone called him Sammy) had chosen to defend a man accused of rape. And not simply one drunken assault after a loutish night, as horrendous as that crime was, even taken in isolation. The man's alleged offences were *multiple* rapes stretching fifteen years back. Planned and executed with a vicious and cruel cunning. The man was guilty of course. Sammy knew that from their first interview, before he had personally reviewed the forensic evidence. That was the problem for the prosecution, the forensics were weak to the point of nonexistent. That was not a problem for Sammy. The rapist had been evilly sly in the way he forced his victims to bathe and scrub themselves down in scalding water, with an added bottle of bleach. He had begun his exploits after the development of more advanced DNA identifying techniques, and so ran his own counter-forensic measures.

His victims were usually left terrified, crippled with fear and vulnerability. It was they who received the life sentence. Which made many of them easy prey for a top barrister at the top of his game. Easy prey for Samir Shah. There were rules to protect rape victims in court, but a skilled lawyer like Sammy could get around those without too much difficulty. Casting doubt being the basis of English jurisprudence. People may not like it, but Sammy knew that if it was them standing innocently in the dock, their whole future depending on the whim of twelve fellow citizens; then they would want a ferocious Sammy Shah on their side.

A week after Sammy had celebrated another successful not guilty verdict, one of the rapists many victims took her own life by throwing herself under a tube train rattling into Piccadilly station. She left a note apologizing to her family, her friends, and the staff of London Underground, for leaving such a mess behind for them to clean up. But she felt she could not go on knowing her living nightmare was going to happen to her all over again at some point to be determined.

It was that message which shook Samir to his immortal soul. He had destroyed her testimony in court, implying that she was a fantasist out for publicity. He was only ever nominally religious before. Going through the motions. Now he returned to praying five times a day.

Sammy's chance for redemption came two months later. The rapist he defended was dead. Caught in the act of another rape by a victim's dad who then chased and hunted him down, before battering his head twenty times with a heavy frying pan from his own kitchen. His latest client was found not guilty on the charge of murdering Sammy's previous client. The man walked from court a free man, a national hero and a book deal. It was Sammy's greatest triumph as a QC. It was also his last case as a defence lawyer, and he took no fee whatsoever.

Sammy walked from court a guilty man with a conscience still to salve. He wanted to pray, meditate and rethink where he was going in this life. And even more importantly to him: the next life. He ignored all the material lure (easy to do when you already have a few million in the bank) and praised God that he had shown him the true way.

Sammy joined the Crown Prosecution Service, and added his star power to prosecuting the guilty to the maximum extent of the law. Naturally Sammy assumed that at some point he would be running the whole shop as the Director of Public Prosecutions, appointed by the Attorney General himself on behalf of a grateful nation.

Something was not right. Samir Shah knew that.

He had felt it for a long time. Nothing tangible, only a nagging doubt, and it always seemed to revolve around the same department in Scotland Yard. He had a nose for these things. Now that he had risen to Deputy Head of the Special Crime Division he was making a concerted follow-up. Like most converts to any cause, he was also rather fanatical about his revised beliefs.

Sammy had joined the Crown Prosecution Service the year following the murder of fifty two people on the London underground. He had no doubt his name and background accelerated his progress to date. So what? That's real life, get over it. The bombers had all died, so there was no prosecutorial element. He was still getting up to speed on being that guy: the guy he used to humiliate in court.

That's when the questionable file crossed his desk. Again no prosecution was necessary as it was a final internal case review of a corrupt policeman, a Detective Sergeant Fletcher Everton Hoodeson, had been murdered by one of his gangland buddies. All that remained was for Sammy to sign off on it as a *case closed*. Which he was about to do until he skimmed through the forensic reports on Hoodeson and Billy Ferguson. Sammy loved expert opinion like this. His forte had always been his ability to discredit experts in court. He lived for that. For every expert one side sported he could usually find reasonable doubt with his own expert looking at exactly the same facts. It always comes down to interpretation and probabilities. That's reasonable doubt. That's why he never depended upon some listless junior to go through the boring minutiae and report back the headlines to the big boss. God was in the details. Everyone should know that.

In this case he could not get past the non-fatal bullet wound to the left side of Hoodeson's head. A 9mm shell had miraculously ricocheted off the man's dome, leaving a groove in his skull, without penetrating. Not such a lucky bastard though, proved by the second bullet penetrating his right eye socket, before tearing through his brain.

The problem? How could it be a contemporaneous wound to the kill shot through Hoodeson's right eye socket, when the forensic examination had indicated the presence of a disinfectant on the first bullet wound, and other superficial facial abrasions? To Sammy the most obvious reason, was the obvious. What was disinfectant used to do? Clean a wound. Which led to the logical next question, how did a man shot twice in the head in a derelict barn get up and clean the non-fatal first wound?

No one wanted to even ask that question, let alone answer it. There were enough cases to prosecute without creating more.

It reminded Sammy of a case he had lost a few years back when he was defending Martin Forbes, charged with strangling his ex-lover Adam Hanna. He hated losing of course. But you win some, you lose some. He had never lost like this though. The prosecution case was a slam dunk. More damning DNA and other evidence than you could shake a judge's wig at. Sammy knew guilt. He could smell it on the accused, no matter how hard they tried to disguise it. He smelt ruthlessness. He smelt ambition. He smelt despair. One thing he didn't smell on Marty Forbes was guilt.

Sammy had his private investigator check out the Met's lead copper on the Forbes case, Detective Inspector Bill Hickman, to see if any unknown connections popped. The Met may have cleaned up its act but it did have a history of corruption to live down. Nothing. Unlike now. The one salient fact that Sammy could not possibly see at the time. Detective Sergeant

Hoodeson had worked as part of the same D.I. Hickman's team briefly, before being seconded to work undercover on an international investigation into the importation of cocaine and illegal arms. Hickman was a direct connection between two cases. Sammy believed in God. He didn't believe in coincidences. It was a sign.

He was disappointed but not surprised when the jury delivered the guilty verdict against Forbes. All he could do was appeal for as long as possible on behalf of his client. Each one rejected right up to the final rebuff by the then final arbitration of the House of Lords. The case against Forbes was airtight and appeal proof.

What to do next was Sammy's dilemma. He was already unpopular with his new colleagues. Jealousy no doubt. He had been parachuted in above most of them. Sammy was golden. He prayed for guidance. He needed to tell someone of his suspicions. Someone he could trust. Alex Furlough, his friend and leading Silk at Advocacy Chambers, his former home.

When Sammy phoned Alex, it wasn't a good time for his former colleague. He had recently had very energetic sex with his new, fifteen years younger lover. Not only was she a phenomenally aggressive commercial litigator, she was also pneumatically limber in bed – and insatiably game for round two. Luckily for Alex, the Viagra did exactly what it said on the bottle. Sammy ran through his suspicions about the Hoodeson case to his distracted former colleague. Mainly to get rid of him, Alex agreed to meet the following week at White's for a late supper. Sammy would have preferred sooner, but Alex said he was off to the states to visit Advocacy Chambers recently acquired Washington D.C. based commercial law firm. Sammy would also have preferred another venue to Alex's posh club, *Whites*. He hated all the obsequious bowing and scraping. Most of all, now that Sammy no longer allowed himself alcohol, in line with his rediscovered piety, he would have to sit and watch as Alex savoured a fifty year old brandy that was once his own favourite tipple.

That was a small price as Sammy felt able to relax for the first time in a month. Alex was probably the only person whose advice he felt merited any consideration on his own level. Yes, the man was a massive snob, but he also had a forensic-like ability to strip any problem down to its base elements and thereby discover its true meaning.

The evening before he was to meet Alex at Whites, Sammy was late home to his swish Knightsbridge pied-à-terre, off Sloane Square, a stones throw from Harrods. Since he and his wife Georgina had split, he tended to spend most of his time there. Alone. Unfortunately she had not shared Sammy's newly rediscovered religious zeal. She had been baptized Church of England, attending to her soul by attending her local church twice a year: Christmas Day for the Birth and Easter Monday for the Resurrection. More than sufficient for God to spot her and the children keeping the faith. The year Sammy spent *finding himself* had been the final straw for her.

They grabbed him as soon as he closed the front door. Three men in black boilersuits. One of them pressed a handgun hard into his cheek and raised his finger to his mouth to give the international sign for *don't say a fucking word*. Sammy mutely complied.

One of the others forced a glass of water down Sammy's throat. Not long after that, his head started to feel woozy and his muscles ceased to function properly. Sammy was half-conscious of being carried to the bathroom and stripped naked, before one of them took his electric shaver and shaved every hair from his body. Why would they do that? It half reminded him of something but it was hard to remember what.

They carried Sammy into his bedroom and fully redressed him in traditional Pakistani tribal garb: a baggy white Salwar Kameezto, like his great-granddad used to wear back in Hyderabad. Sammy was like a floppy rag doll as two of them manhandled him onto his knees next to the side of the bed. Naturally he flopped forward, face-down into the duvet. When Sammy started to choke, one of them turned his head sideways so that he could breath. That's when he noticed the rucksack on his bed.

From his position Sammy could also see the small television perched on the chest of drawers. It was showing Sky News. One of the men put a pile of DVD cases next to the flatscreen, before sliding a disc into the slot on the TV. Arabic writing appeared on the screen, followed by some disturbing handheld camcorder footage of American and British military vehicles being blown up with roadside bombs. Sammy recognized that all right. It was the type of sick Jihadist DVDs unfortunately available in many street markets in Britain. He had been warning about this disgusting stuff for years.

Why were they doing this? One of the men dropped a large transparent plastic bag of four inch nails next to the rucksack, together with a similar bag full of shiny ball-bearings. One of the others carefully placed a large plastic food-container next to the rucksack.

By now Sammy half-realized what was going on. He had read enough about the London Tube bombing to recognize the signature. Inside the container there was probably a significant amount of highly volatile acetone peroxide wired into a detonator to provide the heat-spark necessary to initiate the unstoppable reaction. Sammy knew acetone peroxide is very powerful explosive that can be home manufactured out of household stuff off the shelf at any supermarket, like drain cleaner, acetate, and nail varnish. With a small amount of skill and massive care, the chemicals can be mixed and reduced into a crystallized form. Add a little sulphuric acid and it's—KABOOM.

The men left shortly after that, scattering random Jihadist pages downloaded from the internet throughout the flat. One of them stuffed the nails and ball-bearings into the rucksack, placing it next to Sammy's head. The plastic container was placed in front of his face. Samir Shah QC (called to the bar in1987, took Silk as a QC in 1997) could see the mobile phone through the opaque plastic. The last thing he thought was *why?* The final thing he saw on this earth was the phone screen light up to indicate an incoming call. He felt the phone vibrate for the shortest time. He didn't hear the explosion, though *that* was heard half a mile away. His head was found quite a distance away, but not quite that far.

Commander Fred Needles of MI6, stood in doorway to what was left of the proto-terrorist's bedroom. Two of his brightest young things flanked him.

He shook his head in savage disappointment. 'Sammy Shah for Christ's sake. Knew him at Cambridge. We were both in the Glorious Vine Society.'

Jenny Sinclair was also a product of Cambridge, two decades later of course, but still? To think a fellow alumnus was capable of this. It stung. Probably even more than Burgess and McLean to those of the dying off generation. Of course, some of the Cambridge brigade thought the old Stalinist commies were heroes anyway.

'Wonder where he was recruited?'

Dave Lowden wasn't stung by Shah's academic antecedents. He was a product of the army via John Moores Uni, and had absolutely *no fucking time* for the Oxbridge boys and girls mutual masturbation club. Though he would do Jenny in a heartbeat, even with her recent engagement to the Hooray Henley banker.

Jenny answered her own question before Dave could weigh in. 'Our friends in Tel Aviv and Langley may have a line on that.'

Needles was not so sure. 'Got a feeling this is a classic lone wolf operation Jennifer. David, initial thoughts please'

He preened slightly. Time to show Army beating Oxbridge bluebloods. 'Bomb, acetone peroxide based. No plastic. Amateur home-cooking night in. No body to speak of, which means he was probably leaning over the device when he Irished it. No indication he was part of a cell planning a coordinated spectacular – or the Islamist version thereof. Probable target Whites, heart of the infidel establishment. Have to go with the Sudden Jihadi Syndrome, lone wolf scenario sir. Guy gets religion. Guy splits with anglo missus and kids, nominally being raised C of E. Guy gets obsessed with Al-Qaeda style beheading porn videos. Guy wakes up one morning. Guy goes full-on seventy-two virgins fanatic. End of.'

Jenny was a bit miffed Dave had come up with the most plausible scenario first, based on what they knew. She sort of liked his rough edges though, and was big enough to acknowledge a colleague's insight. 'I concur, sir.'

'Good, that's the line the political PR bods are pushing. Don't worry sheeple, it's all under control. Merely a lone nutter. Back to sleep now.'

Needles gave the room one last sad scope before

turning to leave. 'Sammy Shah, home-grown terrorist. What's the world coming too?'

40

'Who the bleeding hell are you sunshine? And what's that bleeding frozen body doing arse up, tits down?'

Gunn spun around fast to face his questioner, a sparsely haired, middle-aged man wearing pale green orderly scrubs and a quilted blue anorak. Gunn sized him up. The man was six three, seventeen stone, gut flabby. Gunn was sure he had seen the man around the hospital, and was also sure that his own identity was concealed thanks to his surgeons' cap and OR mask.

Gunn didn't want to hurt some *Ordinary Bloke* doing his job. But collateral violence happened. This was likely one of those times. Gunn edged forward with a half shuffle.

'Don't come any closer you fucking pervert.'

Great—thinks I'm into necrophilia.

The big bloke reached into the pocket of his anorak. That was all the opening Gunn needed. The shock of Gunn's speed in closing in on him put the big bloke back on his heels.

Gunn reached the man fast and sideways on. He was perfectly positioned to plant his feet so he could gain maximize leverage, before savagely punching the OB four times in the belly rapid fire: *right, left, right, left.* The surprised punch-bag sagged down faster than a sadly deflated hot air balloon, dropping onto one knee before toppling sideways, sprawling grotesquely on the ground. The guy tried to speak, maybe even shout out *help*, but all he managed was a strangulated whimper.

One look at the flailing blob satisfied Gunn that the OB was going nowhere fast or slow. He stepped over the winded guy and exited the cold room back into the corridor.

Left and right empty. Gunn ran. But he was not running for his own life. He was running for someone else's life.

As he flashed past the still occupied Forensic Suite 3, the terrible images flashed in his mind again.

An hour earlier Gunn's iPhone had sparked into life with the display informing him he had received one video message, and was asking to either *play or save*. He had pressed play, abandoning all hope as he entered through the gates of hell.

The video opened with a long shot in a dark place. Gunn could barely make out anything. It was dark but not pitch black. There was low level extraneous sound, although not voices. Footsteps on a rough floor. It was definitely inside and not outside. Then someone switched on a light, and the figure in the distance became visible. It looked to be woman, who seemed to be standing naked with her arms in the air. Her hair was dark.

Gunn started to feel lightheaded. Bile leapt into the back of his throat as the horror smashed into his consciousness

Ziya. Jesus lord, it's Ziya.

Slowly the camera zoomed in and up to a close-up on Ziya's restraints. She wasn't *holding* her arms in the air. She was strung up by a steel chain attached to metal manacles on either wrist, dangling from overhead pipes. Her arms had been slashed repeatedly, blood had obviously flowed copiously at first, but by now it had congealed almost black. The camera remorselessly and slowly panned down revealing the gut-wrenching slices and cuts.

Gunn could hardly breathe. His eyes swam watching a pornographic display of cruelty and wickedness. He was disoriented, almost as if floating out of his own body. He was conscious of what was happening with his physiological response. But the knowledge could not help mitigate his unstoppable reaction. He was physically unable to *pull himself together*. He understood that his body and mind had gone into instantaneous psychological shock. The medical term is *acute stress reaction*.

The scene was too much to bear. Imagining what was coming caused his body to swing out of sync: heartbeat, blood-pressure were fluctuating wildly. His body was being hit by acetylcholine released from pre-ganglionic sympathetic nerves, in turn flooding him with epinephrine and norepinephrine from his adrenal glands. Massive jolts of stimulants exploding his body into instant physical reactions, triggering increases in heart rate and breathing, constricting some blood vessels, except where the body needs the over-flow for action: muscles, brain, lungs, and heart. Also known as *flight or fight*. Very useful when he was in Iraq being chased by murderous intent. But right here, right now in his own house, he had no one to fight and nowhere to fly. The problem being the two tablets he just popped: as member of the amphetamine family of drugs, they had also released norepinephrine into Gunn's system, at speed.

The camera had panned down past the strung up arms, reaching the top of the Ziya's head, slumped forward on her chest.

Oh Christ Ziya.

Ziya's slumped head filled the iPhone's small screen and the panning down of the camera stopped at that point. *Ziya*. Gunn eye's filled and he could barely make out what he was seeing through the watery daze. So far there had been no spoken word, but it was not silent. In his diminished capacity Gunn was still aware of extraneous sounds. Was that heavy breathing?

There were other random noises, maybe distant cars passing. They were so faint as to be unrecognizable. From nowhere a surgically gloved hand entered the screen. The hand was attached to an arm covered in a black material, maybe a workman's overalls. Obviously it could not have belonged to the person operating the iPhone video camera. Stuart was not alone. Add in Goolsbee and that made three monsters. Kill Club. It was real.

The disembodied hand grabbed Ziya's hair roughly, mercilessly, and began to pull up her head, as if she was nothing but a piece of meat.

For now we see through a glass, darkly.

In his despair Gunn squeezed his eye lids tightly shut, then pulled up his own hand to rub away the leaking silent flow of tears darkening his vision and clouding his mind.

YOMP IT FUCKER, stop blubbing like a baba, and fucking yomp it bootneck.

Gunn pulled himself back from the ledge and opened his eyes. Dead, eyeless sockets greeted him. He stared at her, twice removed from the absolute horror of Ziya's death at the hands of the ghouls in human form. Then to his everlasting shame and horror, a feeling washed over him. For a second only, maybe, but it was there all the same. It was pure joy that he felt. A momentary surge as he realized that the dead body was not whom he had feared.

It was not Ziya.

He had been fooled by the woman's hair which looked dark from a distance. The blood from the savage, brutal cuts on her arms must have flowed like a swollen river down to her head, matting her hair into a dark sticky mess. Turning her delicate, beautiful strawberry blonde into a dark morass.

The naked body dangling from a meat hook was unmistakably that of Kirsty Smith. The feisty Jockette, so full of life that she dazzled innocent bystanders without sunglasses. Now gone.

The video went blank for a couple of seconds before the screen burst back into depraved life. The camera had been pulled back slightly to reveal a scene almost exactly the same, but with one additional element. Kirsty was still dead, strung up, displayed like a piece of meat to be humiliated again, even in death. That would never change. Gunn clenched his fists as tight as his jaw. Tighter.

Dangling next to Kirsty Smith was the sum of all his fears. This young woman was also humiliatingly naked, arms up, forced to stand open and totally exposed to the depraved indifference of her murderous captors. but unlike Kirsty, she had lengths of grey duct tape wrapped tightly around her head to smother her mouth.

Gunn felt another surge of joy. Her eyes were open and blinking back the tears. He was so connected he could physically feel the very terror gripping her whole body, but Gunn did not despair.

It was Ziya. For some reason she was still alive.

He hadn't been there for Zeke. For Ginny. For Megan. He was there now. And this time he was going to save her.

Or die trying.

41

St. Mike's was yawning itself awake—stretching its collective limbs to tackle another day. Nobody gave a second glance to a scrubbed up nurse, rushing at speed.

Gunn was still running for Ziya's life as he zipped down the hospital corridor, still in his scrubs, hat and mask.

From the forbidden zone at the rear of the hospital, Gunn raced to the chain link fence which formed the boundary of the official hospital grounds. Beyond the fence was a good forty yards of demolished rubble, formerly an old bonded warehouse for the Customs & Excise. The derelict land led down to the river and the old dock landing. A sign proclaimed the land would soon be the St Michael's Cancer Cure Centre for the research and treatment of all cancers.

As he effortlessly scaled the fifteen foot barrier, the only cancer interesting Gunn went by the name of Stuart Roper. He had a cure for him alright. The combination of high motivation, adrenalin, caffeine and meth amphetamine put Gunn on turbo power.

Gunn guessed the only reason why Ziya was still alive: she was the live bait to lure him onto a hook. The video had ended with a close up of Ziya's terror filled eyes clearly pleading for her life, before panning left to the dead eye-sockets of Kirsty Smith. The implication was clear to Gunn, this is what was going to happen to her *unless*.

He forced himself to step back and examine his

predicament. The video was the skilled psychological torture of an irredeemable sadist, that was sure. He remembered the always literary Zeke, aged eleven, quoting him Orwell's description of utter hopelessness: *if you want a picture of the future, imagine a boot stamping on a human face—for ever.* That was it. The whole foul *it*.

It seemed everything was being carefully designed to keep him off-balance and focused on one thing. Stuart Roper was going to kill Ziya no matter what, as soon as she ceased to be a means to the end, an end which he couldn't quite see yet.

Keep that up front marine.

Gunn had stood immobile in his own basement, fists and jaw clenched after the horror video ended. Time had become a nebulous construct at that point. Then the text message. Again the sender was *unknown*. The message was all in capital letters.

> LUV MOVIE? UNLESS WANT DEAD SAD ENDING, GO2 FORENSICS @ST MIKE'S, FIND GOOLS BODY IN C7, RETRIEVE PACKAGE FROM SAME PLACE AS MEDALLION WAS. AWAIT FURTHER INSTRUCTS. TELL POLICE OR EDDIE SHE DIES

He sped across the rubble strewn site, pulling off his surgical mask and hat on the run, trying to appear marginally less incongruous.

Once through the gate into Customs Row, he changed down from running fast to speed walking back to the Saab. The car was parked about fifty yards up the road, near the junction with Hercules Road and Gino's. The very place where he had treated Kirsty to breakfast only a week ago. Now she was gone. Just like that. The delicious Celtic firecracker Kirsty Smith – the pocket Jockette – who was looking for love and found it, but not with him.

That's when the violent aftershock hit. He was strapped to a wall, and a wrecking ball was smashing straight into his chest, over and over and over. Obliterating him. Gunn was leaning against a low wall next to his car. Gasping for breath as he struggled to suppress wave after wave of primal sobs, welling up from deep in his guts. Gunn slumped down against the wall holding both hands over his face. His body heaving uncontrollably as his throat closed up and his eyes squeezed shut.

What's happening to me?

He had felt joy—FUCKING JOY, that it was his sparky, funny friend Kirsty, and not Ziya, hanging dead from a chain, eyes gouged out. It was a hideous truth that would be stomping on his face. Forever. And he couldn't even tell anyone what had happened. Least of all Eddie. Not because of the texted warning not to tell anyone. Fuck that. Under any other circumstance his first and only move would have been involving his best mate. He needed Eddie, with his specialist skills, and tactical nous. But not for this mission. Gunn couldn't involve his skilled marine mucker because when he had finally finished with Dr Stuart Roper, it was quite likely he would be spending time in gaol. Probably a lifetime. He couldn't bear the thought of dragging Eddie into that. No way. He'd need Eddie to look out for Bebba and Ziya while he was gone away.

A gaggle of Japanese tourists had stopped touristing en masse and were staring at Gunn from across the street. This was better than Big Ben. Two of the women started giggling, and then they all began taking snaps of the strange looking white man, dressed all in blue, heaving in silent sobs on the ground.

If only they knew. Ten minutes ago he had his gloved hand shoved right up the arse of a dead man. Two days ago he had observed Rufus Wright extract his secreted away stash of medications. A week ago he was washing excrement off his murdered brother's St. Christopher. As the insane incongruity those images hit him, Gunn's suppressed sobs morphed into a manic laugh, cascading across to the Japanese gaggle making them giggle even more uproariously at this oddball Briton.

Gunn pulled himself together and dragged himself into his car.

42

Gunn had a choice. Pop another speed tab. Or hack it. He slipped the tab back in his wallet. Later maybe. His mind was already clicking away at maximum thrust and he couldn't chance another China Syndrome near-meltdown over Ziya, not unless he was absolutely hanging out, dead on his feet. The distant police sirens were approaching fast as he was heading west past the South Bank. Three police cars hurtled east straight back along Lambeth Palace Road, towards St. Michael's hospital. The big orderly must have finally gotten his second wind and called it in.

He drove with the mobile on his lap. So far he had not received the promised instructions with what he was to do with the memory sticks. It was a fine line, he tried not to think of what they were doing to Ziya. The longer the delay in their next move, the more time he had to work out where Ziya was being held in London's seven hundred square miles. Those solo odds sounded greater than him inventing the universal cure for all cancers within the next day. *No chance.*

Despite his earlier decision about going it alone, all Gunn's marine training screamed one word: *backup*. He couldn't trust anyone to get his back. Except one. He needed Eddie's cunning counsel. If Gunn didn't make it, no force on the planet would stop his friend exacting natural justice somehow. That was an unspoken code between men who had already fought to the death for each other. First though, Gunn had to make sure Eddie knew Stuart was the nail he needed to hammer. But even above that natural thirst for revenge, Eddie's first and only priority would be to ensure Bebba's safety.

Gunn had been so concentrated on his potential next moves, he couldn't recall a thing about driving back. Then like the answer to all his prayers, there it was. Parked on the double yellow near the corner, Eddie's sleek, gleaming black BMW 6 Series Coupé.

The video clobbered Eddie with a kick in the guts.

'God almighty Micah.'

Gunn said nothing. He had relived the horror for the third time.

They sat in silence. Eddie noted how dreadful his mate looked compared to only 12 hours ago. Eyes red-rimmed. Skin clammy. Eddie guessed an amphetamine drop. He had done it himself more that once.

Finally Gunn dragged himself up. 'All in mate.'

'Hell and fucking back. Let's yomp.'

Eddie's first job was trying to access the two memory sticks Goolsbee had taken such pains to hide. It took him less than sixty seconds to see it was no go. The flash drives were protected with an impressive mil spec encryption defence. While it may be possible to crack the encryption at some point, it would not be on Gunn's Apple Mac. He would have to pass it on to a specialist with serious computer gear.

Next Eddie set about analysing the iPhone video. In particular, the audio portion. Although it was Gunn's Apple Mac Pro, Eddie had chosen and installed it for his mate. Naturally he over-loaded it with all the applications he had on his identical machine, given he spent probably a third half his life crashing at Gunn's house.

He was using Wingate ProSound, the same advanced

Digital Audio Analyzer deployed by MI6 and Scotland Yard. Eddie played back the sound he had isolated for the third time. First he had loaded the horror video from Gunn's iPhone straight into the Apple Mac. He stripped off the audio track from the video, before opening it in the Wingate Audio Analyzer. Eddie could have kept them linked but he could not bear to have those images on screen for his mucker to see again.

He called Gunn over and played the sound he stripped from the clutter, boosting to audible level.

Gunn nodded in affirmation. Eddie's dogged persistence paid off again, as it had done so many times as they'd yomped it through badlands. That merest smudge of random sound Gunn first thought he heard was now clear and loud. He could be wrong, it wasn't as if there weren't millions of the buggers around.

But he was dead certain what circle of hell those particular hounds patrolled.

43

Eddie had the plan. Always the man with the plan. They would recce the Dylan Thomas Industrial Estate before executing a flanking assault, Eddie going in through the front as diversion, while Gunn breached the rear to smash and grab Ziya. Gunn was dead set against. He had a high probability of how this was going to end for him. He was going to kill Dr Stuart Roper, not the tiniest shard of doubt and not a scintilla of guilt. He sincerely hoped he would get away with it, but maybe not. There was no way he was going to let his mate get caught up in an accessory to murder charge. If he was taken down for it, he would need Eddie to finance and coordinate his defence.

Then there was Bathsheba. What if they both failed together? He needed Eddie to protect her. If he was dead or banged up then that was the point Eddie could Harry von fuck Stuart over, and zap him three times in the face. Only that would be when Eddie had the tactical high ground and Stuart wouldn't see him coming. Quiet, stealthy and lethal. He had Gunn's blessing for that op.

Every point Gunn bounced at Eddie was bounced right back. Solved. Sorted. Finished.

'Look Eddie, mucker.'

'Stow it marine. Desist with the girl's time. We're yomping home down Heartbreak Lane together. Y'know I'll just second wave you from the rear anyway.'

'I need you to cover my sister.'

'Already got my trusty lads on it mate.'

'Still can't get over you having lads.'

'Bleak Hobbesian world out there, case you hadn't noticed shitehead. Like I said, said lads may be nancies but they're Harry von large, with orders to be von nasty and brutish regarding anyone comes within sniffing distance.'

He gave in. 'Okay Eddie, let's do it.'

'Finally the boy sees sense.'

'We need kitting out first.'

Gunn hurried to one of the two large body height cupboards on the wall. It was the mains electrical supply and fuse box into the house. Gunn reached to the side of the wooden plinth holding the electricity meter, and the mains power cable in from the street and down to the fuse box.

—*CLICK*—

The hinge swung the plinth open to reveal the small safe embedded into the house's original brickwork. It was the second time Gunn had opened the safe this morning. The first time was to secure the 9mm Browning he had liberated from Oliver's scumbag last evening. Next to the Browning were two other military spec handguns picked up on his travels to exotic places like Afghanistan, and Iraq.

Gunn double checked the safety, and pulled back the slide to check if there was a bullet in the chamber. Satisfied, he offered the Browning to his mate.

'You're kidding right?'

'Whaddya mean?'

'Black guy, two foot dreads, driving to Brixton in a factory-new six series beamer, poncey number plate. All tooled up. You da bludclot Babylon.'

Gunn winced. It never crossed his mind. 'Yeah, sorry.'

'This is hand to hand, get the bayonets on lads, Zulu

school.'

Gunn was already opening the lid to his other large trunk, not his Zeke trunk. This was his solid oak, P&O Steamer old style. It had the classic RM battle insignia embossed on top of the lid, complete with solid brass hinges and leather handles. Inside. Sleeping. His accumulated gear. Ten years of loyal service in the Royal Marine Corps. Another life stowed and frozen in sixty cubic feet of space-time. A handmade, solid wood tray rested on top, segmented into sections. Lying in the left-side were his *Blues*: the Royal Marines No. 1 dress uniform, safely stowed in a large clear-plastic clothes carrier.

The right-hand side was further segmented to stow his regimental dress caps and the coveted green beret, with its famed bronze laurel and globe cap badge. Gunn gazed at three hundred years of unparalleled service represented in that simple woollen headgear. For the first time since he left the corps after his wife and child died, he picked up the beret, feeling the history radiate. His history. Words like honour, duty, and sacrifice flashed. It was a world where the very best the country has to offer, willingly swim through a ten mile river of shit to earn this ultimate imprimatur of courage and dedication to the brotherhood.

Swim through shit, endure all pain, bear all loss, for nothing but an idea. For the man standing next to you in the firing line. How can you measure that? How could he measure Eddie standing next to him. *Per Mare, Per Terram.*

He carefully replaced his beret, stroked it crinkle free and reverently lifted the tray out of the trunk. Resting immobile below the surface, the basic hand tools of his lethal trade saw the light of day again. These he grabbed and handled rather less reverently. They felt familiar.

They felt good. They felt loved.
   It was time they went back to work.

44

'Dreads in position, over.'
'Copy that Dreads, One Shot over.'

Gunn's Saab hadn't been washed in over a week since he transported Bebba for her RADA audition. The game old girl was looking sorry for herself: muddy, dirty, down and out. The threatened instructions from Stuart still hadn't pinged into Gunn's iPhone. That was good. All the better to fuck Stuart over after grabbing Ziya. They were in and she was out snatch squad style.

If—Gunn didn't even follow through on the *if*. That was the bare bones of the plan, but Gunn had given Eddie the spare set of Saab keys: whoever ended up yomping out with the girl, had the wheels to go-go-go.

They legally parked half a mile away on Coldharbour Lane before setting out on foot in a circuitous route to the target. Gunn wore his Marine combat boots, a pair of black Levis, black T-Shirt and one of his well-worn old jungle combat jackets. It wasn't much of a change from normal. Eddie carried a kitbag in his beamer as a ready alternative to the very expensive suits he liked to wear. He had on his old marine combat boots, and was kitted out in quasi-military, urban combat black. Gunn re-assured him he looked like Samuel L. Jackson. Fully packed with all the gear they would need, Gunn had his old service issue marine Bergen rucksack in camo material slung over his shoulder.

The day was warming up as they skirted the target,

heading for the train line which ran behind and below, through a deep railway cutting. They had selected the spot as the ideal ingress, as it had the one guaranteed hidden entry point to the Dylan Thomas Industrial Estate.

They paused for a few minutes to get a sense of the train patterns on the London Overground railway lines heading up to Blackfriars Station, down to Brighton and the south coast. It was a busy commuter line with trains passing every ninety seconds to two minutes. They scrambled the twenty feet down the steep grassy embankment, and yomped it fast alongside the down inclining track for two hundred yards. The grassy embankment turned into a vertical brick wall, towering forty feet above them.

—CLACK—CLACK—CLACK—

The familiar rhythm of a fast approaching train forced them to duck out of sight behind a conveniently situated piece of cover – a crumbling concrete bunker.

While they were temporarily stalled, Gunn plopped his Bergen on the glass-strewn ground. He opened one of the pouches on the side and pulled out a set of colour photo print-outs. Back at the house, Eddie had logged into his Google Earth account, zooming straight down onto the Dylan Thomas Industrial Estate. He pin-pointed the optimum spot to ascend up the railway cutting wall and breach the target area undetected by any lookout, real eyed or CCTV. Gunn scanned it again for one final imprint on the target and the likely spot where they would be setting up their surveillance base.

They were both back in the marine minimal speak groove. While Gunn did his thing, Eddie unfolded the mil-spec, hi-tensile steel, three-pronged grappling hook ready for deployment.

'Go go go.'

Eddie went. Sprinting forward the final twenty yards to their chosen spot. Using Google Earth he had pinpointed a three foot tall distance post on the opposite side of the tracks as a rough marker for the ideal breach-point on the wall. Uncoiling about a yard of the strong black-nylon rope, Eddie swung the grappling hook around and around expertly to build up momentum. With a measured sureness he released the rope on the fifth up-swing at maximum velocity. The hook soared skywards to clank over the top first try. Gunn was two steps behind as Eddie pulled down fast and hard to make sure the robust hook was tightly dug into the top and reverse drop side of the wall.

'Go go go.'

Gunn went. Straight up, using the brute strength in his legs and feet to help propel him upwards as he went hand over hand up the vertical brick wall. Reaching the top, he instantly shuffled himself sideways, straddling either side of the wall. Eddie was two seconds behind him. He pulled the rope up, reversed the grappling hook and dropped the rope the twenty feet to the ground.

'Go go go.'

Eddie rappelled at speed downwards, followed instantly by Gunn. Twenty seconds after the hook was first hurtled skywards, both warriors stood silent and unseen within the target's perimeter. They were behind perfect cover at the rear of the farthest building on the estate. It was the same crumbling red brick 1950's construction as the other thirty deserted units. Gunn dropped the Bergen on the ground and started removing some of the gear they would need to complete the mission.

He handed Eddie one of the two twinned Motorola walkie-talkies and an earbud with a PTT (press-to-talk) microphone attachment. Eddie had the rugged comms devices stashed in his car.

As the three barking hell hounds came bounding over, Gunn flung out the still defrosting five pound of sirloin steaks laced with a powerful sedative.

'Dreads in position, over.'

'Copy that Dreads, One Shot over.'

Eddie had inched his way up to the roof of the tallest building on estate. All the units were of a similar crumbling red brick construction, topped by filthy grey corrugated-metal sloping roofs. Except one: a 1980s metal frame building. It was one stroke of luck, the structure was a floor higher, with a convenient flat roof. Thanks again Google Earth.

While Eddie was away securing the estate's highest vantage point, Gunn was edging, ducking and crawling his way, building by building, inexorably towards the site of his first encounter with a member of what he now knew was Kill Club. That had been the Sign-A-Rama unit, which was nearer to the front entrance.

Gunn was using all his enhanced spidey senses honed by years of tracking and neutralizing the cunning Taliban in their own backyard. Ziya was hanging in there somewhere. Alive he prayed.

Eddie was busy assuming his heads up and eyes-on position. Gunn was moving up the line and had already surveilled three buildings. At each seemingly deserted unit, he had stopped and listened, then used a stethophone to listen deeper. Like his hospital acoustic stethoscope, the electronic stethophone picked up the natural soundwaves when the diaphragm was held against a sound transmitting surface. Gunn had the diaphragm pressed against the red bricks of the fourth building checked so far. A stethophone's earpiece in one ear, the walkie-talkie earbud in the other. Eddie came in crystal clear.

'Eye-balling your snurgling One Shot. Hold position, taking a look-see. Over.'

'Holding position Dreads. Over.'

Eddie scanned the buildings. The rubber eyepiece pressing up to his eye was another of Gunn's souvenirs from Iraq: a military grade T14 rifle mounted digital thermal imager. The scope could penetrate brick to reveal the thermal signature of anyone inside generating heat. On his fifth building sweep Eddie found the tell-tale thermal signatures he was scanning for.

Eddie tried to keep the excited urgency out of his voice. 'Multiple targets acquired, repeat multiple live targets acquired, over.'

'Copy that Dreads. Over.'

'Hold position One Shot, repeat hold position. On way.'

Gunn laid the six Google Earth photos on the ground, butting them up together to form a complete overhead map of the estate. Eddie used a red marker pen to draw on the red Xs representing the positions of the heat signatures. He was all business as he gave Gunn the ground and target sitrep.

'Scope's Gucci. This building, four jokers, repeat four, plus our girl. Five targets actual radiating heat.'

Some of the dammed up tension flowed out of Gunn. 'Good. That's dead good mate.'

'She appears immobile, arms up vertical in this ground floor room here. One joker walking around same room. Something in his hand, held up to his ear which I take to be a mobile. Three other jokers in this rear room on the second floor appear seated at a table. Unknown heat source in the next room. Could be a kitchen. Maybe a stove. Hard to say. Not a human though.'

Gunn looked at his mate, smiling a joyless smile. It was the marine smile that launched a thousand shits across the sea to the paradise hereafter, or wherever the fuck they believed they were going. 'Copy mate.'

'We can be heroes, just for one day.'

'One more day.'

Eddie grimly nodded. 'Your call One Shot.

'Do these fuckers final for real. And bring the girl home.'

45

Gunn pushed at the door. Nothing doing. Given the configuration of the heat signatures, there was one person downstairs. Plans change and it made more sense for a two-man sideways assault.

They had methodically hugged themselves tight to the sides of the units, efficiently working their way down to the target location. Each unit faced on to one of the four access roads, criss-crossing or winding through the estate. There was a generous glob of land in front or down the side of each unit for a car park and lorry access. the units were all slightly offset from each other, and not laid out in a strict grid pattern. This gave a tactical advantage as there was no direct line of sight past any one building to the next. But they also had a tactical disadvantage, regarding the fences enclosing the rear and sides of each unit. Having to climb over each one and drop down increased the chances of being spotted.

In double quick time they reached the final building standing between them and their objective. They paused on the other side of the seven foot wooden slatted fence separating them from the side of the target building. The small sign over the door told them it used to be the home of Precision Plastic Extrusions Limited.

Gunn bent down on one knee. Eddie straddled himself behind Gunn's head and across his shoulders. Gunn awkwardly forced himself up, grunting slightly, until he was standing with Eddie's fourteen stone of dead weight perched on top, legs dangling against his rib cage.

Eddie scoped through the thermal imager's eyepiece for one final confirmation of the target's locations throughout the derelict property. Gunn shuffled slowly alongside the fence to provide his mate with as much lateral perspective as possible. The target disposition had changed slightly as far as Eddie could tell. The dangling female, they assumed was Ziya, was still in the same painful spot. The second unknown (Stuart?), who had been pacing around, was no longer visible.

'Shit.' Eddie tapped Gunn on the shoulder and he lowered himself down till Eddie's feet reached terra firma.

'What?'

'The scope won't penetrate up through the floors from this angle. Must be lead, asbestos maybe.'

Gunn dropped the Bergen to the ground and unloaded their final bits of kit. He handed Eddie an injection moulded nylon sheath enclosing a hardened steel combat knife. Eddie pulled out the dagger like blade. He laid it across the palm of his hand to get a feeling for the distribution of its weight and balance. It was a modern copy of the classic Royal Marines Fairbairn-Sykes Fighting Knife designed back in the 1940s. Eddie carefully sheathed the scalpel-sharp blade before clipping the sheath to his belt. Even in relatively unskilled hands, the Fairbairn-Sykes was the world's finest stabbing and slashing weapon, having been designed by the legendary Colonel Fairbairn for maximum silent penetration. Eddie was very skilled, and had been commended by his trainers at Lympstone for his superior unarmed combat and close-in knife work.

For himself, Gunn was strapping a black nylon thigh sheath to his leg. It held a far more robust looking double-edged combat blade with a jagged edge one side, and smooth razored edge on the other.

Eddie had already picked up one of the two telescopic batons laid on the ground. He gripped the stippled rubber handle and flicked his wrist in a well practiced move. The baton shot out from its six inch housing and extended to twenty one inches of aircraft grade aluminium. He swished it around a couple of times. It was a real bone breaker capable of stopping, hurting, putting down and killing the most determined attacker.

They clicked the batons back into collapsed storage mode, stowing them in respective pockets. This was it. Both good to go. Gunn slung on the Bergen across both shoulders. Closed his eyes and took three deep breaths.

The door was on the side of the building, at the top of the six sideways-on concrete steps. When the door refused to swing open on his push, Gunn stepped aside and let Eddie do his stuff. Gunn faced out with his back to Eddie scanning the area combat patrol style.

—*CLICK—CREAK—*

Gunn cringed as the door noisily edged open less than an inch. Eddie instantly stopped pushing and fished around in one of his multiple jacket pockets. He found the tiny can of WD40 and sprayed the two rusty door hinges.

Gunn turned, gave him the thumbs up before hand-signalling they should advance forward. Eddie pushed the door again. This time it silently swung inwards, opening up into the heart of darkness.

46

BLACK

At first.

Gunn and Eddie stood rock still. Tiny slivers of dim light were leaking from a few sources, including a door frame on the farthest side of the room. Gunn clicked on his powerful pencil torch, directing the beam to assess their situation. The floor was covered by dark, worn linoleum. Unlike his previous estate visit in Sign-O-Rama, this room looked empty, with little or no scattered crunchy matter to offer useful audio warnings to bad guys.

He hand-signalled to Eddie to follow his lead, clicking off the torch before sneaking quietly towards the door. The dim light escaping from the one inch gap under the door to the floor made it easy for them. As they reached their objective, Gunn had already inserted his stethophone earpieces, and was about to place the bell against the door.

—*VRRRRRRRRR*—*VRRRRRRRRR*—

Gunn's iPhone vibrated in his pant's pocket. He had put it on vibrate for the duration. He knew who it was before even he pulled the phone out and showed the all caps text message display to Eddie.

> BRING GOODS 2 WATERLOO STATION 1 HR. AWAIT FURTHER INSTRUCS. DON'T DO ANYTHING

SILLY OR BYE BYE BIRDY

Gunn rewarded himself with a grim smile of satisfaction. They had achieved the ultimate goal of any military strategist. The element of surprise with a tactical advantage over the enemy. Stuart had no idea they were almost on top of him.

Eddie pointed the T14 thermal scope at the door and peered through the rubber eyepiece. There was still one body heat source in the same spot, arms aloft. Her knees were buckled and there seemed to be no movement at all. He knew that heat will remain in the body for some time after death. *That poor fucking kid.* For a second Eddie almost lost it too. He handed the scope to Gunn.

Gunn stoically took in the image. Almost there. He placed the stethophone bell against the MDF panelled door and listened intently. Nothing. Then—

Mmmm—Mmmm.

Faint, but proof of life. He gave Eddie a thumbs up. Adrenaline flowed as Gunn unsheathed his combat blade, gripped in his left hand.

The hero isn't the man who is not afraid. The hero is the man who is afraid but hides his fear and acts decisively anyway.

Eddie mirrored Gunn's action but selected the baton instead, keeping it quiescent and un-extended. He crouched on his haunches, leaning back into the wall beside the door, ready to spring. Gunn stood tall, nodded to his oppo, touched his shoulder, and turned the round, pitted brushed-aluminium door handle.

Gunn stood in the open door frame and looked into the large area. It was as gloomy in here, but his eyes were fully accustomed to this low light level. Gunn still had the perfect vision which his very first RM physical confirmed included A1 darkness acuity. There she was, back to him, twenty feet ahead, almost dead on her feet. A few feet away hung Kirsty, facing him. Left hanging like a piece of meat.

Gunn scanned the oblong shaped space, which looked to be about a hundred feet by fifty feet. Two rows of four support pillars were evenly spaced throughout the room. He could make out a number of manufacturing machines abandoned in situ. Gunn tapped Eddie on the shoulder, stepped forward a pace into the room, sidestepping left, back against the wall.

Eddie was already up and entering. He side-stepped right and the two of them stood either side of the door frame. Eddie nodded.

Gunn sprinted the final yardage to Ziya, dodging the pillars and machines which obstructed his path. Standing in the doorframe, he hadn't noticed that the floor was littered with some sort of plastic debris, small extruded items no doubt, scattered on the deck at random. Gunn couldn't help booting a few as he charged, causing them to fly and bounce off the other obstructions. They sounded VERY LOUD.

Ziya's bloodied wrists were locked into steel manacles attached at either end of a long steel chain. The chain had been thrown over a six inch diameter metal pipe attached to the ceiling by sturdy metal brackets extending down about a foot. She had been hanging down for about twelve hours with her own body weight supported only by her hands and arms.

Gunn suppressed his righteous fury, trying to block-out the multiple congealing slice marks on her arms and legs. Grabbing around her tiny waist, he raised her up until her feet lifted off the ground. Gunn had the strength of twelve angry men, and her ten stone felt no heavier than a bag of sugar. He started to pull off the duct tape wrapped around her head, covering her mouth and half her face. Eddie was there besides him. As Gunn stroked Ziya's face and whispered to her, Eddie deployed the heavy duty bolt cutter from the Bergen, snapping the padlocks holding the manacles around Ziya's wrists. Eddie had to tap Gunn on the arm twice before he realized his mate had cut through the padlocks freeing Ziya from the cruel manacles.

Gunn lifted her up in his arms. He held her effortlessly.

'I gotcha love. I gotcha.'

Eddie was relentlessly insistent 'Let's go One Shot.'

'Sorry love I'm gonna have—'

Ziya's eyes fluttered open, then shut again as if the very effort of lifting her eyelids was so great because she had run down like a cheap battery. Speaking was even more of an effort as she croaked out: 'Love you pumpkin.'

Gunn's throat lumped. God love her. Parroting Pulp Fiction. 'You too honey bun.'

'Fuck Gunn, why take so fucken long. Fucker.'

'Move it One Shot, we—'

The first shot slammed into the pillar, less than an inch from Eddie's face. Gunn saw the muzzle flash in the gloom at the other end of the room. Eddie swung around to the other side of the pillar, putting two feet of brick between him and the shooter. Gunn dropped down on one knee out of the firing line, clutching Ziya tight into him. Everything had kicked into hyper drive, fuelled by huge amounts of adrenaline, caffeine, and speed. Unlike his *debilitating acute stress reaction* with nowhere to go but mental, Gunn's body was prepped for a massive fight or flight response. Luckily Ziya had been left hanging in front of one of the old machine parts which stood dormant and abandoned throughout the room.

He eyeballed Eddie behind the pillar to his right. Eddie thumbed up to indicate he was okay, ready to rock and roll. Gunn hand-signalled he had eyes-on the shooter's last locat, then signalling Eddie to retreat with Ziya. Eddie dropped onto his belly and scooted the five feet from his secure spot to cross the exposed gap to the cover with Gunn and Ziya.

'Didn't I fucking say we should go five minutes ago?'

Gunn shrugged, 'You're adorable when you're angry. Anyone tell you that?' He thrust Ziya across to Eddie like a bag of groceries. 'Go on my mark. Fireman's lift.' Gunn re-thought. 'No carry her arms front. Shield her with your back.'

Ziya was too weak to protest. She looked pleading back at Gunn as Eddie grabbed her in both arms. Gunn pulled the Bergen off his shoulders and propped it against the base of the big machine riveted into the floor. He handed Eddie a lightweight camo poncho with a slit hole for the head. As Eddie started to dress it around Ziya, Gunn retrieved the small mirror attached to a telescopic arm. Extending the arm, Gunn raised it above the base of the machine providing their cover. Moving it around, he quickly recced the scene. The convex, fish-eye mirror displayed a good portion of the room. No sign of the shooter, presumably Stuart.

Gunn pocketed the mirror, then picked up one of the small objects he had accidentally kicked as he ran towards the hanging Ziya.

Eddie could see what Gunn intended and readied himself. First he shuffled his feet around so that he was facing the exit door, still holding Ziya in his arms like a baby, across one knee, as he crouched. He could feel her whole body shudder with pain.

'Sorry love, has to be done.'

Eddie winked at his mate. The object was about the same weight as a standard issue British grenade. Gunn over-arm lobbed it from his crouched position towards a spot twenty yards to the left of where he spotted the muzzle flash.

—*CLANG—SCRAPE*—

It was the oldest diversionary trick in the book, but always worked because people react instinctively to sound. The solid plastic tube hit something solid and bounced off hard to skid along the floor. At the first *clang* Eddie was up, hoofing it to the exit door.

Gunn had poked his head up a couple of inches while the plastic was in mid-lob to see if the jumpy shooter might give up his location due to the audio provocation. Right on cue he saw the flash and heard the bang from the same area as before. Gunn glanced back towards the exit door to see Eddie zip fast through the frame. Then they were gone.

Right, you fucker. Time to play.

47

Gunn flicked his left wrist and the six inch ribbed-rubber grip telescoped out to reveal its full twenty-one inches of rigid aluminium. His right hand already gripped his combat knife. Sixty seconds since Eddie had left the building. He was hoping their little diversion had worked, with the shooter still thinking he had them trapped. It could be Stuart, or it could be one of the other three warm bodies Eddie had thermal scoped. Maybe all three.

His first move would be to out-flank the shooter, and take him from the rear. *Oh, is that all? What about his three mates?* The shooter had probably guessed by now that the noise was a deliberate distraction. He knew Gunn's last location and if the bloke had any feel for tactics he would already been changing his position, trying to outflank Gunn. Eddie should be yomping at full pelt right now, straight down the access road and out through the front gate.

Like all marines, Eddie passed Commando training carrying a one hundred pound weighted Bergen on a ten mile march. Ziya was well within his physical capabilities. Even so, there was no way he could carry her back via the railway line. If he felt any threat he was going to zigzag around in a maze pattern, until he was safe to stash her in one of the other deserted buildings. That done he would neutralize the obstacle. In that scenario he'd radio in as soon as with a sitrep. Otherwise it was radio silence until he reached the Saab. Though a six foot three black guy with two foot dreads, racing like buggery for half a mile, lugging a petite, beautiful and a semi-naked Chinese woman, was bound to cause heads to turn. Even in seen-it-all Brixton.

Gunn adjusted his tactics on the fly, poking his head up to scan over the top again. Nothing. He crouched down, shuffling backwards, retreating to the exit door.

Ping. Every hair on Gunn's already epinephrine and norepinephrine bombarded body rocketed vertical.

—*SMELL*—

The live human smell hit him again. Exactly the same as last time. It wasn't the same fragrance, still not quite masking its owner's sour sweat. Right behind. Gunn's back totally exposed. Again.

Fuck. I've been outflanked.

No time for subterfuge this time. Gunn pirouetted and leapt up.

—*BLAM—BLAM—BLAM*—

Triple tap muzzle flash. Three bullets slammed into his chest, rapid fire. Gunn staggered backwards a couple of yards before slipping down, humiliatingly flat on his arse. Gunn registered the silhouette of the shooter: with a piece of kit from his time in Iraq and Afghanistan. The head strap clamping a pair of night-vision goggles to the bloke's face.

The pain was beyond excruciating, but under it he thankfully heard the footsteps scurrying away. Smart move, the shooter didn't know exactly where Eddie was or whether he was armed too. Night-vision goggles or not, he wasn't hanging around to find out. That was way smarter than Gunn lingering after Eddie had beat it with Ziya. Besides he had put three 9mm slugs into Gunn's centre mass from point blank range. Devastating.

Not quite. Gasping for breath, Gunn rolled over and pulled himself up to his knees. Thank goodness he had listened to Eddie when he insisted they both rolled with their old marine issue Osprey body armour under their jackets. He felt his chest. All three slugs lodged right over his heart. Either Stuart was dead lucky or a dead good shot. Even from close range you need a certain level of skill to get a tight grouping. He kicked that thought around as he gasped to suck in the air the bullets had smacked right out of him. With each 9 mil delivering a kinetic force of forty-one thousand pounds per square inch, it was like being kicked by a shire horse. Three times. *Oww, that really fucking hurt.*

So far Stuart had managed to axe him and shoot him thrice in the chest. Gunn was beginning to get even more irritated by the arrogant prick Roper the Groper.

He picked up his blade and baton, and struggled back to his feet, ignoring the savage pain. Either advance or retreat? Gunn advanced fast, heading for the other side of the room in the direction he had heard the footsteps retreat. He closed down the final few feet to the large swinging double doors and pushed through.

Back to black, no leaking windows here. He sheathed his knife, and gripped the baton in his right hand. Clicking on his torch Gunn shone the pencil beam left to illuminate the concrete steps of the stairs leading up to the second floor. He gripped the baton tighter, as if that made it a more potent force against a 9 mil semi-automatic.

The shallow steps led up about six feet, before turning ninety degrees to continue to the second floor. Gunn swept the beam 180 degrees right to check what lay in that direction. A few yards down, the beam picked out the familiar push bars of an emergency exit to the outside.

Gunn banged down on the push bars, and the door opened outwards. Cleansing light as bright as creation flooded in, dazzling him for a second. Now he had a fast way out straight down the stairs. Gunn stepped outside to orient himself in relation to the rest of the estate. He wedged the emergency exit door with a half brick laying on the rubble strewn ground, walking away a couple of yards, sucking in air to his still shocked lungs. He could see he was on the opposite side of the unit where he and Eddie had breached. Satisfied he had the escape route imprinted, Gunn was about to turn back when—

KABOOOOOOOOOOOOOOOOOOOOOOOOM.

The shattering shockwave hurtled Gunn sideways, bouncing him off the wooden fence but missing the concrete pillars which set the boundary to the next building. A nano-second later an immense 2000 degree Celsius fireball rocketed down the stairs and out through the exit in which he had been standing seconds earlier. Had he still been in the corridor, Gunn knew from experience that the pulverizing shockwave would have turned his internal organs into the consistency of sausage filling.

As Gunn lay stunned on top of the fence, flattened against the ground, it sounded as if St. Paul's cathedral was ringing at full Easter Resurrection Monday pelt in his head. He dragged himself together and staggered up unsteadily to his feet.

BOMB. No shit Gunn.

He heard screaming. Then he realized it was him who was screaming, except it was in his head. And he was screaming to make himself heard over the ringing.

He looked up at the formerly boarded up windows on the second floor. The plywood covers and glass had disappeared. Blown halfway across the estate no doubt. Flames were fanning out at a rate of knots from the window shaped holes. Rancid, choking black smoke funnelled skywards as if escaping a witch's cauldron. He swivelled his jaw around and around, trying the equalize the air-pressure in his ears. The ringing was replaced by a roaring, but it wasn't inside his head. The noise was coming from the building. The fire was roaring, like a fifty foot tall lion marking its territory: the whole of Africa. His face manipulations seemed to work. His head was clearing, and it dawned on him he had to get out of there, as of *right the fuck now* boot-head.

Kirsty—he thought of his friend. He would have to leave her behind. Consumed by the flames. Gunn ran.

48

Half-mile away, a gasping Gunn spotted his red Saab ahead. He had booted out of the estate, praying Eddie would be long gone, straight to St. Mike's A&E.

The frantic sounds of sirens from all directions sliced the Brixton air. A fire-engine flashed past. Checking behind, to his right, the black mushroom shaped cloud had to be two hundred feet into the air and rising. Two police cars flew past following the fire-engine, sirens screaming *out of the frigging way muppets*. Bystanders were, naturally, by-standing around with worried expressions.

Joy.

Approaching his car, he could see Eddie in the driver's seat, swivelled around, looking to the back. Seconds later he was inside the car, leaning over the passenger seat, holding Ziya's hand, checking her pulse as she lay across the back seat, eyes shut.

'That bang bang your doing One Shot?'

Still winded. 'You heard?'

'Hard not too.'

'Not me.'

'Stuart and the bad guys?'

Gunn pointed his right index finger skywards. 'That black cloud billowing over Brixton? Them. Far as I know.'

He let go of Ziya's hand and pulled off his jacket, showing Eddie the three slugs embedded in his body armour over his heart. 'Stuart. Believe that fucker? Put three in, then retreated fast upstairs, I think. Had to have been setting the bomb when he Irished it up big time.'

'Boss grouping. Has to hurt.'

'Not as much as the alternative mate.'

'Sorry we never got your friend out too. That's not right.'

Gunn grimaced. 'Yeah, look, Eddie mate, goes without saying—'

'Then don't.'

'You two nancies gonna shut fuck up, gemme to Mike's?'

There was no arguing with that. Eddie fired up the Saab and gunned it.

49

'What was the last thing I told you Gunn?'

Dishevelled, bleary eyed, cranky. That was Detective Superintendent Hickman. Gunn looked and felt far worse.

It had been three days since the bomb went off. Merely the primer for the bomb still detonating in New Scotland Yard, all the way up to Westminster. The one female and four male bodies recovered from the building had been crispied to Kentucky Fried Chicken consistency. Hickman told Gunn the bomb had two main components, both violently powerful. The igniter was acetone peroxide, which can be made with common household ingredients. On its own, acetone peroxide is a deadly explosive. Witness the 52 souls lost to it in the July 2005 tube bombings. In this case, it was merely the initiator to the *Nitromethane* – at least a hundred gallons according to the bomb boys. Turns out *Nitromethane* is used as rocket fuel, and more commonly as racing car fuel. Highly flammable and massively explosive when detonated.

Hickman now knew the identities of all five bodies, two of them had been named by Gunn when he caught up with him at St. Michael's hospital. Kirsty Smith, a paramedic and ambulance drive. Dr Stuart Roper, neurosurgeon, and according to Gunn, the psycho who had killed Smith, as well as murdering his brother fourteen years ago; and God knows how many more in-between those two deaths. Even more appalling for

Hickman was who else was in Stuart's Kill Club. And what that meant for a whole slew of investigations going back to 1999. This was the main reason why Bill Hickman looked and felt worse than Gunn. That and the immense pressure from above, all the way to Number 10.

Hickman had finally tracked down Gunn the day after he had carried in Nurse Ziya Zhang with serious but not life-threatening injuries. She was asleep in her hospital bed in the private room when Hickman entered. Gunn was supposed to be in with her but she was on her own.

Physician in charge Dr Rebecca Lewis was reluctant to let Hickman into Ziya's room. Lewis confirmed that Zhang had suffered extreme and sustained physical trauma including severe dislocations in both arms and shoulders. Mentally she was traumatized having been repeatedly assaulted with knife slices all over her body. As well as hearing the awful, pitiful sounds from the girl dangling right next to her. Kirsty being tortured – begging for her life and finally murdered. The doctor had put her on powerful sedatives to blank out the horrors for a while.

Ziya was a feisty lady with a foul mouth, as Hickman found out when she woke up. Despite Lewis's protestations, it was Ziya who insisted spilling non-stop on how she ended up on the Dylan Thomas Industrial Estate.

Hickman took notes as Ziya recounted how she'd finished her shift and was desperate for a smoke. She was on her way to the forbidden zone at the back of the hospital, when there was a call on her mobile. She recognized Dr Stuart Roper's voice. He said Gunn had been hurt and was outside in his Range Rover, so she didn't think twice about rushing to the car-park. Roper's Range Rover was parked way over on the far side, the part not so well lit. As she approached, the driver's side black-tinted window rolled down, it was Roper sitting behind the wheel.

She remembered shouting *'How bad Gunn?'* when she was grabbed from behind. Hood thrown over her head, hand clamped over her mouth, as she was dragged kicking into the Range Rover. Roper injected her in the neck, and that was he last thing she remembered until coming round, hanging by her arms. Hickman was still cringing at the appalling barbarity of it all, when Gunn rolled in with a steaming delicious smelling coffee and a Ciabatta roll.

'What was the last thing I told you Gunn?'

'Yeah sorry. Needs must.'

Gunn was happy to sit for the third time in a harshly lit New Scotland Yard interview room for over a day now. He'd declined his lawyer. Hickman would come and go. They would talk, he would bring him a plastic cup of the drinks dispenser dishwater they called coffee.

'Crazy Rufus Wright's convinced he was visited by an angel of God. We've nothing on you. And he's retracted his original confession to murdering Ezekiel. Now says it was the Kill Club.'

That was the second time Hickman had come across that odd name. The first time was during his investigation into the deaths of Detective Sergeant Fletcher Hoodeson and drug lord Billy Ferguson. The one thing which had never been adequately explained to Hickman's satisfaction was the torn off piece of toilet roll found on Fletcher. The words KILL CLUB, scrawled in Fletcher's own blood with a small splinter of varnished walnut wood. The forensics team could not source the walnut to the barn where the bodies were found. It was a small inconsistency that was not allowed to disturb the more obvious scenario of what went down between Fletcher and Ferguson.

When Rufus Wright hoarsely whispered the same two words earlier this week, from his secure hospital bed at Oxford General, Hickman's curiosity was piqued.

The evidence, such as it was from a building that had been incinerated, seemed to back Gunn's version of events. In Hickman's initial talk to Nurse Zhang, she confirmed her rescue by Gunn, and a third party they both refused to name. Hickman assumed it was Eddie Bishop. She had confirmed that she heard Smith being murdered right next to her by the men who had grabbed her. She confirmed that they had laughed when they sent Gunn the video and that they intended to kill them both, no matter what.

Hickman did have plenty of other evidence though. All of it against Dr Stuart Roper being the prime mover, instigator and controller of a group of serial killing psychopaths who gave themselves the hideous moniker *Kill Club*. His team had been going through Roper's Streatham house for the past two days, and had uncovered a massive self-incriminating archive on Kill Club. The guy loved his records. Quite obsessional.

In Roper's cellar, they found boxes full of videos, targets, plans. The Kill Club gang were all linked by one common factor: Oxford University in the late 1990s, moving down to London after graduation. Byron Goolsbee had been the first member to surface dead. It was obvious that he personally had been compromised by the Mandy Monroe rape/murder that had been elaborately pinned on the film producer Barry Summers. Now there were four other crispied bodies recovered, including Detective Inspector Sam Wilson.

Hickman almost laughed at the grim irony. D.I. Wilson had led the Mandy Monroe murder investigation, not that he needed to do anything as the Kill Club frame had been perfect, except for that one random CCTV factor thrown up by SPI/GLASS. But as lead investigator, he was also informed that the man on trial could not have done it, and that the prime suspect was an American called Byron Goolsbee. There was no way out of that. There was no way his comrades, including Wilson, could let Goolsbee live to tell.

The forensic bomb experts reckoned Wilson was in the office next to the bomb with two others since identified. Movie producer, Sebastian Melling. And former journalist Jude Cockburn. Cockburn had risen rapidly becoming the Guardian's youngest ever deputy editor, before branching out to form his own internet based alternative media empire. Including Roper and Goolsbee, all five were in and around Oxford University at the same time.

Melling was probably the connection to the Lawrence Summers case. There was a long-standing simmering acrimony between Summers and Melling regarding a couple of movie deals that Melling lost out on. Apparently personal ambition was all it took to get an invite to Kill Club. Petty revenge is easily resolved if you enjoy the process of plotting, killing and framing someone else for the crime.

The theory had Roper priming the bomb in the next office – with the purpose of incinerating the meddlesome Gunn and any other evidence – when it accidentally detonated. Acetone peroxide is a very unstable material in crystal form. It can go off by simple friction, knocking it, or striking it like a match. Hickman was also thinking Roper was closing down Kill Club completely. The others being incapacitated, though still alive according to the evidence of Gunn's thermal imager. Trace amounts of the drug Lorazepam had been found it all bodies, except for Roper. It all added up. Case closed.

Gunn did not have all the answers, but from his time helping Hickman with his enquiries he was formulating his own rough scenario of what went down, and why. Bebba was safe. Ziya was safe. Eddie was Eddie. All was right with his world.

Hickman assured Gunn that his brother's real killers were all dead. Stuart Roper's body had been identified from dental records and DNA. Gunn's continuing paranoid thought was *dental records can be faked*. It was still all circumstantial, but that was firming up by the second as more and more was uncovered. Even Gunn had to accept it was Dr Stuart Roper. In the Saab, Ziya had gasped his name.

It was obvious to Gunn that Roper was clearing house. He ran through everything as he remembered it. Frame by frame in his head. Superior Autobiography Memory. But what if that included Roper faking his own death? The guy was devious enough. Maybe there were other members of Kill Club who remained hidden? The fly in that pudding was the conclusive DNA evidence.

Gunn agreed with Hickman's theory that the whole Kirsty/Ziya kidnapping was a ruse to lure Gunn to a final killing ground where Roper could close down Kill Club completely. *One fell swoop*. That was Shakespeare. Shakespeare was born on April 23rd 1564, or so it was generally estimated as no record existed, and died April 23rd 1616 after writing thirty-seven plays. If one believed he did write them. That's how Gunn's mind worked. He had no special insight into William Shakespeare, or his works, but he did remember almost everything he ever read about him, including a school essay written by Zeke. So when a fact popped, another and another would do the same. It was a gift and an annoying curse, depending on the circumstances.

Gunn could see Goolsbee had become a liability because of the Lawrence Summers debacle. He had to go. But somehow Roper and Kill Club botched that. Goolsbee must have known something was up, why else would he ram three pieces of incriminating evidence up his backside? Literally one place you wouldn't think to look. Insurance policy while he was still alive? Whatever his reasons, the medallion started a chain reaction which led Stuart to conclude he had to kill them all to protect himself.

Hickman was looking very frazzled, not the smooth Detective Superintendent with the Homicide and Serious Crime Command, who first interrogated Gunn about the medallion. He had let Gunn know that the copious evidence pointed to Stuart Roper being the prime mover behind Kill Club. It was likely he recruited the others when he was a resident at Oxford General Hospital between 1998 and 2000. Once Hickman had given up that salient fact, each time he returned to the interview room after consulting with his investigation team, he was more and more willing to share information as a collaborator with Gunn.

Hickman agreed with him that the two 16GB flash memory sticks he had retrieved from Goolsbee must have contained evidence to nail Stuart. They had been destroyed in the inferno when his Bergen went up with everything else. When Hickman mentioned the huge historical archive of material collated by Stuart including videos, Gunn asked straight up if it included anything on his brother. He thought Hickman was going to cry when he affirmed yes, and yes he had seen the ten minutes of footage on VHS tape. And no, there was not any way he could countenance letting him see it, for Gunn's own sake.

Gunn asked how many after his brother. The depravity was off the charts. Thirty-four knowns, beginning in Oxford before they all gravitated to London as a group. Hickman suspected twenty-two people framed for murder, twenty of whom were currently serving life. Six other victims had been killed by a variety of horrible methods and subsequently disposed of, usually ending up in acid baths, two while still alive. Yes, that was on video too. Then there were the six faked suicides.

'Ezekiel was the first killing at Oxford. Plus three others we know of. Though we have found some older footage of an unidentified older female in a garden, with a timestamp for 1990, finding what we assume was the head of her cat on a spike. The camera was dropped but it sounds like she was having a seizure, maybe a heart attack. We're trying to pinpoint the location. Our forensic shrink reckons this was the trigger event.'

'My psychia—my friend Dan Mosser gave me a starter for ten once on the signs to look out for in children as budding sociopaths and psychopaths. Animal cruelty. Decapitations of pets. That's usually how it begins.'

'Time-line-wise after your brother, was a Professor Judith Mundy. Murder staged as a suicide. No idea why yet. No personal connection to any of them.'

Gunn's heartbeat leapt into overdrive. 'Who led the investigations on the other two Oxford confirmed victims after Ezekiel and Mundy?'

Gunn felt the brief hesitation – and was having none of it. 'Spill Bill.'

'Czarnecki.'

So Detective Inspector Walter Czarnecki was the lead detective on all four cases. The man whose step-son Simon Murphy was also a student at Oxford. What's more, Gunn knew Simon moved in the same circles as all Kill Club members and knew his brother.

'Okay one mistake can be explained. Walter Czarnecki arrests the wrong guy for my brother's murder. He's an alcky, not doing his job, step-son who hates him apparently. But another two actual murders. And Judith Mundy's staged suicide? One officer? Isn't that in police parlance known as *suspicious*.'

'What step-son?'

Fucking hell. Gunn's eyes literally rolled. *He's got no fucking idea.* Gunn explained his visit to Ruby Czarnecki, the files and the convergence of people he had unearthed in and around Balloch College in the late 1990s.

Hickman was half biting his lips. Clearly tension as the myriad leads kept overwhelming him. 'Micah, you're too close here, not everyone who knew your brother in Oxford was in this *Kill Club*. Jesus I despise saying those two words.' Hickman took a couple of deep breaths. 'Think about it, why would Czarnecki cover for the step-son you say hated his guts, that doesn't ma—'

'Oh that's easy. Because he was protecting the woman he loved. Simon's mum.'

That was a plausible point but it didn't pop for Hickman, one rotten copper was enough. Now two? 'There's no reference to Simon Murphy or Czarnecki in any of the material we've found at Roper's house.'

'Well yeah. Murphy's the one still walking. Maybe Murphy's the big cheese in Kill Club? Okay. You won't let me see the videos. But see any faces in any of them?'

'Not so far, it's all boilersuits and horror-masks. Like those scary movies.'

'There you go.'

Hickman' week of exasperation and anger and pressure – especially the humiliation over Wilson – exploded again.

'There I go what? We don't see the Easter fucking Bunny either, nor Prince fucking Charlie and Camilla. Don't assume it's them in disguise. We HAVE the guys. They're all thankfully dead Micah. Thank Christ and good riddance in my humble opinion.'

Gunn hadn't meant to press Hickman's buttons so hard after he'd turned out such a top bloke. 'Okay, okay. You say so Mr Hickman.'

The release seemed to calm Hickman a tad. 'Right, on your new information I will be speaking to this Simon Murphy character at some point. By I, it means me, us, the police. Not you, okay. It ends here for you. I have your word on that Micah?'

'You do Mr Hickman.'

50

'Never forget son, yer word's yer bond. That's all you got. All you ever need. Break that and you're breaking your covenant with him.'

'Who's him daddy?'

'You know who.' The man pointed upwards. 'The big bloke upstairs.'

Gunn was sure his dad would forgive him breaking his word to Hickman, for the greater good. His dad the true believer who, when the end came, couldn't even wipe his own arse. He didn't even know he had an arse. *Was that all part of God's plan dad?*

Hickman had finally decided there was no point in questioning Gunn any longer as a material witness. A freshly-laundered near-summer's day greeted Gunn as he stepped out from the Yard into Victoria Street. A day to feel good to be alive. Gunn gazed up to the shimmering blue sky, stained lightly by the white wisps of high cloud. He stood on the pavement and let the rejuvenating sun beat down on his face for half a minute, until he was smacked hard in the shoulder by a scurrying passer-by muttering loudly.

'Out the fucking way tourist.'

Welcome to London.

Simon was a priority, despite his word to Hickman. His initial euphoria at being semi-responsible in killing Kill Club had given way to second-guessing. Paranoia was running deep. It was all conveniently neat. Roper dead.

He had to find out for himself if Czarnecki's step-son was involved. Hands on.

But Simon was his number two priority. Ziya first. Hickman had assured him she was doing fine in hospital, and promised he would take her official statement when she felt up to it. Gunn walked the hundred yards to Victoria station, phone glued to his ear. He took the tube to Waterloo, first the Circle Line, then changing at Embankment to the Bakerloo which took him under the river.

She was still sedated asleep when he walked in her room. Dr Lewis was pleased with the physical progress, assuring him that kicks to Ziya's midriff would not affect her future reproductive choices. *Future reproductive choices*—Gunn bit his tongue hard. He drew blood, stemming the rage. *Stay in control.*

Ziya's arms were a hideous bluey-black, interspersed by a dozen or so healing slices. Gunn lightly stroked her velvet-soft hair, and she did not wake to his touch. He propped the huge Panda next to her on the pillow. It had a cute baseball cap with I LUV LONDON printed on the front. Okay, he'd paid way over the odds from a tacky tourist rip-off shop outside Waterloo Station, en route to St. Mike's. But she loved Pandas and she loved London. It was a twofer. A threefer when she woke later and saw he had been there at her side.

He was wondering how long to stay. His continuing rage against the bastards who did this was in no danger of dissipating. He didn't want his murder face vibe to disturb her recovery. He felt calm sitting there, watching her breathe. Knowing she was safe, and that he and Eddie had saved her.

—*VRRRRRRRR*—*VRRRRRRRR*—

The insistent vibration woke Gunn up. He had closed

his eyes for a second, about an hour ago. He was exhausted down to the bone. His shoulder still throbbed from the original axing. He needed a full twenty-fours hours of non-stop zeds to recharge the batteries. And prime fillet steak. Charred black on the outside, red and juicy in the middle. The phone vibrating reminded him that he had to call Eddie, and check on Bebba. It was probably one of them anyway.

It wasn't. The rage surfaced again.

51

'Better come in suppose. Though why you wanna see me, got no idea. You after money?'

Gunn ignored the insult and entered the smart terraced house in the heart of trendy Islington. It looked like Simon Murphy was doing alright for himself with his three years in a hit TV show, *The Colony*.

What a lucky break his main competitor had broken his back in a car crash while they were casting the part. Simon phoned Gunn in the hospital, demanding to know how he had his private mobile number, and why he kept calling. When Gunn reminded him about Ruby, he heard Simon cursing not so quietly under his breath *fucking mother*.

Simon volunteered he had been away for a few days, out of phone reach, preparing for the biggest role in his life, he didn't need the distraction, and couldn't it all wait till next week, if ever.

Gunn was loving this guy by the second, the way you love genital herpes. Simon was already riffing he had a screen test opposite the young American female lead Madeline Morris. There had to be chemistry apparently. *Yeah good luck with that.*

Simon waxed on about Madeline Morris as they walked down the hallway to the pleasant dining room, with the patio doors leading out into the small walled garden. The hallway was lined with photographs of Simon. Ian McKellan with Simon. Michael Gambon with Simon. Comic Relief Red Nose Day with Simon. His reason for not responding sooner sounded plausible to Gunn. But there was something about the bloke that was rubbing him up. And not in a good way. *Oh yeah. His whole personality. That was it.*

Simon was leaner than Gunn, and taller. His longish blonde hair was the same as his character in The Colony. Though not his natural colour going by the early Oxford photos. Simon indicated a leather dining table chair, and Gunn sat down at the thick glass table, supported by solid wooden legs.

Gunn was wondering how exactly he was going to play this. He could feel his combat knife sheathed and pressing into his side under his jacket. *Don't push your luck with Detective Superintendent Hickman, Gunn.*

'If you're anything like your bro you're a whisky man. Fancy one?'

Ezekiel was a whisky man? One more thing Gunn had failed to know about his brother.

'Bit early. But what the hell.'

What the hell? Driving over to Simon's gaff he had popped a couple more codeine pills, attempting to hold back the insistent throb in his body starting at the tip of his shoulder before radiating up and down in various degrees of pain. That done, he popped another tab of speed to try to stem his overwhelming need to zed it and bliss out. *Stay sharp Gunn, stay sharp.*

Simon retrieved a bottle of Johnny Walker with two shot glasses, pouring them both a drink.

'So what's this all about man? Course I knew your bro, we were sort of mates for a while, but you know how it is at college. Friends, acquaintances. Come and go.'

'Thought you were quite close. What about the Mametaliens?'

Simon smiled, or maybe smirked. Gunn was deciding

which. 'Yeah, when I formed the group he came on board. He wasn't bad. Though not leading man material y'know.'

'Unlike you?'

It was definitely a smirk as Simon returned to what was clearly his favourite topic. Himself. 'Luck of the draw. Okay, I'll admit he was at least as good as me acting wise, but Zeke was always more interested in the directing and writing.'

'It's funny, the way I heard it, the Mametaliens was Zeke's idea, he was the driving force. It was him that was getting all the publicity, what was it the Oxford Express said.'

Gunn flicked over the memory cards to read the article out loud to Simon, verbatim. Simon avoided eye contact now, looking vaguely in Gunn's direction as if a giant abyss had opened in front of him. It didn't get any easier as Gunn thrust in the verbal knife, then twisted it around Simon's guts.

'The invite for the Mametaliens to the Edinburgh Festival, that was where you got your first break right? When people thought it was all you. Wherever would they get such a thought. Oh yeah. You told them.'

Gunn's hardened glare burrowed deep into Simon's skull, totally unnerving him. He applied the technique police used on suspects. Psychiatrists and psychologist used it too. Hickman and Wilson had tried it on him. Stay silent and most people feel compelled to fill in the space. Ten seconds later—

'Okay, okay, you got me. But it was a group decision. We all wanted Edinburgh. Who wouldn't. After Zeke's uh—after he was you know, murdered, so, so sorry mate, we got the invite as the Mamets, what were we supposed to do? We had to have a party line, so we fudged it, you know how little white lies grow, the person no longer there diminishes in the memory, till it's—well, till it's like they hardly ever existed. Eventually you start to believe your own shit smells like roses. And as I was probably the most talented after Zeke, no bragging, and that Goolsbee turned out to be a fucking cultish weirdo. Then there was the girl Beth something, she went nutso, got herself sectioned then up and left Oxford completely. Oliver Boodle, Olli was okay, not great, but totally obsessed about Zeke, and in a very gay way if you follow my drift. So I took the helm, so shoot me.'

Don't tempt me.

'What was that about Goolsbee?'

'Him. Had great teeth. Very white. I see that now, had to get all my choppers redone to stand any chance over in Hollywood. But he was off, you know. Gave me the creeps.'

No kidding. 'Remember any instances of *offness*?'

Simon kicked it around for a few seconds. 'Oh I dunno. Christ man it was years ago. we called him the Ghoul. You know, *Ghouls-Bee*.'

'Yeah I get it.'

'There was something nutso, in the eyes, y'know.'

'Nutso. Like the deranged guy who supposedly killed Zeke?'

Gunn observed Simon's face as he said that. He wanted to see what his reaction to *supposedly* was. He looked genuinely surprised. He was an actor though. Quite a good one. Leading man material apparently.

'Supposedly? What's that mean. They got the guy the next day right? Real nutter.'

'Need a piss. That okay?"

Simon thought about it for a second. 'Up the stairs. Top of the landing on your right.'

—CREAK—CREAK—CREAK—

The varnished wooden stair steps echoed up to the top of the landing. Gunn hesitated. Wooden floor boards not being the ideal surface to creep around on. The moment he had recovered his senses after the bomb detonated, relief washed over him like the inrushing tide, sweeping away the flotsam and jetsam beached on his mind.

All over. Just like that.

He'd rescued the girl and the bad guy was dead. Carbonized to a blackened stump. Less satisfying perhaps, as Gunn would have personally gutted Roper, and not woken up once in the dead of night, losing zeds.

All over.

Except for maybe that one dangling thread. Murphy. Ever since he caught Simon's mum, Ruby, unknowingly regurgitating her son's little bit of self-aggrandizement, Gunn was unsure about him.

Think about it.

Simon was one of two people who had profited directly from Zeke's death. He possibly owed his big break and brilliant career so far to Zeke not being around. Bit of a coincidence. The other being proven Kill Club alumnus Byron Goolsbee, the rapist who coveted and then tries to ruin Zeke's girlfriend. Gunn was still thinking about Hickman's admission that in the videos recovered, not one showed their face. Men in boilersuits and creepy horror masks was all they had seen so far. Sometimes a group of three and four, but never more than the five. The number five matched the total of five Kill Club bodies now resting in pieces. Who's to say it was always the same five. Maybe Roper faked his death. Maybe there was one more. *Simon?*

Gunn turned left and zipped down the corridor. The

first door was slightly open, he pushed it and poked his head in. It was a small space, kitted out as a home office.

He creaked as quietly as possible to the next door. Looked like Simon's bedroom. Nicely carpeted. He stepped in and did a quick recce. Nothing stood out.

The large, classic mahogany wardrobe looked the easiest place. He pulled open the large double doors. No surprise. A row of suits and shirts hung down from the rail.

Time to go. Really. Time. To. Go.

Gunn spotted the leather kitbag at the back. Might as well check it. He pulled it out and opened it.

'Find anything interesting?'

Gunn's hand automatically went under his jacket, touching the handle of the combat knife, sheathed against his side. Jagged and razored, twin edges. Able to do terrible damage in the right hands. His hands.

He dialled back and instead lifted a set of leather restraints, and other bondage paraphernalia from Simon's bag.

''Yeah. These. Care to comment.'

'Care to get the fuck out my house.'

Gunn was up for an *or what*, he was edging himself to that abyss.

Simon's splurge of shame, following Gunn skewering him about Mametaliens, had all but disappeared. Gunn fingered the restraints. They looked the same as the steel manacles and chain used to string up Ziya like a dead cow in a slaughterhouse, nearly ripping her arms from her sockets. He pulled out some of the other contents, which seemed to be the Full Pervy of leather S&M gimp gear. Including the ubiquitous ball gag from Pulp Fiction.

Simon was glowering at Gunn, his territory invaded and some deep dark secret exposed. Gunn was silently daring Simon to do something physical, almost challenging his manhood by dangling the gear in his face. Especially the leather and plastic strap-on.

Simon was not backing down. 'What the fuck is this? So I like a little kink. Fucking shoot me. Not a crime.'

Gunn was back to the rage he took out on the wannabe gangster scumbag at Olli's loft. Rage he'd managed to sublimate since he rescued Ziya, without dissipating it by the satisfaction of personal face to face vengeance.

Great physique or not mate, I will fuck you over, you thieving bastard stole my brother's life.

Gunn finally noticed the phone Simon was gripping, he couldn't miss it when he punched in the three number code.

'Fuck off now and I won't call the cops. Don't know what you're problem is mate but you need fucking help big time.'

Gunn's hand went inside his jacket again. The blade reassuringly still there, cold and hard and ready. The inchoate rage was still there. But he couldn't waterboard the guy, simply to make sure Simon was not involved in Kill Club. Could he?

—*VRRRRRRRRR*——*VRRRRRRRRR*—

Gunn didn't even look at the caller's ID, he almost screamed into the mouthpiece.

'WHAT?'

'Micah, bro, it's me. Bebba.'

'Jesus, sis, Yeah. Yes, sorry.'

52

Fuck fuck fuck.

Gunn savagely booted the slatted wooden fence with his steel toe-capped boots. A young woman pushing a buggy with a toddler, heading towards him. She veered across the road to the opposite pavement. He had scared her. *Shit.* That scared him.

He tried a reassuring smile but the woman didn't dare make eye-contact as she kept a wary eye on him. The cute little girl looked across the road at the funny man. She was clutching her little stuffed Panda, and thought he was hilarious. Adults are so funny at times.

Jesus Gunn, maybe the smug prick was right, you do need help.

He crawled into the Saab, checking his face in the rear-view mirror. Freddy Krueger fright night stared back. He lifted his right arm. A rank, sour, sweaty wave radiated up to fill his nostrils.

He had to back down with Simon. What was he going to do? Turn into Stuart Roper, X-ing him across his chest, as happened to his brother. He wouldn't become a monster simply to confirm that someone else was a monster. There had to be another way. He should go and meet Eddie, get his mate to check out Simon – while he slept.

Fuck.

He had to see Bebba too. Try to explain everything he had found out about the death of her other brother. Then back to St. Mike's to be at Ziya's hospital bed. Then check in with Hickman maybe. See how that's all going.

Fuck, so much to do.

Hickman wouldn't let him see the video of Zeke's torture and murder. His last moments, before he was dispatched like a cow for slaughter. Except he still saw the crime scene photographs from Czarnecki's files. Couldn't get them *out of his fucking head.* Zeke hanging. Body so badly hurt. So abused. How his poor kid brother had suffered on November 2, 1999. While he was in Kosovo, doing what and for what?

Think, think, think, what next?

His head was buzzing with activity. A car revved up and red-lined, with the hand-brake on and the foot-brake pressed to the floor. Going nowhere fast.

Gunn gazed dead-eyed at himself in the rear view mirror. His right lower eyelid was trembling like crazy, not visible enough to spot, but he could feel it spasming and it was extremely irritating. As were the electrical impulses to the muscles controlling his left forefinger firing randomly, pulling it uncontrollably towards the other finger every couple of seconds. This would cascade on for minute or so, before slowly subsiding for a while. Then kicking off again.

He winced. His shoulder still throbbed from the original axing. Must be residual muscle damage there. Time for another codeine hit, even though codeine was notorious for bunging up the gut tighter than superglue. He pushed to one side the unpleasant fact he hadn't been to the shitter for almost a week. There was still plenty of water in his bowser on the back seat, he glugged down a pint with the codeine. He'd move on his bowels later.

Think, think, think, what to do next?

A wave of tiredness hit him again. His hand went automatically to his pants left pocket, pulling out the small plastic pill container. He shook it, and it thankfully rattled with the remaining few methamphetamine pills.

Brainfart.

Hadn't he dropped speed tab while he was driving to Islington?

Jesus.

Gunn couldn't remember. Of course he knew speed can affect memory. But if you can't remember doing something, that probably meant you didn't do it.

Right?

He stared at the tiny white energizer bunny pills for a good few seconds.

Fuck it.

Gunn popped a pill and took another gulp of water. He closed his eyes again. Last one, he promised himself. Just to get back to St. Mike's. Then Eddie's. Then Bebba in the country with her two guardian gays.

Gunn sparked into action, but heading God knows where. Ten minutes later Gunn snapped out of it, on autopilot heading north out of Islington, straight up the Holloway Road. He remembered screaming like a maniac as he almost rear-ended a woman who cut him up. He'd passed under the solid red and cream Victorian ironwork of the Archway Bridge, an infamous suicide spot. Up towards Highgate Hill, London's highest point. The involuntary twitches of his left forefinger were driving him crazy again. Now a muscle in the top of his thigh was spasming too. His electrical system was firing off randomly. Every muscle contraction seemed to be multiplied a thousand fold.

Think, think, think, what am I doing?

He needed help, that was for sure. Then it hit him – but not a two hundred pound Archway leaper. He realized where he was automatically going, obvious really. And it was less than a mile away, bearing west. Maybe his body had a sub-conscious defence mechanism looking after him. He took the next left after the Archway, swinging down Southward Lane towards leafy exclusive Hampstead and its multi-million pound highly desirable abodes.

Gunn pulled up in the shade, on the small oak-lined private lane skirting the north western edge of the lush Heath. This was serious money from serious people. Money that didn't have to shout, merely beckon. Dr Daniel Eccles Mosser's wife must be coining it like the realm.

Wrong business Gunn.

Gunn looked at a pair of arms and hands. His. Disembodied in the third person. They were still clenching the steering wheel like a drowning man grasping onto a bobbing life-ring. His jaw felt the same. His heart was bouncing out of his chest. Racing. Gunn unclenched his hands and checked the pulse in his wrist. *Jesus.* 128 beats per minute give or take. Double his normal resting rate of sixty-four. He didn't even want to think about his blood pressure, but the way he felt his head was pounding and whooshing, it had to be cruising the stratosphere.

He walked into the driveway. More like a cobbled courtyard that used to clatter to sounds of a carriage and horses hooves carrying the local squire and his wife about their squiring business of screwing the poor. The smaller brilliant white Coach House nestling separately to the right of the main house.

The metal pole and wooden board scaffolding were still clamped to the grey brickwork, climbing up the four storied property to the dark grey slate sloping roof. It looked like the attic was being extended either side of two seven foot tall chimney stacks. The large space punched through the roof had a bare timber dormer window frame already in place. No glass yet, the frame being covered by thick opaque plastic sheeting nailed to the wooden frame. A skip full of accumulated rubbish lay directly below, topped by some discarded black iron railings.

There were lots of signs of building work. The only thing missing was any sign of actual builders. He pressed the door bell button. No response. He rang again and waited another minute. *Oh well, seemed a good idea around the Archway.*

Gunn was about to leave when he heard the throb of a powerful engine heading his way. The red Ferrari roared in. *Nice motor. Very nice motor.*

Dan Mosser hauled himself out of a two door Italia 458, able to accelerate from nought to eat my dust in 4.1 seconds.

'Dan. Dan the man. The man that is most definitely number one Dan.'

Dan hurried over to his former patient and friend, touching him reassuringly on his shoulder. 'Mike.'

'Yeah, yeah yeah, s'me. Y'alright Dan?' *Shit Gunn, get a grip.*

'Yeah I'm fine Micah—'

Uh—oh. Now it's "Micah". Sounds iffy.

'You sound—let's say I'm a bit concerned my friend. Professionally speaking.'

Gunn paused for a second, letting Dan hang in the air. 'You're right. Suppose that's why I'm here. Uh—not feeling, uh—y'know, too clever.'

'I was expecting you to call sooner to be honest. Especially after what's been happening.'

Gunn was surprised. It had been all so personal to him, he had forgotten that he had been involved in a public event. He hadn't had time to see or read the news, but a massive explosion and fireball in Brixton had to make a splash.

'What do you know?'

'You mean apart from Radcliffe?'

'That? Not even the half of it mate.'

'The good news is you've recognized that we need a proper session, as in me still doctor, you still patient. You've made such progress in the past few years Mike. Shame to piss it all away. Pardon my Jung.'

'Yeah.'

'Great. You better come in.'

53

'Here, drink this.'

Gunn grabbed the large mug as he sat on the rigid leather Chesterfield chaise longue in Dan's office. It was the deep burgundy *psychiatrist's couch* time-warped from Sigmund Freud's house in Vienna circa 1905. Gunn had caught Dan on one of his very few off days, more like a half day as he'd returned from the ChatterBox radio studio where he'd done his weekly daytime hour on *Gabby 'n' Nic's Megatalk*. Gunn shrugged, embarrassed he had never listened to any of Dan's shows: except that one time driving to St. Mike's from Oliver Boodle's studio.

The earthy aroma wrinkled Gunn's nose, not Gunn's cup of coffee. 'Uh—err, Interesting. What is it?'

'Ginseng for stress. And a couple of other natural herbs to help with a calming state, St. John's Wort.'

'Blimey doc, any brew with wart as a main ingredient sounds yummy.'

Gunn took a long gulp. It tasted slightly better than it smelt, and it tasted like crap.

'Okay, sip on that while I go dig up my old copy of your case file. Can you believe it's nearly four years since our last official session?'

Before Gunn could respond, his friend turned heel and left him alone. Almost immediately the silence came crashing in. Gunn switched on the radio on Dan's desk. The noise was a relief to the savage sounds in his head.

Gunn wondered whether to come clean to Dan about the amphetamines he'd been popping like Love Hearts over the past couple of days. He took another mouthful, on second sip it didn't taste half bad. Caffeine would have been bad idea anyway, especially as the forefinger in his left hand had started to spasm irritatingly again. He stood up and flexed his hand. He could still feel his heart racing away at well above his normal rate.

He took a couple of deep breaths and took in the study again. Unlike the last time he was here, lots of the clocks had stopped. Dan's collection of watches, stored in the velvet lined trays, were out again on the impressive antique desk. It was probably quite relaxing for Dan to sit there, slowly winding the mechanisms, resetting the correct time.

Gunn stifled a small yawn and sat down on the soft leather office chair, on castors, parked behind the antique desk. He took another gulp of the cooling Ginseng. Mind still racing. Should he call Dr Lewis at St. Mike's to check on Ziya? *Nah, wait till Dr Dan's done his thing.* The radio droned on. Gunn closed his eyes. That Ginseng seemed to be working, he was definitely calmer than fifteen minutes ago. An irritating tune blasted up. *Eye of the Tiger*, theme from the Rocky movies. A breezy bright female voice announced over Rocky Balboa.

> *'Mornin London, it's us again. Me the Gabby one, and him quick Nic, raring and revving to go with your daily dose of the Gabby 'n' Nic Mega Show. On today's humdinger we have an exclusive interview with Big Boris, better known as Mister Mayor Sir. Taking your capital questions live on air for the next two hours. Also joining us in the third and final hour, answering your emails, tweets and text messages sent to the show since last week, will be the real life Mentalist himself, the man who knows you better*

than you know yourself, and he's never even met you or your domineering mother, if that even makes sense. Dr Daniel Mosser.'

Obvious to Gunn now. Dan had driven back from recording his piece for the show. Another notion bubbled up noisily into Gunn's conscious mind like a small active geyser pushing hot mud up to the surface. Did Dan do the same for his own two hour show? Seemed reasonable now that he thought about it. No, he couldn't have done that. Gunn distinctly remembered the phone call from Dan while he was waiting for the RAC to check his battery, outside Oliver Boodle's place. Dan had definitely told Gunn he had four minutes before he was back on air. That meant live on air, surely.

Gunn yawned again. Things were catching up with him. He checked his pulse, luckily there was a treasure trove of timepieces from which to choose. Gunn picked up the nearest watch on the desk with a moving second hand. It was from the cheapo tray, and was either a larger lady's or smaller man's watch. The second hand reached the top and Gunn started counting his pulse rate. He did thirty seconds and averaged it down to ninety per minute. Still way above his norm, but better than half an hour ago when he thought his heart was about to burst out his chest John Hurt style from *Alien*.

The watch felt solid in his hand. Gunn turned it over to check the stainless steel case. The watch swam in and out of focus in his hand. Gunn rubbed his eyes and focussed on the case again. He still couldn't see the name of the manufacturer. But by then he had lost interest because of the engraving in the faux elegant old-fashioned script font people choose because they imagine it looks classy.

*To my amazing Judith, for whom logic always dictates.
Your one true love, Malcolm.*

'I know. Keeps trophies. Such a cliché.'

Gunn heard the distant familiar voice echo around his head, which was beginning to feel incredibly heavy, planet like. He tried to look up to the entrance of the study. It was hard.

My head. My fucking head.

The figure was silhouetted with the hallway light streaming in from behind, almost like a blue shadow. But it wasn't a shadow. Even with his head swimming around and around he could clearly make out the same familiar boilersuit.

'Dan?'

54

Tick-tock.

He was the alpha and the omega, the beginning and the end. How many times had he reminded them? Only rule of Kill Club: *Betray Kill Club. You die.*

Dr Daniel Eccles Mosser had known for a long time how Kill Club would die. Almost since he first expressed his darker purpose with *the others*. Yes, *the First* had always known the inevitability of this day, as he had always known he was special. It was a gift he had first understood as a child. Before the boy in the woods. Before the white-haired old witch and her cat in her garden. Even before he had awoken in the middle of the night, aged six. Wondering why his sister wasn't asleep in her bunk bed below him.

He saw the smoke immediately he skipped out of their bedroom onto the landing. At the far end of the corridor, which looked a long way away at height two foot eleven, he could see his sister framed in the open doorway to their parents' room, the dancing orange light bouncing out onto the landing walls. A strange low crackling noise reminded him of the time he crunched through parched leaves on his way to the swings in the park.

His sister was standing stock-still looking into their parents' room. Then turning and running back down the corridor towards him and the stairs beyond. Screaming. Coughing from the smoke.

They escaped through the front door, using a footstool from the living room to reach the lock. Their foster parents were not so lucky, finally leaving in body bags. Although the siblings initially went into care together, the were soon split up and farmed out. He went back to foster care. He was told she had gone to a *special* place. Gone forever, never to be seen again. That was cruel to split them up.

Special. Why was she special? Later it occurred to Dan that he was special too. He become the instigator, the manipulator, the beguiling worm-tongue who planted sweet somethings deep into willing ears. It was a gift that found its full expression in his Kill Club, which had had a good run while it lasted, thanks to his genius. A conveyor belt of victims, strung up, balls-naked, dangling from a meat hooks. Punched. Kicked. Bloody. Gouged. Stabbed. Slashed. Terrified. Resigned. And always about to be very dead.

Nothing lasts forever though.

Tick-tock.

He could also pinpoint to the second when had he started planning for Kill Club's inevitable demise. They were attending their monthly R&R together in the Bysshe Club following the Hoodeson debacle in 2005. One random event had almost scuppered his carefully constructed alternate reality. It was the law of wires. All wires will tangle when brought to together. It is their nature. They want to do it, bind themselves into unfeasible knots.

The same with life. It wants to go wrong. Even with the most detailed planning, one cannot account for the trip wire.

He was watching his carefully chosen ones as they lounged around enjoying themselves. Byron Goolsbee the city trader. Sam Wilson the police Inspector. Sebastian Melling, the film producer. Jude Cockburn the editor and influential alternative media maven. They were very good at hiding in plain sight. On their own they would have still been driven to do what they do. Chances are they would have been caught eventually. The very fact of actual bodies for the police to investigate, with no Kill Club misdirection, would greatly diminish survival chances. But with the support of the group, they were unstoppable. Except, as he now recognized, for the random event that could not be foreseen.

They had had their fun, their addictive fun. They had their method, their modus operandi. Meticulous planning. Flawless execution. Ruthless despatch. It was addictive. Never leave an unsolved crime behind, always leave motivation, opportunity and clues for the police to make an arrest or close the case. No linkage. No trail of bodies leading back to the same person or persons unknown.

It was logical and elegant. This is exactly how Kill Club would end too.

Tick-tock.

He started planning that very night at the Bysshe Club. Almost instantly the perfect poster child for Kill Club popped. It was too obvious and delicious. A blast from the past. The manipulator and the instigator went to work creating the trail of breadcrumbs that would eventually lead to Stuart Roper's door.

After discovering his chosen fall-guy was leaving for Washington D.C. in 2007, the nebulous plan began to shape up into greater complexity. Molecules bumped into each other, they divided and created greater complexity. Evolution. This would be his, and therefore Kill Club's greatest triumph. Because really, he was Kill Club.

He instructed Goolsbee to invite himself to his American uncle's place in Maryland. The guy never stopped talking about his spook uncle, and how he still had ambitions to join the CIA at some point. Yeah, right. Like he could get past the cunning psyche evals. Similar tests to those which he had cleverly tricked Judith Mundy into conducting when he was looking for recruits to his darker purpose. Whilst the CIA was looking to identify and exclude the likes of Byron Goolsbee, he was seeking to recruit them.

Dan didn't tell Goolsbee the real reason he wanted him to glom on to a semi-pal from Oxford days. *Fall guy.* Instead he spun him a plausible story about needing a vanilla figure to head up Casey Property Holdings, a profit making enterprise for Kill Club. They had so much cash accumulated from Billy Ferguson's drug empire, it made sense anyway to diversify into property. While they remained hidden from view by a tangled web of shell companies practicing to deceive. Of course, the only one hidden was Dr Daniel Mosser. A forensic accountant would be able to link the spider's web of companies given time. Nowhere would they find the name of Daniel Mosser. Though they would find all the others and Roper.

Like a good little boy, Goolsbee did as Dan told and pitched the business proposition to Stuart Roper out in Washington. The self-centred doctor took the live bait like a marauding shark, and was hooked. Roper the Groper liked the idea of being the face of something else. He liked his face. Men and women liked his face. And he liked both men and women. Though mostly women since his time in Oxford. Apart from the occasional board meeting, signing a few documents, Roper did no work. All he did was bank the regular dividend cheques he imagined were due on his investment.

Stuart Roper was set up for the long game. *Tick-tock.* The final play for Kill Club when all else was irretrievable.

Or when Daniel finally became bored with the whole effort. Dan had to admit that even for a superior being it was quite hard work keeping so many balls in the air. Mask. Job. Family. Plotting. Planning. *Killing*. But he would press that big red button when the last option was to go all out nuclear. Mutually Assured Destruction. Except for him of course. Dan would be the only survivor of the blast wave, because he had built a nuclear bunker of lies.

Things were in place and he felt relaxed. That's when Micah Ishmael Gunn crashed back into his life. Before it had been by proxy after Dan had killed Gunn's brother Ezekiel. The Kill Club initiation. Not random of course. Dan knew he would kill Ezekiel Gunn the very first time he saw him, holding court. He had the light. Energy. Lifeforce. Something effortless and indefinable. Clever, witty, sympathetic, kind, wise almost. It was sickening. Things he could never truly have, merely simulate to a high level with constant effort. Deep down Dan knew that.

When the medical file of RM Sergeant Gunn dropped into his orbit in 2005, he couldn't resist the delicious irony. The chance to manipulate another Gunn was too good to miss, another planet orbiting his Sun. At that point Dan couldn't see down to his full plan, it merely amused him that he could make Gunn be a part of it somehow.

Samir Shah had been an irritant for a while. Guy gets religion and now he's an avenging angel? What's with that? All Shah had to do was sign off on the official independent enquiry into undercover police officer Fletcher Hoodeson. Could he do that? No, he had to turn all Silent CSI Witnessy. Naturally Shah had to confide in someone about his suspicions. Someone he could trust. Alex Furlough, his friend and leading Silk at Advocacy

Chambers. He could trust Alex. Unfortunately for Shah, Alex couldn't help mentioning his upcoming meeting to a few of his former colleagues. Six degrees of separation is real. Somebody tells somebody who mentions it to the next person who tells one of Dan's Kill Club minions. *Law of wires.*

The idea for the acetone peroxide bomb and the fake radical jihad motive came from Goolsbee. Not bad. As a kid, Byron had picked up the techniques for on-the-fly bomb making from his CIA uncle. Out in the Maryland woods, Goolsbee and Uncle would experiment detonating improvised pipe bombs. Dan was genuinely impressed with Goolsbee for once. He knew that he somehow he had to adopt the bomb making techniques for his Kill Club exit strategy. The July 2005 attacks had pushed home-grown Islamic terrorists into the public consciousness. Shah had recently suffered a midlife crisis of some sort, quit his job, left his family and aggressively rediscovered the religion of his birth.

Tick-tock.

It was so perfect. Dan observed Goolsbee mixing the common household chemicals that go into creating Triacetone Triperoxide: TATP. The hardware needed was frighteningly simple: a couple of glass jars, measuring cup, plastic bowl, lots of ice, coffee filters, digital thermometer, and a small fridge. Basic equipment and you're set to go with the chemical ingredients: acetone (a component of nail varnish), hydrogen peroxide (hair bleach), and a touch of sulphuric acid (drain cleaner).

It takes a few hours to form the mixture into the white crystals of Acetate Peroxide. Following careful filtering and refinement, about a day later the finished article is done. Very unstable, the explosive can be detonated by friction alone with a high explosive yield of one and a half tons per square inch. Goolsbee told Dan how the IRA often used TATP as the primer to detonate a secondary explosive, such as a ton of fertilizer (ammonium nitrate). The IRA's trigger usually being a small light bulb. Again so simple. The bulb's glass is removed to leave the filament exposed, coated in the acetone peroxide mixture. Once a battery current is passed through the bulb, the filament instantly heats to 300 degrees, this ignites the TAPT, which explodes, igniting the main bomb, and— KA-BOOM.

They didn't need all that for Sammy Shah. Just the primary. But Dan now had the larger bomb method stored for later use. There's something about blowing things up that brings out the little boy in big boys. It was visceral, the same high as the night they initiated Ezekiel. The same as he felt with old Mrs Rooney.

Tick-tock.

Standing on Sloane Street in May 2007, a hundred yards downwind from Sammy Shah's flat, new prepaid mobile phone in hand, Dan felt the thrill of the first time again. Goolsbee had shown Dan how easy it was to build the mobile phone detonator.

Dan had the phone number punched in ready to go. Savouring the moment he pressed the green send button. The phone rang on Sammy's bed, next to the nails and bolts, the vibrator rotated, completing the circuit to the battery, which powered the current, which heated the exposed touching wires at the other end, whose three hundred degree centigrade heat was over-sufficient to detonate the highly volatile TATP, which KA-BOOMED Samir Shah half way across Knightsbridge. Dead easy. Problem solved.

Well, that problem.

55

Daniel Mosser sat patiently in the dark. Cool, calm, demented. Members meeting called. He had always suspected Goolsbee kept things. Going right back to the genesis of Kill Club with the meat's medallion. It went missing during the stabbing, kicking, punching free-for-all. Before Dan despatched the meat with one thrust of his Rambo knife.

Tick-tock.

The Dylan Thomas Industrial Estate was dead. Soon to be followed by all his Kill Club members, beginning tonight. Tonight's the night alright. Exit strategy to go. He had created a parallel Kill Club in which all the main actors were the same, except for one. Dr Mosser was replaced by his oblivious doppelganger: leading neurologist Stuart Roper.

In Jewish folklore, a *Golem* is a creature shaped in the form of a man, but created entirely from inanimate matter. The Old Testament alludes to Adam as the first Golem. Until God breathes real life into him. Animating the inanimate. The genesis of Mary Shelley's Frankenstein, of course. It amused Dan to see himself as God breathing real life into incriminating inanimate matter, documents, plans, fingerprints, videos. His Golem being the fictional killer, but real fall guy Stuart Roper.

Tick-tock.

They had used Sign-O-Rama before. Bloody messy affair that one. Dan checked his Kill Club tools for the umpteenth time. The ones about to create a bloody mess.

The clock had began running down with the most recent Kill Club project. Lawrence Summers, the whiz-kid film producer and mini-media mogul. Mandy Moore, the former Page 3 girl celeb, and bit part actress about to be dead famous.

Summers was a bug up KC member Sebastian Melling's backside. Summers was always snagging the better scripts, the hotter talent. The final straw was Madeline Morris, A-List Hollywood actress. Sebastian had her lined up for a small budget Britcom. She had a workable window in-between a 10 week run on the London stage, before returning to the States. This was massive deal for Melling, a supernova event for a guy whose career to date hadn't progressed compared to the other Kill Club members. Finally Sebastian Melling would be lit up like a 747 on Hollywood's radar. Then Summers hijacked the deal.

All Kill Club members had the right to nominate a guest to spend a very special night at the club. In an incandescent rage, he wanted to make a date with Maddy. But Dan's cooler head prevailed. Beset by nutty stalkers she was protected by former SAS guys. Not the sort of people with whom you want to tangle. Dan suggested that instead they tackled something a lot more doable and a lot more pertinent: Lawrence Summers himself.

It was a done deal. Another successful Kill Club project. Trial almost over. Guilty verdict assured. Great stuff. Until a panicked Detective Inspector Sam Wilson, dropped the bombshell. Detective Superintendent Hickman was unofficially looking at new evidence which had come to light. Some new hi-tech surveillance super-computer SPI/GLASS conclusively proved Lawrence Summers was entering his own flat at the time he was supposed to have been despatching Mandy Monroe. The trial was about to fold like a deckchair. But there was worse. Hickman had identified an alternative person of interest caught on multiple CCTV sources in the company of one Mandy Monroe. Kill Club alumnus Byron Goolsbee.

Dan didn't panic. Nor did he think twice. The time had finally arrived to implement *the plan*. As the one direct link back to Kill Club, Goolsbee had to go first. It was only a matter of time before he taken in for questioning over his caught on CCTV meetings with Mandy Monroe. Dan knew he would give it all up in a heartbeat.

Tick-tock.

The others were all going to have to go. He would need at least one alive to assist in the initial phase. He didn't trust Melling or Cockburn when it came to Goolsbee. But Wilson had always despised Byron and his adolescent spy fantasies about joining the CIA or MI6.

Tick-tock.

Other wheels had also been set in motion in Scotland Yard. Wilson informed Dan there was nothing he could do to head off Hickman. If proof existed Summers didn't murder Mandy Monroe, it probably dawned on Hickman there could be but one logical explanation: all the supposed physical evidence was planted. A highly organized sophisticated effort. The main suspect had to be the person of interest revealed by a top secret government spy programme, meeting Mandy Monroe regularly in the month up to her murder.

Dan had Wilson petrified that Goolsbee would betray all of them in a weasel attempt to cut some sort of deal.

He reminded him. 'Rule number one Sam—Betray Kill Club and you die. That goes for intent too'

Dan's phone lit up the dark place.

Wilson:	Goolsbee's on his way, left ten minutes ago in his Range Rover.
Mosser:	Problems?
Wilson:	Not sure. Voice rose when I told him we had a meet.
Mosser:	Noted. You in his house?
Wilson:	Tossing it as we speak. (PAUSE)
Mosser:	(TRYING TO STAY COOL) And?
Wilson:	Oh for fu—as I was about to say, easy-peasy. Stash was in a floor safe.
Mosser:	Good. Check the whole house. Just in case.

The Range Rover with tinted windows was a perk from Casey Property Holdings. It was their signature vehicle. They all had one, even Stuart Roper.

Dan had intended incapacitating Goolsbee with a muscle relaxant spiked in a drink, either Diazepam and Lorazepam. Following Wilson's warning he went for Suxamethonium instead. The instant paralytic is the go to incapacitation drug for mental health professionals. Perfect for subduing distressed psychiatric patients.

Dan injected Goolsbee in the neck as he entered the Portacabin type construction acting as Sign-A-Rama's front office slash reception.

When the short term effects of the Suxamethonium wore off Goolsbee found himself in a familiar position, except this time he was the one strung up. Not balls naked. He still had on his expensive suit pants. Dan was standing in the familiar boilersuit, holding that fucking Rambo knife.

Goolsbee didn't understand the *why*. Though he was very intimate with the *how*. The how that came next.

'Don't do it. For fuck's sake Dan, please, please. Why?'

'Did I ever tell you that you are without doubt the biggest pain in the arse ever, Byron?' With that he sliced Goolsbee from shoulder to waist, twice. Once each side.

Goolsbee was screaming and babbling like a baby. When the deluge slowed Dan could finally make him out.

'Got stuff stashed away, incriminating stuff. You'll go fucking down too you dumb cunt.'

'We got your safe idiot.'

Goolsbee did his best to laugh through the agony. 'Think I'm that stupid.'

'Yes actually.'

'You'll never find it.'

Wilson arrived an hour or so later, Melling in tow. No matter how hard they tried, they couldn't get him to spill where the alleged stuff was stashed. If it even existed.

Tick-tock

Dan had his fun but he was on the clock, with other plans to implement. Goolsbee couldn't speak by now. Not with no tongue, and all. That was very intemperate of Dan, but honest to God, Goolsbee really started to piss him off.

He and Melling left Wilson with the task of finishing off and clearing up. Wilson swore he thought Goolsbee was fish bait when he decided to take a quick kip in his Range Rover. He had been up for 24 hours, and this was an unexpected job. By the time Wilson heard the ambulance siren blaring, it was too late. Melling lived south of the river so he called him rather than Dan to clear up incriminating evidence.

'For fucks sake Dan—had to clear up in case my colleagues came calling. Took us till nine to get everything in my rover. Left Melling and went out to collect Goolsbee's Range Rover parked on the road, when out of six billion people on the planet, who turns up?'

Micah Ishmael Gunn. Melling had the drop on Gunn with an axe, but the ex-marine was still way too savvy for him, nearly breaking Melling's shin in the tussle. Dan had to dose Melling up on powerful painkillers to keep him walking.

After Nurse Zhang gave up Gunn and the medallion plopping from Goolsbee's arse in A&E, the medallion dropped as to where Goolsbee stashed the other evidence. Dan felt like finishing Wilson on the spot after the debacle. But he still needed him a while longer to monitor Hickman at Scotland Yard.

Gunn's involvement was a major complication. But Mosser started thinking maybe it was a good thing. Finish everything once and for all. No battle plan survives its first encounter with the enemy. He'd let Gunn play out a little longer before seeing how he could tie it all up with one tidy package. Besides what could Gunn find out?

Breaking into Radcliffe? Dan had to admit he never saw that one coming. All after visiting him in his Hampstead House, and not a hint. Guess Micah had made progress after all. Did Gunn suspect him: his friend and confidant Dr Daniel Mosser? And what about Gunn's two little groupies Kirsty Smith and Ziya Zhang?

Turns out Smith may know something that she did not know she knew. And Zhang, she was the method to control Gunn, when the time came. Good job he dragged himself to Stringfellows, though he didn't have the time. What with things to do, places to go, people to kill.

It took a few days but Dan finally had the mechanics wound up. One last Kill Club job for *the others*. It was sort of poetic that they would be so intimately involved in their own club cancellation. He took Kirsty Smith himself, twelve hours earlier. Turns out she didn't see anything after all.

Dan's next stop was Stuart Roper. He drove to Roper's house in Streatham, taking Melling along for a two man job.

Tick-tock.

Melling knew Roper was the public face of their growing commercial property empire, CPH. So he was suitably enraged after Dan informed him Roper had not only started asking unwise questions, but had also withdrawn over a million pounds that rightfully belonged to Kill Club. Roper invited his fellow doctor into his house. Melling came in right behind and pointed the 9mm Glock at Roper's head, insisting that Roper sit down and shut the fuck up. While Melling kept Roper compliant, Dan planted the doctored evidence which would convince the police that the soon to be atomized Stuart Roper was the mastermind and prime mover behind Kill Club.

Tick-tock.

The delicate flywheels turning Dan's plan clicked into place. On the way over to St. Mike's, a gun in his mouth convinced Roper to phone Nurse Zhang with some story about Micah being hurt. She saw Roper roll down the Range Rover's tinted window in the hospital car park. She didn't see Melling in the back seat with the gun pointed at his head. She didn't see Dan creep up from behind, throw the hood over her head, stuff her into the Range Rover, inject her with a neck full of Lorazepam.

Tick-tock.

Time to check Gunn's whereabouts as Melling chauffeured Dan and their comatose cargo the few miles to Brixton for Kill Club's final gig. Melling as unaware as all of them of Dan's ultimate darker purpose.

Once again, Gunn surprised Dan with his resourcefulness. In some bizarre leap of logic Gunn had come up with Stuart Roper being involved in Ezekiel's murder. He was actually on his way to St. Mike's but his twenty year old crappy car had broken down. This was wild. How had he managed that? Everything was in place. Maybe Gunn would check Roper's laptop he had left for police to find in his office. Dan had fine-tuned the mechanism on the fly to the very last movement. All the other cogs were moving to his direction. He was the conductor and the symphony was playing in his head.

Gunn had his marching orders. He was already retrieving the memory sticks from the location Dan had finally realized where Goolsbee secreted them.

Ziya was hanging on by a thread. Wilson, Melling and Cockburn were sedated but still breathing. Stuart, well every player has his entrances and his exists. Dr Stuart Roper's exit came soon after they arrived at the factory. A massive overdose of potassium and Roper groped no more as he exited quietly into the night.

Tick tock.

Dan looked admiring at his final creation. All the pieces in place. All bodies soon to be buried. Bomb set for a mobile phone detonation on his call. He checked his £7000 Jaeger LeCoultre Reverso watch. Time to send the final video of the suffering Ziya, giving the surprisingly adept Gunn less time than he needed to get to the estate. Keep him nice and off balance. He wouldn't kill her yet. He'd wait till Gunn was on the—

—PING—PING—PING—

The motion detector panel lit up like Christmas. One of the side doors was breached. *Fuck.* Gunn was here all ready. That boy was continuing to surprise him. *How had he managed?—Eddie.* He knew it had to be both of them working in tandem. Dan had been at Ziya ground zero to film Gunn's final incentive video. Poor girl was almost dead on her feet. Returning upstairs to double check on his sleeping Kill Club beauties, and make sure Stuart was right over the bomb, he had sent the interim text message to keep Gunn off balance.

> BRING GOODS 2 WATERLOO STATION 1 HR. AWAIT FURTHER INSTRUCS. DON'T DO ANYTHING SILLY OR... BYE BYE ZIYA

Tick-tock.

It was happening out of the sequence Dan had carefully planned: annoying. He donned the Goolsbee supplied night-vision goggles, checked his Glock and silently headed back down into the almost pitch black.

They were fast. Gunn was already holding Ziya's weight and Eddie had cut through the manacles with a bolt cutter. They couldn't see him as he raised the Glock and took aim at Eddie's head.

The bullet hit the pillar. *Shit.* Both Gunn and Eddie ducked out of sight. No matter. He had the night-vision goggles and they were tactically blind. A minute had passed and Dan was starting to get anxious. Okay he had the night-vision but perhaps they had automatic weapons with them. Two highly trained marines. Crappy odds.

—*CLANG*—*SCRAPE*—

Fuck, outflanked. Dan was jumpy enough to react instinctively to the loud noise to his right, firing blindly into the green void. Furious now that he had fallen for an old trick, Dan started circling around the factory space to get behind the last visual he had on Gunn. He made sure he avoided the random debris scattered all over the floor.

Mission accomplished. Gunn was on his haunches, back to him, slowly shuffling backwards to the exit door. Dan savoured the moment, should he speak, let him know the awful truth about his friend Daniel Eccles Mosser before he put out his lights for good? Maybe taunt him about his sister? The rapturous hesitation was long enough for the super-fast Gunn to somehow know he was there. Gunn swung around and rose at the same time, a weapon in his right hand. From five feet Dan fired three times into Gunn's chest. Gunn hit the deck hard.

Lesson learned, Dan no longer hesitated. No point in hanging around to check on Gunn's rapidly deteriorating condition. In less than a minute he was terminal anyway.

Seconds later he was through the swing doors leading to the stairway left and the emergency exit doors right. Dan ripped off the night-vision goggles and crashed though to the outside.

Hiking it at top speed Dan leapt into Roper's Range Rover, hidden behind the neighbouring factory unit. As he reached the Estate's main entrance he pressed the green SEND button on his mobile phone. He turned left onto Milkwood Road as the receiver phone, attached to a baseboard alongside two A4 batteries and linked wiring, lit up and vibrated for an incoming call. A nano-second later the acetone peroxide exploded, acting as the detonator to the secondary explosive, one hundred gallons of liquid Nitromethane.

The shockwave rocked the Range Rover sideways. Membership was terminated. After fourteen successful years, Kill Club's doors were officially closed. Well, that was the plan.

56

'Dan?'

The boilersuit-clad figure walked out of the door frame and towards the heavy-headed Gunn. 'Give that marine a gold medallion.'

Gunn tied to wrap his rapidly numbing tongue around his own words. 'Tha drr—drr—ink?'

Dan laughed. 'Lorazepam, ten megs. Your central nervous system's receptors are being flooded. You know the rest, that's a knockout dose for at least an hour. More than enough time for us both.'

He grasped Professor Judith Mundy's watch, still half resting in Gunn's right hand, the hand which Gunn could no longer feel.

Gunn could still hear Dan echoing around in his head. 'Ah yes, the pneumatic Judith Mundy. Tremendous fuck by the way. Don't keep trophies of everyone.'

My God Gunn, the state of this self-serving freak—make yourself listen—don't let it fade down—stay conscious—fight it.

Dan gathered up other watches scattered on the desk, returning them to their correct trays. 'Course, none of them can compare to the best trophy ever.'

Gunn tried to speak.

Dan wasn't talking to Gunn. 'What? You ask what that is? Why you, Micah. You're my best trophy, seeing you. Constant joy.'

Gunn battled against his brain's determination to drift off and close down. *Shut up you demented prick. Ten megs isn't too bad Gunn. Not fatal.*

'Couldn't believe it when your marine case file fell into my lap.'

'Not fatal yet.'

Gunn's fluttering eye lids started to give up the unequal struggle, his head lolling back into the soft leather chair.

The last spacey echo he heard was Dan, whining on like he was the victim in all this.

'Know how hard I worked to get everyone in that building at the same time. That was real precision, years of planning, and you very near ruined the whole thing.'

Oh, boo fucking hoo.

57

Dan had laid out the ten by ten square plastic sheet on the rough concrete floor. The garage extension was still a shell. There were no windows to enable prying eyes, so it was perfect make-do kill spot. Part of him, the Kill Club part, would love to spend time playing with Micah, like he did with his brother. He toyed with an adrenalin shot to wake Gunn; then some Diazepam, as he did all those years ago with Judith Mundy. It was much more fun when his meat was fully conscious at the end yet totally immobile. When he could see the terror as the life drained from them. Live meat to dead meat. The transition.

Nah, for fuck's sake, let's finish this thing. It had been a tiring series of events since the sliced and diced Goolsbee staggered out into Milkwood Road. He had a life to reconstruct, a body to dispose and timescale to follow. It was a tight window. No one would ever find Micah Ishmael Gunn, that was for sure.

He looked over at the meat, still propped up in the plush leather office chair, loosely duct taped around his chest and the back of the chair, more to keep him upright than secured. Micah wasn't going anywhere under his own steam.

Dr Daniel Mosser re-checked his tools for the third time, all neatly laid out on the plastic sheet. Circular saw. Two hand saws. Sturdy plastic bags for body parts. Meat cleaver. Large knife. His old favourite trophy. The Rambo knife that had penetrated Ezekiel Gunn's skull so beautifully. Small metal bath for the blood drainage.

Plastic tubing. Mop and bucket of water. Bleach. Plastic overalls. Welder's helmet and affixed clear plastic visor. All present and correct.

The Lorazepam was Mosser's usual dose for agitated patients, given Gunn's height and weight he approximated that gave him another forty-five minutes of oblivious sedation. Of course, in forty-five minutes Gunn would be in little pieces, so the timing was moot. A thought burrowed in from his obsessive-compulsive side.

—*VRRRRRRRRR*—*VRRRRRRRRR*—

Dan jumped as his phone vibrated in his pocket. 'Fuck's sake.' He checked the display before answering. 'Yes dear—'

Dan absent-mindedly exited the garage extension as he chatted amiably to Alicia, as if he'd was about to do the housework she asked him to finish.

By the time she'd finished, Dan had wandered on auto-pilot all the way into his study. 'Bollocks.' He had an idea, grabbed his medical bag and scuttled back to the garage extension.

Shit, in the movies I'll get back and he'll have ooooo. fucking DISAPPEARED.

The crazy thought had him re-entering the garage warily. Once bitten. He hadn't bargained for Gunn being that resourceful with Nurse Zhang. Him and that huge marine pal of his, Eddie. He'd deal with that meddlesome fucker at some future date, to be determined. Maybe the sister. She was fuckable first though.

No worries. Gunn was still in his chair. Unmoved and oblivious to his fate. He found the phial of morphine he was looking for, filling a syringe with a double Shipman dose. Injected straight into a vein it would be more than enough to kill Gunn rapido.

A task for which the bad doctor required both hands.

He balanced the syringe on the chair's left armrest, leaning in to roll up Gunn's left right sleeve past the crook in his arm, the best spot to hit the vein first time.

—*SPLAT—CRACK—*

The sickening crunch of hard bone smashing soft tissue and cartilage bounced off the bare walls. Mosser heard the sound. Then realized it was his nose splattering back against his face. He hadn't seen the hand movement of Gunn grabbing his shirt, yanking him down at high speed, crashing him hard into the marine's on-rushing head.

An instant blood spray erupted, like pressurized steam violently escaping a superheated car radiator. As Dan staggered back screaming, Gunn gamely lifted his right leg and pumped his boot forward as hard as he could into Dan's reeling torso. He managed to land a blow hard enough to catapult Dan, sending him tumbling backwards towards the plastic sheet on the floor.

Gunn struggled to rip the tape from his chest and climb to his feet, still debilitated from the Lorazepam. But he was part mobile now, having semi-come around from the black oblivion while the *fucking nutjob* was double checking his chop and lop tools. Given the dosage Dan insisted on telling him about, that wouldn't have been physiologically possible unless the subject had previously taken massive amounts of chemical stimulants, like Methamphetamine, and caffeine. *Speed saves.* Who knew?

While Dan was obsessively running though his kill kit check, Gunn had tried to galvanize his hand muscles. They wriggled and felt tingly. He was definitely regaining some motor skills, the way a face begins to de-numb after the dentist has given a shot of novocaine.

Please God, another couple of minutes.

As Dan turned around to face him, Gunn had screwed

his eyes almost shut, leaving just enough open to make him out. Prayer answered, for some reason Dan still wasn't satisfied and he rushed out of the kill room. Gunn frantically began working his limbs, trying to pump his blood and adrenaline through his body.

Gunn swore he could hear Eddie exhorting him to action as Dan reappeared carrying his doctor's bag. *Okay pal, time to earn your One Shot moniker, cos that's all you got, one shot.*

Gunn scrambled to hoick the loosened tape from around his chest and the back of the chair.

Arse in gear One Shot. Move it Marine

He was up on both feet. The room swayed and turned, flipping in and out of focus, but at least he was up. *One shot.* He focused on the shocked Dan who was sprawled across the plastic sheeting on the floor, shirt staining up nicely like an all-red Jackson Pollock.

Time to run Gunn.

More like stagger as he tried to get his legs moving fast enough to get past Dan to the rough hole punched through the original garage wall behind him.

Gunn wobbled forward a few feet, reaching the edge of the plastic sheeting. Mosser was already half scrambling to his feet having grabbed the meat cleaver from the ground.

Dan lunged at Gunn cleaver up, one handed, the other being occupied trying to staunch the red sea parting from his snout.

Already Gunn could feel slightly more control over his subdued body. He instantly shifted his weight onto his right foot and was already swivelling counter-clockwise as the demented eyed Dan was closing in on him, cleaver raised to swing down.

Gunn turned ninety degrees to place himself with his

right shoulder forward to counter Dan's wild swing. It was all muscle memory for Gunn. No thought. One shot. Weight fully planted on his right leg, Gunn was near perfectly balanced as he raised and half bent his left leg, propelling it forward to smash his knee into Dan's belly, following through with a steel-toed boot into his hip bone.

DOUBLE BLAMMO—a second unexpected shock to the special one, knocking the wind out of him again, as a savage pain exploded in his hip.

But it wasn't enough to protect Gunn. Dan's momentum swung him sideways, falling backwards face on to Gunn. In one desperate lunge as he tumbled, Dan managed to slice the razor sharp cleaver diametrically down Gunn's body, slicing through the tendons and muscle in his left arm and right leg.

Fuck. Gunn knew it was bad, though he hardly felt any pain.

The back of Dan's head bounced twice on the concrete, stunning. Gunn hobbled to his prone and semi-dazed attacker. His left leg now dragging behind him, semi-useless.

A fully functioning Gunn would have taken a running start and kicked him in the head. A controlled stomp on his windpipe would do the trick, crush his larynx might even end it there and then.

Mosser had other ideas as he half hauled himself up by one hand.

Change of plan.

Gunn took aim and stomped as hard as he could on down on Mosser's left ankle which was still splayed sideways on the concrete floor. Another satisfying crack on bone shattered against floor, followed a nano-second later by the piercing shriek.

Same time, Gunn could feel his warm blood starting to ooze from his arm and leg.

Time to retreat.

He half legged it from the extension into the original garage. Blood steadily dripping behind him. The metal garage doors were closed, probably locked. He discounted checking them out, heading straight to the side door leading back inside the main house.

Seconds later Gunn stood in the kitchen.

Gotta lock that door. Shit, no key in the mortise lock.

The door between the kitchen and garage had two internal bolts, top and bottom.

—CLUNK—CLUNK—

Door secured, Gunn scanned the kitchen. *Fantastic.* Right there in the middle of the table lay his mobile phone. A wave of nausea washed over him. He slumped down at one of the table chairs.

Not so fantastic. No. That would be too fucking easy.

The phone's display screen was flashing NO SIM CARD. Mosser had removed it. He pocketed his phone before triaging himself, inspecting his arm and leg, checking the movement in both.

His left arm was useless. Tendon slice. Gunn tried to take some weight on his leg, again no go. But the movement wasn't worrying him so much as the steady blood loss.

Tourniquet Gunn. Immediately.

He yanked off his leather belt, strapping it around the top of his thigh as fast as he could manage.

Jesus.

The effort was like dropping down a roller coaster. He felt whacked doing that. The adrenaline spike he got fighting for his life was dissipating fast. That and the slow blood loss. Obviously Dan hadn't hit any major arteries, or else Gunn would now be unconscious, his life bleeding out onto the floor.

Gunn pulled the belt hard to the final hole before buckling it in place. Painful tight indicating it was effective.

Now for the dangling arm. Scanning the kitchen, nothing jumped out. Gunn started pulling out kitchen unit drawers. Nothing.

Fuck it, no more time.

A pair of boots under the table. Gunn undid one of the laces, laying it on the table before constructing a constrictor knot. Slipping it over his arm above the bleed, he pulled it tight.

— *CRASH*—

Get the hell outta here Gunn.

Gunn dragged himself up and hauled slow arse out of the kitchen into the ground floor hallway. Escape through the solid oak front door loomed tantalizingly close, about forty feet ahead.

Gunn semi-hopped his way, to the door. Staggering along like a drunken Long John Silver. All he needed was a parrot on one shoulder squawking *pieces of eight*.

He turned the knob on the standard brass Yale lock, thankfully pulling it forward to clear that final inch – and grateful escape back to the real world.

Shit, shit, shit.

The door refused to budge.

Another mortise lock, to much trouble to ask for a fucking key in situ?

Even in prime condition, to get through this door he would have needed the full door battering kit he used in his marine smash and snatch squads.

Think think think. Living room. Chair through ground floor window. Exit post fucking haste.

Plan B instantly morphed into Plan C with the sharp sound of groaning and splintering wood ricocheting from the kitchen. No way could he head back that direction. No choice. Gunn was funnelled up the staircase, behind him to his right.

He'd reached the first floor landing when he heard the final renting of wood and metal from below.

'Gonna fucking gut you Micah. Exactly like your squeal-like-a-pig brother.'

Nut job alert.

All Gunn's instincts were telling him this was a massive mistake, commanding the higher ground maybe good mil strat, but not in an enclosed space with no escape. He remembered from the outside the roof had been sliced open and the frame for a dormer window was already in place, covered by plastic sheeting. He was boxing himself in, cutting down his own options. He also knew his instincts were heavily compromised on a conflicting drug cocktail of stims and seds.

The second flight of stairs was at the far end of the first floor landing corridor. Hauling himself up the third flight, left leg virtually useless, Gunn glanced back to see a couple of obvious blood drips on the steps. Could he make it any easier for Mosser?

The third floor landing was ground zero for the interior renovations. A random detritus of building materials littered the corridor: paint cans, timber off-cuts, nails, plaster board, a hammer, paint brushes, buckets.

Grab that hammer.

He bent down and stood up again. Too fast, he almost keeled over as the room span around. That lasted until he heard the crashing and banging of Mosser reaching the floor below. With a supreme effort Gunn dragged himself up the final staircase to the very top of the house.

The entire top floor had been knocked through from back to front, stretching the whole depth of the house, about fifty feet. It was like a New York loft space. At the front end, the bare wooden window frame jutted out over the courtyard, the opaque plastic cover diffusing the sun's rays. Various tools lay abandoned on the deck.

The single space had clearly been a separate attic till the dividing wall was punched out. It was filled with a time-capsule of discarded junk from old, well-off houses. Gunn scoped the boxes, tea chests, travel trunks, a child's traditional wooden rocking horse well faded over the years, old mahogany wardrobes, a series of portable clothes racks packed tight with swathes of women's clothes from the swinging sixties as far back as the Flappers from the roaring twenties.

Promising.

He stowed the hammer in his waist band. To the left of the door, a heavy old oak sideboard stood against the brick wall. He hobbled over and sat on the floor, back against the end panel of the sideboard. Normally he would have been able to push it across the door frame by brute force. Not now. Straining everything remaining of his strength, Gunn pushed down with his one good leg, transferring the vertical force into horizontal movement. He was able to move the sideboard a couple of feet then had to stop for a breather. Then again. And again. Somehow he found the strength to push it fully across the door.

That should buy a minute or two.

He dragged himself to his feet again, scrambled around checking the lay of the attic. Looking for something. Inspiration. Anything.

Gunn pulled open the door to the tall, five foot wide antique mahogany wardrobe. It smelt faintly of moth balls and decay. An array of tightly packed men's suits hung from the brass rail, spanning the decades in lapel size, from wide to narrow to back to wide.

It gave him an idea. He clicked the wardrobe door shut. And got his arse into gear.

58

'Gonna fucking gut you Micah. Exactly like your squeal-like-a-pig brother.'

The enraged Mosser grabbed one of the tea towels from the rail, ran it under the kitchen cold tap, and gently held it to his crimson-tide damaged face. *Owwww*. That fucking hurt. As for his ankle, stomped broken.

Fucker Micah. You fucker.

He contemplated slicing off Gunn's nose. Keeping it pickled in a jar. Maybe not. Too on the nose?

The shock was passing. Time to get back to work. He was glad he had locked the house up tighter than a nun's knickers. As for his wife? She was safely out all day leaving him home alone while the kids were packed off to boarding school. The Housekeeper back in Ireland for a week. He had always managed to keep his home life, his professional life and his killing life separate. That was important. Never bring your killing work home. Thankfully there was no way out of here for Gunn. Except—

Fuck.

The blood drips confirmed Micah was heading up. If he could get out of the open attic, he could climb across the roof and down the scaffolding, even with his injuries. The neighbours might see. Anyone might see.

Mosser climbed the stairs, intense pain wracked him every time he stood on his left foot. Three minutes behind his potential Nemesis. He stopped himself screaming in a temper tantrum of frustration. Everything was turning into a Goolsbee level fuck up. Gunn had managed to block off the attic door from the inside, trying to delay the inevitable. Whatever it was, the barrier was proving immovable to his shoulder.

—*THWACK—THWACK—THWACK—*

So much for Mosser's planned stealthy approach. He Lizzie Bordened his axe straight through the top panels of the Regency design door. Better. He gave it a few more whacks, creating a jagged hole large enough for him to slide through on to the top of the blocking sideboard.

Mosser dropped to the floor and looked around. He placed the axe on the sideboard and pulled the leather sheath from one of the many useful side pockets in his overalls.

He flashed back for a second. *Fuck me. It's a fucking Rambo knife.* Mosser liked the symmetry of it all. This was the very knife he used to start Kill Club, and now it would end it too.

'Oh Mikey, come out, come out, wherever you are.'

Dan examined the floor for blood drips. None. Odd.

He crept towards one of the large tea chests, easily big enough for a person to hide. 'Oh goody. Hide and seek. I love that.'

Glancing down he saw it was packed right to the top. An old stained pillow covering what lay beneath. And there it was. Fresh blood. A drop. Mosser violently stabbed down with his knife, slicing through. The air was filled with choking small feathers, as Mosser stabbed a duck-down pillow to death, but nothing else.

'You're really starting to piss me off Micah.'

The clothes racks looked promising places to hide behind. Mosser closed in rapidly. He savagely thrust the wicked ten inch blade through the hanging antique clothes, slicing across and up. All the time looking back and to his side to make sure Gunn wasn't taking a last opportunity to creep up on him. All three racks came up empty.

Where the fuck is he?

A second of panic. Mosser realized he had followed the blood drips to the top of the stairs to this location. They stopped there. What if Gunn had deliberately left a trail of blood crumbs to lure him while he had quietly doubled back, hiding in one of the lower rooms until he was in the attic.

Yeah, but he couldn't lug that heavy old sideboard across the door, then get out as well.

Relief. Until he remembered. The old trap door in the ceiling of one of the rear bedrooms. Mosser couldn't believe he had forgotten it. Goolsbee level fuck-ups must be catching, like the flu. This was so unlike him and his infinite superiority over a lumpen like Micah Ishmael Gunn who, let's face it, wasn't that bright. Certainly compared to his brother Zeke. And look what happened to him.

That was it. Gunn had fooled him. *Shit.* He'd have to search the whole house. He took a breath to calm down. And was about to check the trap door right at the far end of the attic rear, when—a familiar sound. Faint, smothered up, but as clear as Goolsbee's screams.

There is a house in New Orleans, they call the rising sun. And it's been the ruin of many a poor boy, and God I know I'm one.

Gunn's tell tale heart was ringing. The melody was emanating from one of the large old mahogany wardrobes. Mosser steadied himself, then caught his reflection in the one wardrobe mirror on the right double door.

My face. For fucks sake look at my face.

The surreal sound of the song still faintly played over

the scene like the soundtrack to a movie. Mosser yanked the small brass handle on the mirrored door and slammed it open, stabbing wildly at another pile of hanging clothes.

Blitz. Stab. Slash. Thrust. Slice. Up. Down. Left. Right. Middle. Everywhere.

But the only thing the blade penetrated was the wardrobe's back panel. Still the song continued. He poked his head in, and located the source. It wasn't Gunn. Merely Gunn's phone in a suit pocket.

What the—

Mosser slammed the door shut hard: incandescently pissed off.

That's when he saw Gunn reflected in the mirror, right behind him, holding something he couldn't quite—

59

'There is a house in New Orleans, they call the rising sun. And it's been the ruin of many a poor boy, and God I know I'm one.'

Gunn readied himself the instant he heard the faint echo of Eric Burdon. He had set the iPhone's alarm to repeat at four minutes intervals. This was the second time it had gone off, and played for the full sixty seconds. But the first since Mosser had smashed though the top of the door and slid into the attic via the sideboard.

As Mosser stomped across towards the wardrobe, Gunn pushed the same sideboard door from the inside, placed his improvised weapon on the deck, and flopped himself down onto the floor.

'My mother was a tailor, sewed my new blue jeans. My father was a gamblin' man. Down in New Orleans.'

Gunn rose up like a fallen, broken angel.

He thought of his brother, and a Bible passage their dad often quoted, from the Book of Ezekiel: *'The land is full of blood, and the city full of injustice. For they say, "The Lord has forsaken the land, and the Lord does not see." As for me, my eye will not spare, nor will I have pity; I will bring their deeds upon their heads.'*

Mosser was fully distracted at the wardrobe, convinced he had his adversary trapped as Gunn inexorably advanced upon him. The music playing on.

'Oh mother, tell your children, not to do what I have done. Spend your lives in sin and misery, in the house of the Rising Sun.'

There he was, blitzing, stabbing, slashing, and thrusting. And here was Gunn, right behind him, five feet at most. He stopped advancing while Mosser poked his head inside. Nada. In a fit of unconsummated homicidal rage, Mosser slammed the wardrobe door shut and saw—

Gunn reflected in the mirror, right behind him. Something in Gunn's right hand, dangling by his side, something he couldn't quite make out.

'Jesus Dan, you look like shit.'

A shaken Dan turned and raised his hand in total surprise. 'I look like shit, have you seen—'

Before Mosser could get out another word, Gunn raised the nail gun, stepped forward and fired. The three inch long steel finishing nail slammed through Mosser's right palm, burying itself into the mahogany, impaling Mosser against the wardrobe.

Bollocks. Gunn was aiming at his head.

Mosser let out a howl of agony. 'Fuckkkkkkkkkkkkkk,' before releasing an inventive tirade of bravado, 'Gonna carve you like baby bro, then your sister—'

Gunn calmly adjusted the angle of his aim to take into account its imprecision. He was going for the biggest target, centre mass. 'Don't think so shithead.'

He pulled the trigger again.

—CLICK—

Mosser smirked through his semi-crucifixion agony. 'Ooops.'

Gunn quickly scoped the makeshift weapon. Mosser grunted as he tried to pull his hand away from the wardrobe door.

A half bent nail was protruding from the firing mechanism. Dropping down onto his good knee, Gunn used it to pin the nail gun to the floor. He pulled the hammer from his belt.

Mosser was almost fainting from the agony as he tried to pull his impaled hand away from the door, the flat head nail resisting his attempts.

Gunn slammed the gouging end of the hammer under the bent nail and applied pressure.

'Fuckkkkkkkkkkkkkk.' Mosser pulled hard on the nail as the flat head stubbornly refused to rip past his metacarpal bones.

The jammed nail popped from the firing mechanism and flew past Gunn's shoulder.

Same time: Mosser rips his hand away from its impalement.

Mosser threw himself forwards – Rambo knife first – as Gunn was raising his weapon to waist height, firing it in an upwards trajectory.

—*SPLAT*—

Another three inch nail embedded itself in Mosser's left shoulder, leaving him bellowing like a wounded bear.

The impact stopped him as Gunn backed up towards the window.

Mosser rushed him again. This time Gunn held back until Mosser was almost on him before firing. His aim was bang on and he nailed Mosser straight through his windpipe.

Mosser's eyes widened – big as the full moon. This shouldn't be happening. This couldn't be happening. He staggered back trying to speak, clutching at his throat with his left hand, still gripping his knife in his right.

Gunn continued hobbling backwards, his back was now a yard in front of the almost open window frame. A sudden shaft of sunlight blazed and diffused through the plastic sheeting, bathing Gunn in a soft righteous glow. As Mosser's throat filled with blood, his body started to go into shock, eyes filling with wet pain. Maybe that's why at that moment, Gunn appeared to be surrounded by a whole body halo, seeming for all the world like an avenging angel sent from on high to render justice here on Earth. A prosaic nail gun transformed into a mighty sword.

Mosser shook his head to clear his clouding vision. That was all nonsense, a trick of the light. There's no God. There's no judgment. There was only the rule of the fittest, the rule of the superior being. His rules. He lives. Others die. That was the natural order.

Knife outstretched, Dr Daniel Eccles Mosser made one last lunge forward.

Weapon extended fully, Gunn fired once more, straight for the monster's left eye. The nail penetrated the soft ocular tissues and nerves, burying itself deep into Mosser's frontal lobe.

Not quite enough to kill him outright. Not even enough to stop his forward momentum. Gunn sidestepped Mosser's uncontrolled tumble, and with all his remaining strength, swivelled and smashed himself against the killer's back.

Mosser crashed through and out of the window frame, hurtling fifty feet to his own personal ground zero. He would have made it too, except for the skip – and the perfectly placed vertical spiked railings which he hit back first.

Gunn likes to think the last thing Mosser saw in the moments before his worthless life expired was him and Ezekiel looking down at his shattered body from on high.

Gunn looked down at his brother's killer for a long time.

The sun shone bright and hot. A distant plaintive cuckoo echoed from the Heath. Other birds chirped and sung, calling out to each other. Nearby a lawnmower cut through the still air. A church clock chimed. The melody of young children playing came and went.

Gunn finally gave up his perch and moved back inside, satisfied this Lazarus would not be rising. He half collapsed down and laid his head on the dusty wooden floorboards. So tired.

After a long while, he removed his wallet from his jacket pocket, taking out the photograph of Zeke and Beth together on the bench in Balloch quad. Forever young Zeke with his dreamy smile inherited by his baby sister. Beth gazing at Zeke, dreaming of a bright future together. So much promise in a life barely lived. His kid brother whom he never saved.

Now Gunn understood with dazzling clarity. Once Zeke had been dragged to the event horizon of the abyss by Dr Daniel Mosser, Gunn could never have saved him, no matter what. He thought of his dad, Holy Bible in hand gently giving him and Ezekiel homilies. One of his favourites: John Chapter 8, verse 32, or John eight, thirty-two, as his dad paraphrased it. *'Then you will know the truth, and the truth will set you free.'*

The dust dissolved and ran from his tears splashing onto the floorboards. Finally, the truth had set Gunn free.

60

12 Days Later

'Cor blimey, yippeekayfuckinyay—'

Gunn grinned and laughed. Oh yes, the girly girl was back. Apparently a two week classic hospital TV diet of Eastenders, Only Fools and Horses, Minder, The Sweeney and The Professionals had made a slight dent in Ziya's American movie inspired vocabulary.

Gunn had collected her from St. Mike's. Her left arm was still slinged, but she had gained almost full movement in her right limb.

That was her physical recovery. Her mental status was an entirely different timeframe. Gunn caught a brief glimpse of the marshmallow that lay beneath the hard, in your face, say anything to shock shell she had created for herself since her mum's murder by the Chinese regime.

His own wounds were healing up nicely. It took nearly a week for the effects of the multiple drugs to work their way out of his system. The combined effect of amphetamines, caffeine boosters, painkillers and sedatives had screwed him up big time. The mood swings and the twitches gradually passed as his mind settled on a normal equilibrium.

Eddie had found him at Mosser's place two hours after the violent confrontation in the attic. When Eddie couldn't make contact, he checked out Gunn's location by pinging his mobile phone. Even though Mosser had removed the SIM card, the GPS locator was still operating.

Finding the Saab on the road, it didn't take him long to detect Mosser's body grotesquely impaled in the skip. Eddie scaled the scaffolding and entered through the attic window. He found his mate semi-unconscious from blood loss, the drug cocktails and the whole killing Kill Club thing. Eddie slung Gunn over his shoulder battlefield fashion, lugged him to his Beamer, then on to the nearest hospital. On the way he phoned Sarah Olongo-Hitchens who phoned Hickman at Scotland Yard.

A massive fire storm was piled on top of the ongoing shit-storm which had begun with a huge explosion in Brixton. It took Hickman a while to wrap his head around the fact that while Kill Club had been real, Stuart Roper had not been the instigator, but merely its final dead victim in one final project from the real killer. Gunn and Ziya being the only known survivors of Kill Club.

That fact became irrefutable when the police unearthed Mosser's copious and very detailed Kill Club archives. The real ones this time, and not the expertly doctored versions planted by Mosser to frame Stuart Roper. The cunning Mosser had begun planning his exit strategy in 2005. Examination of a bank account separate from the three joint accounts with his wife, showed a monthly mortgage payment that the police linked to a two-bedroomed flat in Camden Town. One search warrant later, Hickman supervised the flat door being smashed in to reveal Kill Club HQ.

It was serial killer central, where they targeted, plotted and planned with a quasi-military precision. Fortunately Mosser had an obsession for keeping records. Mosser kept everything. Notes, photographs, targets, plans and, most gruesomely of all, video recordings of the killings.

They were always careful to keep on the Kill Club uniform of horror-mask and black boilersuit. The one time a face was revealed was not a gruesome murder but a despicable rape of Beth Monteretti, when Goolsbee deliberately removed his mask to camera while the girl was still drugged unconscious.

The *evidence* Mosser had planted at Roper's house was a crude approximation of Kill Club's deeds, missing him of course.

As to Mosser's wife Alicia, Hickman was cynically sceptical that she could have been unaware of her husband's psychopathic proclivities. Not even a hint? Maybe a partner in crime? Was she the glamorous Rosemary to Mosser's Fred? He interviewed her at Scotland Yard for twelve hours solid without lawyer, at her insistence. She seemed to be in a genuine state of shock, truly devastated about her husband's betrayal of her, his kids and his profession. Protecting her children was her one concern now. Hickman assessed her demeanour as indicating Alicia Mosser was as much fooled as anyone who knew Daniel Mosser. She was distraught, inconsolable, couldn't believe it. Hickman observed closely as he interviewed her. Then again with the Yard's team of forensic psychologists as they analysed the multiple angle recordings of her every movement, dissecting every facial tick and body posture. It wasn't even close. They all agreed that no one was that good an actor, and Hickman had interviewed many who believed they were. But he always knew the genuine emotion from the faked.

The clincher for him over Alicia Mosser was the evidence at the family house in Hampstead, or rather, the lack of evidence. Apart from the watch trophies discovered by Micah Gunn, there was nothing in their home which could be linked to Kill Club. It seemed Mosser had kept his two lives running in strict parallel. They never intersected, except for a litany of victims, which no one knew about, thanks to the most cunning modus operandi Hickman had ever encountered.

In the end, Hickman felt sorry for Alicia Mosser. How could she continue with her high flying career with all this tied to her feet like a cement block in a mafia hit. No smoke without hell fire. Despite her best efforts, Hickman didn't even want to think about the two small children growing up with the nightmare sins of their father over them.

Ziya's eyed bugged. 'Cor blimey, yippeekayfuckinyay. You buy flower shop Gunn?'

Not quite. Before he went to collect her he nipped down to the local flower emporium and bought as many bunches as he could cram into the Saab. He turned Ziya's flat into a fragrant garden of delight, strewn with vibrant life affirming colours.

They had the desired effect. Sobbing gently and laughing simultaneously, Ziya hugged Gunn with her one better arm. He held her gently and squeezed back.

'Make me fucken cry. Ruin makeup.'

As if she needed any beauty enhancers to her silk-perfect skin. 'Yeah, sorry doll. Just don't eat them, you know you Chinese.'

Ziya laughed, and feebly smacked his back with her fist. 'Not funny Gunn. That racial stereo. Everyone know that Koreans.'

He laughed back at her before reluctantly pulling away from her. 'And now I've gotta run.'

Ziya over-pouted and burrowed her brow in disappointment. But he had explained in the car ride from

St. Mike's how important today was for his sister—and for him, of course. They had never visited Zeke as a family together. After everything that had happened in the past few weeks, it all seemed so petty and pointless.

He made sure Ziya was comfortably settled in the bed they had shared (sort of) once. Pillows fluffed, television on one of those TV channels where she could get her new daily fix of Arthur and Terry larking around with lovable rogues and bloodless crimes.

All nicely tucked up with the telly on, after two weeks of hospital food, Ziya had been hit with a sudden desire for a bacon sandwich, slathered in tangy HP sauce, washed down by a nice milky cuppa, and three sugars. No problem as he had already stocked up her kitchen with food basics.

He heard the letterbox clang as he was in the kitchen waiting for the kettle to boil, and the electric grill to do its job. Tray in hand he collected the post to add to the pile accumulated while Ziya had been away. It was now a stack of two. Gunn thought it was odd she had only received one other post. Even odder, neither was addressed to her, but to someone called Xiong Ming-Ming. Who was that? A Chinese boyfriend? He hoped not. Both had American stamps, so it was a long-distance relationship. He hoped—Gunn hoped for a lot of things in the future. But it reminded him that he could write what he knew about Ziya on the back on her tiny hand. Those few intimate details of her sad life in China, were all she had ever let slip, to him anyway. That hard shell again. He placed the tray on the bed.

'Yummy yummy for my tummy. Ta Gunn.' She attacked the sandwich with focussed enthusiasm. She caught him watching her, something he found he rather enjoyed doing.

'What Gunn?'

'Nothing.'

It was the most animated he had seen her since that early morning when she dragged him down the bloody rabbit hole to check out the body of one Byron Goolsbee.

He could have sat around all day, watching the box, being next to her. Clearly a sentiment she concurred with when she saw him glance at his watch before pouting mid-chew on the last bite.

'Shit Gunn, go already?'

'Don't worry, I'll be back.'

She pouted again. 'Yeah right. That's what Arnie said before he got fucking arse melted.'

61

Gunn checked his watch again though he was in the one place where time had ceased to be of any consequence for residents: Kensal Green Cemetery, last resting place for all-comers.

He had been standing by the black marble memorial stone for fifteen minutes. Any second he was expecting his sister and mother to emerge from the path edging a line of mature Ash trees.

The good news was Detective Superintendent Hickman's private, and as yet unofficial, confirmation that the Director of Public Prosecutions would not be preferring charges against him in the death of Dr Daniel Mosser. It was accepted that Gunn acted lawfully and in proportion when he fired several long nails into the Kill Club killer's body, before he accidentally fell fifty feet to be impaled upon antique iron railings. The fact that the DPP had been a personal friend of Shamir Shah, and had learned how his former friend had been shredded by an acetone bomb with two hundred nails, and framed as an Islamic terrorist, didn't harm Gunn's case. Besides, the man had more than enough on his plate in having to reopen and reinvestigate thirty-four homicide convictions going back fourteen years. The tabloids were in a piranha-like feeding frenzy. And the DPP was bleeding live bait.

The eternal hum of the throbbing metropolis was silenced by a lush tranquillity. Life abounded, surrounding the dead. A parade of song birds, butterflies, honey bees and other flying insects criss-crossed the sweep of wildflowers. A fox languidly trotted from one line of shrubbery to another, stopping for a second to give him a disdainful glance as she went about her foxy ways.

He checked his phone, no messages or missed calls. Time to phone Bebba. It went straight to voicemail.

'Hey, you know who. Knew I should have picked you both up. I'm here. Waiting.'

Fifteen minutes later, Gunn placed a splash of flowers under each of the three headstones, place markers in a single row of sorrow. His dad. His brother. His wife and child. Family. That's all we have at the start and the end of our journey.

This was silly. He had made up his mind to make his peace with his mother. For him, and not for his persistent and effectively guilt-tripping sister. So if his mum wouldn't bend and come to him, on today of all days, the mountain would move to her.

62

The house looked more diminished than in his most vivid memories as a child. He'd grown while his past had shrunk. In west London, Kensal Green was always a mixed buffer between the tougher, poorer areas like Kilburn and Harlesden, and the nearby central wealthy Notting Hill, Lancaster Gate and Bayswater.

The road was on the road to gentrification, as those who could no longer afford houses in the trendy likes of Notting Hill, trekked west, encroaching into former working-class locales, a couple of miles north of the West End.

He walked the few yards up the tiny front garden path of the white pebble-dashed corner terrace. The substantial green privet hedge was bushy and overgrown, curving down the side of the house. Gunn had a front door key, but wasn't sure whether to barge in unannounced.

He was about to ring the bell when he thought no: Archie would race down the hallway with his hysterical barking. At fourteen, the poor little bugger had to be on his last legs, even though Bebba assured Gunn the tan and white Yorkshire Terrier was as nippily feisty as ever.

Without any more calculating, he had the key in his hand and was inside the hallway, clicking the door quietly shut behind him. The first thing he spotted was the small trail of blood, leading to the body of a Yorkshire Terrier, Archie, laying deadly still on the carpet.

Bathsheba.

Gunn's world vibrated on its axis before splitting in two, and crashing back together with a cataclysmic jolt. *Now I am became death, the destroyer of worlds.* He pulled it together. The one loose end he still couldn't reconcile, but had put to one side after Hickman assured him there was no evidence anywhere he was involved in Kill Club: *Simon.*

There were two doors in the hall, before the staircase up to the three bedrooms and bathroom. Gunn glanced at poor faithful Archie. Gunn felt the dog's fur, he was still living warm but not breathing. The foul deed was minutes old.

Creeping down the hall to the front parlour door, Gunn scoped it. No one inside. The second door down opened into the rear dining room, which in turn gave access into the kitchen. The dining room was also empty, so he advanced cautiously towards the door into the kitchen. He heard the soft, almost inaudible moan before he saw the legs on the floor.

Dear God.

His mother was sprawled on the kitchen floor, face up, unconscious, blood oozing from a wound to the back of her head. A bloodied steam iron lay near, one side smeared with blood and hair. Three mugs were on the kitchen countertop next to the kettle.

I'm here mum, I'm here.

Gunn felt her neck for a pulse. It was weak and thready, but she was breathing, all dressed up in her Sunday best.

Bebba.

Moving fast, Gunn fought back the horror as he gently wrapped a kitchen towel around his mother's head, before turning her on her side to stop any chance of her aspirating vomit and blood. Improvising, he ripped open a four-pack of thick absorbent kitchen rolls, placing them under her head.

Hang in there mum.

He used the kitchen phone to call 999 stating ambulance as the nature of his emergency. He knew by using the landline, the emergency services could track the call to the address no matter what. After quickly detailing the head injury and the address, Gunn instantly hung up before he could be questioned further.

He touched his fingers against one of the mugs on the countertop. Earl Grey Orange Blossom teabag. Bebba's tea brew of choice. The liquid was warm. Three mugs meant she had let the person in the house.

He grabbed a kitchen knife from the wooden block next to the kettle. Now it had two of its slots missing a blade.

The house was silent. Sidling his way up the stairs he was gripped by an intense dread at what he might find. Heading straight for his sister's bedroom overlooking the small back garden, the first thing he saw was blood on the handle.

Fuck.

There were obvious signs of a struggle: a lamp knocked off the dressing room table lay trampled on the floor. Bebba would put up a fight but against a bigger male, no chance. She was gone. Taken.

There was no other blood around to indicate a severe injury. He had to assume she left walking, under duress. Gunn quickly rifled through her handbag, pleased he couldn't find her phone.

The persistent wail of an approaching siren kicked him into high gear. He rushed down to the kitchen to check on his mother, she was breathing steadily. Hurtling out to the front gate he flagged down the ambulance. The two paramedics calmly followed him into the house, Gunn filling them in on what had happened, and his nursing status. He knew the police wouldn't be far behind. As the medics worked on his mum, he shipped out. He didn't have time to hang around, he had one chance to find his sister. Right now.

His car was parked around the corner. First priority would have been to call his best mate. Right this very second Eddie and Sarah Olongo-Hitchens were probably taking an early morning dip in the warm waters off the Maldives. It was a spur of the moment thing. Eddie having told Gunn *life's too short mon* to waste any more time.

He pulled out his iPhone which he hadn't checked since the cemetery. He'd missed Bebba's call. And a text reminding him he had one new voicemail message from Bebba.

Calm calm calm.

Gunn phoned his voicemail box. All he could hear was the sound of a car (he assumed it was a car) moving. The traffic noise lasted for sixty seconds, then cut off. Clever girl. Somehow she had managed to speed-dial him, which meant she definitely had her phone hidden on her. She didn't speak, so she was probably gagged, which also meant she was tied. But she was alive. At least she was twenty minutes ago, based on the time stamp.

Gunn silently thanked himself. Before Eddie had left on his paradise break, Gunn asked about the big black brother GPS tracking gizmo which he had used to save Gunn's arse. Five minutes later Eddie had the EyeSpy mapper app installed and registered on Gunn's iPhone. All he had to do was log into the servers to ping the location of any other mobile phone with a GPS locator, like Ziya and Bebba. His phone indicated a strong internet signal as he logged into EyeSpy server. On the locate page, he entered Bathsheba's mobile number and waited. The little hour-glass rotated for a few seconds then a map page popped up.

Fucking fantastic.

The red dot flashed on and off to show the exact location of her phone. She was on the M40 motorway, passing junction 4 at High Wycombe, heading north.

Now followed by Gunn, thirty minutes behind. Moving fast to catch up.

63

Gunn's blood chilled when his phone lost the internet connection between junctions five and six on the M40. It's a notorious blank spot for mobile coverage, the knowledge didn't console him. Keeping the phone gripped tight up against the steering wheel, he could drive and still see signal connection for the network.

The bars popped back as he passed the junction six exit for Watlington. Gunn veered hard onto the hard shoulder, slamming to a stop. This was an emergency alright. A minute later he had the reassuring red dot on the display screen. It had left the motorway at junction ten, heading west along a narrow B road. From what he knew of the area and the map display, it looked all countryside heading into deepest Oxfordshire. Unthinkable nightmare thoughts were thought. Countryside. Body dump.

Fucking Simon. Fucking dead no matter what.

The old girl was made for driving fast down winding country lanes. Gunn pushed her as fast as he dared. The GPS signal from Bathsheba's phone hadn't moved in five minutes. Wherever she was being taken, she had arrived. It was about fifteen miles west from the motorway exit, nor far past the tiny village of Little Crowle in the rolling hills of the Cotswolds. The location looked a miniscule blip on the EyeSpy map, a dozen or so properties clustered near and around a small crossroads, or cross lanes probably.

Twenty minutes later the Saab rolled slowly past a perfect Cotswolds village of thatched roofs atop the soft yellow limestone local to the area. Attached to the few cottages and houses was a pub, a village shop and—that was it. The red dot was still pinging strongly. Half a mile past the village the high hedgerows concealed the fields either side, until they sloped upwards onto the hills.

Gunn saw the semi-concealed turning, the old metal white road sign with the rough black lettering announcing Spennycopse Mile. Another half-mile up this heavily rutted dirt road would bring him to his sister. A hideous thought could not be kept at bay. The only thing which he knew was still alive, was her phone.

The lane was one car wide by a foot either side. He decided to ditch the Saab and hoof it the rest of the way across the fields, using the hedgerows to mask his approach and catch the abductor off guard.

He had already traversed a ploughed field, then over a sty into another field laid out to pasture. In the far corner of the hedged field, about a hundred yards away, three grazing horses looked up as he hurried across their dinner table. Forging ahead, Gunn saw the group of stone buildings in the distance.

Hang in there sis, coming.

The sheep panic-scattered as Gunn raced across the pasture grass, the final field before he reached the red dot target. Two crows (not quite a murder of) wheeled overhead in an adjoining field shopping for dead meat, their eerie cackle renting the air. Approaching the final above head-height hedge, the cluster of stone farm buildings loomed ahead. Pausing to peer through a natural gap in the tangled vegetation, the farm buildings looked ramshackled and abandoned. All that remained of the main farmhouse was a burned out shell open to the elements. The grim stone walls scorched black by the fire which had consumed the whole building.

A black Range Rover with *fuck you* tinted windows, stood in the small yard in front of a fully standing, lengthy stone building. He recognized it instantly. Identical to the one parked outside Simon Murphy's Islington house.

The other building was thirty yards to the right, behind the derelict main farmhouse. Its red-tiled sloping roof had an upper window located dead centre, overlooking the countryside like an all-seeing eye. Wooden double doors in the left hand corner of the building were swung open. Half way along the front, were two large water troughs.

Maybe an old cattle shed? Stable? Barn? Doesn't fucking matter Gunn. Move your fucking arse marine.

Gunn looked at the blank phone display. The signal had given out. CONNECTION LOST flashed and taunted him.

He decided to follow the straight line of the hedgerow extending thirty yards to his right, before flanking around through the next couple of fields, approach from the rear.

Racing at full marine yomp Gunn made rapid progress and was soon leaning against the back wall of the barn, unobserved as far as he knew. There was no rear ground floor access at the back, but twelve or so feet above his head, framed by the sloping roof, was the mirror image of the front window, its glass long since shattered and missing. Ten years ago, with his marine super-fit body, he could have taken a run and leap to grab hold of the bottom of the window frame; dragging himself up by brute strength. As fit as he was, no chance today. He did a quick recce of the immediate vicinity.

He spotted the perfect solution, half-jutting up from the ditch running behind him. He quickly rolled the rusting black oil drum the twenty yards from the muddy ditch, hearing liquid sloshing around inside. Gunn righted the drum under the window and clambered on top. Not as easy as he hoped, but he finally managed to haul himself up and through the window frame, quietly dropping down onto the filthy floor boards, layered in rat droppings.

Gunn scoped the scene. His entry point was plumb centre of the building, which stretched fifty feet in both directions. The sunlight, filtering through the wooden slats covering the front window, illuminating the swirling dust cloud his entry had thrown up. The low ceilinged space was empty, except for a heap of horse feed sacks. They were printed with a friendly horse's face and the words *Daley's Horse & Pony Feed Cubes* in a large bold typeface: definitely a clue.

To his right Gunn could see another source of natural light at the far end of the storage area, beaming in from the cut-out space in the floorboards. As quietly as he could, Gunn hurried towards the top of steps. The ten narrow flagstone steps were boarded either side by a limestone wall. Gunn was halfway down when he tasted—

What the?

The unmistakeable acrid tang of petrol fumes. Gunn lingered at the bottom of the stone steps, the floor was hoof-worn concrete, cracked and dusty. Fifteen feet in front was the shed's large entrance into the yard. The sliding wooden stable door was open, and he could see the Range Rover's front poking into view. To his left, down the length of the stable, a row of seven individual wooden stalls beckoned. Each was closed off with a wooden half-gate supporting a vertical metal rail top half, tapering into a horse head sized middle section.

The smell of petrol was nose-on, front row of the

annual Petrol Huffers Convention. Gripping the handle of the kitchen knife in his jacket pocket, Gunn balanced whether to check the stalls or the rover first.

'Mmmm.' The faint, but unmistakable sound kept him inside. Nothing for a few seconds. Again.

'Mmmm.'

Gunn was already moving down the stalls at the second sound, knife in front, glancing in through the open rails to see inside each stall.

First empty. Second empty. Third empty. By now the fumes were overwhelming, sickening.

Jeez, where's that petrol smell coming from?

He saw the trail of filthy rags, almost as dark as the floor. They led from the last stall, then back out towards the far end of the stables.

'Mmmmmmmmmmm.'

No doubt now. Straight ahead. Another few strides. One more second. There she was. Bathsheba. Head covered with a pillow case, but unmistakable in her leather jacket and Doc Martens. No time for the horror of the scene to register as Gunn rushed to her at the back of the stall.

'Gotcha sis. Hang on.'

At the sound of his voice Bebba thrashed her head from side to side trying to shout out but only managing the same. 'Mmmm.'

A petrol-sodden trail of flammable materials led straight to her, up against the wall, hands behind her back. She'd been secured to the bucket-shaped metal attachment fixed to the stone wall, three feet off the ground. Bebba was trapped like some 17th century witch, about to be burned at the stake by the Witch Finder General. A mound of petrol soaked wood off-cuts were heaped around Bebba's legs, surrounded with another pile of petrol soaked rags. One spark and the whole place was primed to whoosh up into an hellish inferno. The fire fuelled by the scattered four-pint plastic milk cartons filled to the brim with liquid.

Gunn yanked the pillow case off Bebba's head. *Fucking bastard.* Also doused in petrol. The look of terror in his sister's eyes would haunt him for a long time. She tried to speak again, or shout, or scream but was incapable of opening her mouth though she wasn't gagged. Gunn touched her lips.

'Super glue?'

Bebba nodded her head frantically. Her hands were bound by a strong nylon rope, pulled tight around her wrists. The rope was looped a couple of times around her waist, then knotted before being lashed hard to the metal horse feed holder.

'Okay love, we're outta here.'

Bebba shook her head in amazed relief that her big bro was there to save her. Gunn sliced through the rope around her waist.

Bebba's eyes bugged out. *Oh shit.* Someone was coming up fast behind her brother. *Look out.*

Gunn clocked her non-verbal scream like they were connected telepathically. Turning fast into the on-rushing threat, the blur of the boilersuited assailant's arm flashed as the business end of a shovel smacked hard against his protective raised right forearm, the knife smashed from his hand, bouncing on the concrete next to Bebba's feet.

Gunn was swivelling fast now, perfectly balanced, weight on his right leg. Left leg was high, and propelling forward with great force. Gunn caught the assailant smack in the belly and carried through with the flat of his boot. Half pushed, and half kicked. His attacker was propelled backwards at speed. The blow forcing the bloke to bend double, winded. As the shovel flew sideways from his hand it crashed through the milk cartons, their petrol filled content glugging out onto the concrete floor.

The attacker refused to go down first time, so Gunn advanced fast. He couldn't believe was he was seeing. The same Kill Club uniform, black boilersuit, matching horror-mask. How many of these fuckers were there?

Gunn bounced in fast on his toes, both hands up in chopping mode as he homed in on the still staggering target. But he didn't intend moving in for close action combat. In one elegant movement he sidestepped slightly, swinging around sideways before wrapping his right leg round the back his assailant's left ankle. Carrying on through, Gunn executed a perfect foot sweep throwing the attacker's legs from under him, then tossing him up into the air.

—*THUD*—

Bad guy crashes back down into the concrete. Gunn heard him gasp as he was dropping knee first onto the guy's chest in a powerful crush blow. Gunn knew he could have killed him had he gone in full force. The life seemed to sag out the attacker for few seconds, as Gunn kept him pinned down. Maybe he should have gone through his chest as he felt a hand struggle to grab Gunn's leg, the assailant's own his own legs trying fitfully to kick out.

Fuck that.

BLAMMO—Gunn smashed him in the face.

Then again, because the first time felt so good. That seemed to subdued the bloke. Following up Gunn pressed his left forearm into the man's windpipe. Not full choke hold pressure, but enough to cut into his airway and reduce his flow of oxygen. Gunn had established full physical control, and felt confident. Right handed he gripped the horror-mask on the top of his head and ripped it off.

He saw the blonde hair first. Simon Murphy. *Fucking knew it.* Gunn had always had that lingering doubt and now it was answered.

But it wasn't Simon. It wasn't even a man. Gunn looked at the face with its two rapidly bruising punch marks.

'Alicia? Mrs Mosser?'

64

Case closed.

It had been a few years since the doctor had last seen the little girl. *Little girl?* Was Alicia Greene ever a little girl, even at six years old? When she finally disappeared from care, aged thirteen, Dr Patricia Mundy wasn't surprised. Worried yes. But not surprised. And not worried for the welfare of the girl. Worried for the welfare of anyone who had the misfortune to come across her. Even Mundy's own family, in particular her own brilliant daughter Judith.

Patients come and patients go. It's the cycle of care. Dr Mundy had been doing professional house cleaning and was transitioning her case files from active to archived, and then on to these exciting new small computer thingies, PCs some people called them.

She hadn't thought about the girl for a while, out of sight, out of mind. Maybe not the most sensitive of metaphors for a psychiatrist. Alicia Greene's case file was quite substantial. And it was sitting on her desk, glowering at her. Mundy had never doubted that she would be coming across the name again, but it would be unlikely to be in a professional capacity unless it was to give background testimony in court. Alicia would be 16 now, and Dr Mundy, MB ChB, MRCPsych, BSc, MSc, PhD, was still Medical Director of Child and Adolescent Psychiatry for the county of Oxfordshire.

Patricia didn't need to check the Alicia files, but she seemed drawn to them like flies to a freshly dead body.

She had always recorded her sessions and had them transcribed and typed out for reference. When she first started practicing medicine, it was audio recordings; but by the mid-80s, domestic video recording cameras had become widely available, so Patricia had switched over.

She picked up the first transcript and flicked through it, quickly scanning portions, reminding herself. Each page had the letterhead:

Dr Patricia Mundy, MB ChB, MRCPsych, BSc, MSc, PhD,
Medical Director of Child and Adolescent Psychiatry, Ashurst Hospital, Oxford OX10 8YT
Tel: 01865 555777. Fax: 01865 678123

Patient: Greene, Alicia
D.O.B: 1976 (estimated)
Session: Assessment
Date: 5th Sept, 1982

PM: *Date. Fifth of September, ninety-eighty two. Dr Patricia Mundy, Director of Child and Adolescent Psychiatrist services, Ashurst Hospital. Patient for assessment is a six year old female child, Alicia Greene. Foster parents died in a suspicious fire at their home three nights ago. The child is reportedly non-communicative, traumatised. Currently in the care of the social services awaiting an immediate placement to a care facility or foster home until a final decision on her future is made.*

(Time Gap)

PM: *Hello, my name's Pat. And this little chap here.*

He's called Bertie. Bertie Bear. I think Bertie wants to play with you. Do you want to play with Bertie? (PAUSE) What's that Bertie? Whisper it to me. You do want to play with the beautiful little girl in the pink dress. And you'd love to know her name. Do you want to tell Bertie your name? (PAUSE) No? (PAUSE) Okay then. Do you want me to tell Bertie your name?

AG: *I want my brother. Where's my brother?*

(Time Gap)

PM: *My initial observations about Alicia Greene. The child seems detached, which is not unexpected given the circumstances of escaping a raging house fire which killed her foster parents. She made no enquiry about their wellbeing and where they are. Her only emotional concern is for her twin brother Daniel, from whom she's been separated for the first time in their lives. She has an age advanced understanding of the concept of death, and seems capable of grasping the idea that once a person has died, they will never return.*

Patricia remembered that first session as if it were yesterday. As far as she knew then, the unfortunate child had suffered another in a series of life-blows at such a young age. She and her fraternal twin brother had been found abandoned in a doss-house aged approximately three. No one knew their names. Despite extensive publicity no one ever came forward to identify them. Her own daughter Judith was still young at the time, now the love of her life was researching her PhD at Oxford at the start of her own brilliant career. Time flies.

Adult psychiatric disorders are never diagnosed on children. Officially there are no six year old psychopaths. All Dr Mundy could do at that age was note traits that may lead to adult conditions if not addressed. Of course, there are some children who are beyond this intervention, even aged six. All psychiatrists knew that, even if they would not acknowledge it.

Patient: Greene, Alicia
D.O.B: 1976 (estimated)
Session: Assessment
Date: 25th April, 1984

PM: *Patient placed in foster care with a view to adoption together with her twin brother following the accidental deaths of their previous foster parents in a house fire. Following a serious incident involving the natural born 5-year old daughter of the foster family, it was decided to remove Alicia Greene from the family pending my recommendations. Unfortunately there seems to have been a pattern of anti-social behaviour developing in the female sibling, which seems to have not been manifest in the male sibling, although they do seem highly attached to each other, which is not an uncommon trait amongst both identical and fraternal twins.*

(Time Gap)

PM: *Hello Alicia, I'm Pat, which is short for Patricia. Do you remember me?*
AG: *No.*
PM: *I remember you. We met a while back. Remember when there was a terrible accident at your farm house,*

when you lived with Mr and Mrs Greene? Do you remember that? The fire and the smoke, and you escaping with your brother?

AG: *(POINTING AT PHOTO ON DESK) Who's that?*

PM: *In the photograph? Well, that's me, of course, at bit younger. And that's my little girl, when she was about your age. She's a big girl now.*

AG: *She's pretty.*

PM: *Thank you. But you're very pretty as well. And we are here to talk about you.*

AG: *Why?*

PM: *Well, why do you think? Has something happened recently?*

AG: *Dunno.*

PM: *Let's think then. The new mummy and daddy you live with, they have a little girl, Hannah. You know Hannah don't you?*

AG: *Course. She's stupid.*

PM: *She is? Why is that? Why do you think Hannah stupid Alicia?*

AG: *Dunno.*

PM: *Okay. Did you go to Hannah's birthday party last week, it was her fifth birthday I think.*

AG: *Dunno.*

PM: *I'm sure you did. You wouldn't be left out of that, she's almost your sister.*

AG: *No she's not. She's not my sister. Never be my sister. I only have a brother.*

PM: *Daniel. Yes he's your brother. Was Daniel playing with Hannah, at her birthday party?*

AG: *She's always playing with him.*

PM: *Really? I bet that can be annoying for you.*

AG: *Dunno.*

PM: *Did something happen then. Between you and Hannah?*
AG: *Can't remember.*
PM: *Okay. Because Hannah's mummy says she heard Hannah scream and when she came to see, little Hannah was cut. You cut Hannah with a knife.*
AG: *Liar. She's a dirty liar, she hates me. She wants to get rid of me and keep my brother all to herself and her stupid bitch Hannah. She's a cunt. They're both cunts.*

(Time Gap)

PM: *I am very concerned about this child who exhibits seriously irresponsible behaviour. Her current foster parents have indicated that they are no longer prepared to continue with the adoption procedures of both siblings, due to concerns for the welfare of their natural born daughter Hannah, who suffered a serious stab wound to her left arm at the hands of Alicia. They are prepared to continue adoption of the male child, and although I am usually reluctant to split up siblings, in this case for the developmental good of the male child I am seriously considering removing Alicia from single family foster care and placing her in a managed care facility with twenty-four hour supervision. In addition, I am now gravely concerned Alicia Greene was involved in the house fire which killed Mr and Mrs Greene. This has to be considered given the subsequent behaviours of the child.*

Patricia shuddered as she reread the transcript. She was now convinced of her assessment. She had produced a standard Risk Triangle to analyse her patients. The three axes of the triangle supported Self, Self and Others. The risk assessment along each axis indicated the risk of Self to Self, Others to Self and Self to Others. Alicia Greene's Risk Triangle was all based along the Self to Others risk axis.

Patricia went to the bottom of the pile and skimmed through their last session, skipping to her summary.

Patient: Greene, Alicia
D.O.B: 1976 (estimated)
Session: Assessment
Date: 3rd February, 1989 .

PM: *The patient continues to display occasional abnormally aggressive behaviour towards her Managed Care Facility support workers, and to other members of the outside community. In the latest incident of acting out, the patient was on a supervised outing to a local supermarket, when she attempted to choke an elderly man whom she accused of 'letching her' after he enquired as to where he might find the toilet rolls. It took two accompanying male staff to pull her off the victim. As a calming measure it was necessary for the trained nurse to administer intramuscularly, a small dose of Lorazepam in situ. The police were automatically called, as it is store policy in any incidence of violence on the premises for insurance purposes. It appears the man may wish to press charges. In the past, she exhibited no remorse for her actions or empathy with those her actions may potentially harm. Any harm that may befall others would be their fault, and not her fault. For instance, aged eight, the patient seriously injured the natural daughter of her prospective adoptive foster parents. Aged ten, she kidnapped (although she insisted she captured an intruder) the six year old girl who lived in the house adjacent to the Care Facility. The young female was kept bound and gagged in the basement of her Care Facility for almost five hours, until a police search found her. Alicia does exhibit some emotional response to her actions in her sessions with me, and in the immediate response to her care workers when challenged over her behaviour. However, having been involved with the patient since she was aged six, I am confident that this is a learned expected response. The patient is simply mimicking what she now knows is the expected emotional response of a personality which falls within the norm. This behaviour indicates a highly manipulative personality. In an adult this would be a base line indicator of a psychopathic or sociopathic personality disorder. Her manipulative traits are a disruptive influence on the other five girls in the facility. In particular, her most obsessive outburst is focussed on her brother Daniel Greene, from whom she has been separated for over five years. Unfortunately the patient focuses her anger over this upon me. Her brother's adoptive family has long since moved from the area, and the patient has no means to trace her brother. Her continued occasional references to my own daughter gives me concern, even though I have long since removed all personal items from my office prior to the patient's attendance. Were my daughter still a child, this would probably be a cause of some worry. At the moment I see no real progress in the patient towards a healthy psychiatric future.*

Patricia Mundy closed the final file. Shortly after that

session, and before the supermarket incident could reach court, Alicia Greene disappeared from her Care Facility, vanishing from the face of the earth. Four months later, Patricia heard from the police that her twin brother Daniel Greene had vanished from his adoptive parents, who had moved to Tintagel in Cornwall. How cunning was that for a thirteen year old girl to obsessively track down her brother almost at Lands End.

She put all the files in the special delivery box ready to be sent off to be digitized. It killed her to think the thought, especially of a child. But Patricia hoped with all her heart that this would be the last time the name Alicia Greene would ever cross her path.

And in a way it was. Pretty soon, Alicia Greene's name would disappear forever, along with Daniel Greene. Patricia Mundy would never knowingly intersect with either of them again.

As to her incredibly bright and clever daughter, Professor Judith Mundy, D.Phil, D.Sc, logician, grammarian and all round professorial brainiac, with a speciality in statistical analysis?

She was not so fortunate.

65

'Alicia? Mrs Mosser?'

The image of Dan Mosser's wife lying there didn't fully compute. Not Simon. 'Alicia?' He repeated it like a slow learner waiting to be praised. Realizing she wouldn't be able to speak with his forearm pressed hard into her windpipe, he released the pressure a smidgeon.

Alicia Mosser looked at him with a blank detachment. Odd, as he had the upper hand, as well as the upper body strength keeping her secure. At the same time he was half aware of his sister trying to shout behind him.

'What the—I mean, why, what the—this is crazy.'

Her voice was raspy and gaspy which was to be expected given the pressure Gunn had been exerting on her windpipe. It was nothing like the smooth corporate lawyer elegance when they had first met in her crazy husband's study. Back when Mosser-world seemed normal and not some giant twisted loony bin.

'You killed my brother. I kill your sister. It's Greek, not crazy.'

'Killed your brother? What the fuck are you—'

Oh right. CLUNK. The twisted penny dropped for Gunn landing with a *you gotta be kidding me* thump.

'Mmmm.' Bebba was still frantically screaming as best she could with her lips super-glued together.

Yeah okay Bebba, all under control.

Alicia Mosser was pinned hard to the ground and he was in control. Even a tall woman is no physical match for a battle-hardened marine.

Gunn unthinkingly relaxed his grip as he processed his surprise. It hardly mattered that Alicia was still feebly flailing around with her right hand. No worries.

Except that's not what Alicia Mosser was doing. And that's what Bebba was frantically trying to tell her brother. She saw the silver Zippo lighter glint in Alicia's right hand.

Micah. Her hand. Lighter.

She saw Alicia spark it once. No ignition. Again. The Zippo sparked but no ignition. Again.

The butane fuelled bluey orange flame shot up from the Zippo. At 1400 degrees centigrade, butane burns at twice the temperature needed to flash ignite petroleum vapour.

Gunn saw Alicia's smirk a nano-second before he heard the tell-tale WHOOSH as the freshly spilled fumes air-ignited to his left, rushing downwards to light the liquid pooled on the concrete deck.

Bebba.

Nothing else mattered. The floor rags, leading to the wood surrounding his sister, blazed up into a wall of flame. Gunn leapt off Alicia, scrambling past the instant inferno to reach Bathsheba. The furthest pieces of timber were already ablaze, throwing out choking thick white smoke.

The knife. where's the fu—

Gunn grabbed up the kitchen knife from the ground, hacking through the rope secured around Bebba's waist. The wood under her feet sparked into fire. As best as he could, Gunn kicked away the loose timber already burning. Finally he sliced through the cord attaching Bebba's wrists to the wall bracket.

Fire is a living being. And a malevolent one at that. It moves and shifts and speaks menacingly. The low moans and hisses and high pitched wails as the wood twisted, screamed at Gunn to get the hell out of there.

In one movement he lifted Bebba from the rising flames and threw her across his shoulders, fireman's lift style. His right arm across the back of her knees, reaching around to grip her right leg with his hand.

Where was she? The bitch had bolted, but he didn't have any time to second-guess as he had to go go go. The flames had engulfed the entire petrol doused wooden stall in the few seconds it took him to cut his sister free from her bindings. They were already shooting vertically up the wooden panelling.

Gunn rapidly exited the burning stall, turning right, leaving the way he entered. He was half way out when Alicia came after him again, sideways on from one of the stalls. Shrieking like an inchoate banshee in almost pitch perfect harmony with the sound of the rapidly engulfing conflagration.

He did the one thing he could do. Momentarily letting go of Bebba's legs, Gunn pirouetted around a tremendous speed, whirling dervish style.

—THWACK—

Bebba's involuntary flying feet caught Alicia full face, hurtling her back into the iron rails of the stall door. Her head bounced onto the hard metal, and she careened sideways, landing hard on the concrete floor for the second time.

Not looking back Gunn sprinted the remaining distance to the stable entrance, a dull roar revving up. He was out, Bebba clinging on as he cleared the stables by twenty yards, heading towards the rough stone wall enclosing the stable yard. Only then did Gunn afford the luxury of looking back to see if the crazed banshee was following for a third Rasputin attempt.

Smoke was venting the first floor window, the first licks of orange flame bursting through the haze. Gunn gently lowered Bebba feet first to the ground. She was breathing fast through her nose, her mouth still glued shut. The panic in her eyes beamed out like a lighthouse as she looked ready to hyperventilate at any point.

Gunn grabbed her hand, and stroked her face, feeling the racing pulse in her neck. 'You're safe. You're safe. Relax. Relax. Deep breaths sis. Through the nose okay. Relax. Don't panic okay. Deep breaths. Bit of solvent will soon unglue your mouth.'

He could feel her fill her lungs and breath out. Once more. The near death panic was slowly dissipating, for both of them. Gunn shuddered. Hideous images of Lt. Mackie burning alive in Iraq danced like cruel flames across his memory. The man's doomed screams reverberated in Gunn's head. But these screams were real and they came from the rapidly exploding inferno engulfing the stables.

Gunn looked at Bebba, eyes speaking wordlessly to her. Realizing his crazy intent, she violently grabbed him with both hands, pulling him to her. *No, no, no.* Her forcibly shaken head spoke the words she couldn't articulate. But Gunn had no choice.

Why does the scorpion sting? Why does the shark attack? It is their nature. This was Gunn's true nature to his very essence. He could no more refuse that call than a sociopath could feel empathy. Never going to happen.

He almost ripped Bebba's leather jacket from her body. Then he was gone from her side.

Gunn raced back as another awful scream rent the air. He quickly reached the two foot deep water trough. Gunn vaulted straight into the rank, green slimy liquid, soaking his clothes down to his skin, and through Bebba's jacket. Head and face under as well.

Leaping out, he threw Bebba's dripping leather jacket over his head, filled his lungs, held his breath and marched back into hell.

Life-taking black smoke billowed about his head, as if the immense heat wasn't suffocating enough. He forged ahead deeper inside. Flames illuminated the smoke, but he could barely see an inch in front. Ahead a flaming beam crashed to the ground into one of the stalls.

Another desperate scream rang out, located a few feet away. As if in response, the fire bellowed, demanding to be fed. Then movement. There she was, Alicia Mosser writhing on the ground, one of her arms ablaze, a blazing fallen beam pinning her legs.

Gunn pulled the jacket from his head, the heat wave slammed into his face, furnace hot. Dropping down to his haunches, Gunn used the jacket to smother out the flames eating into Alicia's arm. She didn't seem to notice him, half unconscious from the smoke already inhaled. No time for niceties, he viciously dragged her by both arms, an all in effort for a one time only go.

This doesn't work I'm outta here while I can, no regrets.

The burning beam scraped down her legs and then it was off. Face feeling as if the skin was being blowtorched off, he threw the jacket back over his head for whatever protection it could offer. Mosser lay motionless at his feet, either gone or passed out. He didn't investigate, simply scooped her up, and for the second time in minutes exited a blazing building with a woman in his arms.

Bebba was there as he staggered out, half spluttering up his guts, clothes ready to ignite, ripping the jacket from his head, gulping country air. She'd found a bucket from somewhere and had filled it to the brim with the foul slime. She threw the contents over his head. Nectar.

He dropped Alicia Mosser onto the ground, feeling for a pulse in her neck. He looked down at her limbs, bone showed through the right leg where the timber had scorched through. Gunn started chest compressions, thirty in each twenty-four second cycle, followed by two mouth-to-mouth rescue breaths. This despite his own breathing being forced and laboured. Bebba indicated she wanted to help, but there wasn't much she could so. So she watched as her brother tried to save the life of a heartless psychopath.

Alicia Mosser coughed back to life on Gunn's third CPR cycle.

Gunn collapsed onto his back for a few seconds, gasping for his own breath. His panicked sister dropped to his side, so he hauled himself back up.

'I'm alright kiddo.'

She would have liked to respond, but there was still the whole mouth glued up thingy. Instead Bathsheba grabbed her Micah and hugged him. Her big brother with a heart bigger than Texas.

Her hero.

66

'Six.'

'Seriously Ziya? Six minutes a side?'

'Blimey. What wrong with that Gunn?'

'Err, everything. Which is why we men have always been in charge of cooking steaks. Since cavemen times and medium rare dinosaur.'

For emphasis he gave himself a double-fisted Tarzan chest thump. 'Arrrrgghhhhh.'

'Luvaduck. What you talk about Gunn, you fucken crazy monkey man.'

'Oh, I'm the crazy one? Succulent prime Aberdeen Angus fillet steak. Forty pound a pound. Not dog. And you wanna incinerate it to chewy cardboard.'

'Oh you so funny man Gunn. Plonker think all Asians are same. Everyone know Koreans eat dog, not Chinese. South Koreans. North eat rat, if lucky.' She punched Gunn in the arm, hard with her small fist. This was more like the old Ziya.

'Oww, that hurt Ziya.'

'Fucken A.'

Gunn gently touched her arm. She half flinched involuntarily again. Still not there. It had been two weeks since he had brought her back to her flat from St. Mike's. Physically Ziya was almost fully mended. Psychologically she was in deep pain. She hadn't ventured out and was nesting inside. He had virtually moved in, platonically sleeping on a blow-up mattress on the floor. He was happy to be Ziya's pet Golden Retriever fetching for her.

She was on compassionate leave from St. Mike's. He was supposed to return to neurology in a week, though he wasn't sure if that's what he wanted. Maybe it was time for a change. Not merely a change of hospital, but perhaps a change of profession too.

Bathsheba was still looking after their mother in her pebble-dashed house at Kensal Green. Her fractured skull was healing up nicely. Eddie was still in the Maldives, at this rate he and Sarah would be there for the birth of their first child. There are worse places to live. Gunn had phoned Eddie to let him know about Alicia Mosser. Sarah had immediately called her good friend Octavia Simmonds, one of the best criminal defence lawyers in London. She was now Gunn's lawyer and was dealing personally with the Met on all outstanding issues regarding the criminal activities of Daniel Mosser and his twin sister Alicia Mosser as they affected her client (and public spirited hero) Micah Ishmael Gunn. That meant he had been pretty much shielded from the continuing investigation.

Eddie was as gobsmacked as Gunn had ever known when he sit-repped the twisted tale, as far as he knew. Alicia Mosser had not said a word since she was placed under guarded custody in the Burns Unit at the Middlesex Hospital, treated for the severe burns to the lower half of her body. At the moment, the police did not even know how they became Daniel and Alicia Mosser. The history of the two Greene children from aged 3 to 13 was known. After that was a mystery. The house in Hampstead had been owned by an eccentric rich recluse, the real Daniel Eccles Mosser born in 1919. He inherited his father's vast fortune made from textiles in the North of England, based in Eccles, Lancashire. He never married, and apart from a distant cousin in Canada, he had no living relatives, certainly not two thirty-something adult children. The last known sighting of the real Mosser was a meeting with his solicitor in 1991. There was no record of his death.

Both the ersatz Mossers studied for their respective academic degrees at university. But neither attended the schools claimed, and their school records were forgeries. Gunn didn't even want to think of the two Mosser children. It was too hideously awful.

He was in Ziya's kitchen when the dispute over the steaks broke out. He wasn't a great cook in Eddie's Masterchef league, but he did steaks and he did them delicious. The baked jacket potatoes were crispy skinned and meltingly soft inside. The leafy avocado salad was tossed with an expensive Italian dressing. The condiments included various mustards and ketchups. The thirty quid 2006 bottle of Stag's Leap/Napa Valley Merlot was breathing quietly on the dining room table. While they hyperventilated over cooking times and the mad cow disease Ziya was convinced she would contract this side of cremating the beef. She had watched a classic 1980s episode of *Minder* and the subject came up between Terry and Arthur.

Gunn prevailed and banished her from the kitchen. He had let the two fillet steaks stand for an hour at room temperature, having kneaded in a drop of corn oil (olive oil burns at a lower temperature than he needed). He turned the gas hob up to maximum and let the non-stick frying pan stand to take the heat until it was smoking. Two minutes a side, and perfection. The intense black seared outside, pressing in the still slightly red, moist interior.

Ziya squealed with delight after her first mouthful. Followed by a gulp of the Californian red. God she was so freshly gorgeous, it almost hurt his eyes. They chomped their way noisily and messily through a simple meal made great with the best ingredients. For Gunn, the very best ingredient being Ziya.

To finish off, they attacked the fresh English strawberries and clotted cream, washed down with a chilled matching 2007 Stag's Leap Karia Chardonnay. He felt stuffed, like the old family Sunday lunches of his childhood, when he was six, or seven. His dad would fall asleep in front of the television till early evening and Church. He and Zeke would play Cowboys and Indians, or Paras and Argies, or Spacemen and Aliens. Always something involving running around shooting imaginary guns at each other. Eventually the big Sunday meal would catch up with them too. They would slow down, eyes would flicker shut, they would nap in their bedroom for an hour or two, brothers next to each other on the bottom bunk bed.

Stuffed, he lay on Ziya's bed, shutting his eyes for a moment or two. Ziya had insisted on clearing the table. When he opened his eyes again, the table was tidy, and she was lying alongside, on her side, with her delicate back facing him. He wondered if she was asleep.

'Admit I was right.'

He felt the pout in her reply. 'About what?'

'Steaks.'

She mock-kicked him with her heel on his calf. 'Your fault my mind goes mad cow mush.'

Gun had noticed the small pile of letters on the bedside table earlier. They seemed to include the two he had seen the day he left for Kensal Green Cemetery. And all were addressed to the mysterious Xiong Ming-Ming. Now was as good a time as any to ask about them.

'So who's this Ex eey, ong Ming Ming person then,

supposedly living here with you? Boyfriend?'

'Cor fucken blimey Gunn, you muthafucken jealous?'

Yeah, sort of. 'No way. Just curious.'

Ziya turned to face him. She looked into his eyes, then laughed mischievously. 'Oh yeah you jealous big time Gunn.'

'Am not.'

'Are fucken too.'

Ziya sat up, leaning across him to grab the letters from the table. Her breasts brushed against his arm. Twice. Once on the way there, once on the way back. She didn't seem to flinch. And neither did he.

Sitting upright on her knees, Ziya indicated the spelling on the envelope. Laughing. 'Xiong Ming-Ming. That me, me Gunn. Letters from cousin in Los Angeles America, want me to go live there, get good nurse job easy.'

'You're not Ziya Zhang?!'

'No dipstick plonker. That name of very famous Chinese actress. You no hear?'

'Of course, Flying wotsits, hidden thingamabobs, but why change—'

'Xiong? English peoples can't even say it Gunn. And Ming-Ming. Like bleedin giant panda?'

'Ming-Ming is beautiful. I love Ming-Ming.'

Out of nowhere, Ziya's eyes teared up. 'Why?'

'I love everything about you Ming-Ming. The real crazy you, whatever that is.'

They looked into each others eyes again. Gunn wondered what he was waiting for. This gorgeous, foul-mouthed, funny-sad, crazy, and damaged girl was kneeling right next to him on her own bed, that he was also occupying with her willing consent. But he knew. He hoped she trusted him completely. It wasn't up to him to make the first move. Again. A level he was now fully ready to rise to. Her call.

Ziya leaned in and pressed her lips to his. She smelt as deliciously evocative as an English summer's day in the countryside: fresh mown grass, scented flowers, a taste of honey. Ziya sat up and began to unbutton his shirt. Hand wobbling. He returned the favour and unbuttoned her blouse.

Naked. Kneeling together on the bed, they pressed into each other, tight. He pressed his nose into her rich black hair and breathed her in.

'Gunn. I—I—you my first. I never been, you know. Pretty pathetic huh pumpkin?'

Gunn smiled. 'Me too honey bun.'

'No fucken way.'

'Well, first since. You know.' Gunn paused for effect. 'Even so, I gotta say. I'm pretty great.'

Ziya laughed and punched him again. Softly this time.

'Better be.'

Afterwards, they snuggled into each other for what seemed hours. Taking each other in. Talking. Laughing. Messing about.

The light was diminishing, the lengthening shadows eating unstoppably into the remains of another day, slowly fading down to bleed into the fog of memory. Another passing footnote in London's endless story.

There are many Londons. 2000 years of them filled with a countless throng of humanity who will never meet. Yet bound in winding lives whose paths endlessly converge and diverge. Part of a virtual *Londiverse* forever branching off into endless re-creation and untold memory. This was already a great memory for him and Ziya. The first of many he hoped.

Time to truly live it again mate.

His mobile had vibrated pleadingly into *answer me* mode a few times. Not wishing to break the spell, he had let it go straight to voicemail. Eventually he would check them and get back to the callers.

When he did, would they guess he was different to what he was, when the messages had been left Bee Zed. Before Ziya, or should he call her Ming-Ming? Would anyone notice the difference in his voice. His demeanour. Gunn reborn.

Ziya padded softly to the kitchen to get them both an ice cold coke, dressed in his extra large sweatshirt and nothing else. This was good. This was more than good. This was fantastic. This was a life.

She wiggled back and they nestled together on the bed. Connecting.

'Hey Gunn, we go on holiday. Okay.'

'Sure babe. Together?'

The punch to his arm was hard. 'Oww, that hurt.' It felt great.

Ziya picked up the glossy magazine next to her on the bed. She pointed to an inviting double page spread. Groups of beautiful tanned people having fun on a pristine white beach with an azure blue sea backdrop. The life.

'Let's fucken go here. Looks superfucken great. Club Med.'

Gunn winced, absentmindedly rubbing the St. Christopher medal hanging by the sterling silver chain around his neck.

'Wherever you like, doll. But not anywhere, at any time, with the word Club in the name, Got it?'

'You fucken say so Gunn.

ABOUT THE AUTHOR

DJSmith is a former advertising creative director and copywriter.

He was born, bred and raised in Liverpool, then moved down to work in London for a few years.

David currently lives happily in North Wales with his trusty laptop, while also following his beloved Liverpool Football Club.

Printed in Great Britain
by Amazon